Outstanding praise for
MATTHEW DUNN
and the *Spycatcher* novels

"Dunn's exuberant, bullet-drenched prose, with its descriptions of intelligence tradecraft and modern anti-terrorism campaigns, bristles with authenticity."

The Economist

"Great talent, great imagination, and real been-there done-that authenticity make this one of the year's best. . . . Highly recommended."

Lee Child, author of *Personal*

"Matthew Dunn's third Will Cochrane novel is a complex work, with a twisting and turning plot that moves ever forward, loaded with the double—and triple—crosses that readers who follow the author have come to expect. . . . Should be added to the must-read lists of all fans of espionage thrillers."

Bookreporter.com

"How close do you think any of us can get to knowing what it's really like to live the life of a spy—to walk and talk like one, to see the world the way he or she must, to run assets, to hunt and track a target, to outthink brilliant opponents? Well, one way would be to meet a real spy. But then, of course, they might be a bit hard to spot. Or better, read an excellent new novel by a former spy, one who has the gifts of a born storyteller. . . . Matthew Dunn is that very talented new author. I know of no other spy thriller that so successfully blends the fascinating nuances of the business of espionage and intelligence work with full-throttle suspense storytelling."

Jeffery Deaver, author of *The Skin Collector*

"[Dunn has] a superlative talent for three-dimensional characterization, gripping dialogue, and plots that feature gasp-inducing twists and betrayals."

TheExaminer.com

"The general is a terrific villain—strong, sly, scheming, sick, smart, and really, really evil. And as Dunn spins out the story, the whole scenario seems to become more and more believable. . . . While reading them, the reader starts thinking, 'I wonder if Dunn actually was involved in a battle just like this.' I'll bet he was. And on top of all that, there is a fascinating shocker at the climax."

National Book Examiner

"As a former member of British MI6, Dunn is familiar with the cat-and-mouse game of espionage, where the loyalties of agents can never be taken for granted, as he shows in a truly dynamite ending."

Iron Mountain Daily News (MI)

"Dunn, a former MI6 field officer, skillfully handles the usual spy business—uncovering high-placed traitors, blowing the other guy up, fighting one-on-one, and crossing and double-crossing each other."

Publishers Weekly

"You can thrill to the high-pressure intrigue as CIA and MI6 agents bumble into each other, unfortunately rubbing out the wrong principles in their haste to save their ideals. . . . *Sentinel's* characters are thoroughly and irresistibly believable."

Examiner.com

"An exciting novel that will keep you in suspense right up to the end . . . Espionage at its best."

Yahoo Voices

"Terse conversations infused with subtle power plays, brutal encounters among allies with competing agendas, and forays into hostile territory orchestrated for clockwork efficiency but vulnerable to deadly missteps . . . A stylish and assured debut."

Washington Post

"[Dunn] has created a plot with plenty of action and lots of twists and turns . . . nonstop action and relentless danger."

Associated Press

"Dunn, a former M16 officer, fashions a Nietzschean hero who looks poised to give Lee Child's Jack Reacher a run for his readers. . . . Cochrane is a powerful, efficient killing machine, but his menace is leavened by some warm and appealing traits. . . . This is [a] twisty, cleverly crafted work."

Kirkus Reviews

By Matthew Dunn

DARK SPIES
SLINGSHOT
SENTINEL
SPYCATCHER

Novella
COUNTERSPY

MATTHEW DUNN

DARK SPIES

A SPYCATCHER NOVEL

HARPER

An Imprint of HarperCollins*Publishers*

This book is a work of fiction. References to real people, events, establishments, organizations, or locales are intended only to provide a sense of authenticity, and are used fictitiously. All other characters, and all incidents and dialogue, are drawn from the author's imagination and are not to be construed as real.

HARPER

An Imprint of HarperCollins*Publishers*
195 Broadway
New York, New York 10007

Copyright © 2014 by Matthew Dunn
ISBN 978-0-06-230948-8

First Harper premium printing: May 2015
First William Morrow special paperback printing: October 2014
First William Morrow paperback international printing: October 2014
First William Morrow hardcover printing: October 2014

HarperCollins ® and Harper ® are registered trademarks of Harper-Collins Publishers.

Printed in the United States of America

Visit Harper paperbacks on the World Wide Web at
www.harpercollins.com

10 9 8 7 6 5 4 3 2 1

*To Margie, my children, and the spies
who carry secrets to their graves*

PART I

ONE

Prague, 2005

It was no easy task to identify a spy and make that person betray their country. But that was what the Russian man was here to do.

Wearing a black tuxedo, he entered the Inter-Continental hotel's Congress Hall and fixed a grin on his face so that he looked like every other insincere diplomat who was attending the American embassy's cocktail party. There were hundreds of them, men and women, beautiful, plain, and ugly, from at least forty different countries. The less experienced of them were huddled awkwardly in small protective groups, pouring champagne down their throats to ease the pain of being here.

The Russian wasn't interested in them.

Instead he was here because he wanted to watch the people whom he termed "the predators":

the seasoned, clever, heads-crammed-full-of-juicy-secrets diplomats who glided through events like these, moving from one person to another, offering brief, charming, inane comments, touching arms as if the act conveyed profound meaning, before floating effortlessly to the next person. Diplomats called it "working the room," but the Russian understood that wasn't what they were doing. They were controlling the room and everything within it, watching for a moment when they could snatch a vital piece of information from someone weaker than themselves, or choosing the right moment to speak a few carefully chosen words and manipulate vulnerable minds.

The Russian knew the predators, and some of them thought they knew him—Radimir Kirsanov, a forty-something, low-level diplomat who was on a short-term posting to the Russian embassy in the Czech Republic. The women in the room liked Radimir because he had cute dimples, sky-blue eyes, blond-and-silver hair that was styled in the cut of a 1960s movie star, and the physique of a tennis player—the kind of shape that was not particularly good or bad in the naked flesh, but that wore a suit with rapierlike panache. Plus, they thought his dim mind made their superior intellects shine. The men, on the other hand, briefly glanced at him with disdain, as if he were a brainless male model.

Radimir grabbed a glass of champagne from one of the dozens of black-and-white-uniformed waiters who were navigating their way across the vast room, dodging diplomats, and skirting around tables covered in immaculate starched white cloths kept firmly in place by heavy candelabra and artificial-flower arrangements. The Russian held the glass in front of his chest, with no intention of drinking from it, moved past a bored-looking string quartet, and walked into the party. All around him was the sound of laughter, manifold languages, and women brushing against men who were not their partners.

Radimir made sure he didn't glide with the confidence and precision of a predator. He wasn't supposed to have the skills to do that. Instead, he meandered his way across the room, smiling to show off his dimples. He stood in the corner, shifting his weight from one foot to the other, sometimes smoothing a hand against his suit, as if he were fidgeting because he was ill at ease and had sweaty palms.

For a while, people noticed him. Beautiful people get that kind of attention. But as with gorgeous art, there's a limited period of time one can stare at a good-looking person before it becomes boring. After thirty minutes, he was sure he was invisible.

He moved to another part of the room, not too far, just a few yards to the next table, where he could pick at some canapés and fiddle with part of the flower display. He kept his gaze low, as if to avoid the embarrassment of having to talk to someone cleverer than him. Thankfully, the demigods around him knew that Radimir was aware of his limitations, so they left him alone. It was the only good thing they did for him.

Holding his champagne glass with two hands

so that he looked like an amateur at this type of event, he walked to another table, then another, then several more. Forty minutes later he returned to his starting point in the corner of the room. Poor Radimir, he imagined the pros would think if any of them had seen his awkward and pointless amble around the room, though he doubted any of them had noticed. The predators were moving up a gear, pouncing on late and desirable new arrivals, placing firm arms around them and guiding them to people they didn't know but just had to meet, cracking jokes, whispering in ears, kissing cheeks, flattering, nodding with sage expressions, and all the time acting to hide their agenda: pure lust for information.

The Russian placed his full glass on a table, leaned back against the wall, folded his arms, and smiled his very best pretty and dumb smile. He'd practiced the expression many times in front of mirrors and he was convinced he'd perfected the look. It was an expression that he hoped said, I'm resigned to the fact that my looks are all I have.

It kept people away. Even the ones who were as dim-witted as he was, because no one wants to stand next to a man who's as stupid as they are but four times more attractive.

Radimir momentarily closed his eyes.

When he opened them, he was the cleverest person in the room.

A man who was not called Radimir.

Instead, someone who was known to a limited number of people as Gregori Shonin, an SVR intelligence officer. And a predator with skills that were way beyond those of the other predators around him.

There was a third side to the Russian, one that did not carry the false names of Radimir or Gregori, one that was the truth, but right now that was buried so deep inside him that he gave it little thought. This evening, being Gregori undercover as Radimir was sufficient for what he hoped to achieve.

Gregori's huge intellect was processing a vast amount of data, all gleaned from his forty-minute walk through the room. Hundreds of voices and sentences, many of them in English, some in other languages he understood fluently, only a few in tongues he didn't understand or care about. He spent several minutes doing nothing more than deliberately forgetting most of what he'd heard. Ejecting the crap, was how he liked to term the cognitive process. It was an arduous task, but necessary, because at the end of it he would picture himself standing in this huge room, not with hundreds of diplomats from all around the world, but instead with one or two officials who worked for countries he loathed and who'd said or done something interesting.

Something that suggested they had the potential to spy on his behalf.

He continued the process of ejecting. Introductions, pleasantries, small talk, lots of "How long have you been posted here?," several people lying about how beautiful the American hostess looked tonight, a few jaded comments about last week's G7 summit, bad humor, and a fairly amusing anecdote from an Italian diplomat about her experience at a Mongolian tribal feast. All crap.

Gregori stared ahead. The room was still buzzing at full capacity, but in his mind he imagined that only one American couple was in the place. Both were predators. They were standing still, frozen in Gregori's radar as he walked around them, staring at their faces from different angles as he sought a glance into their eyes and their very souls.

The husband was an experienced CIA officer who'd previously been posted to the Agency's stations in London, Abu Dhabi, and Pretoria. He'd been in Prague for two and a half years and was due to return to Langley in six months. He was thirty-seven years old, no doubt smart and capable, and had met his wife while both were studying at Harvard. She too could have gone on to have an excellent job in government, though early on they had decided that the overseas life of an Agency spouse would preclude her having a career. So, she'd agreed to be the good wife, accompany him on his overseas postings, and support him in every way, and in return he could give her a couple of kids. But so far they'd been unsuccessful in having children.

Gregori was interested in them for two reasons. One was a hushed and angry comment made by the husband to his wife.

"Are you sure that's where you were this afternoon?"

The other reason was perfume.

The wife loved Dolce & Gabbana perfume, so much so that she would never step outside of her home without applying too much of it to her throat and wrists. At events like these, one didn't have to stand too close to her to smell the unmistakable rich scent on her skin. But tonight was different, because she wore no such scent. Where had she been this afternoon? Gregori thought through the possibilities. A place she'd gone to clutching the ball gown she'd collected from the dry cleaners. A venue where she could get dressed in comfort, fix her hair, and put on makeup that she'd brought along in her handbag. Some location that didn't allow her time to rush home before meeting her husband at the party. And she would have desperately wanted to go home when she realized she'd forgotten to pack her beloved perfume.

Where was that place? Like all top spies, Gregori used his instincts and imagination to fill in the gaps. Of course, that place was another man's home. The woman had been unfaithful to her husband. She'd dressed for the party after she'd made love.

Gregori smiled.

Her infidelity could give him leverage over her husband.

Perhaps it would make her husband betray the United States.

TWO

Norway, Present Day

Will Cochrane crouched on the frozen ground, removed his gloves, and withdrew two metal tubes from his rucksack. Each tube was two and a half feet long, ten centimeters in diameter, and branded with the name of the fishing equipment manufacturer Orvis and a label denoting that one tube contained an eight-foot-four-inch mid-flex Helios 2 fly-fishing rod and the other contained a ten-foot tip-flex variant of the same precision distance-casting model. He laid the tubes side by side on the ground, pulled out binoculars from his jacket, and examined his surroundings.

The tall man was alone on a mountain escarpment along the stunningly beautiful northern coastline. Around him were large azure-blue fjords that cut through the snow-capped mountain range, low areas of barren land carved into numerous islands by thin stretches of seawater, patches of mist hanging motionless over sea and earth, and above him a windless clear sky that looked heavenly and yet was cold enough to kill an ill-equipped man in less than an hour. But there were no signs of life out here save for an occasional kittiwake bird gliding close to water.

Carefully, he moved his binoculars until he spotted an area of lowland through which a thin meandering mountain river led to the sea. It was an excellent place to cast a lure and tempt a salmon or sea trout. But it was approximately one thousand yards beneath him; one would need to be dressed in appropriate clothing and be at the very peak of physical condition to reach the area and fish there at this time of year. Thankfully, Will was supremely fit and had come fully prepared to stay out all day in this remote place. He was wearing a white woolen hat that was pulled down tightly over his close-cropped dark hair, a jacket and fleece, thermal leggings and water-resistant pants, and hiking boots covered with rubber galoshes. In these parts, an angler needed to dress like someone who was hiking to the North Pole.

As he further examined the distant stretch of river, his vision locked on the only evidence that any person had been here before: three log cabins and a track leading away from them. He wondered if the owners of the buildings had long ago deserted this place, or whether the cabins were rented out to vacationers during the summer months. He imagined clambering down to the river, preparing one of his rods, and making a few casts before being confronted by an angry owner of the cabins who would be shouting at him to leave.

Still, it would be worth the risk to try to fish there, as it would be a once-in-a-lifetime experience.

But that experience would have to take place on another day.

Because the MI6 operative wasn't here to fish.

He unscrewed the caps on both tubes and withdrew pieces of metal equipment that had been designed and handcrafted by specialists in England before being couriered in a diplomatic bag to the British embassy in Oslo. Carefully, he slotted each piece together. One minute later, the sound-suppressed, high-velocity sniper rifle was fully assembled. After putting his gloves back on, he lay flat on the ground and stared at the buildings through the gun's powerful telescopic sight.

He spoke into his throat mic. "In position."

And immediately heard an American woman's voice in his earpiece. "Okay. We got you."

The woman was a CIA analyst, operating in the Agency's headquarters in Langley, and was temporarily seconded to the highly classified joint CIA-MI6 Task Force S, which Will worked for as its prime field operative. She wasn't very experienced, but didn't need to be, as today her job was simply to sit at her computer and make notes of what Will could see.

Getting on this assignment had infuriated Will because it had come on the back of his being told without explanation that he was to cease his hunt for Cobalt. He'd spent the last eleven months chasing the financier—a man without a name or identifiable nationality, but one of the most dangerous men on the planet due to his funding of terrorist activities across the globe. Cobalt was all the more dangerous because he had no causes beyond seeking profit; his support of terrorist cells bought him their allegiance and gave him access to opium and coca plantations under their control. He transformed the crops into salable drugs, used his extensive network to smuggle them out of the countries, made vast fortunes, and in return gave the terrorists a cut of the profits. It was a deal that suited him, and suited them. And it was one that ordinarily would require someone like Will Cochrane to put a bullet in Cobalt's brain. But the powers that be in Washington and London had decided that Cobalt needed to be left alone.

So here he was, on a routine job that should have been given to one of the Agency's many paramilitary Special Operations Group officers.

In the largest wooden building below was Ellie Hallowes, the CIA's best deep-cover officer. Will had never met her, but he knew she was thirty-five years old—the same age that he was now—and was an excellent and courageous operator whose job required her to live in near constant danger. Today, he was here to watch over her while she met a Russian intelligence officer who carried the CIA code name Herald. The Russian was her spy, and during the last two years they'd met many times without the need for protection. But this meeting was different. Two days earlier the CIA had received signals intelligence that suggested the Russian intelligence services had suspicions about their officer and the real reasons for his trips overseas. The Agency was worried that the meeting could be compromised and that Ellie could be attacked. If that happened, Will was under orders to do whatever was necessary to ensure Ellie escaped to safety.

It was a straightforward job for a man like Will.

As a younger man, he'd spent five brutal years in the French Foreign Legion, initially in its elite 2e Régiment Étranger de Parachutistes before being handpicked to serve in the 11e Brigade Parachutiste's Special Forces unit, the Groupement des Commandos Parachutistes. Upon completion of his military service, he'd returned to England and studied at Cambridge University. After being awarded a first-class degree, he'd briefly considered a career in academia, though others had different plans for him. MI6 tapped him on the shoulder and said it was very interested in someone with his skill set. He could have turned the intelligence agency down and hidden away from the world in an ivory tower, surrounded by books and with human contact limited to students and other lecturers and professors. But MI6 knew it was an impossible dream for someone like him: a man whose CIA father had been captured in Iran when Will was five years old and incarcerated in Tehran's Evin Prison for years before being butchered, who'd fled to the Legion aged seventeen after witnessing the brutal murder of his English mother, who'd killed her four assailants with a knife to protect his sister from a similar fate, who'd been deployed not only by the GCP behind enemy lines but was also used by France's DGSE as a deniable killer, a man who was not completely at peace with the world.

Within the first few weeks of training alongside
other recruits, MI6 had singled him out as having
attributes that were even greater than expected. He
was removed from the course and put on the top-
secret twelve-month Spartan Program. Only one
person at a time was permitted to take the mentally and physically hellish selection and training
course and, if successful, carry the code name Spartan. Despite the fact that all other applicants before
him had either voluntarily withdrawn from the
program, failed, received severe physical or mental injuries that prevented them from continuing,
or died in selection and training, Will passed the
program. He was awarded the distinction of carrying the code name, and the program was shut down
and would remain closed all the time Will was
operational and alive. He'd spent the subsequent
eight years on near continuous deployment in hostile overseas missions, and was tasked on the West's
most important operations. Throughout that time,
very few people knew he was an MI6 officer, let
alone the nature of his work and his achievements.

He sighed, concluding once again that today's
babysitting job should have been given to someone
else. After slotting a magazine containing twelve
rounds into the rifle, he trained the weapon on the
track leading to the cluster of buildings. That was
the route Herald would take to drive to the meeting. He checked his watch. Ellie Hallowes was a
stickler for exact timing, and she'd told the Russian
that he was not to arrive a minute before or after
the allotted time. The Russian wasn't due to arrive
for another eight minutes.

Will relaxed and thought about other things. A year ago, he'd moved into a new home in West Square, in the Borough of Southwark, south London. It was a two-hundred-year-old house that had been converted into four apartments. For the first time in his adult life, it was a place where he felt he was putting down roots. A sudden panicked thought hit him. Had he paid the latest council tax bill? He thought he had, though—shit—he couldn't be sure. The local council was becoming a bastard with people who didn't pay up on time. Well, there was nothing he could do about it until he got home tomorrow. He thought about his three single neighbors who lived in the converted house: stubborn Dickie Mountjoy, a former major in the Coldstream Guards and now a retiree; Phoebe, a thirty-something art dealer and lover of champagne, high heels, and middleweight boxing matches; and David, a recently divorced, slightly flabby mortician. They believed Will was a life insurance salesman. That false cover seemed apt, because today he was here as insurance that Ellie lived.

He glanced at his watch again and put his eye back against the scope. A black sedan was driving along the coastal track, at exactly the right time, easily visible against the backdrop of the tranquil blue sea. Will moved his weapon millimeter by millimeter to keep the crosshairs of his sight in the center of the vehicle. It stopped, and a man got out and walked fast into the largest of the three buildings.

"Our man's arrived. He's in the building."

"You're sure it's him?"

"It's him."

He flexed his toes and his muscles. Not for the first time this week, he tried to decide if he could afford the nineteenth-century sheet music for Bach's Lute Suite No. 1 in E minor. It was for sale in a tiny basement store in London's Soho district. He'd paid the elderly proprietor of the store a £50 deposit to take the music temporarily off the market, with the promise that he'd settle up the balance of £750 after his next paycheck had come through. Still, as desperate as he was to place the sheets on a stand, pick up his German antique lute, and expertly play what was in front of him, he had to reconcile the high cost with the fact that he was a man who was on government salary, could obtain the same music for free at a library or off the Internet, and in any case knew every note of Suite No. 1 by heart. But the score had been produced and edited by Hans Dagobert Bruger, meaning the papers were a rare and beautiful thing. That was decided then; he'd eat beans on toast for a month to ensure he had enough cash to pay for the sheets. Will had made many similar decisions in the past. His new home was crammed with antiques and rare items he'd picked up during his travels, including a Louis XV lacquer and ormolu commode, Venetian *trespoli*, a pair of Guangzhou imperial dress swords, a German chinoiserie clock, an Edwardian mahogany three-piece suite and chaise longue, woven silk rugs from exotic markets, and vintage vinyl records of Andrés Segovia guitar recitals. He shouldn't have bought any of them, because every time he'd done so he'd nearly bankrupted himself, but he'd always done so because life was too short to ignore beauty in favor of financial well-being.

He tensed as he saw movement in the distance.

A man walking awkwardly over rough ground, using a walking stick as an aid.

Will trained the scope on him and watched him move toward the cabins, stop approximately two hundred yards away from them, and sit on a boulder on ground that overlooked the cluster of buildings and the sea beyond them. The man had his back to Will, so his face was not visible, though Will could see that he was wearing tweed and oil-skin hiking gear. His walking stick also seemed to be from another age; it was nearly as long as the man and at its head was a curly ram's horn. Judging by the way he'd been walking, it was clear that the man needed the stick, meaning he was either old, weak, disabled, or all of those things. The man rested his stick beside him on the rock, withdrew a metal thermos flask, poured liquid into a cup, and drank.

Will relayed what he'd seen to Langley.

"Suspicious?"

"Impossible to know." Will moved his face away from the scope. "I'm going to look at his face."

Carrying his rifle in one hand, Will ran while keeping his upper body low. Two minutes later, he threw himself onto the ground, then crawled until he reached the summit and could once again see the distant cabins in the valley. The man was still there, a tiny speck to the human eye. Will looked through the scope, moved the gun until he located the man, and saw that he was still sitting on the rock. From this angle, Will could easily see his face.

He studied it, felt shock, and muttered, "Hell, no!"

Antaeus dabbed a handkerchief against the corners of his mouth to absorb any traces of the coffee he'd now finished, rested his weaker leg over the stronger one, and rubbed the disfigured side of his face before realizing what he was doing and abruptly stopping. It was a habit he'd had for years and he was trying to break it, because no amount of massage would get the muscles on that side of his face to work properly. His carefully trimmed beard helped to hide the lower part of the disfigurement, and the thick rims of his glasses covered most of the area where his left eye drooped. From a distance, he looked normal. But up close there was no mistaking what he was: a man who was ugly on one side.

He'd long ago gotten used to it and no longer cared. All that mattered to him was his mind. It was perfect and beautiful.

He stared at the Norwegian log cabins and gripped his walking stick.

The performance was about to begin.

And he was going to be its conductor.

Ellie Hallowes desperately wanted to cut to the chase and find out whether Herald had any useful intelligence for her, but knew that her Russian spy would consider it rude of her to do so. He was a showman, one who took pleasure in feeding her an hour or so of small talk before getting down to business. She was his audience, and he liked to keep her waiting for the good stuff.

During the third meeting she'd had with him after the start of their case officer–asset relationship, she'd tried to circumvent the crap to get to business, but had received a sharp rebuke from the Russian together with threats that if she did this again he'd come to the subsequent five meetings with zero interest and plenty of lessons about how to be civil and conduct meetings in a manner befitting their respective countries' officer classes.

As well as being a showman, Herald was a pompous ass.

He was already thirty minutes into the meeting, sitting cross-legged in a chair facing her, occasionally glancing at his manicured fingernails or checking that his bow tie was horizontal.

She moved to the sea-facing side of the cabin and gestured to a bench containing a half bottle of vodka and two tumblers, while trying not to yawn as Herald was telling her that he'd discovered a fine restaurant in Moscow where all the staff were only permitted to speak in French.

Something caught her eye as she casually looked out of the window while unscrewing the bottle.

Movement in the sea.

Men.

Seven of them expertly emerged from the sea in scuba gear, dumping some of their equipment on the thin beach, and moved silently on foot toward the log cabins while keeping their SIG Sauer handguns at eye level.

Spinning around, she barked, "Shut up! We're compromised!"

Herald's face went ashen. "What?"

"Compromised! We've got seconds!"

Herald jumped to his feet and looked around, confusion all over his face. He walked quickly to Ellie, glanced out the window, grabbed Ellie's arms, and spoke fast and loud. "Listen to me! Trust no one. There's a mole in the CIA. Works for the Russians. And he's sitting at the very top!"

Will's heart and brain were racing as he spoke into his throat mic. "I'm looking at a man who's supposed to be dead."

"Who is he?"

"High-ranking SVR officer. Code name Antaeus. I killed him three years ago."

"Means nothing to me."

Will kept the crosshairs of his scope on Antaeus's head, placed his finger on the trigger, and made ready to put a bullet into the brain of a man who'd consistently outwitted the West's attempts to counter his actions; a man Will had spent years hunting, an individual who'd thwarted every attempt to neutralize him, a brilliant spymaster who was one of Russia's most influential and powerful men. Until Will had finally managed to track him down three years ago and detonated a bomb under the car that Antaeus was driving in a Moscow suburb.

Will pulled back on the trigger.

Then stopped as he heard the unmistakable sound of pistol fire near the log cabins.

Antaeus smiled as he watched his Russian team approach the log cabins. He removed a small rectangular box from his jacket and withdrew from it a cheroot cigar, which he lit with a gold Zippo lighter. The doctors had told him that he mustn't smoke anymore, and for the most part he followed their instructions. But there were moments when a smoke made complete sense. Doctors didn't understand that; spies did, and now was one such moment. He inhaled the rich tobacco and blew out a long stream of smoke, the volume of which was accentuated by the icy air. As he did so, four of his men kicked in the doors to the two smaller buildings and entered; the remaining three operatives forced entry into the larger cabin.

Then he heard two shots.

Though he'd permitted his men to shoot to wound their targets if necessary, the SVR spymaster wondered if the CIA officer had made the shots the moment she'd seen men burst into the cabin, or whether her Russian agent had done so. Still, if two of his men were now dead, it wouldn't change anything. His other men would easily overpower the American woman and her asset. They'd dispose of their colleagues' bodies in the sea, but even if they were later discovered, that wouldn't matter, as Antaeus had instructed his men to use CIA SOG equipment and carry documentation showing they were residents of Virginia.

He tapped ash from his cigar, raised an old telescope to his good eye, and waited.

Will pointed his sniper rifle at the cabins and the ground around them. Two shots had been fired, but there were no signs of any assailants. He knew there could be only one possible explanation: men had assaulted the cabins from the one blind spot he had—the sea. Had he been complacent? He had considered the possibility that an assault on the meeting could take place from the coast, though he'd decided that at this time of year it would be done so with boats that would be easily visible to him from his position on the mountainside. Plus, he thought that no one in their right mind would swim in the icy waters to the coastline where the cabins sat. And yet, he of all people knew that Special Forces could operate in Arctic waters all year round. Yes, he had been complacent.

As a result, he'd probably failed a routine assignment that he'd believed was beneath someone of his capabilities. "Shots have been fired. Don't know what's going on. But I'll make sure Antaeus and his men don't leave here."

"Negative." The analyst sounded unsettled.

"What?"

"Repeat, negative. You have no authority to proceed."

Will couldn't believe what he was hearing. "I can do what I like."

The analyst sounded on the verge of panic. "I've checked our system. Don't know what it means but the instructions are clear. It says, Antaeus must not be touched. Further inquiries require Project Ferryman clearance. My search on the system must have been flagged, because I just had a call from the duty officer asking me what's going on. I told him. He told me to pull the plug. You're under orders to withdraw."

"No way."

"Your orders are clear. Get out of there."

"No fucking way!"

"I . . ." The analyst was breathing fast. "I . . . the DO told me it would be a breach of category one Agency protocols if you proceed. Please . . ."

Men emerged from the smaller cabins and a moment later the rest of them came out of the larger building. Two of them were dragging Herald, and it looked as though he'd been injured. The others were gripping Ellie's arms and walking her to a clearing in front of the cabins. They stopped. The Russian was forced onto his knees and winced in pain as one of the men yanked his hair back to lift his head. Ellie was pushed to the ground next to her asset, and a man placed a boot on her back to keep her still. The men looked toward the distance. Will urgently swung his rifle toward Antaeus's position. He was still there, calmly smoking his cigar.

What was happening?

Antaeus was motionless for a moment. Then he lifted his stick high in the air.

Of course.

Antaeus had told his men that he needed to be sure the Russian was the man he was after.

If he was, he'd give them a signal to proceed.

By lifting his stick.

"It's an execution!" Will swung his weapon back at the man holding a pistol against the Russian. But he was too late. Two bullets were fired into the back of Herald's head. His killer released his grip on the dead spy and let him slump face-first toward the ground.

"Our asset's dead." Will gripped his gun tightly as he saw the man who was pinning Ellie to the ground lean forward, yank up her head, and look in the direction of Antaeus.

Will darted a look at Antaeus.

The spymaster was raising his stick.

Will trained his gun back on the man who was now lifting his gun toward Ellie's head.

"You're under orders to withdraw. If you don't, you'll be—"

"Enough!" Will pulled his trigger, and his bullet sliced through the Russian operative's eye and exited through the back of his head.

The remaining six operatives immediately sprang into action, five of them dashing for cover while one of them coolly remained still and raised his gun to complete Antaeus's orders to kill the CIA woman. Will's chest shot made that man flip backward. When he was on the ground, a second round smashed through his skull.

Ellie was crawling forward, staying low to give Will sight of her captors. But she was still an easy target for them. Will got onto one knee, fired five rounds at the areas of cover the Russians were using to remain hidden from his sniper

rifle, ran fifty yards farther along the mountainside, got onto his knee again, and looked through
his scope. The different angle put three of the
men in his sightline. He took a deep breath, half
exhaled, held his breath, and fired three shots in
three seconds. Each bullet hit its target; the three
men were dead.

He ran again, desperately hoping that the remaining two operatives could no longer see Ellie, then
stopped and examined the area around the cabins.
It was no good. The men were staying out of sight,
and Will knew why: they stood no chance while
Will was out of the limited range of their handguns; their best hope lay in forcing him to come
nearer to them, to a distance where close-quarter
pistols would be far more effective than a rifle.

Ellie was still inching away from the clearing in
front of the cabins. No doubt she was waiting for
the moment one or both of the men broke cover
and shot her in the back. Will had to get to her, and
fast, but while the men were still hiding there was
one thing he had to do first. Kill Antaeus.

He pointed his gun at the area where Antaeus
had been sitting.

The spymaster was no longer there.

Will urgently scoured the distant mountainside
for signs of the Russian.

Nothing.

He silently cursed.

After fixing a fresh magazine into his rifle, he
ran down the escarpment toward the buildings,
leaping over clumps of heath that were renowned
for twisting or breaking hikers' ankles, hearing the

gentle whoosh of the sea grow louder as it eased back and forth over the seaweed-strewn coastline's pebble-and-sand beach, the rich and salty air causing his nose to sting and his lungs to feel that they had acid inside them as he sucked in the brutal air to fuel his exertions.

The cabins were now five hundred yards away, still too distant for the men to pose any threat to him. He slowed down as the incline lessened and he was confronted by round white rocks as high as his waist, haphazardly scattered on the heath as if dropped there from the heavens by playful child gods. Moving at a walking pace between them, he removed the weapon's scope and raised his rifle to eye level, using the fore and rear sights to try to spot the men.

Nothing.

Then he sensed movement to his right, and he flinched, crouched, twisted, and readied his gun. But it was only a white-tailed eagle, launching itself off the ground with a small writhing rodent in its beak. As the bird rose higher, it was able to glide with only the occasional flap of its majestic wings. Will recalled watching a similar bird of prey circling high above him in a remote part of Russia, while he was putting a brave, dead colleague's entrails back into his body.

He wondered why that memory had come to him now, of all times.

Was he about to die?

Maybe. On this routine operation. One that he'd believed was beneath him. What an idiot he'd been.

The CIA analyst spoke again, something about him having to surrender to CIA custody because he'd disobeyed orders, but her words barely registered. He turned off his radio and moved beyond the boulders onto flatter land.

He felt each step was drawing him closer to death.

He could see Ellie clearly now with his naked eye. She'd stopped crawling and was staring at Will with a calm expression. Most people in a similar situation would have bolted from the scene in fear. And they'd have been killed in doing so. But Ellie was very different; she knew exactly what she was doing.

Remain motionless.

Put her faith in Will.

Only attempt to escape if Will failed.

Will was two hundred yards away from the cabins. Though it would take a very lucky shot to hit him at this distance, his breathing was fast, and his temples throbbed.

And as he moved farther forward, he kept asking himself, Are you sure you paid that council tax bill? Really sure? Because if you haven't, you'll be summoned to court and will be fined a hefty sum that will preclude you buying anything by Hans Dagobert Bruger. He didn't know why this thought was in his head, but did know that thinking about it was far preferable to thinking about getting to within range of two men who'd kill him without hesitation or remorse.

One hundred yards.

Kill range for an expert shot holding a handgun.

God, was he facing such men? He was. Antaeus only surrounded himself with excellence, so the two men before him were no doubt expert operatives.

He walked toward Ellie, his gun moving left and right to cover the two areas beyond her where he thought the operatives were hiding—small grass-covered mounds that were fifteen yards in front of the largest timber cabin, places where at any moment two men could break cover and put bullets in his heart and brain. He'd never thought he would die in a beautiful place. Instead, he'd always believed it would be in a dingy hotel room, a war zone, or a Third World gutter.

He made a decision. If he died here, his soul would stay nearby, drifting along the rugged coastline and fantasizing about casting a line into one of the rivers as the Atlantic salmon made their run. It was a lonely place, yet stunning. He would be at peace here.

When he reached Ellie, he crouched beside her while keeping his gun fixed on the mounds. Her drawn face was covered in grime, though her eyes were glistening and focused. He made ready to move on, but she grabbed his arm and yanked down on his jacket.

She whispered, "Got a spare handgun?"

Will shook his head.

To his surprise, Ellie smiled, winked, and said, "Then there's a lot resting on you being able to do your job." Her expression turned resolute. "Good luck."

Will moved toward the cabins.

• • •

The Russian SVR operative glanced at his colleague twenty yards to his left and nodded to indicate that he was ready. He didn't need to make the gesture, as both men had served together in numerous Special Forces and intelligence combat situations to the extent that they could read each other's thoughts in situations like this. They could operate anywhere—land, sea, air, rural, urban—but excelled in the places that could break an otherwise tough man. Though rugged and cold, this place was a walk in the park compared to the weeks-long training exercises and operations they'd done in Siberia and the Arctic Circle.

And it would be a pleasure and a mere formality to deal with the man coming toward them. Though the Russian knew snipers could be useful, he felt nothing but contempt for them. Killing a man from a distance was an easy thing to do; it was not until you'd experienced putting your hands around a man's throat and watching his eyes nearly pop out, or wrenching a knife upward in his belly while smelling his breath as you held the back of his head close to yours, or seeing a flash of fear in his eyes as you walked quickly toward him and made two shots into his chest, that you really understood what it took to extinguish a human life. Snipers rarely got their hands dirty. They didn't understand close-quarter combat.

The Russian and his colleague did.

He heard footsteps.

Now the footsteps were faster, the noise of them growing louder.

The sniper was coming for them.

The Russian raised three fingers to his colleague, then two, then one.

They broke cover from behind the mounds, their pistols raised toward the encroaching sniper.

But he wasn't there.

The Russian stopped and held his handgun before him, twitching it left and right to search for the sniper. Where had he gone? Movement from near the cabins to his left. He changed stance, pointing his gun in that direction, and for half a second saw his colleague being dragged backward while still upright, his feet desperately trying to keep up with the rest of his body because a big hand was on his throat, and another had two fingers in his colleague's nostrils. The rest of the sniper was obscured. His colleague was being used as a shield. The Russian had no clear shot before they disappeared into the largest cabin.

That's where the sniper had run to, and where he'd emerged from to attack their flank when they broke cover.

The Russian operative dashed to the buildings, entered the cabin, and saw his colleague on the ground, his neck at an odd angle and clearly broken.

He felt an almighty punch to his chest.

Another punch struck him on the jaw.

A hand slapped him in the throat.

A knee smashed into his ribs. His hand was

grabbed, twisted so that his arm muscles were in a lock and were weak, and he was forced to the floor and held there in a viselike grip. He knew what was coming next.

Will Cochrane's boot slammed with brutal force into his throat and held him there as his legs thrashed and his life was crushed out of his body.

Before he died, the Russian's last thought was that he'd totally underestimated his assailant.

THREE

Standing in the same spot where Will Cochrane had momentarily crouched beside her, Ellie Hallowes watched the tall officer emerge from the cabin holding one of the Russian's pistols.

He stopped and stared at the five men who'd died outside of the buildings. Ellie thought he looked haunted by what he'd done. That surprised her, because she'd met enough paramilitary men to know that they were totally focused while doing a job and acted like overexcited kids when the job was done. This man was clearly different.

He tucked the pistol under his belt, knelt beside Herald, rummaged through the dead spy's pockets, and removed his wallet and ID documentation, which he secreted in his jacket. She frowned as she watched him take off her asset's overcoat. It was the same one that Herald always wore when he met Ellie during the winter months—knee-length, expensive, Royal Navy blue, hand-tailored in Savile Row by an émigré called Štěpán. Will held it by the shoulder pads, moved to her side, and put the coat on her.

He lowered his head.

"What happened in there?" she asked.

Will looked up, but didn't answer. His greenish blue eyes were bloodshot but nevertheless shining and alert. He was, she decided, a handsome man.

She lit a cigarette and stuck it in the corner of her mouth. "I'll recommend that you get a commendation." Her cell phone rang. The number was withheld, though she knew it was the Agency calling because only it had this number. As she raised it to her ear, she thought she saw the tiniest smile on Will's face.

A man spoke to her with a deep, strident voice. He didn't introduce himself, although Ellie knew exactly who he was: Charles Sheridan, a senior CIA officer who'd proven throughout his career in espionage that he was in equal measure very capable, ruthless, and, in Ellie's opinion, a complete dick. He told her that it annoyed the fuck out of him that the duty officer had needed to call him in on his day off because it sounded like a Category 1 protocol was about to be breached by one of their own. He asked what had happened. She told him while looking at Will. Sheridan went silent for five seconds before muttering in a more deliberate tone that Cochrane *had* been in breach of the protocol and had disobeyed orders to withdraw, that she was to tell him that his Agency exfiltration route out of Norway was now going to be shut down and that the most important men on both sides of the pond were in complete agreement that Cochrane was to surrender himself to either the British or American embassy in Oslo. Sheridan said he'd send a team to the area to try to clean up the mess, though he couldn't guarantee they'd reach the location before Norwegian cops arrived on the scene, so either way Ellie was to get out of there and return to Langley.

She closed her cell and looked at Will. "Charles Sheridan says you disobeyed orders. Why did you do it?"

"It seemed like a good idea at the time not to let them put a bullet in your brain. I'm prone to being impetuous."

He was English. She wasn't expecting that. "I thought you were SOG. Who do you work for?"

Will shrugged. "As of right now, sounds like no one." His expression became serious. "What do they want you to do with me?"

She told him what Sheridan had said.

"The embassies?" He laughed. "Nice and discreet. Tie me up, put me in a box, fly me back to the good old U.S. of A., rendered as a traitor who'll face the gallows."

"You did nothing wrong."

"You just worry about yourself now."

"You'll go to Oslo?"

"Nah, never liked the city. Beer's too expensive."

Ellie blew out smoke and tapped ash onto the ground. "Then I'll have to bring you in myself."

Will didn't respond.

"Disarm you. Put a gun to your head. Walk you out of here." Ellie's expression was focused as she kept her eyes on him. "Trouble is, that's not an easy option."

Will held her gaze. "I'm not in the business of hurting female colleagues."

With sarcasm in her voice, Ellie said, "How very chivalrous of you." She dropped her cigarette onto the ground and extinguished it with her foot. "No. The option's not easy because . . ." She left her sentence incomplete as she nodded toward the bodies of the men Will had killed to save her life.

Will momentarily followed her gaze. "I just did my job."

"Yeah. *Your* job. Not an Agency job. At least, not after it told you to back down."

"Perhaps I should have backed down."

A large part of Ellie wanted to disagree and tell him that nobody had ever put their neck on the line to save her in the way that Will had done today. But she was still attempting to get the measure of Will, and responded, "Perhaps you should have." She folded her arms and repeated, "Who do you work for?"

"I'm a joint MI6-CIA officer."

"Joint?" Ellie frowned. "Paramilitary? Freelance?"

"No. Full-time intelligence officer."

Ellie's mind raced. Though the Agency and MI6 frequently ran joint missions and shared freelance assets, she'd never heard of an individual being used as a full-time employee of both organizations. The man before her had to be highly unusual. "I think you're in a classified task force."

Will was silent.

"Not one run by Sheridan. But maybe one that he'd dearly like to shut down because he wasn't given the glory of running the force."

Will said nothing.

"And today you gifted him that opportunity by disobeying orders. But it goes beyond that, doesn't it? Because those orders have to relate to some serious shit. What's this about?"

Will nodded toward the cabin where Ellie had met Herald. "I could ask you the same thing. What happened in there?"

Ever the consummate actor, Ellie shrugged and lied in a totally convincing way. "It's as we suspected: Herald was under suspicion by the Russians. They came here to permanently shut his mouth."

"I don't believe you're telling me everything."

Though she didn't show it, Will's perception caught Ellie by surprise. "Why not?"

"Because you're standing here talking to me, when instead you should be getting as far away from here as possible before cops show up."

"Maybe I just want to spend a few moments with the man who saved my life."

"Touching, but impractical. I doubt a deep-cover officer like you wants to get anywhere near a Norwegian police cell."

"Jail doesn't scare me."

"No. But having your cover blown does." Will admired the great strength of character Ellie had shown by winking at him when she was faced with the likelihood of her own death. Moreover, for the first time in his life he believed he was standing before someone who, like him, truly understood what it was like to operate in the very darkest recesses of the secret world. Plus, he liked her on sight. But, he knew that he had to be mentally one step ahead of her.

Ellie felt the same way about Will.

Will continued, "You're standing here because you want to know why the Agency was prepared to let you die."

"Obviously."

"Less obvious is the possibility that you're in possession of information that's unsettled you. Information that maybe you want to share with me, if you decide to trust me. Herald information."

Ellie held her fingertips together against her mouth and studied Will. Should she tell him what Herald had said before the Russian team stormed the cabin? Say nothing and walk away without knowing why the Agency had been willing to sacrifice her? Leave Will to the dogs? Help him? It all came down to a matter of trust.

Trouble was, trust was a dangerous concept in her line of work.

Will knew what she was thinking. "It's a judgment call."

"It is indeed. And what's your judgment of me?"

"My judgment's incomplete and therefore flawed. But we're running out of time. Maybe you have something for me and I have something for you. And maybe they're linked. We have to make a decision."

Every instinct told Ellie to keep her mouth shut and walk away. She'd survived her entire deep-cover career by making it a rule to never put her faith in others in the field. Today should be no exception.

But it was.

The CIA had been willing to have her killed. Herald had told her that there was a Russian mole at the top of the Agency. And she was standing before a man who'd not only risked his life to save hers, but was also paying a huge price for doing so.

She was silent for one minute before making a decision. "Herald told me the Agency is compromised. A Russian mole's sitting in Agency senior management."

Will's eyes narrowed. "Identity? Other details?"

"Nothing else, aside from Herald telling me to trust no one. We were then snatched before he could tell me more."

Will shook his head and muttered to himself, "Shit, shit."

"Does it mean anything to you?"

"On face value, nothing. But I'm trying to put the pieces together of what happened here today, and maybe that will help me understand more about the mole. Have you heard of Project Ferryman?"

Ellie shook her head.

"It's what nearly got you killed and why Langley wants to cut off my balls. It's a CIA operation, by all accounts highly classified. I reckon even the duty officer who told me to back off wasn't cleared to know about its relevance to what happened here. But I'm also betting your man Sheridan *is* Ferryman cleared, considering he was called in." He pointed toward one of the mountains. "Earlier, a senior Russian spy sat there, watching over everything. The men who attacked you were doing so under his orders. His code name's Antaeus. I had him in my sights and should have been allowed to kill the bastard. Ferryman protocols blocked me from doing so." He shook his head. "Antaeus will be long gone by now."

"Do you know what Project Ferryman is?"

"No. But here's the thing . . ."

Ellie interjected, "Top Russian spy turns up in person here to oversee the execution of Herald; Herald knows there's a high-ranking Russian mole in the Agency; you're told to back down because of an Agency operation called Project Ferryman. Ergo . . ."

"Ergo there's a link between them all, and as a result I'm fucked, the Agency's fucked, and"—Will smiled—"you came very close to a fate worse than being fucked."

Ellie laughed. "I sure did." Her expression changed. "I could take this to the FBI."

"You could."

"But Sheridan told me our countries' leaders personally authorized your incarceration for breaching protocols. That means . . ."

"They've bought into the significance of Ferryman and you could be in danger of compromising Western security if you go to the feds and try to blow this open."

Ellie walked to Herald, crouched beside his dead body, placed his hand in hers, and whispered, "Thanks for the coat." She looked at Will. "Herald could be a pain in the ass, always waffling on about crap, loving the sound of his voice. But I liked him. He gave me invaluable insight into Russian secrets. And he put his life on the line for me."

"As you did for him."

"Yeah, as we all do. And on and on it goes until we all fall down." She gently rested Herald's hand on his chest, stood, and asked, "What are you going to do?"

"I'm not sure I should tell you."

Ellie shrugged. "Why not? We've done the foreplay, moved to second base, might as well go the whole distance."

Will faced west toward the mountains. "I'm going to try to get to the States and find out what Ferryman is."

Ellie moved to his side. "You think you can make it that far? European agencies will be put on your trail."

"I've got to try."

"Even if you make it to the States, they'll shoot you before you get anywhere near Langley and the answers."

"What other choice do I have?"

"Two choices. Either give yourself up and I'll support your actions. Or disappear, get a new identity, and forget all about Ferryman."

"Is that what you'd do if you were in my situation? Surrender or vanish?"

Ellie followed his gaze toward the mountains. "Surrender? No. But vanishing's something I excel at."

"And you'd do it now if you were in my shoes?"

"I . . ." She turned to face him. "Look, I don't know what I'd do." She smiled. "But I do know that there's no more 007 days for you, Mr. Bond. You've just had your license to kill revoked. No chance of you getting access to Project Ferryman."

"I could track Sheridan down and make him talk."

"Tough-guy stuff? You could end up being put in jail for laying a hand on such a high-ranking U.S. official."

"True. It's also unworkable. For the same reason you can't go to the feds, I can't confront Sheridan until I know the details of Project Ferryman. It seems Ferryman's of vital importance to our countries. I can't just blunder into the States to get answers. I could compromise something that's beyond our comprehension."

"Beyond my life, judging by what happened today."

"Exactly," Will said. "Sorry, that was insensitive. I—"

"Stop." Ellie fixed another cigarette in her mouth, lit it, and winked at him in the same way she'd done before. "You want to be insensitive, then start patronizing me."

"Fair point."

Ellie nodded. "There. Fourth base achieved—first lovers' tiff." She exhaled smoke and said in a measured and cold tone, "There is another potential option open to you."

"I know."

"You'd considered it already?"

"I'd considered it, and rejected it."

"Why?"

"Because, like you, I don't put my faith in other people."

Given that Ellie had been internally wrestling with her lack of faith in others only moments before, it made her uneasy that Will had the very same thoughts. With her back to him, she walked a few paces closer to the mountains and thrust her hands into Herald's coat pockets.

Will watched her as she stood motionless, just staring at the stunning vista. Large snowflakes began to slowly descend in the windless air.

"I've spent ten years as a deep-cover operative." Ellie's voice sounded distant. "You know what that means?"

"Yes." Will knew that it meant she'd spent five years longer than the maximum time an intelligence officer could expect to operate under-cover before the constant state of paranoia and fear would finally take its toll on even the strongest mind. "Why have you stayed in the field so long?"

"Because I was never interested in a desk job in Langley."

"Is that your only reason?"

Ellie hesitated before answering, "Thought I was doing some good."

"For the States?"

"For the people who live there, yeah."

"The Agency should have pulled you out of the field. You're on borrowed time. I'm surprised you're not dead in a ditch somewhere with a bullet in the back of your head."

"Thanks for the mental image."

"It's one you've thought of every day during the last ten years."

"It is." She turned to face him. "And you know what I've concluded about that image?"

"You've accepted it, and that's how you survived so long in the field."

She nodded. "But the thing is—"

"You never thought you could be shot with the blessing of the Agency."

"Or needing to be rescued by a guy who's on the run." She pulled out another cigarette, stared at it, and replaced it in the pack. "You saved my life. That matters. But what also matters to me is that I've gone above and beyond what the Agency should have expected from me, and in return they've stuck the knife in me. So, I can no longer put my faith in the organization. And that means I'm faced with the choice of putting my faith in nothing or something."

"Something?"

"You." She folded her arms. "The only option that makes sense."

That option was for Ellie to return to Langley, pretend to senior management that she'd tried to persuade Will to surrender to the embassies in Oslo, somehow gain access to the Project Ferryman files, and relay what she'd discovered to Will if he made it to the States.

"If you get caught they'll—"

"Oh, come on!" Ellie made no attempt to hide the sarcasm in her voice. "Don't give me a pep talk about risk, okay? I know this stuff backward. Just don't."

Will made a decision. "Okay. Get a pay-as-you-go cell phone. Not in your name. Deposit its number at a DLB in Washington, D.C." He gave her the precise location of the dead-letter box. "If it rings, it'll only be me. But you might not hear from me for a while. No idea how long it's going to take to get to America. Given you're a deep-cover operative, I'm assuming you know how to get stuff? In particular, disguises and people's home addresses."

Ellie nodded.

"Okay. I'll need a lockup or an apartment in D.C. Someplace on the outskirts and cheap. And I'll need you to procure and store some things for me there." He told her what he had in mind, and drew out his wad of cash to give her money.

But Ellie walked up to him and said, "You'll need every cent you've got. I'll get you what you want. We can settle up later."

Will held out his hand.

Ellie shook it and held it for a few seconds, staring at the scars on his fingers. It surprised her that holding his warm hand made her feel so good. "We need to go."

"We do." Will looked at the place where earlier he'd had Russia's best spymaster in his sights. "Antaeus was here in person to make sure we didn't learn about his mole." He fixed his gaze on Ellie. "Be *very* careful. Trust no one."

FOUR

Eighteen hours later, Alistair entered a large boardroom in the CIA headquarters in Langley. The MI6 controller, co-head of the joint CIA-MI6 task force, had been summoned here because he was Will Cochrane's boss. The other co-head, CIA officer Patrick, was already in the room, sitting on a chair facing three people on the other side of a large oak table. The room was nothing like the others in the sprawling headquarters: it had oak paneling on the walls, leather-upholstered chairs, and ornate oil lamps that emitted a flickering bronze glow through their tulip-shaped glass bulbs; on the table was a tea set and doilies that would have looked at home in the Claridge hotel. Alistair had been in this room twice before, once to talk in fluent Arabic to a visiting Arab prince who was young and charming and naive to the nastier ways of the world, and latterly to advise the head of the Agency that MI6 was certain the Chinese had recruited an employee of the NSA.

On each occasion he'd been here, the room reminded him of the officers' quarters on a seventeenth-century man-of-war ship.

The slim, middle-aged controller was, as ever, immaculately dressed, wearing a blue three-piece suit, a French-cuff silk shirt with a cutaway collar, a tie that had been bound in a Windsor knot, and black Church's shoes. His blond hair was trimmed and lacquered in the style of an Edwardian gentleman.

Patrick looked similar to Alistair and was the same age. But today, the CIA officer had not opted to match Alistair's immaculate look; he wasn't wearing a jacket or tie, and his shirtsleeves were rolled up to reveal his sinewy and scarred forearms. Alistair knew from experience that his informal attire meant the CIA officer had contempt for the men opposite him and was pissed off.

Alistair sat next to him and studied the three people on the other side of the table. Though he knew of them, he'd never met them in person before. The man directly opposite him was Colby Jellicoe, a former high-ranking CIA officer and now an influential senator who sat on the Senate Select Committee on Intelligence, an oversight body that was tasked with ensuring that the CIA operated within the rule of law. Next to him were CIA director Ed Parker and senior CIA officer Charles Sheridan.

Jellicoe spoke first. "The Norwegians got there before we could, and they're saying there are dead American spies on their turf and they want to know why."

Alistair placed the tips of his fingers together. "Dead Americans? Oh dear."

"Yeah, well, they've been made to look like Americans, anyways." The senator picked up a pen and jabbed it in the direction of Alistair. "We're now at the diplomatic shit storm stage of a cluster fuck."

"What a delightful turn of phrase." Alistair was analyzing Jellicoe. Probably mid-fifties, short, fat—no, fat in places, wrists were normal size, face was jowly rather than round, probably he'd lost and gained weight throughout his life, but he wasn't naturally fat. What did that mean? He was a binger, yes, a man who at times couldn't resist being a gourmand, a pig. That was decided then: Jellicoe was a pig. "I'm sure you can placate the Norwegian government with a little honesty and perhaps a reminder about the nature of false-flag operations."

Jellicoe looked over the top of his glasses with an expression of utter hostility. "That's providing we want to try and placate anyone."

"Try *to*."

"What?"

"Try *to*. Never mind." Alistair smiled. "Let me guess—you'd like to use this . . . cluster fuck to enable your own agenda."

"And what might that agenda be?"

"There are many possibilities, but I've not yet settled on one. But don't worry, it'll come to me. All I need you to do is to keep opening your mouth."

Jellicoe leaned back in his chair, huffed, and tossed his pen onto the table.

Ed Parker picked up the reins. "You can't protect Cochrane."

Alistair nodded. "Of course we can't, because we don't know where he is."

"You got a number where we can call him?"

Alistair answered truthfully. "No. We had to have him completely off the radar in Norway."

"Has he called you?"

"No."

"Likely to?"

"I sincerely doubt he would."

"Why not?"

"Because he'll assume my phone is being monitored by people like you."

"Doesn't matter. We will inevitably get him."

"Inevitably?" What did Alistair think of Parker? Honest face, no anger or hostility in his voice, instead his tone was quiet and resigned, and a moment ago he'd made the briefest of glances at Jellicoe with an expression that said he was uncomfortable with what the senator was saying, or with the situation, or with Jellicoe himself. Alistair decided it was all of those things. But Parker was here because he followed orders. Despite being one of the eight directors who reported to the Director of the CIA, and despite his good nature, he was a weak bureaucrat, a plodder. "Patrick and I have direct lines to our respective premiers, men who've always been very keen to ensure that Mr. Cochrane's free to do his work. Because we've no means of getting hold of Cochrane, you'd be doing us a courtesy by *inevitably* capturing him. But that's where it will end. We'll whisk him away and put him back in the field."

"No you won't." This came from Charles Sheridan.

"And why not?"

"We'll come to that."

"Oh good, because I do like suspense." His eyes took in everything he could see of Sheridan. Tall man, early forties, a full head of brown hair that was short at the sides and back, probably meant he was ex-military, the type who thinks that all civilians need a few toughen-you-up years of national service so that the world can be a more disciplined and simpler place. Though they were physically entirely different, his expression matched the hostility of Jellicoe's, and so far he'd not looked once at the senator; instead his eyes were fixed on the men before him. Sheridan completely agreed with everything Jellicoe represented in this room. He was his ally. No, that was an overly generous assessment. There was no doubt that Jellicoe was running the show, and that meant Sheridan was his pawn.

Pig. Plodder. Pawn.

Alistair wondered which of the three men would speak next.

It was the pig. "We need to know more about the task force you guys run."

Patrick exclaimed, "No fucking way!"

Alistair glanced at his colleague. Oh dear God. His face was flushed, his eyes wide, and the sinews in his neck were jutting out like knife blades. When Patrick became like this, it usually meant he wanted to rip someone's head off and eat it. "What my friend means is that in order for us to comply with your request, we'd need written clearance to do so and from the highest authority."

"And that authority ain't going to give you clearance, Jellicoe!" Patrick was leaning forward.

Alistair patted a hand on Patrick's leg, knowing it would only further fuel his colleague's anger—anger that was useful in situations like this. "Gentlemen, let's sort this out amicably. I've had a rather long and turbulent flight to get here to understand why you're on the warpath because my officer wanted to kill enemy number one when he had him in his sights, and because in killing Antaeus's men he breached Project Ferryman protocols. What is Ferryman?"

Jellicoe and Sheridan laughed, and Parker averted his gaze.

"Written authorizations or otherwise, you can't expect us to tell you anything about our task force and the nature of Cochrane's work if we don't understand the implications of his actions in Norway. What is Ferryman?"

The senator composed himself. "I'll tell you exactly what Project Ferryman is. It's something much more important than your shitty little *special relationship* task force, or your loose-cannon lone wolf for that matter."

Patrick leaned back. "Thankfully, the president and British prime minister don't share that view."

Jellicoe seemed unflustered by the comment. "You think so?" He loosened the knot of his tie, undid the top button of his shirt, and rubbed his flabby throat. "Task Force S, formerly known as the Spartan Section, has been in existence for eight years, ever since Will Cochrane passed the Spartan Program." He pointed at Patrick. "Two years ago, Cochrane landed in your lap and needed your help. You and some of your Agency colleagues started working with the Section and as a result of that work a decision was made from on high to make the unit a British-American collaboration." Jellicoe picked up his pen and started twirling it around his fingers. "I can give you a blow-by-blow account of the three joint task force missions you've conducted if you like. Actually, make that four missions, if you include Cochrane's unsuccessful hunt for Cobalt."

The menace in Patrick's voice was unmistakable as he asked, "How do you know that information?"

For the first time since arriving in Langley, Alistair felt angry. "I too want to know the answer to that, before making a decision on whether to report you to my superiors for obtaining highly classified information without clearance to do so."

"Clearance?" Jellicoe withdrew a sheet of paper from his jacket, unfolded it, and placed it in the center of the table. "Your superiors?" He tapped the sheet. "You mean these guys?" He pushed the paper toward Alistair with one finger. "Take a moment to read that. Might put things in perspective."

Alistair read the brief note, recognized the two signatures at the bottom, momentarily closed his eyes while feeling utter dismay, and handed the letter to Patrick.

"This can't be possible." The Task Force S

co-head's voice was trembling with rage and shock. He slammed the note onto the table and sat in stunned silence.

As did Alistair. The president and prime minister had personally signed a letter stating that Project Ferryman had nearly been jeopardized by the actions of Will Cochrane and Task Force S, that an international warrant for Cochrane's arrest had been issued and would remain in force until Cochrane was caught and dealt with away from public scrutiny, that Alistair and Patrick were to give full assistance to Senator Colby Jellicoe in his efforts to apprehend Cochrane, and that with immediate effect Task Force S was permanently shut down.

Jellicoe grinned. "You're lucky Ferryman's still intact, or you would have been strung up rather than disbanded. Try and"—his smile broadened— "try *to* understand that Cochrane's a dead man walking, and his bosses have just had their balls cut off."

FIVE

Even though the sun had started rising only minutes earlier, the occupants of the Norwegian coastal home were clearly awake, with smoke billowing from one of its chimneys and interior lights switched on. It had two small outbuildings and a barn, and in front of them a small trawler boat was moored alongside a jetty on a thin inlet of the sea. The place was in a flat valley, carpeted in snow and an icy early-morning mist, and was surrounded by hills. Will was on one of the hills, staring at the isolated encampment. He'd walked forty-two miles north to reach the location.

Shivering violently, he watched the place for four hours, saw an older man and three younger men coming and going from buildings, and a woman and a teenage girl doing chores. Will's physical situation was bad. He'd had no food for two days, and his weak state meant his body was struggling to generate heat.

By midday the sun was up high in the cloudless sky but the temperature was still dreadfully cold, at least fifteen degrees below freezing. Will saw the men get into a pickup truck and drive off the property along its only track. When they were gone, Will rose to his feet, brushed snow and ice from his face, and shuffled painfully down an escarpment until he was in the valley. Keeping the outhouses between him and the main residence, he carefully moved forward, desperate not to be seen by the woman or the girl. He reached the jetty, moved along it in a crouch until he was beside the trawler, and searched the boat's metal hull. He found what he was looking for, close to the bow on the vessel's port side. Crouching lower, he looked at the fist-sized circle that had been scratched on the hull's paint. He took out his handgun, ejected the magazine, and used the gun clip to scratch a cross within the circle. Replacing the magazine in the gun, he carefully made his way back off the jetty, past the outbuildings, and back up the escarpment.

Three hours later the vehicle and men returned. Will's teeth and jaw were shuddering uncontrollably, but he didn't care because nobody could hear him here. The men exited their truck and went about their duties.

After a further two hours it was dark. Will was lying on his front, his arms wrapped around his chest even though they did nothing to get him warm. His breathing was shallow and he could taste blood in his mouth; his eyeballs throbbed in agony from the cold; the shaking continued. The house was fully illuminated again, with two exterior lights switched on as well as tiny lights lining the jetty. Will imagined that the occupants of the settlement were sitting down in their house to a hot dinner and drinks. He desperately wanted to go down there, to find any shelter and warmth, but he knew he had to wait.

Seven hours later, it was midnight. Only one light was illuminated within the house, but the outside lights were still switched on. The older man stepped out of the house's sea-facing door, stopped, lit a cigarette or cigar, and blew smoke before walking along the jetty. He moved to the front of the pier, turned toward the trawler, crouched down for a brief moment, stood again, walked back to the house, and disappeared inside. Will hauled himself to his feet, staggered, collapsed onto his knees, raised himself up again, and took agonizing steps down the hill and into the valley. His mind was a daze and he barely knew if things around him were real anymore. He desperately tried to stay conscious but felt that he was minutes away from losing the last remaining mental strength he had. Using a hand against the walls of the outbuildings to steady himself, he staggered to the jetty. He collapsed to the snow-covered ground, silently cursed, knew that he could no longer stand, and instead used his hands to pull himself inch by inch along the jetty. Snow entered his mouth; he tried to spit it out, gave up trying to do so, but kept pulling himself along the walkway until he was by the trawler's bow. He looked at the circle and cross scratched on the hull.

Three horizontal lines had been engraved over both.

It was the covert signal telling him that the Norwegian captain of this trawler knew the British intelligence officer was nearby, that it was safe for him to approach the house, and that the captain was ready to sail him out of this country.

Will rolled onto his back and stared at the spectacular star-filled sky before his eyes closed without him wishing them to do so. He wondered how long it would be before the captain found his frozen dead body.

SIX

FBI director Bo Haupman had long ago decided that the CIA was a rootless entity because it wasn't law enforcement, military, or civilian. Its officers reflected that amorphous state; they were soulless creatures who, when asked to explain what results they'd achieved and how those results mattered one bit to the man on the street, would look coy and use the excuse of secrecy to avoid the question, when in reality they just plain and simple didn't have a concrete answer. For sure, post-9/11 the Agency had taken the lead on counterterrorism work, turning many of its young bucks into John Wayne wannabes who relished the prospect of swapping their suits and attaché cases and diplomatic life for a dishdasha, an AK-47, and a tent on an Afghan mountainside. Right now, they had a bit of tangible purpose—we shot this bad guy, did a predator drone strike against this bunch of crazies, put this leader into a cell with only a blanket and a bucket of water and three burly men for company. But you could see in their eyes that they knew the party wouldn't last forever, that pretty soon they'd be going back to the world of paper reports, cocktails, agonizingly boring analysis, and the only highlight of their lives being the opportunity to listen in on a telephone intercept and learn that a terrorist's wife wants her husband to pick up some potatoes, chicken, and cabbage for dinner.

That's not to say he disliked all Agency officers. Put them in a room with a drink in their hands and they could be great company, because they'd go out of their way to talk about anything other than their work. Put a bunch of feds in a room and within five minutes all of them would be talking about how the perps are getting away with murder because the Bureau's snowed under with paperwork. Yes, Agency people could be light relief.

Charles Sheridan wasn't.

On more than one occasion, Bo had gotten himself to sleep by fantasizing about clubbing the high-ranking CIA officer to death and dumping his body in the middle of a lake.

Not that Bo could actually do that. Despite having shot a few scum in his career, and being the size of a bear that was a few years past its prime, Bo was a gentle man, and it had come as a relief when promotion had enabled him to swap his sidearm for a desk.

Still, the fantasy remained, and he imagined doing it to Sheridan right now as the CIA officer placed his leather bag on the floor, removed a raincoat that matched the style Agency and Secret Service characters wore in the movies, slumped into a chair, and gave Bo his sternest Chairman of the Joint Chiefs of Staff look. A look that was undeserved, given that Sheridan had retired from the infantry with the rank of major before joining the Agency.

They were in a small room in the Bureau's headquarters in the J. Edgar Hoover building. Bo had chosen the room as it had no table in it, and was informal and unimpressive. That would grate on Sheridan, because he would have expected the red-carpet treatment for someone of his seniority and power.

Bo gestured toward the woman next to him and asked Sheridan, "You don't mind if my secretary takes notes, do you?"

"I'd rather she didn't."

"I only asked out of courtesy."

"Do what you want, then."

"And what do *you* want?"

Sheridan glanced at the secretary. "You sure she should be in the room?"

Bo smiled, hoping he looked condescending. "The last time you and I spoke without notes being taken, you reported the content of our conversation to the head of the Agency. I didn't mind, though I was concerned when I heard that your interpretation of what was said was . . . less than truthful." Bo placed his ankle on his other leg. "In any case, she's security cleared."

"Not by us."

Bo waved a hand dismissively. "But she is by me, so she stays. What do you want?"

Sheridan stared at the secretary for a few seconds before locking his gaze back on Bo. "I want a bloodhound."

"A Bureau bloodhound?"

"No, a frickin' NYPD bloodhound," he huffed, causing small flecks of spit to stick to his lips. "Of course a Bureau bloodhound. Otherwise I wouldn't be wasting my time in this shitty place."

"Would you like a cup of coffee?"

"No."

"Tea?"

"No."

"Water?"

"No."

"Anything else that might put you at ease?"

"I am at . . ." Sheridan looked irritated as he scratched fingers against his hair and examined his nails. "Look, let's just get this over with. I need your best officer."

"To do a manhunt."

"That's what I said on the phone."

"On U.S. soil?"

"I doubt it."

"Then why don't you guys take up the challenge?"

"Because this is a matter that's being overseen by the Senate committee, and the SSCI doesn't like it when the Agency plays cops."

"Of course, plus there's the small matter that you're not very good at it." Bo continued to imagine swinging his baseball bat at Sheridan's head. "Who is he?"

Sheridan pointed at the secretary. "Tell her to stop writing!"

"I will do no such . . ."

Sheridan leaned toward the secretary. "You can

listen to your boss, lady, or you can listen to me. Keep taking notes, and I'll ensure you're put in prison for threatening national security."

The secretary darted a look at Bo, raising her eyebrows.

Bo held up his hand. "It's okay, Marsha. Let's leave the notes until Mr. Sheridan is feeling a bit more . . ." He looked directly at the CIA officer. ". . . calm."

Sheridan leaned back. "His name's Will Cochrane. British Intelligence, but he's joint with us. Last seen in Norway two days ago."

"What's he done?"

"Compromised an Agency operation. That's all you need to know and"—Sheridan raised his voice before Bo could interject—"that's all you will *ever* know."

"Have the Brits given you authority to apprehend him?"

Sheridan nodded. "You'll get the green-light paperwork and the signatories to the task. But I'm here because before I draw up those papers, I need to know if you've got an officer who's up for the job."

"A bloodhound."

"A man who hasn't failed before."

Bo was deep in thought. "Would Cochrane kill my officer to evade capture?"

Sheridan seemed to consider the question. "I think he'd prefer another way out." He shrugged. "But if he's backed into a corner, then who knows."

"His capabilities?"

Sheridan glanced again at the secretary to ensure that she was continuing to obey his instructions. "Three years ago, he covertly entered an African war zone, shot dead the deposed dictator while he was on the run, made it look as though rebels had killed the man, and exited the country without anyone but a handful of MI6 officers knowing he was there. It was the easiest job he'd done in eight years of service."

Bo frowned. "That dictator had to be . . ."

Sheridan pointed at him. "Exactly who you're thinking of, but you keep your mouth shut about that or you'll be in a cell next door to pretty missy here."

Bo ignored the threat. "What resources does Cochrane have in Europe?"

"He's got ten thousand dollars of cash on him. Plus an alias passport and credit card, but he'll be flagged the moment he uses either."

"Then he'll stand no chance of evading capture."

Sheridan laughed. "You got much experience of hunting black-ops guys?"

Bo rolled his eyes. "You're not going to get all melodramatic on me now, are you, Charles?"

Sheridan looked unsettled; clearly he had been warming up to a bit of melodrama. "Well, either way, you don't know shit, so I'll tell it to you straight. Typically, deniable operators have three preplanned options to escape a country. The first is pretty standard: they enter a country with a false passport, they leave the same way. Providing the wheel's not fallen off, it's as straightforward as that. But if something goes wrong and we think the officer's blown, the Agency will always have in place a covert exfiltration route—cross-border, sea, air, assets in situ to help him."

"Presumably that's no longer an option for Cochrane."

"No." Sheridan grinned. "We fucked him on that one."

"So that leaves . . . ?"

Sheridan's grin vanished. "That leaves the it—annoys-the-hell-out-of-me option. See, black–ops guys and girls are a bunch of paranoids. Everyone's out to get them. Trouble is, sometimes they're not wrong."

"They put in place backup contingencies?"

"Yeah."

"Without telling the Agency?"

Sheridan nodded.

"Because it might be the Agency that's tryin to . . . fuck them?"

Sheridan was motionless. "Cochrane will have at least one or two assets in Norway that we don know about. They'll try to help him get out of the country."

"Where will he go?"

"East or south, but most certainly not west."

"Yes, I can see that west wouldn't be a particularly desirable option. You know that if you approached me two weeks ago, I'd have told y straight that we didn't have the resources to another manhunt. Know why?"

"Sure. Every fed under your control was alrea tasked on a manhunt. Trying to find Mr. Cobal

Bo frowned. "Last intel we had on him was that he was moving major capital between Turkmenistan and Algeria. I still don't get why we, and every agency we know outside the States, were told to shut down that operation." His frown vanished. "You know anything about that?"

Sheridan grinned. "Not much I don't know."

"So why . . ."

"We'll get Cobalt, rest assured, but not the way we've been going about it so far. That's all I'm saying." Sheridan checked his watch. "You going to capture Cochrane, or not?"

Part of Bo wanted to tell Sheridan to give the job to another agency, because any enemy of Sheridan's couldn't be all that bad. No. That's exactly what Sheridan wanted to hear so that he could go back to the SSCI, tell them a bunch of crap, and try to persuade them that the Agency should be given the task. "Okay, we'll do it."

Sheridan looked momentarily annoyed before composing himself and giving his most insincere grin. "Great to hear, but you should know that I've been given authority to sit in your bloodhound's team and watch progress. Officially, the term is 'adviser.' But better for you to think of it as 'pain in the ass.'"

Bo had expected this. "It's an FBI operation, meaning we have primacy up to the point when we capture him. After that, you can do what you want with Cochrane. Do you know what primacy means?"

Sheridan didn't answer.

"It means that you're not an adviser or a pain in

the ass. It means that for the duration of the man-hunt, you're my bloodhound's *employee*."

Sheridan didn't like that description one bit. "Well, you better get your man in here, so I can meet my new *boss*."

In Bo Haupman's fantasy, he stopped beating Sheridan around the head. This was turning out to be much more fun. "When you called me to say that you needed to speak to me in person about a potential manhunt request, I thought I'd alert my best officer that you were coming."

"Good, get him in here!"

Calmly, Bo replied, "Oh, there's no need." He pointed at Marsha Gage. "My best bloodhound's been in the room with us the whole time."

SEVEN

"Can you hear me?"

His eyes were shut but he could feel his body moving up and down. He could smell coffee, tobacco, and the sea.

"You need to wake up."

He moved his fingers; they touched cloth. He moved his feet; they were in boots.

"It's time."

Will opened his eyes. His vision blurred at first but then he saw a man, the older person he'd seen light tobacco before walking onto the jetty. He was in his fifties, was thick-set and looked very strong, had a beard and sandy-colored hair with streaks of gray, wore a turtleneck sweater and oilskin waders, and had a cigar fixed in one corner of his mouth. His muscular hand was outstretched toward Will. Will grabbed it, pulling his body up until he was seated. Looking around, he saw he was on a bed in a tiny cabin containing four other beds. Two windows were on one side of the cabin, beyond which sea pounded their glass. He was on the trawler, and to judge by its rolling movement they were far out at sea.

The Norwegian captain spoke in a deep, thick accent. "You've been asleep for twelve hours. That's more than enough rest for any man, even though you were in danger of getting hypothermia. My wife's been looking after you."

Will released the Norwegian's hand, looked down and saw that he had been dressed in a sweater, jeans, and boots. He frowned. "Twelve hours?"

The captain shrugged. "Seems you needed the rest. Plus, my sons and I didn't need your help to get this far. But we're about to exit Norwegian waters, and I need you awake in case we spot a coastal patrol heading toward us and"—he smiled—"we need you to jump overboard before they search the boat."

Will stood gingerly, worried that his legs might buckle. But they were strong and steady. He had needed the sleep. He also knew the real reason why the captain needed him to be awake before they entered international waters.

The captain needed every person on the boat to be on hand to throw stuff into the sea if they saw a naval or customs vessel approaching them.

The captain was a smuggler—mostly precious metals, counterfeit money, stolen goods, though Will wasn't blind to the fact that the man sometimes smuggled nastier stuff like drugs and weapons. Four years ago, he'd learned about his activities by reading files belonging to the MI6 division that targeted international organized crime. He'd had no interest in the ongoing efforts to monitor and one day thwart the activities of criminals, because that task was in the safe hands of other officers, but he was most certainly interested in the people in the files: criminals he could approach without MI6 knowing and whom he could help if one day they'd do the same for him. The trade was simple—I tip you off if I think the net's closing in on you; you get me out of your country if I need you to do so. Over the years, he'd handpicked and recruited dozens of men like the Norwegian captain, spread out across the globe; people who could get him stuff, who traveled off the radar, who had overriding reasons not to tell a soul about their secret pact with Cochrane.

No doubt it was a morally ambiguous thing for Will to do, but Will had long ago given up attempting to grapple with the ambiguities of his line of work.

Right now, all that mattered was going west, and the captain's smuggling route was going to do that for him. "Thank you."

The captain waved a hand while puffing smoke from his cigar. "I don't need gratitude." He looked up at the ceiling. "Come on, make yourself useful on deck. Providing the weather holds, two days until we reach Greenland."

EIGHT

Ellie Hallowes pulled up the collar of her overcoat, thrust her hands into her pockets so that they were dry and one of them could grip the metal box, and hunched her shoulders, because rain was pouring out of the sky and it was cold and dark. Hunching her shoulders did nothing to stop the wet and chill, but it made Ellie feel at least a bit like the many people around her who'd been caught in the sudden downpour in Washington, D.C.'s small Chinatown.

All of them were tourists who should have been tucked up in bed in their hotel rooms. Adults and kids jostled for space to move onward while gawping at the primary-colored glow from the twenty restaurants and their window displays of Peking ducks on rotisseries and neon signs in Cantonese, and inhaling the rich aromas of soy and oyster and hoisin sauces, aniseed, Szechuan pepper, cinnamon, ginger, garlic, and cloves.

Ellie liked Chinese cuisine. But tonight, the pungent smells from the restaurants seemed out of place, because they reminded her of her safe places—the havens where she could shut her door at night, not fear the moment when she might inadvertently say something that compromised her undercover work, kick off her shoes and watch TV, and eat stir-fry noodles out of a cardboard carton.

Right now, she wasn't in one of her safe places.

She wondered if she was doing the right thing by finally laying the tiny metal box to rest. Twenty-two years ago, her father had placed it gently in her hand while they were watching ballet at the Kennedy Center. She was thirteen, and was wearing a ball gown that her father had bought from a second-hand store and had arranged to be altered by a seamstress who refused payment for the job because her daughter was at the same school as Ellie and she knew Ellie's father had it tough. He was wearing a bow tie and old tuxedo, one that would have looked good on him when he was younger but now was shiny with wear. She remembered smiling at him and noticing a few flecks of dandruff on the black shoulders of his jacket. Poor Dad; he'd made such an effort to look smart for her, but had forgotten to brush down his suit. Her mother would never have let him go out like that. But she had died the year before and they were here to commemorate the anniversary of her death by attending her favorite ballet, *Giselle*.

Inside the box was a plain nine-carat necklace with a heart pendant. As she'd held it with her fingers, he'd leaned toward her and said, "Your Mum told me that I had to be smarter than usual when you got to the teen years, that I wasn't to get all awkward just 'cause you were becoming a woman, and that I needed to buy you pretty things."

He'd sat back in his chair, pretending to watch the performance, but Ellie could see that he was tense. No doubt he'd rehearsed what he'd said to her, and was now wondering whether he'd used the right words. Ellie had placed the necklace around her throat and kissed her dad on his cheek. His rigidity vanished, replaced with a big grin and look of utter relief.

He'd died when she was in college, and it was sometime then that she'd lost the necklace. The guilt over losing it made her hang on to the necklace's box, as if doing so made everything okay. Over the years it had sat on mantelpieces or in the corners of drawers. But all the time, she'd known that the box had meant nothing to her father. He'd wanted her to feel pretty; boxes don't do that.

So tonight, while rummaging through her hotel room in D.C., looking for a suitable container for the job, her eyes had settled on the box and she'd made a decision. It was time for the box to go.

Odd, though, that she wasn't just throwing it away; instead, she was giving it to another man. Did that mean she wasn't really letting go?

She walked out of Chinatown, south along Seventh Street NW, staying close to buildings to avoid the spray from passing vehicles. Less than a mile to her right was the White House. Twelve years ago, she'd stood in front of the building with a letter of employment from the Central Intelligence Agency inside her jacket, marveling at the center of power and feeling pride that she was being brought into its inner circle of trust. Like all college graduates about to embark on life in the real world, she'd been naive back then. Doubly naive in her case, because upon completion of her Agency training, Ellie was told that she had to resign and set up her own Agency-funded consultancy so that she could be a deniable undercover operative. One without the name Ellie Hallowes, because the real her would be kept at arm's length from the inner circle.

High-ranking Agency officers had told her that she'd been selected for the task because she'd displayed an exceptional ability to operate alone and make independent decisions. She'd believed them, and in fairness they were being truthful. But a year into being undercover, she'd realized that another reason she'd been selected was because she had no one in her life. There'd be no big Thanksgiving family dinners for Ellie, ones during which she might look around and think, I can't live this lie anymore.

She moved into a dark side alley, wondered if someone was waiting in there, and briefly recalled what she'd been taught by an ex-Delta unarmed-combat instructor at the Farm. *Fancy ninja moves don't work. Go crazy. Hit eyes, throats, and balls. Do it fast, then run.*

But the narrow alley seemed empty and quiet.

She stopped in the exact same spot she'd reconnoitered yesterday during daylight. After withdrawing a tiny flashlight, she cupped her hand over the beam to minimize the possibility of it being seen by passersby and searched the building's wall. It took her only a few seconds to find the loose brick, at which point she switched off the light and continued her task in complete darkness. Her fingers felt along the tiny gaps between the top and bottom of the brick. Fingernails would have been useful right now, ones that weren't chipped and ragged. Instead she had to use the tips of her fingers to grip the few millimeters of brick that she could reach, press hard until her fingertips were in pain, and pull the brick out.

She let it fall to the ground, quickly secreted the jewelry box in the hole, and picked up the brick to put it back in place and hide the box. Inside the box was a slip of paper containing the number of her new pay-as-you-go cell phone. It was her lifeline to Will Cochrane.

But it was only of use if Will could covertly enter the States and if she could somehow illegally access the Project Ferryman files.

Even for professionals of Ellie and Will's caliber, right now both tasks seemed near impossible.

NINE

At ten thirty the following morning, Marsha Gage entered a large rectangular hall in the FBI HQ. The room was typically used by temporary task forces and contained many desks and chairs, whiteboards, phones and computers, sophisticated imagery of parts of the United States pinned to walls, and spot ceiling bulbs that sent pillars of blue light to the floor and made the hall look like it was filled with electrified prison bars. No one else was in here because no other FBI officer had yet been assigned to Marsha. Right now, she alone was the task force. But Bo Haupman had given her the room in case that changed.

She unrolled a large map of the world and stuck it on a wall. Directly beneath the map was a large desk. Marsha decided it would be hers and started unpacking items from her bag—stationery, five cell phones, a directory containing the names and contact numbers of her key contacts in every European intelligence and security agency, and a holstered handgun; all symmetrically laid out in front of a computer terminal and landline telephone.

"Is the room okay?"

Marsha barely glanced at Haupman as he walked up to her carrying two mugs of coffee. "It'll do just fine."

The director placed one of the mugs on Marsha's desk and stared at her new map. "Like looking for a needle in a haystack."

"It is if you think that way."

Haupman laughed. "Right now, I can't see an alternative to thinking that way."

Marsha took a sip of her coffee, her expression focused as she looked at Europe on the map. "My starting point is to cut the haystack into manageable segments. Norway, Sweden, and their surrounding countries are the first segment. I've already spoken to my contacts in the Politiets Sikkerhetstjeneste and Säkerhetspolisen"—Norway's Police Security Service and Sweden's Security Police—"and they're hitting the ground running. Not just covering their own turfs, but also getting the word out fast to their counterparts in other European agencies, plus law enforcement, hotel security, transportation security, you name it. All of them know Cochrane's traveling under a passport in the name of Robert Tombs, but they also know it's highly unlikely he'll use that ID."

"Sounds like they're being cooperative."

Marsha shrugged. "Ever since we all got pulled off the Cobalt case, they're as desperate to get back into a full-blown manhunt as I am."

"They realize the risks involved?"

Marsha nodded. "Everyone in Europe I've spoken to so far has asked the same question: What do we do if we close in on Cochrane but he won't go down without a fight?"

"What did you say?"

"Kill him."

Haupman's smile vanished. As ever, this was the Marsha he knew. A great colleague, and as honest as they come, but also a woman who'd not hesitate to put a bullet in your brain if you'd done some serious messing with the law. That's why he'd appointed her as lead agent of the team that was trying to locate Cobalt. He'd reckoned she was getting close to the terrorist financier when Haupman had received the call from his boss and was told that the president himself wanted the mission to immediately abort.

"You've alerted our European-based Bureau stations?"

Marsha sighed with impatience. "Of course."

"Your husband and kids going to be okay while you're on this assignment?"

She turned to face the director and gave him a withering look. "One of the upsides of Paul being made redundant is that he's got plenty of time on his hands to look after Kimberly and Jack. You don't need to worry about my private life."

"Fair point."

"All I need from you are resources when they're required, and to be left alone to do my job."

"Don't worry, I've spread the word that you answer to me and me alone, and that no one in the Bureau is to interfere with or obstruct your assignment."

Marsha raised an eyebrow. "Answer to you?"

Haupman was momentarily unsettled. "I mean . . . well, that you *technically* answer to me."

"*Technically* is a good word." Marsha's expression softened. "You need to go up two sizes on your shirt collar. You look like you're being strangled."

The observation made Haupman's good humor return. "Yeah, I know. Just can't build up the courage to tell Mrs. Haupman that she's deluding herself that I'm still the shape of her high school prom date."

Marsha smiled. It had always touched her that Bo had been devoted to Lizzy Haupman all of his adult life. Her expression changed. "Whether we capture or kill Cochrane, I'll be in Europe when it happens."

"Damn right. Just make sure you do it without that bastard Sheridan being around."

"Yes, no Sheridan . . ." Marsha's voice trailed as her mind raced. She stepped right up to the map and placed a finger on Norway. "South or east. There's where Sheridan assumes Cochrane will go."

"Correct."

"I like facts, love possibilities, but hate assumptions."

"I know."

Her finger moved west away from Norway, over Iceland, before stopping on Greenland. "Maybe Cochrane is attempting something that Sheridan hasn't anticipated." Marsha nodded as her heart raced fast. "Thanks for the coffee. But with all due respect, *boss*, I need you to get out of my office. I've got some fresh calls to make."

TEN

Will Cochrane was standing on the deck of the trawler. In the distance he could see the snow-covered, mountainous coastline of Greenland. The boat wasn't drawing nearer to land; instead it was sailing parallel to the coast as it headed south toward the tiny port of Tasiilaq. Though the sky was now clear and had stopped yielding snow at least thirty minutes ago, large flakes were all around him, held in the air by sudden gusts of wind that were preventing them from reaching the sea.

Will gulped down tea that was stewed, nothing like the loose-leaf Assam blend that he liked to delicately prepare with no milk or other accompaniments. But out here it tasted as good as anything else he'd drunk, and in any case he knew the captain's wife would give him a stern telling off if he didn't drink and eat everything she prepared for him. The hardy crew consumed anything they could to survive out here; it was as simple as that. Will was not permitted to be an exception.

The three adult sons were also on deck, preparing the vessel as it neared port. Though a few years older than them, Will blended in with their appearance—warm clothes and boots, and faces that were covered with a few days' growth of beard. They ignored him, as no doubt the captain had told them to do, and got on with their chores of lashing ropes, removing seaweed from nets, hosing and scrubbing the deck, and squaring away anything that wasn't tied down.

The boat changed direction. Will glanced at the cabin and could see the captain inside, holding the wheel with one hand and a radio mic in the other while speaking inaudibly. Will knew the captain was radioing ahead to the Tasiilaq's harbormaster, telling him they were approaching the port, would need a berth, and had all necessary papers ready for inspection. The captain knew from previous experience that the harbormaster usually took his time before coming to the berthed vessel to check all documentation was in order, because the captain had always proven to be meticulous with his papers and cooperative. Most international smugglers are.

His vessel had only been boarded once by the customs officer who worked alongside the harbormaster, and that was only because his boss in the Nuuk HQ had decided he needed the practice. He hadn't found any contraband on the boat and he never would, because the captain had good hiding places in the vessel. But on this occasion, the only illegal thing he was carrying was Will Cochrane.

The captain had told Will how it would happen. He would be first off the vessel and would do his normal routine of walking down the jetty carrying a crate of bourbon, which would be his gift to the harbormaster and those who worked alongside him in the port. The captain's wife and sons would stand beside the boat. At that point, the captain would have completed his job of covertly getting Will to Greenland. How Will got himself off the boat was of no interest to the captain.

Will rubbed his nails through his stubble, wondered if he should shave before they reached land, and decided that anything that made him look less like himself should stay. He checked his watch. They were only three-quarters of a mile away from the port and would arrive in less than thirty minutes. He placed a hand over the handgun secreted under his belt and watched the Danish province of Greenland draw nearer.

Danish police officer Daniel Møller placed the remains of his thick raw beef and egg sandwich on his plate and put a fist on his chest while holding his breath to try to suppress a burp. The only other Rigspolitiet law enforcement officer in or anywhere near Tasiilaq was Johanne Lund, and she was sitting exactly 2.5 yards away from him at her desk in the small office that overlooked the port. Since they'd been working together for the last eleven months, Møller had burped sixteen times in front of her and always at lunchtime. Not deliberately; just that he'd been manning the office on his own for a year before his superiors in Nuuk decided to second a newly qualified officer to his post, so that she could experience what the force described as "community policing." Before then, Møller's work habits had no consequences. After the female officer arrived, the thirty-two-year-old Møller had made a conscious effort to share the shoebox office with Johanne in a way that was respectful to his new cohabitant. But sometimes he just plain forgot. After the sixteenth time, Johanne had plucked up the courage to tell her boss that perhaps he should purchase some medicine to ease his digestion.

He looked at her and she was head down typing a report. The trapped wind abated; this was good, no embarrassment to be caused in front of the woman who he was beginning to take a shine to. His phone rang, and he picked up the receiver, opened his mouth, and involuntarily let out a loud burp. Damn. "Officer Møller."

A woman introduced herself. American. FBI. She asked, "You speak English?"

"Better than Kalaallisut." Danish through and through, Møller had been struggling to learn the native language of Greenland at night school for the last two years since he was transferred to the country. Thankfully for him, Danish was also widely spoken. "How can I help, Ms. Gage?"

"Mrs." Marsha Gage spoke to him for ten minutes. "Strikes me your port is the only one on the east side of Greenland where a boat might head to from Norway or Iceland."

"It is." Møller looked at his sandwich, considered taking a bite, but thought better of it. "It's rare for my office to get calls from the FBI."

"Rare?"

"Unprecedented."

"I'm sure." The woman sounded tense. "You got weapons there?"

"Of course." Shit, when was the last time he'd cleaned his sidearm?

"A team?"

Møller looked at Johanne. "A team, yes."

"Who runs the port?"

"Papik Zeeb, harbormaster."

"Can he be useful to you?"

Møller smiled. "He's seventy-two years old, and before you ask, he's never held a weapon, let alone got one."

"Anyone else?"

"Salik Knudsen, our customs guy. He's capable enough, and we go hunting together in the summer months. I'll give him a handgun." Møller saw that Johanne had stopped writing and was staring at him. "How likely is it that the man's heading our way?"

"Can't answer that. But I can say that some of the world's most sophisticated security services haven't spotted him in Scandinavia or Europe."

"And who is he?"

Marsha hesitated, then told him.

Møller's face paled, and sweat began to drip down his forehead. "This most certainly is . . . *unprecedented*." He replaced the handset and called the harbormaster. "Any boats due in from Scandinavia or Iceland?"

Zeeb answered, "We've had nothing for weeks and only one due in during the next month."

"When will it arrive?"

"About twenty minutes' time."

"Twenty minutes?!" Urgently, Møller said, "We're on our way. Get Knudsen to meet us at the harbor." He ended the call, stood, and looked at his colleague. "We need three sidearms from the gun cabinet, plus spare ammo. I'll get the car." He paused, felt breathless, and quickly said, "I was going to ask you to join me for a drink after work. Sorry. Stupid, I guess, but thought you ought to know. Just in case . . . in case."

Salik Knudsen stared through binoculars while standing next to the harbormaster at the base of the long jetty. The blond-haired, blue-eyed customs officer could easily see the trawler slowly heading toward the berthing station at the head of the narrow pier. "Møller didn't say anything else?"

Papik Zeeb shook his head. "Just that there's a slim chance the boat might be carrying illegal cargo." The old man looked uncertain. "What should I do?"

"Go back to your office. Put a call into my HQ telling them that I'm about to conduct an on-board search alongside police officers Møller and Lund." He glanced at Zeeb. "Stay there until one of us calls you once the search is complete."

The harbormaster smiled. "Bit of action at last, eh, Salik?"

"Oh, at best it'll be contraband cigarettes and booze. But I'll take what I can get."

The trawler captain expertly steered the vessel toward the tip of the jetty and slowed the boat to five knots. At the far end of the pier, standing on the harbor wall, was a solitary figure. Though he was too far away to be distinguishable, almost certainly it was the harbormaster, eagerly awaiting his usual gift of liquor.

The captain imagined walking down the pier, holding his gift in two arms, greeting Papik Zeeb with a big smile, strolling alongside the old man to his car, and helping him put the crate into his trunk while Will Cochrane ran down the jetty and vanished before the captain and Zeeb returned to go through the formalities of checking paperwork.

That's how he'd told Will Cochrane how it would happen. Easy for a man of his talents. But the MI6 officer had said nothing in response, just looked at him while checking the workings of his handgun with an expression that made even the captain feel considerably ill at ease.

Møller stopped his car and said to Johanne, "With me. Fast."

The two police officers ran to the part of the harbor wall that hid them from the sea. Salik Knudsen was only ten yards away from them, still rooted at the base of the jetty.

"Salik! Over here," Møller beckoned him when the customs officer looked over, and crouched down even though there was no need to do so. Johanne handed Møller a pistol and spare cartridges, which Møller in turn thrust into Knudsen's hand. "You may need these."

Knudsen asked what was going on.

Møller told him.

"What's a black operative?"

Møller answered, "Apparently, someone who can kill everyone in Tasiilaq."

The captain turned off the boat's motor, shoved a cigar into the corner of his mouth, and smiled. The trip had earned him two thousand dollars. Cochrane had objected to paying the sum, but the captain had rightly pointed out that their deal was to get Cochrane out of Norway and dump him in adjacent Sweden, Finland, or Russia, but for some reason Cochrane had wanted to head west and enter Greenland. That was above and beyond the captain's duty. It meant a financial deal needed to be struck.

Two thousand dollars didn't sound like much, but it was to a fisherman who only occasionally could top up his income with more lucrative and illegal activities. And right now, the fishing catches were poor and the supply and demand for smuggled goods was going through a dry patch. Two thousand dollars would go a long way to keep him and his family alive until the warmer months produced full nets of herring and cod, and the hull of his vessel could once again contain gold, counterfeit fifty-dollar notes, and maybe some white powder.

He exited the cabin, picked up the wooden box of bourbon, stepped onto the jetty, and frowned as he saw three people in the distance walking slowly toward him.

• • •

Møller gripped his handgun tight as he cautiously stepped along the pier. He glanced at Johanne, then Knudsen. "You know him?"

The customs officer nodded. "He's the captain. I boarded his vessel a year ago. Probably he's got his wife and sons with him."

The captain stopped. He was approximately one hundred yards away.

Møller whispered, "He might be about to bolt."

Knudsen looked at the calm sea either side of the jetty. The nearest land and other vessels in the port were at least seventy yards away from the jetty, and the water around it would quickly kill anyone who dived into it without wearing a scuba dry suit. "Where to?"

"Drive his boat out of here; head home."

Knudsen shook his head as he continued onward with his two colleagues. "He'd easily be picked up at sea. He's trapped."

Møller imagined Cochrane waiting inside the boat with a weapon, cornered, with no intention of giving himself up. His voice shook as he said, "Trapped? Oh good."

They moved closer.

The captain remained motionless.

Forty yards away.

Møller shouted, "Get your crew out here."

The captain placed his box on the jetty. "What's this about?"

Knudsen answered, "Just routine. We're checking

all boats coming into Tasiilaq. We can get this done in minutes and be on our way."

They moved closer to the captain, stopped when they were a few feet away from him, and kept their pistols pointing at the decking so as not to antagonize the burly sailor.

The captain glanced over his shoulder, placed two fingers in his mouth, and emitted a high-pitched whistle. His three sons and wife stepped off the trawler and looked puzzled and anxious as they moved to the captain's side.

Knudsen smiled, and tried to keep his voice calm and jovial. "You got anything on board we should know about?"

The captain did not smile. Instead the broad man momentarily looked like he was going to step forward and rip Knudsen's head off. "Like what?"

"Like a man who wants to get into Greenland unnoticed."

The captain spat on the jetty, his saliva brown from cigar residue. "We're not a fucking ferry service. We fish."

"I know." Knudsen shrugged, hoping the gesture made it look like they were all in this together and that this was a procedural load of nonsense. "Nuuk's up its own ass. Told us we had to check every vessel. No exceptions." He laughed. "My bosses have spent too long away from the sea." His smile receded. "But I got no choice. Need to know if"—he nodded toward the trawler—"there's a man in there."

The captain was silent, his eyes darting between the three people in front of him.

Møller felt his sweat slime between his hand and the pistol's grip. "You looking to cause us trouble?"

"Trouble?" The captain's voice boomed. He kicked the box, inside which bottles clanged against each other. "I was looking to give you boys a good time, not trouble. You're the ones with guns."

Møller glanced at Knudsen. "You keep them here. We'll go on board."

As Møller and Johanne walked past the trawler crew, the captain lit the stub of his cigar and shouted out, "Good luck with that."

It was the last thing Møller wanted to hear. He glanced at his rookie colleague, nodded, gripped his pistol, and moved toward the vessel feeling sick with fear.

Will Cochrane slid the workings of his handgun back and forth, placed the pistol in his lap, flexed his muscular fingers, and arched his back. He could hear seagulls and waves gently lapping against the boat, but he had no care for the tranquillity of his surroundings. He could sense that danger was drawing closer to him.

As she stepped onto the trawler, Johanne thought three things. One, she'd never searched a boat before; two, community policing wasn't supposed to be like this; and three, perhaps she should go for a drink after work with Daniel Møller—providing of course they weren't hospitalized or dead.

Daniel seemed nervous. His hands were shaking and his face was covered with perspiration, though she could see that he was making every effort to stay in control. He was a scared man who had no choice but to face up to this situation and act brave, and that appealed to her. Less so his office habits, but guys can be like that, and she knew he meant her no disrespect. He needed a woman to make him better lunches.

Might be too late for that.

She followed him into the hold, recalling a jumped-up firearms instructor yelling at her during police training that she was the worst shot he'd ever had the displeasure of teaching. Officer Møller was in front of her, his upper body hunched, breathing fast as they entered a small cabin with bunk beds. He stopped by a narrow ladder, and pointed at his chest and the ceiling. He was going to somewhere above them, on his own. Oh yes, the place where they sail the boat, or steer it, or drive it, or whatever was the right term. That was good, bad, and bad. Good that she didn't have to go up there, bad that Daniel might get his throat slit the moment he reached the top of the ladder and stuck his head into the tiny cabin, and bad that she'd be left on her own with a weapon that didn't deserve to be in her hands.

She shook her head, eyes wide, at Daniel. What noise would he make if he were stabbed in the gullet? Worse, she decided, than the noises he made in their office.

But Officer Møller looked sternly at her and proceeded to climb. He must have been petrified.

As his legs disappeared from view, she spun around a full 360 degrees, too quickly, and her head felt momentarily giddy. She heard boots clanging on the metal ladder, the noise growing louder. Daniel coming back down? Or a murderer?

She trained her gun on the ladder. Her hands were shaking so much that she decided she'd have to fire at least three shots to stand a chance of hitting anything near the stairway.

Boots came into view, then legs.

Then Daniel.

Thank God.

Officer Møller shook his head. The cabin was empty. Did that mean they could leave now? Clearly not, because Daniel was moving onward, now holding his gun in two hands, his breathing louder than ever. Officer Møller obviously knew more about boats than she did and was leading her to a place they'd not yet searched.

He stopped by some steps, leaned right into her, cupped his hand over his and her mouth, and whispered, "The hold." His breath smelled of raw beef and eggs. Johanne decided she definitely needed to wean him off that filth. "It's the last place to check and most likely where he's hiding." He tried to smile, but the fear and tension on his face made it impossible to do so. "Drinks on me?"

Johanne nodded. Strange time and place for her to agree to a date, but under the circumstances, why not?

She followed him down metal stairs into the dimly lit base of the boat, swallowing hard while praying to God that fear didn't make her suddenly burst into tears.

• • •

Will tensed and looked at his handgun. Any moment now. Had to be ready, move quickly, get the job done, then get out of here. No time to think now. Everything's instinctual. No matter what comes your way, use maximum force, no hesitation, no guilt, no compassion toward anyone carrying a weapon.

Møller reached the bottom of the stairs, his pistol held at eye level, and braced himself for a gunshot to the chest or head. If that happened, he hoped Johanne had time to turn around and run away. It was her best option, and she should just keep running, away from the boat, the jetty, Tasiilaq, and her job in the police. At least his death wouldn't then be pointless.

The boat's cargo hold stretched the length of the trawler, not much bigger than a regular-sized living room, but was cluttered with crates, nets, lobster pots, tools, blankets, oilskin clothes, ropes, lanterns, and buoys. There were plenty of places for a man to hide.

He had to search the place thoroughly while acting like Johanne's superior officer, even though he wasn't even up to a bit of acting, let alone professional policing. Moving between the crates, he could hear Johanne behind him, breathing as fast as he was. The air was salty and fetid, from damp clothing and rotting fish and mollusks, and made him gag. Or maybe it was the wretched feeling inside.

His head banged against a low-hanging naked lightbulb, which swung wildly on its single cord, throwing haphazard light into the hold's dim recesses and causing Johanne to shriek. He grabbed the cord to steady the bulb, silently cursed, and continued moving around the room. Both officers checked behind anything that could conceal a man, lifted blankets and nets, kicked stuff to see if it prompted a killer to bolt from his hidey-hole, and finally used whatever tools they could find to lever open every crate in the room.

When they were finished, Møller looked at Johanne. Tears ran down his cheeks as he said between sobs, "He's not here. No one's here. Thank . . . thank . . ." He could no longer speak, and instead stepped forward and hugged Johanne. They were alive.

Will Cochrane scrutinized the coastline and felt relief. No cops, no others, no danger.

He thrust his pistol into his jacket, leapt from the small rubber dinghy into knee-deep water, flicked open a knife, and used it to slash the rubber. He watched the strong ebb take the shredded boat quickly back out to sea, grabbed the two oars that were floating by his legs, and walked onto the thin strip of pebbly beach. After five minutes, both oars were buried under stones. Within a couple of hours, the wash would probably expose them again, but by then it wouldn't matter. He'd be long gone.

He ran off the beach, up higher ground until he was on an empty area of ice-covered flatland, beyond which were mountains. Spinning around, he went down on one knee, pulled out the scope from the sniper rifle he'd left in Norway, and stared through it. Three-quarters of a mile away was Tasiilaq. He could see the port's jetty, the trawler, the captain and his crew, and a man he didn't know standing close to them while holding a pistol. A man and a woman, wearing cop uniforms, exited the boat and joined the group. The woman was smiling, the man was speaking, and both were holstering their pistols. The other man gave him his handgun and slapped him on the shoulder before turning toward the captain and holding out his hand. The captain hesitated, then beamed, shook the man's hand, reached down into the crate by his feet, and pulled out a bottle of bourbon, which he uncorked with his teeth. He passed the bottle around and everyone on the jetty took a swig. The male cop held his hand to his chest and vomited onto the pier before smiling and shaking his head. The female cop laughed, then she too threw up. Their bodies were reacting to the fear and adrenaline they'd felt moments ago.

Will had known he might have trouble getting off the vessel once it had berthed. That's why he'd insisted that instead the trawler crew lower a dinghy alongside the boat while they were still out at sea, so that Will could row to a place on the shoreline that was out of sight of the port.

He was glad it had happened that way and that the people who'd come looking for him had ended the day's adventures with nothing worse than a glug of the captain's awful liquor. And he was also relieved that he hadn't needed to confront any other potential danger on this bit of coastline.

He pulled his jacket hood onto his head and ran toward a destination in Greenland that contained people who were infinitely more deadly than those he'd seen a moment ago.

ELEVEN

CIA director Ed Parker was standing on a Washington sidewalk. Next to him were Senator Colby Jellicoe and his Agency colleague Charles Sheridan. Cars moved slowly past them with their windshield wipers and headlights on full because the torrential downpour made visibility poor, though it was only midafternoon. On the other side of the street was the imposing Dirksen Senate Office Building, renovated fifteen years previously to make its numerous committee hearing rooms more television friendly. In thirty minutes, Jellicoe would be sitting in one of those rooms, with cameras pointing at him while he testified to some of his colleagues.

Parker raised his umbrella so that he could see Jellicoe's face. "You shouldn't be doing this."

Jellicoe smiled.

Sheridan did not. "Shut up, Parker."

"Don't talk to a senior officer . . ."

"Senior to me by one grade, and only 'cause your paycheck says so." Sheridan flicked a finger against the tip of Parker's nose. "Having a fancy title doesn't give you the right to get all ladyboy on us."

Parker was about to respond but knew there was no point. Sheridan loved conflict, and a retort would play right into his hands. He looked at Jellicoe. "Your mind's made up?"

Jellicoe nodded, his grin still fixed on his flabby face. "Back channel, the deal's already been done with the Norwegians, so we might as well make it public."

"Why?"

Jellicoe didn't answer, and that confused Parker even more. The senator had told the Norwegian government the truth about what had happened in Norway and had given them Will Cochrane's name as the rogue officer behind the fiasco, though he'd naturally omitted any mention of Antaeus and Project Ferryman. In doing so, he'd completely defused political tensions between the States and Norway to the extent that the Norwegians were fully cooperating with Marsha Gage to hunt down the MI6 officer. But Jellicoe couldn't be so candid in a televised hearing. Instead, he'd have to say that a classified Agency operation in Norway went wrong, that the Norwegians were on our side, and that an investigation was under way into why the operation nearly caused a diplomatic furor. Some of the senators facing Jellicoe would naturally ask him for further specific details, but at that stage Jellicoe would have to keep his mouth shut on the basis of national security.

So, what was the point of airing a drastically sanitized version of events at a public hearing?

Perhaps, Parker speculated, this was about nothing more than Jellicoe getting his ambitious face back in front of the cameras. Yes, that was it. For a long time, Jellicoe had ridden the crest of a wave because of Ferryman. Parker could tell that Jellicoe was ready to take another step up the career ladder, perhaps to chairman of the SSCI. Or maybe— Parker shuddered at the thought—to head of the CIA.

That evening, Ed Parker entered his home in Arlington and poured himself a large Scotch. He didn't always drink whiskey after work, but he'd had a bad taste in his mouth all day and needed something fiery and toxic to burn it out.

Catherine was in the garden greenhouse, tending begonias, achimenes, and cyclamens while singing to the plants. Gardening was a relatively new hobby for her and made her smile and relax, and anything that made Catherine happy and contented was a damn fine thing as far as Ed was concerned. She was wearing a gray woolen cardigan with leather elbow patches and her favorite "hippie chic" skirt, which reached her ankles; her raggedy gray hair was kept in a bun by two knitting needles. She described it as her pottering look, though in recent years it was rather more the predominant Catherine look. Ed didn't mind. She looked gorgeous, the way that many middle-aged women do when they relax into life after surviving all the crap. Moreover, Catherine was not only Ed's loving wife; she was also his perfect antidote to the pissing contests he had to put up with in the Agency.

He knocked a few times on the kitchen window until she heard him, looked up, and smiled. He raised the full glass of liquor to the window, pointed at it, mimicked gulping it down in one, then crossed his eyes, stuck out his tongue, and wobbled his head as if he were blind drunk. Catherine laughed, knowing that it was her husband's call to arms to share an aperitif with him after a bad day at work.

His cell phone beeped, and to his amazement he saw he had an SMS from Sheridan. He'd never received a message from him before, and didn't even think the man knew how to send them from his phone. Probably Sheridan's long-suffering wife had finally succeeded in getting the grumpy bastard to learn how to use the cell, even though she barely spoke to him after their marriage had nearly fallen apart during their last overseas Agency posting. Given that they had no children, there was no one else in the Sheridan household who could have taken on the unenviable task. The image made Ed smile, and he imagined Sheridan huffing and puffing about civilian technology being just for kids. Of course, Catherine had rightly pointed out several times that Ed was equally useless with technology, and recently she too had needed to explain to him the basics about texts, contact lists, and how to press Send. He took a sip of his whiskey, read the message, and frowned.

Did you see him in action? Jellicoe nailed it.
Screwed the bastard to the wall.

Catherine entered the kitchen, pulled out the knitting needles, bent over, and swished her long hair to release raindrops gathered during the short walk between the greenhouse and their home. "Cocks In Agency day?"

That put the smile back on Ed's face. "Yeah, one of them."

Catherine walked to the refrigerator. "Well, there's only one thing to do." She grabbed a bottle of Sauvignon Blanc and a chilled glass and poured herself a drink. "Pizza delivery, followed by me taking a soak with a bit of *50 Shades*, and"—she blew him a kiss—"see where it goes from there?"

Ed loosened the knot of his tie. "What about Crystal?"

Their nine-year-old daughter.

"Last-minute sleepover at Debbie's place."

Ed shrugged. "We'd better make the most of it then." He walked into the living room, flicked on the TV, and started trying to find the right channel while muttering, "Fucking . . . fricking . . . shit . . . why, why, why do they make this playback thing so damn complicated?"

Catherine took the controller from him, pretended to be exasperated, and asked, "What program?"

"Senate hearing. Four o'clock this afternoon."

It only took her a few seconds to find. "I'll call for the pizza. Usual?"

"Yeah, but extra jalapeños."

"Not concerned about heartburn?"

"Least of my worries."

Catherine laughed as she walked out of the room. "On your head be it, but don't let it spoil our fun later tonight."

Ed slumped into the sofa and pressed play. God, there was Jellicoe, sitting behind a desk and microphone while facing seven senators, his ridiculously expensive suit only serving to make the plump man look like a 1920s mafioso with a heap of cash but no taste.

Ed turned up the volume.

Fifteen minutes later, he turned off the TV and briefly considered resigning from the Agency. Because Jellicoe had told everyone watching the hearing that the Agency was hunting a British intelligence officer named Will Cochrane, had pulled out a photo of Cochrane and held it up so that the room's cameras could zoom in on it, and had concluded that it would be better for anyone who saw Cochrane to kill him on sight rather than risk attempting to capture him alive.

Though Ed had as much vested interest in Ferryman as Jellicoe and Sheridan, and had agreed that Cochrane needed to be captured, he'd wanted the manhunt to be done under the radar and Cochrane to be punished by due legal process. Plus, he'd learned that Cochrane had an incredible history of serving Western intelligence. Whatever reason Cochrane had disobeyed orders in Norway, he still deserved to be treated with respect. Now, his name and face were blown and Jellicoe had encouraged everyone who owned a gun to shoot to kill if they spotted him in their backyard.

Catherine sat next to him. "Everything okay?"

Ed shook his head in disbelief. "Our best . . . best operative. We . . ." He gestured his glass toward the television, spilling whiskey on the carpet. "We . . . It's not right. We shouldn't be doing this to him."

Lindsay Sheridan looked at the silver-framed photo of Charles and her standing together in their college graduation gowns and couldn't decide if the image was making her feel sad or regretful. They looked so young then, happy, her with the nice engagement ring Charles had given her a week before the photo had been taken, Charles with his arm around her and an expression of pride and contentment. What a nice man he'd been then, before he'd joined the Agency, before they'd gotten married, and before they'd been posted overseas several times, culminating in her indiscretion with a fellow diplomat. She couldn't blame him for being angry about that—not at all—but she could blame him for what led to her being unfaithful. Over the course of years, he'd become a changed man, distant from her and sharp-tongued. She'd lost count of the number of times she'd wanted just to run away from him. All right, they had joint ownership of their home in Montgomery County, but that was the only complication they'd face in a divorce settlement, given that they had no kids. That, and the fact that he had an almighty psychological hold over her.

She placed the photo next to others on a

mahogany side table, rubbed a duster over all the frames, and sighed. A world-class education, and yet she was reduced to dusting a house for a man who showed no signs of loving her.

She heard the sound of tires on the gravel driveway and glanced across the sumptuous living room. Outside, she could see a limousine. One of the men in the rear was her husband, the other was Senator Colby Jellicoe. Oh Lord. That meant brandy and cigars stinking up her home, with her being banished from the living room while the men spoke in hushed voices about world affairs and how to spy on them.

It was a shame Ed Parker wasn't with them. At least then these types of meetings were bearable. Ed was a nice guy, would help her prepare drinks in the kitchen, chat to her, raise his eyes in disdain when Charles or Jellicoe would be barking orders at her from the other side of the house, tell her that she'd lost ten pounds even though she hadn't, and say that his wife Catherine sent her love and dearly hoped that Lindsay was fucking her way through the neighborhood just to spite her ungrateful bastard husband.

The difference between Catherine and Ed's marriage and her own couldn't have been more stark.

How times had changed since their days on the diplomatic circuit. Then she'd be at her husband's side, wearing a ball gown and gorgeous perfume, looking radiant, and working the room to support her husband's work for the CIA.

Now she was reduced to being treated with contempt and locked away from all things glamorous, interesting, and intelligent.

God, she wished she could turn back the clock and undo some of the things that had happened. Too late now. She was condemned to this life.

TWELVE

Alistair and Patrick knew for a fact that if they stood side by side they'd be the exact same width as Bo Haupman, because they were standing next to each other and were in front of the FBI director in Marsha Gage's ops room.

As usual, Alistair was immaculately dressed, though on this occasion he'd opted to turn up wearing a three-piece tweed suit that, together with his slicked-back blond hair and good cheekbones, made the MI6 controller look like an early-twentieth-century royal who'd decided that a weekend in the Scottish Highlands was in order.

It was a deliberate look—one that played up to the English gentleman stereotype but also unsettled the established norm of bland attire within the FBI HQ.

Patrick's image was also chosen with care. His suit jacket was off, slung over his shoulder and held in place by one sinewy finger; his shirtsleeves were rolled up and his tie was loosened. The CIA officer looked like he was about to administer rough justice to a terrorist in a top-secret Agency facility in Southeast Asia.

Haupman gestured toward Marsha. "This is Marsha Gage. She's running things."

Alistair stepped forward, smiled, and held out his hand. "Delighted to meet you, young lady."

Marsha placed her hand in his and didn't know what to think when Alistair lifted it and kissed the back of her hand. "Ain't been young for a while, sir, nor called a lady for as long as I can remember." She turned to Patrick.

No kiss from him, instead a firm handshake, a wink, and the comment, "Bet you're delighted that you got three dinosaurs assigned to your team."

Haupman said to Marsha, "Let me know what you need." He smiled. "And don't let these spooks do their Jedi mind games on you."

After Haupman left the ops room, Marsha placed her hands on her hips and nodded toward two desks that were facing each other in the middle of the room. "These are yours. Sheridan's desk is over there, and I hope you appreciate that I didn't sit you next to him. Thankfully, he's not here right now."

Alistair rubbed his hands and faked enthusiasm. "Wonderful. So what do you want us to do?"

Marsha frowned. "Help."

"To do what?"

"Catch your boy."

Patrick asked, "How long we gotta be here playing cops and robbers?"

"Until the robber's captured."

Alistair glanced at Patrick with a faint smile on

his face before returning his attention to Marsha. "Considering that we could be here for a while, can we request some things?"

Marsha shrugged. "Sure. Whatever equipment or data you need."

"Excellent."

Both men whipped out pens and paper and wrote lists. They handed the sheets to Marsha.

Marsha tried to keep her expression neutral as she read the notes, though she desperately wanted to smile. She looked at the two men before her, spies who she'd been advised had been two of the more powerful individuals in Western intelligence, before they'd recently had their horns removed. But now they just seemed to be a joke, particularly the crazy Englishman. "Really?"

Patrick nodded. "You did say anything."

Alistair added, "When you get to our time of life, it's the little things that keep us going."

She looked at the lists again.

Patrick wanted a chess set, De'Longhi espresso machine, menus of the best Italian and Indian delivery services in D.C., a picture of a nice sunset or something like that to keep him calm, a once-daily visit from a sports masseur who could loosen the knots in his upper back, a bottle of single-malt whiskey and two cut-glass tumblers, and a sound-proofed cubicle to put around shitty Sheridan.

Alistair had requested a wine refrigerator, a box of Cuban cigars and a humidor, matinee tickets for the National Theatre in case there was a lull of activity in the manhunt, Darjeeling tea and a high-quality tea set, and a catapult with a range of no less than half the length of this room with pellets that would sting but not cause serious injury.

Marsha sighed. "I'll get you *some* of these things."

"Splendid." Alistair walked over to Marsha's map of the world. "I had one of these on my wall when I was a boy at Eton."

"Eton?" Marsha joined him. "Why doesn't that surprise me?"

Alistair's expression turned icy, and he lowered his voice so that only Marsha could hear him. "Jellicoe has to all intents and purposes issued a death sentence for Cochrane."

"He was authorized to do so."

"Not by me."

"Seems others have a bigger say right now."

"Quite so. You agree with them?"

"Not on a shoot-first, ask-questions-later basis."

"You'd do it properly?"

"Yes. But make no mistake—if Cochrane wants a fight, we'll fight back."

"I'd expect nothing less."

"Kinda not sure that it's in my interest to have you two here, because . . ."

"We might hinder."

Marsha nodded. "I get it, but it's a fact that you've got a vested interest in keeping Cochrane underground."

"Not anymore."

Marsha frowned. "Why?"

Alistair did not answer, instead asked, "No sightings at all?"

Marsha followed his gaze at the map. "I threw

in the wild-card option that he might be heading west. We had a possibility in Greenland, but that turned out to be nothing."

"The world's his oyster." Alistair's eyes rapidly took in everything he could see on the map. "You assure me that you're going to do this professionally? That you'll take him alive if you can?"

"Yes, but I can't assure you that the mavericks think the same way." She was referring to the CIA.

"I wouldn't ask you to assure me on a matter that's beyond your control." He was deep in thought. "Jellicoe's appearance at the Senate yesterday has changed everything." He turned his gaze to Marsha. "Patrick and I will help you in every way we can, because we want *you* to find Cochrane, before the mavericks close in."

Marsha momentarily wondered if Alistair was trying to flatter her, but rapidly decided not. The MI6 controller's blue eyes were cold, piercing, and gleaming with intelligence. She'd been wrong about him. He most certainly *wasn't* crazy or a joke. "Okay, I buy that."

"I'm so glad you do."

"But you're putting a lot of faith in me. Cochrane could be anywhere."

"Does that challenge daunt you?"

"No."

"That's what I'd heard. And I'd also heard that you were head of the Bureau task force hunting Cobalt."

Marsha hesitated before asking, "Haupman told you that?"

Alistair nodded. "I told Director Haupman that you and Cochrane had Cobalt in common, because I'd tasked Mr. Cochrane to capture Cobalt."

In a near whisper, Marsha asked, "Do you know why they pulled the plug on the Cobalt operation?"

"No. I asked, and was told to mind my own business. I kept asking, and kept getting told the same thing. I do know it was authorized by our prime minister and your president. But why they made that bizarre and downright dangerous decision is beyond me. By my calculation, Cobalt's money has enabled terrorists to kill at least seven thousand people during the last five years."

"Our most conservative assessment is three times that figure."

"And you could be right."

"I should still be looking for Cobalt."

"I agree, but like it or not, we've both been given a different assignment." Alistair took a step closer to the map and put on his reading glasses. "What's motivating Cochrane right now?"

"To stay alive, evade capture, vanish, probably change identities and live out the rest of his life in a country without a U.S. extradition treaty."

"Maybe. Come closer."

Marsha took a step forward.

Alistair pointed at the map. "It was a good hunch to look west."

"Just covering bases. It produced shit."

Alistair turned toward her, and in a flash his icy demeanor was replaced with a look of utter charm. "My dear, you underestimate yourself that easily?"

"Hell, no."

"That's my girl." His icy expression returned. "It's quite possible that Mr. Cochrane has an altogether different motivation. Have you heard of a CIA operation code-named Ferryman?"

"Means nothing to me."

"Nor us, but Ferryman protocols are responsible for putting my boy on the run. And he won't like that one bit." While keeping his eyes fixed on Marsha and without looking at the map, he stretched out his arm and placed a finger on a country. "Keep looking west, because I think Cochrane's motivation is to find pure gold."

Marsha looked at the map. Alistair's finger was positioned in North America.

THIRTEEN

Despite his best attempts not to, Will imagined that the noise of his boots crunching over ice was rather the sound of his vertebrae grinding together. Though it wasn't carrying anything aside from the weight of Will's muscular physique, his back was in agony from his efforts to get across a landscape that was equal parts beautiful, undulating, frozen, and terrifying. He'd trained and operated in places like this many times before, but this was different because he had no backup, no job, no identity, and no purpose beyond establishing why his former employers had turned on him.

For years he'd felt dislocated from the real world. But it was perverse compensation that the secret world had made up for that by embracing his flaws and unique talents. Now that that world no longer wanted him, he felt more alone than ever, and he could feel the weight of the planet crushing him with the heel of its boot.

At some point soon it would snap his spine in half, but not yet, because Will had to keep going to find the truth about Ferryman. Whatever the CIA operation was, there was no doubt that it had a vested interest in keeping Antaeus alive. Getting to the bottom of that reason had been plaguing Will ever since he'd walked away from the aftermath of the gunfight in Norway. He'd considered the possibility that Antaeus had been recruited by the CIA, but had immediately discounted that option because the spymaster would never betray his motherland or, more important, abandon his achieved ambition of being the West's most formidable espionage opponent. Perhaps the Agency needed Antaeus alive as part of a bigger operation to disrupt Russia, one within which Antaeus wittingly or unwittingly played a crucial role.

No. That too just felt wrong. Antaeus couldn't be manipulated by anyone, knowingly or otherwise, because he was always several steps ahead of even the brightest minds in Western intelligence. That left the bad-taste-in-the-mouth option. One that dovetailed with Herald's declaration. Antaeus had recruited a high-ranking mole in the Agency, someone who was powerful enough to warn Antaeus off if danger was drawing close to him. Perhaps, given who was called in by the Agency duty officer when Will had the spymaster in his sights, that person was Charles Sheridan.

But that still didn't explain what Ferryman was and why it was deemed so important that the U.S. and U.K. leaders had decided to hang Will Cochrane out to dry. Sheridan might be on Antaeus's books, but it would be impossible for him alone to pull the wool over everyone's eyes, protect

Antaeus, and put Will on the run. This was about something bigger than a mole, and that left an even nastier taste in Will's mouth.

Nor did it make sense that Antaeus was alive. Three years ago, Will was given independent confirmation that Antaeus was found dead in a decimated vehicle, after Will's bomb had gone off. The man he'd seen in Norway looked much older and more fragile than the one he'd watched getting into his car in a Moscow suburb. But there was absolutely no doubt it was the same man whose body had been blown to pieces.

Up to two weeks ago, everything had been so very different. He and Task Force S's team had been scouring Europe, Africa, and South Asia for Cobalt. The objective was clear: kill him on sight. Will had support to conduct a mission of overriding importance. Then Alistair had called him and said that he was to abort the mission, effective immediately. Will had argued with Alistair, saying that he was sure they were closing in on the terrorist financier, but Will's controller had won the argument when he told him that the British prime minister had ordered that all efforts to find Cobalt were to be ceased.

Everything had gone wrong since then. And nothing made sense. So Will continued walking, determined to get answers even though he now wondered whether he'd get to the United States to do so.

According to the trawler captain's map, Will had traversed fifty-two miles of Greenland's landmass. But such was the arduous nature of the journey that it had felt three times as long. The clarity of the air didn't help—mountains that appeared to be only one mile away were actually fifteen miles distant. Reaching them seemed to take an age and made his mind cry out for variety.

Not for the first time during his trek, the thought of Christmas entered his rambling mind. After all, he was in Greenland, though that shouldn't have brought Christmas to the forefront of his mind because Christmas hadn't had any meaning to Will for as long as he could remember. Every year, he'd either been working overseas during the festive season or sitting at home on his own. Right now, either seemed preferable to what he was doing. Seeing Santa Claus's alleged base of operations up close and personal in winter was frightening. It was a lonely place to be. Maybe that was apt.

Dean Martin's "Let it Snow" began playing in a loop in his head. He didn't know why, as snow was the very last thing he wanted, but he let the jingle continue while thinking about tree lights and warm log fires: anything that took his mind off the fact that it was getting dark, the headwind was becoming stronger, and if he collapsed to the ground it was unlikely anyone would find his body until spring.

He wondered what his neighbors at his new home in Southwark did at Christmas. Perhaps David the mortician invited art dealer Phoebe and retired major Dickie Mountjoy into his apartment for some home-cooked mince pie and a glass of mulled wine. Maybe David would extend the invitation to Will.

He'd like that.

Shards of ice hit him as he moved alongside the base of a mountain and encountered a stronger wind. Visibility was very poor now; no more clear air playing tricks on the mind, instead a dark sky and weather that was howling.

Then lights were ahead of him, exactly where they were supposed to be, illuminating SUVs, a house, a track, and a small Islander aircraft.

His destination.

But as he looked at the isolated settlement, part of him wondered if it was preferable to walk on by and take his chances with the elements.

The four people who operated out of the remote place had always said that they'd help him so long as he continued to keep his mouth shut about their work here and in Canada. The protocol to get in touch with them was a call from a specific pay phone in Greenland's west coast town of Maniit-soq, a message placed in a dead-letter box in the same settlement, followed by one of the men clearing the DLB and leaving instructions there as to how to make human contact. Will had no ability to get all the way across the country to follow this protocol, so he had no choice other than to turn up uninvited at their home. That would make them ill at ease, and rather than help him, it was just as likely that they'd club him over the head, chop his body into small pieces, and scatter his remains in the surrounding countryside where they would be quickly eaten by wildlife.

He was sure all four of them were here, because the tiny Islander aircraft was next to the house.

Were it not here, at least two of them would be out of the country, meaning he'd have a chance to negotiate with the remaining two and get their help or overpower them and flee if they refused to aid him. With all of them here, he might as well be walking into a lions' den.

He wished he had other options, someone like the trawler captain who could hide him in a boat and sail him across the Davis Strait to Canada. But he didn't, so he continued toward the lights while holding his pistol underneath his jacket.

Many times during his journey here, he'd considered different scenarios of approaching the house—waiting for one of the men to exit the place and approaching him while he was away from the others; placing a message through the front door or under the wipers of one of the SUVs and then retreating to a place of his choosing where he could watch them approach while he had his gun trained on them; maybe grabbing one of the men and holding a gun to his head while he negotiated terms with the others. But all these options were too aggressive, considering that he needed their trust and significant help. He had to put his life in their hands, even though the thought of doing so made him feel sick.

Nor was he willing to wait for two or more of the men to get in the Islander and fly off before he made contact with the remaining team. Waiting for the right time to approach the captain's homestead in Norway had nearly killed him. He wasn't going to put his body through that agony again.

• • •

Marsha Gage made a call to Assistant Commissioner Danny Labelle of the Royal Canadian Mounted Police. After she told him about her role in hunting MI6 officer Will Cochrane and explained that she was already in contact with his compatriots in the Canadian Security Intelligence Service, she said, "It's a long shot, I know, but there is a chance he may be trying to reach the States by infiltrating the east coast of Canada. Can you let me know if you spot anything suspicious?"

Labelle laughed. "You have any idea how long our eastern coastline is? There aren't enough Canadians, let alone Mounties, to cover that area."

"I know. Just want you to let me know if anything lands in your lap that doesn't feel right."

"Okay. I'll put out the word, plus speak to our Coast Guard. Why Canada?"

Marsha stared at her map of the world. "Like I say, a long shot. But I'm wondering if I missed Cochrane in Greenland, and if so whether he's headed to the next nearest landmass. And that would be Canada."

Will approached the house, knocked on the door, and took five quick steps back so that he was partly bathed in darkness. Other lights came on in the house, movement could be heard from inside, and the door was opened.

A person, silhouetted in the doorframe, said in Danish, "Yes?"

Will hesitated, then responded in the same language, "Thomas Nigh. I need your help. I'm sorry that . . ."

"You're sorry?" The man laughed.

Will gripped his handgun tighter. "Yeah, I'm sorry. Actually, desperate."

"That doesn't excuse you being here."

"I know."

Silence.

"You want me to leave? Forget this happened?"

The man's face was now visible in the hallway light. "Too late for that."

"It's never too late."

"Oh, it is." This was another man's voice. From behind Will.

A gun barrel against the back of Will's head was unmistakable. "I see."

"Bet you do."

The man in the hallway said, "I think you'd better come in so that we can decide what to do with you."

Will was sitting at a kitchen table, his hands flat on its surface. His handgun was lying on a bench on the other side of the room. Next to it were rolled-up charts, maps of Greenland, compasses, a sextant, microscopes, plastic bags containing soil samples, a pile of academic papers, a jar of loose rolling tobacco, and a laptop. The four people were standing, watching him. One of them was smoking; the second was making hot drinks; the third was twirling a butcher's knife; and the fourth was standing stock-still while pointing a handgun at Will's head.

The person making the tea was the leader of a team that the scientific community of Greenland believed was Finnish and here to carry out research in geophysics and climate change. Nobody paid them any attention during their frequent expeditions north and to the west coast, as Greenland was awash with similar scientific outfits. But even if anyone took an interest in their activities, the trips within Greenland were purely for show. Their low-level flights into Canada were most certainly not.

They were a covert team of Russian GRU military intelligence operatives who used their cover in Greenland to make secret sorties into Canada, where they would refresh buried caches of weapons and supplies, monitor the activity of Canadian and American naval deployments in the Arctic, and report back to Moscow anything of interest that could support a Russian assault on the United States via Canada. It was a task for a bygone era; now the Cold War was over and Russia had no appetite or ability to engage head-on with America. But there were still some in the Russian high command who yearned for the good old days, hence this team was under direct orders to maintain and observe the Canadian flank. Though it was a futile task, it did nothing to diminish the risks the team took or the hardships it endured, particularly at this time of year. Typically operating in two-man teams, they would spend days and sometimes weeks in Canada's harshest terrains, usually in the northern archipelago, before being picked up by the Islander and returned to Greenland. Will admired their professionalism, even though he was also well aware that they were highly trained killers.

The team leader was called Ulana. She slammed

a mug of tea in front of Will and said in English, "You brought others along with you?"

As Will looked at her, he wondered how she coped being a woman alone out here in charge of three men. She had a whippet-thin, sinewy physique and was as strong as any of the men she commanded, which no doubt helped. That, and the fact that she wore a permanent reminder to anyone that she was extremely dangerous—a vivid scar across her throat that had come from a man who'd tried to decapitate her before she broke free and used his knife to gut him. "Thanks for the drink. No, just me."

"You sure?"

Will glanced at the man pointing a gun at him. "Nothing else would make any sense."

Ulana nodded. "That's true. But you're a tricky bastard and it wouldn't be the first time that you'd deliberately done something that didn't make sense."

"Not on this occasion. Our agreement remains fully intact."

An agreement that was two years old and was initiated shortly after Will had been told about the GRU team in Greenland by one of his GRU double agents. He'd considered telling CSIS, the Canadian intelligence service, about the unit's activities in the northern archipelago, but had decided their activities were harmless, and in any case they could prove useful to him. So instead, at a time when Alistair thought Will was on vacation, he'd observed the team and approached its leader when she was alone. They'd agreed on terms, though Will and Ulana both knew it was a precarious deal.

The man with the knife stopped twirling it and pointed the blade at Will. "You know this isn't the way to go about getting our help."

Ulana agreed. "Your being here may compromise us. The rules are in place for a reason, and they're your rules."

They were. Will looked again at the man holding the gun and saw that his finger was now over the trigger. "I can assure you that no one knows I'm here."

The smoker stubbed his cigarette out. "Good. Then we get rid of you and go back to business."

"I'm hoping you might consider another option." Will took a gulp of his tea. It was sickly sweet and made with cheap tea bags, but God, the hot liquid felt good as he swallowed it down. "I need transit to Canada."

Ulana laughed.

Her men did not.

One of them said, "Not a bad idea. Bury his body there, away from us."

Ulana moved to the table and leaned in close to Will. "Or just drop you out of the Islander midway across the strait."

Will held eye contact with her.

She smiled before moving back to her mug of tea. "You been a naughty boy?"

Will didn't answer.

"Of course you have, or you wouldn't be here." Ulana clicked her fingers at the smoker. Without taking his eyes off Will, he hand-rolled a cigarette, lit it, and gave it to his boss. She inhaled deep on the tobacco, blew out a stream of smoke, and asked, "You know why you're not dead already?"

Will shook his head.

"Sir Tim Berners-Lee."

Will frowned.

"Inventor of the World Wide Web."

"I know who he is, but what's he got to do with—"

Ulana gestured for him to shut up. "You remember the days before the Internet? Grubbing around in archives, or libraries, or speaking to assets just to try to find out some crappy piece of information?" She patted the laptop. "Now we've got Google."

Will nodded toward the laptop. "You won't find any trace of me on there."

"Really?" Ulana typed on the laptop and placed it in front of Will. "Who's that then?"

Will made no attempt to hide his shock. On the screen was a photo of his face. "What the—"

"Seems an SSCI guy called Senator Colby Jellicoe doesn't like you very much, and to all intents and purposes he's told the world as much. Actually, it's worse than that. He's put the feds and all their European pals onto you and thinks it's best that you're shot dead. Gave the media a photo of you. This one's from the front page of the *New York Times*, but you'll find the same one all over the Net and in a pile of other U.S. and non-U.S. papers." She snapped the laptop shut. "Seems you *were* a naughty boy. And seems your real name is Will Cochrane."

Will couldn't believe what he was hearing and

what he'd seen on the computer. "Did the senator say what I'd done?"

"No. Just you disobeyed Agency orders during a mission in Norway, and that the only reason U.S.-Norwegian relations hadn't turned to rat shit was because the senator had promised the Norwegian government that you would be brought to justice."

Will nodded slowly. Of course, no mention had been made of Ferryman or Antaeus. But that didn't change the fact that he was now royally screwed. "I didn't think they'd go . . . this far." His mind was racing. Did this change everything? Should he turn around and vanish for good?

Ulana seemed to be reading his mind. "Still want to go to Canada?"

"I . . ." Will settled on one thought—Ferryman—and made a decision. "Yes. More than ever." He looked at each person in the room, knowing that this could go either way, and that all it would take for him to be killed was for Ulana to snap her fingers as if she were requesting another cigarette. "Please. I'm on my own. In every sense."

"You were set up in Norway?"

"No. But it appears that I came very close to severely pissing some people off."

"People we might dislike?"

Will lifted his hand to rub his weary face.

The man with the gun cocked the hammer.

"Maybe." Will lowered his hand. "I don't know. How would I know?" He tried to smile. "You'd have to meet them first to see if your personalities jelled."

Not his wisest comment. The man with the

pistol was now standing next to him, looking at Ulana while holding the barrel against Will's temple.

Will spoke quickly. "This is nothing to do with GRU. I promise you that."

"You promise me it's got nothing to do with Russia, full stop?"

Smart, Ulana.

Will responded, "Nothing to do with anything other than me wanting to get my hands around the throats of some bastard Agency people."

Ulana tapped ash from her cigarette. "Difficult situation, this, isn't it?"

"Yes."

"Why?"

"Because people like us lie for a living."

"Correct. And did you just lie?"

"No."

Ulana laughed. "You could have said yes."

"And that could've been a lie."

"So, round and round the mulberry bush we go." She stared at him, her expression now cold. "But I don't think I have time for any of that."

She turned her attention to the colleague next to Will.

And clicked her fingers.

FOURTEEN

Antaeus raised his old rifle to eye level, focused on the moonlit area of woodland, and pulled the trigger. The shot echoed over the surrounding countryside, causing night wildlife to shriek as it made for cover. He ignited his oil lamp and limped toward the place where his bullet had struck flesh.

His breath steamed in the cold air as he stopped on an area of heathland beneath a tall birch tree and held the lamp low, scouring the ground around him. It took him only a few seconds to find the dead body. He moved to it, felt pain in his bad leg as he crouched, and smiled while smoothing a hand over the warm carcass. His shot had been precise—straight through the breastplate, no mess, instant death.

His rifle's aim had been as true as it had been in the hands of a Boer, over a century ago during the siege of Mafikeng. After slinging it onto his back and putting the lamp's handle on his forearm, he placed two hands under the body, lifted it to his chest, and walked to the large building that was positioned on stilts over a glistening and tranquil lake. The house was the only sign of human life for miles around in the countryside, and that's why he liked living here. Plus, it was only fifty miles beyond the outskirts of Moscow and so gave him easy access to the SVR headquarters.

He entered the house, kicked the door shut behind him, and went to the kitchen. On the table was a copy of the *Washington Post* that was open on a center-page spread about Senator Jellicoe's appearance at the Senate hearing. An SVR courier had delivered the paper to him one hour ago. As soon as the courier had left, Antaeus had read the article in silence, his vast intellect attempting to process hundreds of thoughts, before deciding that hunting his supper was the best way to focus his mind.

He placed the dead rabbit on top of the newspaper. Blood from the bullet's entry and exit wounds dripped over the article's photo of Will Cochrane's face, quickly making the image saturated and crimson. Antaeus smiled and went to his study.

The room was small and cluttered with wall-mounted shelves, a set of drawers, leather chair and oak desk, books, a scorched wooden ashtray, pre-WWII metal coffee tin containing cheroots, gloves and scarves hanging from the ceiling, print photographs of Captain Scott and his ship *Discovery* during the Antarctic expedition in 1902, stationery and papers containing his ongoing research into a Stone Age settlement that was once located in his property's expansive wild grounds, a reptile tank, and a blackboard that was fixed on the wall above his desk.

The spymaster sat at his desk, picked up a piece of chalk, and stared at the board.

Many times he'd used the board to make notes.

This evening was different, because the stakes were the very highest.

He reached with the chalk to the left side of the board, wrote four names, and studied them while deep in thought.

Senator Colby Jellicoe. Totally dedicated to Project Ferryman, but he'd blurt the truth if pain was inflicted on him.

Charles Sheridan. He hated his wife, Lindsay, after their last overseas posting. How much did she know? A weak link? Or could Sheridan keep her mouth firmly shut?

Gregori Shonin, Antaeus's best SVR agent, who years earlier had spotted the Americans at the embassy function in Prague, and as a result had enabled the spymaster to commence Project Ferryman.

And Ed Parker. Loyal to his wife, the Agency, and Ferryman.

He drew a line from the names to the center of the board, where he wrote PROJECT FERRYMAN.

Above it he wrote COBALT. The code name of the financier who spent more money funding terrorism across the globe than all other terrorism-financing schemes put together. A ghost. A repulsive man driven solely by profits. An enemy of the motherland, America, and all others who loathed anarchism and dogma. A man who was the complete antithesis of professional operators like Antaeus or his opponents in the West. And yet one who was inextricably linked to Ferryman.

From there, he drew another line to the other side of the board, his chalk screeching as he did so. He wrote one name.

WILL COCHRANE.

Antaeus looked at the reptile tank. Inside was a chameleon. Its markings had adapted to mimic the color of its surroundings. He imagined the chameleon was Ellie Hallowes. The creature was alive because Antaeus chose to let it live; Ellie Hallowes was alive because Will Cochrane had disobeyed orders by choosing to protect her.

Her Russian SVR agent had met her in Norway with knowledge that the CIA had been totally penetrated by Russia. Did he communicate that to her? Or was he gunned down by Antaeus's men before he could do so? Time would tell. Plus, Ferryman was still in place.

He stared at Cochrane's name. Thanks to Ferryman and what the man had said at the senatorial hearing, Antaeus now knew that Cochrane had had Antaeus in his sights in Norway. How galling it must have been for the MI6 operative when he was ordered not to shoot Antaeus.

But Cochrane wasn't a man to back down from danger. He wouldn't flee.

Antaeus nodded.

Will Cochrane would head to North America to ascertain why he'd been made to go on the run. And that meant there was a threat—just a potential that he could destroy Ferryman.

He picked up a photo of his wife and six-year-old daughter, and felt a moment of utter sadness. They were his beloved darlings, and to his unexpected delight had helped him discover and reveal a genuine kindness inside him. That had all ended on the evening when his daughter twisted her ankle while shopping with her mother. They were supposed to have caught the train home, but it was raining hard and his daughter's injury made it impossible for them to reach the station. So his wife had called him on his cell when he was leaving work. Every day since then, he'd wished he'd ignored the call. But he hadn't, and had made a quick detour to pick his family up. It was the only time they'd ever shared a car journey with him while he headed home after work. He remembered his daughter's excitement overshadowing the pain in her leg. That had made him momentarily happy, an emotion that had been instantly replaced with dread when Ferryman called in a state of panic. Antaeus had stopped the car, rushed out, and moved to the rear passenger doors while screaming at his family. His hand was on the door handle when the bomb went off and threw him halfway across the Moscow street. Despite the severe burns and lacerations to his leg and half his face, he'd tried to crawl back to the vehicle, even though it was a mangled wreck of burning steel and corpses. But the flames were too fierce, and in any case there was nothing he could do. His wife and child had been blown to pieces.

Antaeus touched the photo, two tears running out of his eyes, one of which coursed erratically down the disfigured side of his face.

He'd never allowed anyone to travel in his car to or from work in case something like this happened. But on that day, his wife had implored him and in the background he'd heard his daughter crying. He just couldn't bring himself to leave them stranded. So he'd taken a risk.

To this day Cochrane didn't know they'd been in the car, because their presence and their deaths had been carefully covered up by the SVR. Had he known about Antaeus's unplanned detour that evening, Cochrane would undoubtedly have done everything he could to get the spymaster's family out of the car before the MI6 timer triggered the bomb.

But that made no difference to the fact that they were still goddamned killed by the bastard.

Antaeus wiped the tears away and now felt nothing but burning anger. He took out his cell, spoke to a man for eleven minutes, ended the call, and drew an arrow pointing at Will Cochrane's name.

The anger receded and was replaced by fast thinking and a cold resolve. He held the chalk at the base of the arrow, wondering what he should write. Not their real names, of course; instead appropriate code names that only he knew. Looking around the room, his gaze settled on the framed print photographs of the Antarctic expedition.

He made a decision and wrote on the board.

SCOTT. SHACKLETON. OATES. AMUNDSEN.

Four early-twentieth-century Polar explorers.

The very toughest of men, who were able to withstand unimaginable hardships and could only be stopped by death.

Just like his four top assassins. And like the explorers, two of them were British, one of them Irish, and one Norwegian.

He'd just told the assassin code-named Scott that the team was to immediately deploy to the United States.

His instruction was as precise as his shot that hit the rabbit.

Kill Cochrane.

PART II

FIFTEEN

Wind and ice rushed into the house as Ulana opened the door, and she had to use all of her body weight to resecure the entrance once she was inside the kitchen. She removed her ski goggles, balaclava, and gloves, jumped up and down to shake the snow off her clothes, placed her bare hands around the kettle, and shuddered as the warmth aided her fingers' circulation.

From the other side of the kitchen, Will said, "Thank you."

"For what?"

"For not putting a bullet in my brain, cutting my body into pieces, and scattering my remains in Greenland."

Ulana smiled. "It took a lot of my willpower not to do that."

"What changed your mind?"

Ulana folded her arms and looked at him. "You knew what we were doing here and in Canada, and yet you never told anyone."

"It suited me not to."

"Even so, you could have sold us out at any time."

"Yes."

She drummed fingers against the wall, thinking. "I'm going to take you to Canada."

Though he was hugely relieved, this was the last thing he'd expected Ulana to say. "Of course, I'm delighted you said that. But why would you do it?"

Ulana answered quietly, "Every month I fly my guys into Canada. Fat generals in Moscow tell us it's important work, but we're not stupid. It's all a load of crap. And providing we don't freeze to death first, doing crap work doesn't change the fact that if we get caught, it's life imprisonment in a high-security Canadian prison after the Mounties have interrogated us." She hesitated, then said, "Of course, we'd try to escape before that happened, though things rarely go as planned." Her voice trailed. "I don't envy you."

Will kept his mouth shut.

"I spent most of last night trying to decide why I wanted to help you. In the end it came down to one thing—people like you and I have worked for so long in the field, it no longer seems relevant that we're Russian, American, or British; GRU, CIA, or MI6. Because we're not really any of those things, are we?"

"No."

"Instead, we're just weird people doing weird things in weird places, and all the while we rarely have a clue if what we're doing is of any use to anyone. And when we go home we . . ."

"Aren't like the people around us."

Ulana nodded. "I'm helping you because you know what it's like to be me. And maybe one day you can return the favor and help me."

"I'd like that." He was about to elaborate.

But Ulana held up her hand. "Kicking up out there. It'll be a very bumpy crossing."

"You tell me if it's safe to fly."

"It's never safe to fly. Not in these little birds. I think all that first-class 747 spy travel has made you a bit naive."

Will recalled that the last time he'd been in a small airplane it had been torn apart during an emergency crash landing, moments before a sniper shot him and all of his men.

Ulana tossed him a small document.

An American passport.

He turned to the page containing the photo. "You're certain this won't be missed?"

Ulana shrugged. "Out here stuff gets lost, or ruined by the weather. I'll just request another one. Moscow won't think twice about it. Just make sure you keep the beard."

The alias passport belonged to one of her men, also bearded. While the photo and Will looked reasonably similar, he doubted there was a sufficient match in their looks to pass the scrutiny of a border crossing. But Will wasn't intending to thrust it into the hands of a professional immigration officer; instead, if needed, it was solely for use in-country. "You didn't need to pull out all the stops for me."

"Dumping you midwinter in Canada with

nothing but a passport to back you up is hardly *pulling out the stops*." Ulana started preparing herself a hot drink. "You got yourself a woman yet?"

"No."

"Occupational hazard, I guess."

"You seemed to have cracked it with Filip," he said.

"Not anymore. He couldn't stand the wait."

"I thought he knew the deal. That doesn't make any sense."

"Obviously not." She poured sugar into her tea. "Not much sense about today, is there?"

"None."

Ulana burst out laughing.

"What's so funny?"

Her eyes twinkled. "I've just realized that we're finally putting this shit task to some use. Not quite what my superiors intended though."

"You sure about the cache?"

"I'm sure. We have to replenish them with new supplies into Greenland, and often as not we have to chuck out the old stuff because it's become damaged over time. Warn you though: not much in this cache."

"I'll take what I can get."

Ulana studied him while frowning. "You sure you should be doing this? America? Things are about to get considerably worse for you."

"It's a better option than hiding out in a bar in central Africa, drinking shooters just to numb the boredom."

Ulana sipped her tea. "You could come and live in Russia."

"No thanks."

"Why not?"

Will chuckled. "Where do I begin to answer that?"

"At the end."

"My end wouldn't be living in a pretty dacha. It would be a Russian president one day realizing that he could hand me over to the West in return for big favors."

"True. By the way, you were lucky to reach us when you did. We're being pulled out in a few weeks—back to Moscow; team change over."

"What are you going to do?"

Ulana beamed. "I'm adopting a little Russian boy. All the paperwork's been approved."

"Wow! That's wonderful news." Instinctively, Will wanted to step forward and embrace her, but stopped himself doing so because Ulana wasn't the cuddly type. Still, he felt genuinely pleased for her, his smile matching her own. "Are you staying in GRU?"

"Have to. Our economy's still fucked and who else would want someone who can fly planes under the radar, sit in ice holes for days on end while looking through binos, and shoot a man in the head from a distance of over one thousand yards?"

"Oh, I can think of quite a few *employers* who'd jump at the chance of having someone like you on board."

Criminal bosses, among others.

"Seen too many of my pals going down that path. Most of them are in prison or dead. No, I'll apply for a cushy training job in GRU. It'll keep me in Moscow; let me be a mom." She checked her watch. "Hope you don't get airsick, because I'm going to have to fly low. Weather aside, this is a risky flight—I'm taking you to Nova Scotia. It's the farthest south we operate and there's a far greater risk of compromise. But dropping you in Newfoundland, Labrador, or anywhere farther north would be a death sentence."

Will was relieved. From the Maritime province of Nova Scotia, he could travel northwest to New Brunswick and then cross the border into Maine.

"You got assets in country who're going to help you travel south?"

"None that I can use."

"You got a plan though, yeah?"

"Actually, no."

"Jesus."

Will shrugged. "Having a plan is too risky on U.S. soil. I've got to be unpredictable."

"Or stupid. Either way, we leave in sixty minutes. I suggest you use that time"—she nodded toward her laptop—"to research Nova Scotia and its surroundings."

"Who's coming with us?"

"No one else. I can't afford to have them killed."

The sound of the Islander plane's engine and propellers was nearly drowned out by the wind as Will forced his way through its icy blast toward the stationary craft. Ulana was in the cockpit, making a final check of her instrument panel. Behind her were two passenger seats, both empty. He entered the plane, slammed the door shut, and was grateful for the warmth inside the tiny compartment.

Though she was only three feet in front of him, Will had to shout to be heard. "When does the cabin crew bring champagne and canapés?"

While continuing her checks, Ulana replied, "Because you're first class, seat 1A, that's already been taken care of. Look next to you."

Will glanced down and saw wrapped sandwiches and a thermos flask that no doubt contained sickly sweet tea. "Splendid. In-flight entertainment?"

"That'll be me. Buckle up." The Islander began taxiing along the track. "If we go down anywhere over the strait, better to shoot yourself before we hit water. End of safety announcement."

Retired major Dickie Mountjoy looked at the *Daily Telegraph*'s photograph of Will Cochrane. The seventy-one-year-old desperately wanted to believe that the man in the image merely bore an uncanny resemblance to his Southwark neighbor, who lived in the West Square apartment block's third floor, above him. Trouble was, Will Cochrane was mentioned by name eight times in the article.

His intercom rang, meaning someone was at the communal front door of the two-hundred-year-old converted residence. Briefly, he wondered if Phoebe or David would answer, though he knew from experience that his two neighbors rarely did. Right now, Phoebe was probably lying on her couch, nursing a hangover after an evening out watching a middleweight boxing match while hoping to get lucky with some disreputable ruffian; and recently divorced David was quite possibly continuing to cook his way through a famous French chef's collected recipes while listening to Dixieland jazz on full volume.

Anyway, need a job done, ask a soldier. Dickie pushed himself up out of his armchair and marched to his intercom. "Yes?"

A man answered. "Metropolitan Police."

"Good for you. I'm ex–Coldstream Guards. Now we know each other's vocations, what do you want?"

The police officer hesitated before asking, "Can we come in?"

Dickie was ramrod straight, his clothes pressed to the standard of parade grounds, and asked in the clipped tone favored by British army officers, "Did I forget to pay my library fine?"

"This isn't about you."

"Then why are you speaking to me, sunshine?"

"We just need someone in this house to let us in."

"We? You come mob handed? Want to bang some heads together?"

"There's just two of us."

"Maybe you want to plant some evidence. Fit me up, then take me away in the blues and twos."

"Blues and twos?"

"How long you been in the force?"

"We call it service these days."

"My school dinner ladies used to do service. You a dinner lady?"

The officer sounded exasperated when he replied,

"No. I've been in the . . . force for fifteen years; my colleague six years."

"Twenty-one years combined. Same length of time, I fought in four conflicts and stood in front of Her Majesty thirty-seven times. You know what Guardsmen think of coppers?"

"I'm sure you're going to tell me."

"Damn right, young man. We think you're undisciplined bullies who'd never have cut the mustard in the army."

"Please. Just let us in. It's not about you. It's about Will Cochrane."

Dickie glanced at the *Telegraph*. Beyond it, lights from his small Christmas tree flickered over his neighbor's image. It added a surreal festive flavor to the spread. "Very well then. Just make sure you don't steal anything." He pressed the intercom's buzzer.

Will looked out of the small airplane's window and saw Greenland's coast move past and be replaced by an inhospitable gray sea. The Davis Strait. The plane shook from the wind as it flew a mere two hundred yards above the water, but Ulana expertly turned it in new directions to work with the weather rather than let the icy blast toss the aircraft onto its back like a discarded toy. As he watched her motionless head, he had no doubt that she'd be able to navigate her way through parenthood with equal skill.

He recalled a day during the Spartan Program when he had received a briefing from two surviving

members of the Special Operations Executive, both
in their eighties. During World War II, one had
been a Lysander pilot, the other an agent who'd
helped rally resistance in Holland and France. The
pilot had described how he'd needed to fly the agent
across the Channel and land on tiny strips. His biggest fear hadn't been being spotted and attacked by
the Luftwaffe, but rather making an error and flying into the sea. The agent had concurred, saying
that he was always relieved when they safely landed,
even though it was in a place of extreme danger, and
that he felt utterly useless during those flights.

Right now, Will knew how that felt.

If Ulana made a misjudgment, there was absolutely nothing he could do.

He was willing her to reach Canada and touch
down successfully.

Detective Superintendent Barclay handed his
police ID to Dickie and watched the widower scrutinize it before handing it back to the officer.

"Special Branch?"

Barclay nodded. "Based in Scotland Yard." He
gestured to his uniformed colleague. "This is
Police Constable Evans. He works in Southwark
Station. I thought it best to bring along a local
friendly face."

Dickie's eyes narrowed as he looked at Evans.
"Friendly face? Never seen you before. Not sur-
prising. These days, you lot spend all your time
driving around thinking you're in some American cop flick. Forgot you got legs. Tell you what
though: pop over some time for a cup of tea so we

can get to know each other. I can teach you how to properly iron your uniform. You look like a bag of shit tied up in the middle."

Barclay sighed. "It would be most helpful if you had a spare key to Mr. Cochrane's flat."

"Why? Thought you liked kicking doors down."

"We'd rather not."

"Scared he might be in there and get a bit peeved if you damage his property?"

"Is he in there?"

"Haven't seen him for weeks."

"That's what we thought. But we would like a look inside his apartment. We do need to find him."

"Think he's left a holiday brochure lying around, telling you exactly where he's popped off to?" Dickie was standing to attention, his arms locked tight against his sides, and felt every bit as if he were dressing down a bad recruit on the parade ground in Wellington Barracks. "Don't have a spare, but Phoebe might. Come with me." He eyed Evans. "You single?"

The police constable nodded.

"God help you."

"Forty-five minutes, give or take, until we reach Canada." Ulana banked the Islander as a blast of wind came from a different direction, causing the plane to shudder. Dense snow and ice particles were racing past so quickly that Will wondered how Ulana managed to remain oriented. She leveled the craft. "Conditions are getting worse."

Will gripped his seat while trying to smile. "Great to hear."

"At least it means we stand less chance of being detected. Visibility's bad; plus no one would expect a plane to be flying low level in this shit."

"There's always a silver lining." Will stared at the sea and imagined what would happen if they crashed. Would they drown or freeze to death? Either way, it would be agonizing. Yes, a bullet into the brain would be preferable.

Superintendent Barclay, Constable Evans, and Dickie reached the first floor and stood outside the apartment. Dickie knocked and called out, "Phoebe. It's the major. I'm here with company. *Male* company."

After a five-second delay, Phoebe replied, "Just give me a minute." There was rapid movement inside the home. "Fuck . . . damn . . ."

Phoebe never liked to answer the door to men unless she was looking her best.

"Shit."

The three men stood patiently.

"Bollocks."

Six minutes later, the door opened. Phoebe stood before them, her hand on her hip, wearing a little black dress and heels. It was her sultry look, and all the more remarkable for the fact that a few minutes ago she'd had no makeup on and had been wearing a dressing gown.

Though they had absolutely nothing in common, not for the first time Dickie thought that his Guardsmen could have learned a thing or two from Phoebe. Most of them needed at least an hour to get themselves into their number-one uniforms. Phoebe could do so in a fraction of the time.

Dickie pointed at the men by his side. "Coppers, looking for our boy Cochrane. Bloke in uniform needs motherin'; probably can't tie his own shoelaces."

Phoebe eyed the constable, a slight smile on her face, her eyes wide and penetrating. "Do you need mothering?"

Dickie interjected, "They want to do some snooping. Need a key to Cochrane's place." He glanced at the officers. "Lost the use of their legs."

Phoebe frowned. "What has Will done wrong?"

Dickie clasped his hands behind his back. "Seems Mr. Cochrane's been living a lie, and Plod here wants to punish him for that."

Will opened the flask, poured himself a drink, and was surprised to see that his cup wasn't filled with bad tea; instead it contained soup. He took a sip of the liquid. It was homemade and he could taste beef, vegetables, fennel, paprika, cream, and a hint of lemon. Ulana was right; during his service in MI6, he'd done a lot of first-class travel and had availed himself of food that was as refined as it could be at thirty-seven thousand feet. The soup tasted just as good as anything else he'd consumed in a plane; actually, better. He wondered if Ulana had prepared it especially for him. Most likely, yes.

Holding the mug in two hands, he eased back into his seat while trying to stop the soup from spilling out as the plane was buffeted. Alongside a

British passport and credit card in the blown name of Robert Tombs, a dodgy American passport, eight thousand dollars, and a handgun and spare clip, the soup was all he had. It was important. Something good that was here to help him.

He thought about his home in West Square. It was now just as he wanted it: a place that was homey, safe, and contained his treasured art, antiques, and musical instruments. A year before, he'd taken his possessions out of storage so that they could be prominently displayed, partly to cheer up his new place, but more important, to barrage his senses with beautiful and interesting things. They were healthy distractions from the wholly unhealthy sense of feeling utterly alone and unwanted. He dearly hoped he'd be back home sometime soon.

As Phoebe, Dickie, and the police officers reached the top of the next flight of stairs, David opened his door and asked, "Everything okay?" He was wearing a chef's apron and holding a large knife; Kid Ory's "Society Blues" was in full swing within his apartment.

Barclay eyed the knife. "Best you put that thing away."

David glanced down, looking embarrassed. "Oops. Sorry." The flabby mortician smiled. "Don't worry—I only use knives on dead things. What's going on?"

Phoebe told him.

"A spy? On the run? That can't be right."

Dickie said, "Read the papers, Sunny Jim."

"They're always full of shit."

"Not this time." Dickie nodded toward the officers. "They want us to let them into his flat so they can search the place. We're here to exercise our civic duty to ensure they're not bent coppers who're going to nick stuff. Care to join us?"

Barclay pointed at the blade. "By all means join us, but you're coming without that thing."

"Sure." David placed the knife on a shelf and rubbed his hands over his food-stained apron. "How exciting. Cochrane a spy. Who'd've thought?" He winked at Phoebe. "I always thought he looked like one of them boxers you fancied. Makes sense though. All those trips away. Who does he work for? Communists? Terrorists? Please tell me, not the Chinese."

Barclay ignored the questions and strode up the final flight of stairs.

Despite her heels, Phoebe kept pace and unlocked the door. After it swung open, she held her hand to her mouth and exclaimed, "Oh no!"

They all moved into Will's apartment. The beds in the bedrooms had been overturned; drawers had been pulled out and upended, their contents spilled on the floor; and the clothes in the closets had been slashed with razors or knives. The living room was in an even worse state. It had been comprehensively torn apart to the extent that all around them was carnage. Will's German lute had been smashed; his paintings had been ripped from their frames; foam had spewed out of his chairs and sofa where they'd been cut; everything had been damaged beyond repair.

Dickie was visibly shocked and disgusted. "Vandals? Burglars?"

Superintendent Barclay calmly moved around the room, examined the barred windows, went back to the front door and got on one knee to scrutinize the lock, reentered the living room, and methodically examined everything within the room. A few minutes later, he asked, "Does anyone else have a key to his front door?"

Phoebe shrugged. "Apart from Will, don't think so. He told me never to lose my key copy, because he didn't have or want any more spares."

David pointed at the lute. "Bloody idiots. Reckon they could have sold that for a few thousand quid."

Dickie huffed. "We're dealing with scum here. Might be able to pick a lock but, sure as eggs are eggs, whoever turned this place over didn't have two brain cells to rub together. Wouldn't have any idea about the real value of things. No discipline. Utter scum."

Barclay stood in the center of the room. "That's one possibility."

"*Possibility?*" Dickie's face was flushed with anger. "Think you've spent too long in an office. Forgotten what it's like to live among"—he swept his arm—"parasitic vermin."

Barclay's eyes flickered as he rotated around, staring at the damage. "I've been to thousands of burglaries and places of mindless vandalism. They're either one or the other, but never a combination." He looked at Major Dickie Mountjoy and smiled. "You know what *coppers* think of most military men?"

The old soldier held his gaze with stubborn resolve. "That we put our lives on the line to keep civvies like you safe in their warm beds?"

"I'm sure most of us think that way. I'm also sure we think that you're hindered by a hierarchical need for order and discipline that requires you to be linear thinkers who can't visualize anything outside of a tiny box." Barclay looked around one last time, while deciding that he needed to get back to the Yard to make an international call. "A professional entered this property, and that person, most likely with the help of other professionals, did all the damage you can see." He crouched down and picked up a battered French viola by its broken neck. "This isn't vandalism or burglary. It's a systematic search. And I think I know who authorized them to do so."

The coastline was barely visible through the inclement weather, but it was most certainly drawing nearer and looked as rugged as the seaboard vista that Will had seen as he'd approached Greenland. But this was Canada. He'd have zero help here and would somehow need to travel west and south to reach America.

He screwed the thermos shut, opened the sandwiches, and took a bite. The bread tasted home baked, and inside was salmon that had been smoked, drizzled with lime juice, and sprinkled with cracked peppercorns. Again, not what he expected. After he swallowed a mouthful, some of it was involuntarily squeezed back up his gullet as the plane repeatedly bounced midair. He winced, desperately trying not to vomit out the food that Ulana had prepared with care and most likely a desire to ensure her passenger died with a full and contented belly. Thankfully, he managed to swallow it back down, though the bodily action had left an acrid sensation in his throat and mouth.

Ulana shouted, "Make ready. We're landing on a deserted track. It's going to be a bumpy landing. You can sue me later." She turned the plane and flew even closer to the sea.

The lower altitude meant Will could no longer see the land; instead it looked like Ulana was going to put the Islander onto water. He put on his jacket, gloves, balaclava, and ski goggles. Then a thud, followed by staccato jolts as the plane's wheels came into contact with land. Will lurched forward as Ulana slowed the aircraft, thrust out his arms to prevent him from head-butting Ulana's seat, and forced his upper body back as the Islander came to a halt.

Ulana turned the engine off, quickly donned her winter gear, jumped out of the plane, opened Will's door, and shouted, "Come on. Duty Free's open."

Will stepped out of the plane and was nearly knocked off his feet by the force of the wind. It was even stronger than it had been in Greenland. And as he looked around, the place looked more desolate and barren. Mountains were at least twenty miles away; most of the land around him was relatively flat, windswept, and covered with snow and ice that was being whipped into a frenzy by the gale. There were no buildings here, no sign of any life.

Ulana reached into the craft, opened a compartment, and withdrew a spade. "Quickly, now."

Will ran alongside her for 150 yards until she abruptly stopped and thrust the spade into the snow.

"X marks the spot. You'll need to go down at least two feet and four by three feet wide." She checked her watch. "Start digging. I'm going to inspect the aircraft for any damage."

As she sprinted back to the plane, Will grabbed the spade and began his task. His wrists and arms jarred in pain as he slammed the spade into the frozen ground, making him wonder if he'd be able to remove much more than a few inches of snow and soil. But he continued anyway, knowing that he'd die out here if he didn't access the cache. Ten minutes later, he'd gotten down to one foot.

Ulana reappeared, cupped a hand next to his head, and shouted, "I'm good to go."

A fresh gust of wind pushed her back so quickly that Will had to grab her arm to stop her from crashing to the ground. "You should wait until this dies down!"

"Too dangerous. This kind of weather usually hangs around for days." During which time, she'd freeze to death or be captured. "I've got to make the flight back before it gets worse."

The wind sounded like the howl of a wolf, though many times louder.

"Please, Ulana! Come with me. We can lay low somewhere until it's safe to come back here."

Ulana shook her head. "Never done that before

and I'm not going to start now." Though Will couldn't see it, underneath her balaclava she was smiling. "As tempting as it may be to lay with you for a day or so."

Will was about to make further objections.

But Ulana held out her hand. "Goodbye, Mr. Cochrane. Word of advice: if it doesn't work out, don't do prison. Every wannabe hard man will want to test himself against you. When you're exhausted, one of them might get lucky."

Will could see that Ulana's mind was made up. He shook her gloved hand. "Be safe and take a risk by going back at a higher altitude."

"High altitude, low altitude. Different risks. Same outcome."

Will didn't know how to respond, then settled on "What are you going to call your boy?"

"I haven't decided yet. Something strong." She patted him on the arm. "Just occurred to me— there's one good name I can think of." She pointed north, shouted, "Nearest road's eight miles that way," turned, and ran back to the plane.

Will watched her while continuing the excruciating dig. The task in hand made Will admire Ulana and her team even more. Most others would have found the futile yet backbreaking and fraught task of maintaining the Canadian border a soul-destroying job. Not so these Russians.

Ulana started up the Islander's engine, gave Will the thumbs-up just before a blast of snow momentarily obscured her and the craft, turned the plane around, and immediately accelerated away before taking off.

Will saw the plane get smaller as it commenced its journey back to Greenland. He counted each dig, rationalizing that when he got to one hundred he'd be finished.

On the fifth dig, Ulana's plane was at least one hundred yards over the lethal sea.

On the sixth dig, the plane flipped sideways, crashed into the strait, and was tossed on the waves.

Will screamed, "No!" and sprinted as fast as he could through the driving wind until he reached the water's edge.

Jump in there?

Die in seconds?

Didn't matter.

He began removing anything that would slow his swim down.

The plane began to sink into the freezing depths.

In a state of panic, he tore off his jacket.

He stopped.

He couldn't hear the sound of the gunshot. But he could see its result. Blood splattered over the inside of the aircraft's windows.

Ulana had taken her own life.

SIXTEEN

It was 6 A.M. as Marsha Gage strode along a Bureau corridor toward her office. Her cell phone rang. London number. What time was it there? About five hours ahead, she reckoned. "Marsha Gage."

"Agent Gage, this is Detective Superintendent Barclay."

"Hi, Terry. How did you manage at the apartment?"

"Not well."

"Damn it, was hoping we'd get at least one lead there."

"We didn't get any leads, but Cochrane's place was trashed. *Expertly* torn apart." He told her everything.

Marsha snapped her cell shut and walked faster.

Bo Haupman smiled as he saw Marsha walking toward him, was about to greet her, then saw something in her expression and body language that warned him he should give her a very wide berth. As she strode past him without uttering a word or giving him a glance, her face looked thunderous.

She entered the FBI ops room and slammed the door shut. "Alistair! I need a word. Right now."

She didn't give the MI6 controller a chance to respond, instead walked fast into an adjacent small room, leaned against the desk, and folded her arms.

Alistair entered, looking completely unperturbed by her evident anger. "What is it, my dear?"

"Don't you *my dear* me."

"Breathe, Mrs. Gage. It'll do you a world of good."

"So would slapping someone right now."

"And who would be top of your list?"

"You!"

"Of course I would."

"You know what this is about?"

"Haven't the foggiest. Milk and one sugar, isn't it?"

"I beg your pardon?"

Alistair held up one finger, stuck his head back into the ops room, and called out in his well-spoken voice, "Charles, be a darling and bring us two teas. Both with milk and sugar."

"Fuck off."

Alistair clicked his tongue and smiled at Marsha as he closed the door. "Seems Mr. Sheridan's not predisposed to making us a nice cuppa." His expression changed. "What's wrong?"

Marsha pointed a finger at him. "Someone got to Cochrane's home before the Metropolitan Police. Systematically ripped it apart."

"I see. And you think I commissioned a team of MI6 operatives to do the job?"

"Damn right. Superintendent Barclay thinks the same."

"And why would you believe I'd do such a thing?"

"Your patch. Your boy. If you can find out where he is, you can warn him off."

"Quite so. But I had no reason to search Will's home."

"That's a lie."

"It's the opposite. There'd have been no point, because I'd never have found anything remotely interesting there. Will's not the kind of chap who leaves clues about his life lying around. He stores everything important inside his head." He frowned. "How badly damaged was the place?"

"Bull in a china shop bad."

"His antiques and other stuff?"

"Ruined."

"That's awful." Alistair moved to the window and stared out at nothing. "He loved his things."

"I'm sure that's the least of his worries right now."

"I know, but when this is over he'll—"

"When this is over he'll be in prison or dead." Marsha frowned. "You still think he might have some kind of future?"

Alistair smiled, though his expression remained unsettled. "For the last nine years he's been working for me, I never once thought it was certain he'd have a future."

"At least then he had somewhere to retreat to. That's all changed."

"It has." Alistair turned to her. "Being Will's controller has required me to do more than issue orders. I've had to wear many hats—psychologist, defense lawyer, confidant, motivator, provocateur, and guardian. I know him better than anyone, though there are still parts of his mind and character that I've yet to fathom. He keeps me on my toes, always going in directions I least expect. But there's one thing I know for sure: his home and possessions were about putting down roots and trying to connect with humanity. I'd *never* have issued orders for his things to be touched, and now that it's happened I've got no idea what it will do to him if he ever gets the chance to find out."

Marsha kept her eyes on the controller while deep in thought. "This one of them Jedi mind tricks Bo warned me about?"

"Quite apart from the fact that I've got no idea what Jedi means, a mind trick would serve no purpose given the fundamental principle that Will would never have left anything compromising at his home."

Marsha nodded. "Guess that makes sense."

"And yet somebody did think they'd find something at Will's home. Any further thoughts as to who?"

"Yeah, one."

"No doubt the same one, I suspect." Alistair was once again all charm. "Would you like me to make you a cup of tea, my dear? Unlike Sheridan, I don't think any task is beneath me, plus it would be a pleasure."

Marsha smiled. This guy talked like he was in a

black-and-white movie, but it was kind of refresh-
ing and made her feel nice. "No thanks."

Alistair hesitated on his way out. "You're doing
an excellent job."

"Bo Haupman should have told you I don't like
praise."

"He did."

"So why ignore his advice?"

"Because I know he's wrong."

"Yeah? How!"

"Because of seven things you don't realize you do
that betray the fact that you secretly enjoy praise."

"What are they?"

"I'm not telling, Mrs. Gage."

"Now that *is* a damned mind trick."

"No. The mind flip is that I now know something about you that you don't. You'll wonder if
others can see the same. And that leaves you with
two choices—continue to perpetuate a lie, or be
honest with yourself and others." His smile was
warm and his eyes held compassion. "*That* is the
Jedi mind trick."

Marsha laughed. "Tell you what—bring me that
cup of tea when I'm done. Think I need one."

"Of course. By the way, don't stand for any nonsense, but do keep your powder dry."

Sheridan entered the room two minutes after
Alistair had left.

"Yeah?"

Now this was someone Marsha really wanted to
slap hard, just for being Charles Sheridan. She told
him about Superintendent Barclay's call and what

he'd discovered at Cochrane's apartment. "You know anything about that?"

"None of your business."

"Meaning you do."

"Meaning my business is my business. It's called logic."

"It's called being uncooperative."

"Never said I was here to help."

"Bit boring and predictable though, isn't it?"

"What?"

"Bureaucratic, interagency infighting."

"I ain't bored with it. Anyway, Patrick isn't a fed, and he's helping you."

"Yes, but Patrick's as much in the dark as I am. You're not."

"Yeah, life sucks for all but the rich and powerful."

Marsha tried to stop her voice from becoming audibly angry. "Discreet call to our U.K. embassy? Get our London station to deploy an Agency team to Cochrane's place before the cops went there? Endgame: find something that might locate Cochrane so you and your crony spooks could get to him before the Bureau did? That sound about right?"

Sheridan walked right up to her and held a finger close to her chest. "Keep your nose out!"

"Don't touch me!"

"Why not?" Sheridan's face was inches from hers, his expression utterly threatening and hostile. "You want equality in the workplace, you got it!"

Marsha held his gaze, even though he was at

least a foot taller than her. "Equality? You touch lots of men in the workplace, do you, Charlie boy?"

"Fuck you." Sheridan stepped back. "Senator Jellicoe's authorized me to cover all bases, and if that means checking out Cochrane's pad before the Brits get there then so be it."

"You had no right . . ."

"I had every damn right, Gage! You help us or you don't. Doesn't matter. But nothing's going to get in the way of us finding Cochrane."

"I'll make an official complaint."

"To who? Haupman?" He laughed. "Maybe you'd like to have a little whine to the president. Want me to get him on the phone? 'Cause I can."

"Has the president *really* bought into you, Jellicoe, and Parker?"

"Not us, you fool. What we can deliver."

"Something called Ferryman?"

"Who told you about that?"

"Alistair. Want to go threatening him as well? Good luck. Maybe *he'll* make a few phone calls. I've heard the Brits are world class at getting rid of people they don't like."

Sheridan pointed at her. "Alistair knows shit about Ferryman, meaning the same is true for you."

"You—"

"Shut up! I ain't *threatening* you, so don't go getting your panties in a twist. You just ain't worth the hassle. But I am telling you this: you think I'm some spineless dick who's going to let himself be talked down, then think again."

Marsha forgot about slapping Sheridan. Instead, she wanted to pull out her sidearm and shoot him. But she remembered what Alistair had said to her, and instead breathed deeply and kept her powder dry.

SEVENTEEN

Ellie Hallowes introduced herself to the security guards in the foyer of CIA headquarters in Langley and scrutinized her surroundings, because her deep-cover role made her feel exposed within the prominent high temple of espionage. "You should have me down for a pass. Director Parker's expecting me."

The guard made a phone call, got her to sign paperwork, and gave her an electronic swipe card that had the inscription TEMPORARY. "Wait here. Someone's coming to get you."

That someone arrived five minutes later, all smiles and handshakes. Ellie had no idea who he was, and didn't care.

"Come with me. Been a while since you were here, right?"

"A while. Yes."

"Nothing's changed." The man's smile broadened. "Coffee's still lousy."

Just like the lame jokes. She followed him through the security gates, keeping her gaze low while desperately hoping she didn't bump into someone who might shout out something like, "Ellie Hallowes, as I live and breathe!"

But no one took any notice of her as she rode an elevator and was guided along corridors that contained rooms with initials and number codes designating which teams they belonged to. She wondered if hostile intelligence agencies knew what these codes meant, because everyone in Langley did, and that meant there'd be a good chance someone had leaked their meaning. Langley was anything but deep cover—too many people, only one set of loose lips needed to damage the place. That said, there was a part of Langley that was a steel-plated fortress of secrecy.

She was ushered into a spacious room containing a large desk, computer, conference table and chairs, walls containing framed photos of Presidents Obama, Bush junior, Clinton, and Bush senior, and windows overlooking part of Langley's manicured grounds. Ed Parker stood from behind his desk, walked to her, and shook her hand. "Great to see you in one piece, Ellie. That was a shitty deal in Norway."

Senator Jellicoe didn't get up, smile, or offer any greeting. He just stared at her from his seat at the conference table.

Parker pulled out a chair at the table and gestured toward it. "Can we get you anything?"

"No." Ellie sat, wishing she could be a few feet farther away from Jellicoe—actually, wishing she weren't in the same room as him.

Jellicoe kept his eyes on her. The scent of his pungent cologne was mixed with sweat.

Parker sat next to her so that they were both opposite Jellicoe. Ellie knew it was Parker's way of saying that he was on her side. It was bullshit.

Parker asked, "Did Welfare visit you at your hotel?"

Ellie nodded.

"Much use?"

"I hadn't realized the Agency's Welfare Department had gone all amateur psychologist. Seems they want everyone to have PTSD so that they can sit down, have a chat, and share the horrors. All that kind of stuff. Not much use when life's a little more complicated than that. I preferred it when they came over with a bag of groceries and a bottle of Scotch."

Parker laughed. "Me too. Sorry. I just wanted them to check you were okay during your week off. Before you came here."

"Make sure I wasn't losing my mind? Put me on suicide watch?"

"Just check you were okay."

"I'm fine, and I'm here. Reporting for duty. *Sir.*"

Jellicoe took out a pink silk handkerchief and began twining it around his flabby fingers. "You being sarcastic, girl?"

She glanced at Parker. "Is the senator cleared to speak to me?"

Parker nodded.

"About specifics? Norway?"

"He is."

Jellicoe wrapped the handkerchief tight around a finger. "What do you think happened in Norway?"

"Russians killed my asset and tried to kill me."

"How do you know they were Russians?"

"They spoke Russian, looked Russian, and after all, we had advance intel that Herald was under threat from the Russians. You telling me I got it wrong?"

"No. Just wanted to hear what you thought happened."

"Well, that's it in a nutshell."

"Not quite."

Ellie was silent.

"More to it than that."

Ellie held Jellicoe's gaze.

"You did the right thing telling Sheridan what Cochrane had done." Jellicoe yanked hard on the scarf as if he was attempting to strangle his finger. "But I want to know what Cochrane then told you."

She shrugged. "He said that a senior Russian spy had ordered the hit; that Cochrane had disobeyed Agency orders by killing his men; and that he wasn't going to comply with Sheridan's instruction to give himself up to the U.S. or U.K. embassies in Oslo. Then he left."

"Why didn't you stop him?"

Ellie darted a look of incredulity at Parker before returning her attention to Jellicoe. "Should I have fought him? Not that easy, given I'm just"—she smiled—"a *girl*." Her smile vanished. "But I did tell him to comply with Sheridan's orders. And just so you know that I'm giving you a balanced account, I also thanked him for saving my life."

Parker responded, "That's understandable."

Jellicoe removed the handkerchief from his fingers and patted his jowls. "You curious as to why we had orders in place for Cochrane not to open fire on the Russian spy and his team?"

"Of course I'm damn curious! Those orders would have had me dead! Are you going to tell me what they're about?"

"Nope."

"Thought not."

"Cochrane give the Russian spy or our orders a name?"

Antaeus. Ferryman.

"No," Ellie lied.

"Say where he was going?"

Ellie had predicted this question, and days ago had decided on an answer that she thought the Agency might swallow. "He seemed confused. I asked him what he'd do, and he'd told me that he had to go someplace safe. My guess is he's laying low for the time being, trying to decide what to do. Probably Europe or Middle East. But I could be wrong. Maybe he's trying to get as far away from Norway and the States as he can. Don't blame him."

"You feel compassion toward Cochrane?"

"A bit. Yes."

"Damsel in distress rescued by knight in shining armor?"

Regardless of the events in Norway, Ellie hated the idea of being viewed as a damsel in distress. Then again, Will Cochrane was the first man to have saved her life. She recalled the way he gave her Herald's coat. The memory made her feel wanted, even though the sensation seemed strange. She feigned annoyance. "I told him to give himself up and that in return I'd put in a good word for him."

"You'd take a polygraph test so that we can check your version of events?"

"Sure." Ellie meant what she'd said. Polygraph tests were wholly unreliable and she'd proven in the past that she could easily manipulate them. "I can do it today if you like."

"We'll let you know."

Ellie drummed her fingers. This was the moment she'd been leading up to. "No denying, at first I was major league pissed that you were willing to sacrifice me for something I'm not cleared to know about. But I've had a week to get my thinking straight. I get it. Doesn't mean I like it, but hey, it's a game I've played as well. What bothers me now is why Herald was killed and why a senior Russian spy turned up in person to oversee it being done."

"Could be any number of reasons."

"Maybe. But seems to me this Russian spy's very important to you, because you wanted him kept alive. Supposing Herald had wanted to meet me because he knew something about the spy, something that could have threatened the spy's interests, perhaps something that could have threatened *your* interests."

"Doesn't matter now, because your asset's dead."

Ellie nodded. "That's fine, as long as he's taken his secret to his grave."

"Herald didn't say anything to you before you were attacked?"

Something like, All the Agency's biggest secrets are being leaked to Russia by a high-ranking mole.

Ellie lied. "Nothing important. We were just catching up, pleasantries, small talk, warming up to the reason he wanted to meet me. I always let him do that; he hated being rushed into business. Then the Russian operatives kicked down the door."

Jellicoe and Parker were silent as they momentarily glanced at each other.

Ellie asked Parker, "Whatever interests you have in the senior Russian spy, is it important stuff? Stuff that I'd buy into?"

"Ellie, I can't—"

"And you don't have to. I just need to know if it's something good."

Parker looked at Jellicoe, who hesitated before giving the slightest of nods. "It's *very* important. The president takes a personal interest."

"Then that's all I need to know. What plans do you have for me?"

Parker seemed relieved with the question. "I was thinking a few more weeks' leave, followed by putting you back in deep cover. Another name, change of dress and hair, lose or gain a bit of weight, different continent, usual drill."

Back to a life that wasn't her life.

Ellie nodded. "I'm not very good at twiddling my thumbs, doing nothing. Why don't you make use of me during the next few weeks? Keep me in Langley before I go back out into the field."

"Doing what?"

"I know my asset inside out. I can read through his files. See if there's anything there that could suggest he might have put a fail-safe in place that could mean his secret information about the Russian spy *wasn't* taken to the grave. Maybe something similar he's done in the past. If I find something, I just present it to you and leave you to decide what to do. Job done."

Ellie expected to find absolutely zero of interest in her asset's files, but that wasn't relevant. Having a pass to camp in Langley was.

Jellicoe asked Parker, "She security cleared to read those files?"

Parker snapped, "She was his case officer, for God's sake." He composed himself. "Sorry, Mr. Jellicoe. Yes, of course she is."

Jellicoe eyed Ellie. "You find something, you bring it to us and shut the door on your way out. But I warn you: start looking in places you shouldn't and it'll trigger an automatic red flag. Our security boys will be all over you. It won't be pleasant."

"I understand."

"Good."

Parker went to his desk and made an internal call. "Get Miss Hallowes a room on the third floor and extend her pass to three weeks. I'll give you a list of her security clearances"—he looked at Ellie—"together with a list of what she's *not* allowed to read. She's ready to go."

A few minutes later, Ellie was escorted out of the room by the man who'd met her in the lobby.

After the door had shut behind her, Jellicoe

stuffed his handkerchief into his expensive suit and asked, "You trust her?"

"No reason to think otherwise."

Jellicoe shook his head and said with contempt, "You'd never have made director if it weren't for Ferryman. You're too damn naive."

EIGHTEEN

As soon as Will spotted the road, he removed and secreted his goggles and balaclava, grimaced as icy rain struck his face like needles, shoved his hands into his jacket, and adopted the posture of a man who was severely pissed that his car had broken down north of here and had to walk to the nearest civilization to get help.

He stepped onto the road and headed south, his only hope being that a passerby would stop, take pity on him, and drive him to someplace warm. No one would fail to spot him—the road was deserted and quite flat, either side of it was open snow-covered countryside. Plus, though the route was remote, there was no doubt that vehicles had recently driven along it, since the road had recently been plowed. Didn't mean anyone would stop, though; they might just err on the side of caution and keep driving in case he was a serial killer.

Did Nova Scotia have serial killers who'd be stupid enough to chance their luck in these conditions and with very few victims around? Will had no idea; nor did he have much experience of attempting to hitch a ride. He decided that if he heard a vehicle, he wouldn't stick out his thumb. Instead, he'd just keep walking while looking as pathetic as possible. Hopefully that would make him look less likely to be a killer who was desperate to get inside someone's vehicle. Perhaps the passerby would think through options as he continued onward, decide that the walker wasn't a threat, then stop and back up.

Not that Will wasn't a threat. As well as the Russian pistol he was carrying, the cache had given him another handgun and spare ammunition, army food rations that would feed him for a few days, two thousand Canadian dollars, a lockpick set, and a military knife, all hidden in his jacket. There had been other stuff in the cache that would have been extremely useful for a man going to war, but too conspicuous for someone who just wanted to blend in. So he'd left the assault rifles and most of the other military supplies behind. Even though there was every possibility that he *was* a man going to war.

Most likely a futile war.

One that would see him being mowed down the moment he stuck his head out of the trenches.

His stomach was cramping, partly because he was tired and hungry, and partly because he was tense. Not knowing what lay ahead was making things worse, and it was an unusual sensation because secret agents are trained to be in control of everything around them, even when things go wrong. But this was different because he was no longer an agent, and had no support and safety net.

All of this was new to him. Not even the Spartan training program could have prepared him for what it was like to be a homeless criminal on the run in a world full of people who wanted him dead.

Part of his brain was telling him to move into the countryside, remove his outer clothing, sit down, and wait for the elements to take away the pain by killing him. But he kept going, each step taking him closer to his destination.

It would have been reasonable for anyone watching the four people walking briskly across the concourse of the Arrivals section of Washington Dulles Airport to assume that they were businessmen in their early thirties who broke up their high-pressure days with intensive cardiovascular workouts. Further, the observer might have noticed their casual, confident smiles, which, together with the expensive-looking overcoats, suits, and suitcases, suggested they were wealthy playboys who exuded the joie de vivre that is often prevalent in the successful and rich. No doubt they'd inherited good genes—high cheekbones, lean and athletic builds, above-average height, straight hair—but money had made them look even better. Only expensive dental work could have gotten their teeth that white and straight; professional stylists had spent a lot of time getting their short hair into cuts that made them dashing, charming, and full of sex appeal; and their lightly tanned Caucasian faces were marble smooth. These, the observer might have concluded, were Forbes 400 men who would look right at home on the front cover of *Esquire* or *GQ*.

The observer would have been wrong.

Because the men were assassins.

Code names Scott, Shackleton, Oates, Amundsen.

Antaeus's best.

Scott and Oates were English, both ex–Special Air Service; Shackleton was Irish, formerly of the counterterrorism Army Ranger Wing; and Amundsen was a Norwegian whose career included ten years in Norway's premier maritime special forces unit, Marinejegerkommandoen. None of them had spent one minute of their adult life sitting behind a desk studying profit-and-loss spreadsheets, investment portfolios, or share-price fluctuations. But that's not to say that they couldn't talk the talk of businessmen. If taken to one side by airport security and questioned, all of them could speak effortlessly about the nuances of their faux businesses. It was their usual cover for getting in and out of countries, though they were equally adept at covertly crossing borders from sea, air, or land.

But today, they were merely asked a few perfunctory questions at passport control, then allowed to proceed to X-ray machines where their luggage was scanned and deemed to contain absolutely nothing of concern.

The men would never risk bringing anything compromising through airport security, and today was no exception. Plus, there was no need. A local asset would be supplying them the weapons to kill their target.

NINETEEN

Lindsay Sheridan entered her living room, carrying a tray containing three glasses of brandy, a bowl of ice, a jug of water, and Cuban cigars. She placed the tray on a table between three leather armchairs occupied by Senator Colby Jellicoe, her husband Charles, and Ed Parker. The fire was burning well and there were plenty of extra logs beside it in case it needed replenishing. That was good; it meant she wouldn't be called to fetch more wood.

Charles and Jellicoe didn't acknowledge her presence and were talking directly to each other in hushed tones. Parker, on the other hand, beamed at her and asked, "That your usual perfume?"

Lindsay patted her throat, darted a look at her husband, who was still taking zero notice of her, and smiled. "No. Chanel. Thought I'd try something different."

"Suits you. By the way, Catherine says pop over sometime." Parker winked at her. "Think my wife wants a drinking partner. Someone to grumble to about being married to the Agency."

"Well, that would be great."

"Looks like you've lost a few pounds since I last saw you. You been on that five-two diet thing?"

Lindsay smiled. "Always flirting with me, Mr. Parker."

"Someone's got to." Parker reached for a brandy, and said in a quieter tone, "Don't worry, I'll look after them. Just make sure you get on the phone to Catherine and get that all-men-are-bastards drinking session in the diary. It'll do you a world of good."

Her smile still on her face, Lindsay nodded, momentarily forgetting that her husband actually was a bastard.

When she had exited the room, Colby Jellicoe asked, "Marsha Gage?"

Sheridan took a sip of brandy. "I treat her like crap, but *she's* good."

"So why treat her like crap?" Parker stared at his drink, wishing he was going to partake of it at home with Catherine.

Sheridan smiled. "To keep her on her toes and focused. She thinks I'm a shit just for the sake of it. Truth is, I need her to think that way so she doubles her efforts to get to Cochrane before I do."

"How can that be a good thing?"

It was Jellicoe who answered. "Because the president's given me written authorization for Cochrane to be handed over to us the moment he's in FBI custody."

"Okay, that *is* a good thing. Where's Gage looking for him?"

Sheridan shrugged. "Far as I can tell, mostly Europe."

The senator nodded slowly. "If you capture him alive, he's to be immediately executed. Do it somewhere private."

Parker frowned. "President's comfortable with a shoot-to-kill policy while Cochrane's on the run. But I don't recall him saying anything about a cold-blooded execution."

"Neither do I. But that's what's got to happen. You okay with that?"

Parker didn't know how to respond, then settled on the truth. "No, I'm damn well not okay with that."

"You happy for national security to be breached?"

"What?"

"Got no problem with Cobalt's drug money being used to blow up civilians and soldiers?"

"You know—"

"What I know," Jellicoe said, raising his voice, "is that Cochrane caught and kept alive means a trial. Secret, of course, but a trial nevertheless. Someone's going to leak what was said in the courtroom. Always happens. Public will get to hear why Cochrane's been a bad boy. Ferryman will come to light. Then everything will be fucked, including national security."

"You *need* to get authorization from the president."

"You think he'd want me to pose the question

to him? Force him to give me an answer?" Jellicoe drummed the tips of his fingers together in front of his bloated body. "I got to read between the lines, second-guess what the president ain't saying but *is* thinking."

"That doesn't mean he wants an execution."

"Doesn't mean he doesn't want one, either."

"Oh, come on!"

"You got better ideas, Parker, then I'm all ears."

"I . . ." Parker's voice trailed off, because he had no other ideas.

Sheridan leaned forward and jabbed Parker's knee. "You don't need to get your hands dirty. I'll take care of things. Just keep your mouth shut."

Jellicoe ran a finger around the rim of his glass. "I gave the president the latest Ferryman intel."

Intel that was from the United Kingdom. It stated that an MI6 officer had been tasked with flying around Afghanistan to hand out bags of cash to opium growers in return for them destroying their crops and turning their backs on the drug trade. A tribal elder who ran one of the largest plantations told the officer that his money was no good, because someone else had made contact with him and had offered to buy his crops for three times the price. Everyone in MI6 and Langley was in no doubt that that someone was terrorism financier Cobalt.

"What did the president say?"

"What I expected: keeping Ferryman intact remains an absolute priority. Cobalt *must* be killed. Ferryman will do that for us."

• • •

Four thousand eight hundred miles away from Washington, D.C., Antaeus was sitting in his study in the rural outskirts of Moscow. On his desk was a leather-bound notebook, bought for him by his wife five years ago, his gold-embossed initials on its cover. The book was open to a page that contained his elegant handwriting in blue fountain pen ink. At the top of the page was the heading DOMINOS. His pen hovered over the page as he read his notes.

2010. FSB double agent tells Germans that Russian security services are hunting major terrorist financier, code name COBALT. Financier strikes terms on terrorist-controlled opium and cocaine plantations; manufactures and ships drugs using sophisticated network; sells drugs; gives terrorist plantation owners cut of profits. Germans share this intel with Western allies.

2011. FSB freezes account in Bank of Moscow, moments after $80 million was transferred to account in Algeria. British GCHQ intercept encrypted burst from SVR's London Station, saying, "Cobalt's moved his money. We're too late."

2012. FBI meets FSB and asks if

Russia has heard of a major terrorism financier, code name COBALT. FSB says it believes Cobalt is financing more terror operations around the world than all other sources of funding put together. But FSB is wary of cooperating with FBI.

2013. Security services from States, Europe, and Russia conduct independent and joint operations to try to locate and capture Cobalt. But Russian-American cooperation still tense. Americans suspect Russians are withholding information.

2014. Pakistani ISI tells America that it has captured and interrogated a Taliban fighter, and he's confessed that he'd been contacted by the Islamic Movement of Uzbekistan who said that a financier called Cobalt was making arrangements to travel to the Afghan-Pakistan border to meet the Taliban leadership, and that he was to be given safe passage.

Antaeus moved his pen underneath the last paragraph and wrote two sentences.

MI6 officer tries to buy off major opium plantation in Afghanistan as part of ongoing operation to rid country of drugs.

*Plantation owner refuses, says Cobalt has
made far better offer and will be taking
possession of crop soon.*

Antaeus capped his pen, rolled an ink blotter
over his latest entry, and closed the notebook. In
approximately two weeks' time, Project Ferryman would know the exact location and time that
Cobalt was going to be in Afghanistan to secretly
meet senior Taliban and al-Qaeda leaders. Ferryman had already told the CIA about this meeting,
that it was going to be heavily guarded by upward
of three hundred combat-experienced jihadists,
and that Russian intelligence had decided it was
too risky to infiltrate the country and attack the
meeting. The Americans, on the other hand, had
decided that the scale of the defenses precluded
a SEAL or Delta assault to kill Cobalt, but that
didn't matter because they'd use an unmanned
predator drone to drop a bunker-destroying bomb
on the location. And a minute after they'd done
so, they'd go public to the world's media with the
success story.

The Ferryman intel had prompted the premiers
of Western countries hunting Cobalt to agree that
all existing efforts to find him should cease, for
fear that if they continued they could drive him
further underground and prompt him not to travel
to Afghanistan. All they needed to do now was wait
for Ferryman to obtain the final piece of the jigsaw
that would pin down Cobalt. Then America would
blow Cobalt to pieces.

Ferryman had to remain untouched for that to happen.

Antaeus looked at his chalkboard containing the names of the major parties who were wittingly or unwittingly involved in the Ferryman project. His eyes settled on the name Will Cochrane. The MI6 officer was the biggest threat to Ferryman and could not be allowed to get closer to the truth.

Antaeus smiled.

Because the truth was that the Americans didn't know that dropping their bomb would cause a catastrophe.

TWENTY

Will didn't turn around when he heard the vehicle behind him draw nearer. Instead, he continued walking along the slush-filled edge of the road, his hands in his jacket pockets and his collar pulled up to give him some protection from the driving rain. The vehicle sounded like a car or an SUV, but he couldn't be sure because the wind was loud and hitting his ears from different directions, and he was dog tired and not thinking straight. He hoped the vehicle didn't contain a woman or child—no driver of either would stop for a stranger—and that wherever it was headed, it would be driving through a place where he could be dropped off and rent a room for the night.

The vehicle's engine grew louder.

Please slow down, drive alongside me, lower your window, and look concerned.

Please.

The vehicle was close now, changed into a lower gear, and was slowing for sure.

He kept walking, his feet aching from fatigue,

boots full of water after he'd witnessed Ulana's plane sink into the icy strait.

The vehicle was right behind him.

He carried on.

So did the vehicle. But it remained behind him, matching his speed.

Jeez, it would be ironic if the person behind him turned out to be precisely what he hoped he didn't look like: a prowling serial killer.

It turned out that the vehicle was something even less welcome. Blue lights flashed over the ground around him, followed by a short burst of siren and a man's voice on a microphone saying, "Police. Stop where you are. Turn around."

Will's heart and mind were racing. The broken-down-car story wouldn't work with the cops. They'd drive him back there with the intention of radioing for a tow truck. He turned, keeping his hands in his pockets, because only soldiers, special operatives, and experienced criminals would automatically put their arms out if someone had a gun trained on them from a distance.

There were two cops, both standing behind the cruiser's open doors, hands on their holstered pistols, one of them holding a mic close to his mouth. "Hands where we can see them."

Will put his hands up and flat in front of his chest, as if he were about to play patty-cake and had never confronted someone with a gun before. "I'm glad you guys are here." The words were spoken in an East Coast American accent. Before she'd been murdered, his English mother had frequently told the adolescent Will that he sounded just like his

CIA father. Not that Will had copied his father's accent. He'd been incarcerated in Tehran when Will was five years old. But like his father, Will had grown up in Virginia.

"You in trouble?"

Will smiled. "You could say that. Woman trouble." He nodded toward the road behind the cops. "About five miles that way, my girlfriend kicked me out of our van. We had a bit of a . . . disagreement."

"You on vacation?"

"Yeah. Well, that was the idea."

"Where you headed?"

Will shrugged. "Anywhere that'll give me a bed for the night. Debby gets like this sometimes. Never lasts more than a day. I'll text her, she'll probably pick me up in the morning." His smile broadened. "All I said to her was that her driving was crappy."

The policeman near him tried to suppress a laugh. "Bet you regret saying that now."

"Yep. I wondered if it was Debby behind me. Not guys with guns."

"Seems it's not your day. You tried calling her?"

"Several times. Goes straight to voice mail. She'll turn it back on when she calms down."

"Dumb move getting out of the vehicle this time of year. You can die out here."

"I realize that now, but staying in the vehicle might have been just as dangerous. Debby's got a crazy temper."

The cop with the mic asked, "She going to be okay?"

Will nodded. "The van's got a full tank plus

spare gas, and lots of food. We've done plenty of touring before. Debby knows what she's doing."

"Vehicle registration number?"

"No idea. It's a rental car, and Debs sorted all the paperwork out in New York."

"You take the Maine–New Brunswick route in?"

"Yeah. Crossed at Vanceboro eleven days ago."

"Okay, lower your hands. We'll need to see some ID."

"Sure. You able to drop me off someplace?"

The cop glanced at his colleague, who nodded. "We're heading back to Truro. That do you?"

"If Truro's got a diner and a motel, it'll do me just fine."

"Center of town's got Holiday Inn, Willow Bend, Best Western, and Glengarry hotels. You have options. Identification, please."

Will pulled out the American passport Ulana had given him. "I got other ID, but it's in the van."

The nearest policeman stepped up to Will, took the passport from him, and leaned over the ID so that his upper body shielded it from rain as he flicked through the pages.

As the cop opened the page containing the photo, Will mentally rehearsed what he'd do if the officer reached for his gun because he realized that the man in the photo wasn't him or because he suddenly recalled seeing a nonbearded shot of Will Cochrane in a newspaper after the Senator Jellicoe hearing.

But the officer closed the passport, handed it back to him, and said, "Okay, Mr. Jones. All seems good. We'll get you to Truro, and we should be able to get the plates of the van from Vanceboro immigration. During your crossing, it will have been logged alongside your passport. It'll take a few hours though. If you don't hear from your girlfriend by morning, it's vital you call the RCMP station in Truro. We'll go looking then."

"Sure."

The cop beckoned him forward. "Afraid we've finished our flask of coffee and we got a good hour before we reach Truro. Still"—he smiled—"since you look like shit, I'm betting you won't mind getting a bit of shut-eye during the drive."

Marsha Gage was sitting at her desk in the FBI task force room and had her cell phone pinned against one ear and a landline handset against the other. On one line was Sorocco Fonseca of Spain's Centro Nacional de Inteligencia; on the other was Bianca Dinapoli of Italy's Agenzia Informazioni e Sicurezza Interna. Both were telling her that there'd been a few possible sightings in southern Europe of someone matching Will Cochrane's description, but all of them had proven to be false. Behind Marsha, Patrick and Alistair were playing chess, while Sheridan was on the phone to Senator Jellicoe. Not for the first time since the three men had graced the room with their presence, Marsha thought that at best they were useless and at worst downright counterproductive. Regardless, it seemed that they enjoyed doing nothing while she worked her ass off.

On the screen of her landline, she saw that she

had a call waiting from Assistant Commissioner Danny Labelle of the Royal Canadian Mounted Police. She ended the other calls, picked up, and said, "Commissioner. You got something for me?"

"Might be nothing, but you told me to report anything odd."

"Wish half the people I work with could be as forthcoming. What is it?"

"Our Coast Guard's found a crashed Islander plane on our Nova Scotia seaboard. Only reason they spotted it was due to the tide being out."

"That happen a lot where you live?"

Labelle laughed. "Not where I live. But yeah, it happens in parts of Canada where there aren't many roads but there are plenty of high winds that'll knock you sideways."

"So, why suspicious?"

"Pilot was still inside the plane when the Coast Guard found it. And she's got a bullet in her brain."

"ID on her?"

"American passport. My guys have already put a call in to your Department of State. Turns out the passport's a fake."

"Drug runner making a delivery that went wrong?"

"Could be."

"Anything else on her to suggest this isn't just some criminal matter?"

"Can't say there is, but you wanted to know about any suspicious transportation movements into east coast Canada."

"I did indeed. Thanks anyway, Commissioner."

"My pleasure. Oh, and Marsha?"

"Yeah."

"Her body's now at the Nova Scotia Hospital. Just a formality because she's been dead for at least twenty-four hours. But doctors examined her anyway. She's got a tattoo on her upper arm. Odd looking. Not the sort of thing women generally go for."

"Probably a prison thing." Marsha drummed her fingers on her desk. "Can you fax a picture of it over to me?"

"On its way."

Two minutes later, the fax machine printed a single sheet with the letterhead ROYAL CANADIAN MOUNTED POLICE—*MAINTIENS LE DROIT*, NATIONAL HEADQUARTERS, HEADQUARTERS BUILDING, 73 LEIKIN DRIVE, OTTAWA ON K1A 0R2. On it was the photo image of an upper arm, and next to the limb was a handwritten note stating, *Dead female pilot. Still no luck identifying her. Not seen this kind of tattoo before. She liked hunting, maybe? D. Labelle.*

Marsha took out a magnifying glass from her desk drawer and examined the tattoo. It was a picture of a bear; an eagle with outstretched wings looked to be landing on its back. Like the commissioner, she had no idea if it symbolized anything or was just an innocuous cartoon that signified its wearer was prone to moments of illogical whimsy.

She swiveled in her chair and eyed Patrick and Alistair. Both were still engrossed in chess. "Unlike you, I'm kind of busy right now. So, *gentlemen*"—she folded the fax sheet into the shape of an airplane and tossed it at them—"I wouldn't mind if you tapped Spooksville—Stateside and old country—on the shoulder to see if that tattoo makes any sense."

Patrick picked up the fax with one hand while moving knight to take bishop with the other. The CIA officer unfolded it and held the image in front of Alistair, then thrust the fax toward Sheridan and called out, "You know what this means?"

Sheridan looked bemused. "I have no idea."

"That a statement about your raison d'être?"

"What?"

"Never mind, idiot."

Marsha gestured toward the paper and told the men about the downed Islander airplane. "Most likely it's nothing, but I really would like it if you could find out if that tattoo means anything."

Alistair shrugged while positioning a rook as bait to tempt Patrick's knight to take it and in turn leave the knight vulnerable to attack from a bishop. "We don't need to."

"Just because I'm not paying by the hour doesn't mean . . ."

"Shit." Patrick stared at the chessboard, knowing that Alistair was thinking ten moves ahead. He adjusted his thinking, moved a rook, and called out, "It's a military tattoo."

"Russian." Alistair's rook took his opponent's rook. "A version not too dissimilar is popular among Special Forces paratroopers."

"This one's unusual though, because it's on a woman and because the bear and eagle aren't fighting but instead are cooperating." Patrick's brain was racing because he knew Alistair had thrown in a new strategy. "You only see it on specialists."

"GRU specialists." Bishop defends queen.

"Who've been given advanced airborne training." Pawn move to feint attack on queen.

"Secret training." Queen retreats two squares.

Patrick's knight puts Alistair's queen and rook in jeopardy. "Seems your dead pilot was very unusual."

"A highly skilled paramilitary intelligence officer."

"Unlikely to be a drug runner who'd let petty criminals get the better of her."

"More likely she was conducting a covert infiltration."

"And something went wrong on her return journey."

"Plane malfunction." Alistair moved his queen. "Or got hit by some godawful weather."

"And put a gun to her head rather than let the Atlantic do its work on her." Patrick smiled as he moved his bishop. "Your king's got nowhere to run. Checkmate."

Alistair rubbed his hands together. "Didn't see that one coming, old boy. Congrats."

"Reckon that's nine wins each so far." Patrick turned to Marsha. "Also reckon you'd better be wondering what the GRU woman was delivering to Nova Scotia."

The police cruiser stopped outside the Best Western hotel in Truro. One of the Mounties opened the rear door and gestured for Will to get out. "Remember—call us in the morning if your girlfriend doesn't make contact with you."

"Sure, and thanks again for the ride." Will exited the vehicle, shook the cop's hand, and walked into the hotel lobby. He had no intention of staying here or anywhere else in Truro. A few minutes after the cops had gone, he'd leave the hotel and head farther west.

TWENTY-ONE

Ellie Hallowes walked down a corridor inside Langley that housed the Directorate of Intelligence, specifically its Russian and European Analysis division. On either side of her were large, open-plan rooms that housed researchers and analysts whose task was to support the work of the Agency's National Clandestine Service as well as the dissemination of all source intelligence to key government and military customers in the United States. When not working in the field, it was common for members of the Clandestine Service to stalk the halls of this wholly separate directorate with the intention of trying to browbeat analysts into upgrading the importance of their sources' intelligence. Though they were different shapes, ages, and sizes, you could differentiate officers of the Clandestine Service from the desk-bound ranks of the Directorate of Intelligence. They had an unusual way of looking at people, exuding confidence and an air of superiority. When one of them walked past, analysts would frequently stop what they were doing and stare at them in awe, jealousy, and resentment that they were responsible for a lot of the paperwork and crap the analysts had to put up with. But nobody took any notice of Ellie, because she averted her gaze from others and wanted to be invisible.

She entered a vast room containing at least two hundred desks and computer terminals, with people sitting or walking around, talking to each other or on the phone or working in silence. It was a cluttered and vibrant atmosphere, similar, Ellie assumed, to those found in newspaper head-quarters, investment banks, and telemarketing companies.

She had to ask three people where to go before she found the desk of the female analyst.

Alongside the Director of the CIA, Sheridan, Parker, and Jellicoe, Ellie had ascertained from her computer's file request database that four other officers were cleared to access Ferryman files. All were analysts. Three of them were no good to her because they were male. The fourth had potential, not just because she was a woman but because she was also cleared to read the Herald files.

"Ellie Hallowes." She held out her hand to the woman, who was a few years older than Ellie, plumper, and wore thick-rimmed glasses. "Thought I'd introduce myself to you while I'm in town."

The analyst didn't get up from her seat. She looked quizzical and hesitant before shaking Ellie's hand. "Helen Coombs."

"I had direct involvement in the Herald case. Wanted to thank you in person for processing my intelligence reports, before he . . . well, you know."

Helen's mouth widened in surprise. "You were Herald's case officer? I often wondered who you were, because your name was never mentioned in his files."

Nor would it be. Unlike their peers in the Clandestine Service, deep-cover officers were never identified in official reports.

"Glad to hear that. I'm going to be pulling some of Herald's files from archives. Director Parker's given me written clearance to do so, but I thought you ought to know." She smiled. "In case you thought they'd gone missing."

"They're *your* files, my dear. The rest of us can stand in line. You take as long as you like reading them. Know which archive department they're in?"

"I'm told six corridors down."

"Yep." Helen looked concerned. "Were you with him when he was killed in Norway?"

"I . . ." It was time for the waterworks. Fake waterworks. Ellie held a handkerchief to her mouth and nose, and nodded.

"You poor thing." Helen got up from her desk and put her arm around Ellie. "Nobody should have to go through that."

Ellie cleared her throat and inhaled deeply, as if trying to compose herself. "Guess that's why I wanted to meet you. I don't know anyone else here. Certainly no one else who was in on Herald."

"It must be so hard for you." Helen patted her hand while looking around the bustling room. "Want to have a chat somewhere more private? We could grab a coffee."

This was excellent. Ellie thought she'd have to

make the first move, but Helen had suggested precisely what she was hoping for. "That sounds like a great idea. How about after work today?"

"Of course. I finish in two hours."

"As long as it doesn't annoy your husband."

"I'm single. Live alone. I can do what I like."

Ellie looked like she was about to get emotional again, though all she was thinking about was that she'd have to move quickly to get home first to sort through her array of disguises. "In that case, is it possible we can get something a bit stronger than a coffee? And go someplace away from here?"

Helen smiled. "I look forward to it. Tell you what—it's work related, so let's put it on expenses and make the Agency pay."

Later that evening, Ellie drained the remainder of her wine and smiled. "Thanks for this evening, Helen. I needed it. Think I had to lay Herald to rest."

"You calling it a night?" Helen's words were a bit slurred, her face flushed. "Place's just livening up."

The bar was indeed getting lively with young office workers; the men had ties loosened and were speaking too loudly, trying to hold court; the women were cackling and gulping wine, all of them displaying the booze-fueled hubris of individuals who were relieved to be set free from work. Ellie wondered if Agency people came here, since the bar was close to Langley. She hoped not, because being seen out with one of the Agency's analysts was the last thing she wanted. "Actually, it's just a bit noisy in here. Feel like there's too many people around."

"I understand."

"God, it feels good though to be off duty. Have you got anything decent to drink at your place? I could do with a few more glasses, but somewhere a bit less party-party. Still feeling very emotional, and the last thing I want to do is break down in front of these folks."

Helen slapped a hand on the table, a broad smile on her face. "In that case, girl, let's you and me make a night of it. I've got *plenty* to drink at home."

"Great." Ellie grabbed her overnight bag. "That's more than can be said for my hotel room. Can you hail a cab while I make a visit to the ladies' room?"

"My pleasure." After Helen put on her overcoat and grabbed her handbag, she walked to the exit, her footing a little unsteady.

Ellie waited until she was outside before approaching one of the waiters. "Found this by our seats. Someone's going to be pissed when they realize it's gone missing."

She handed over Helen Coombs's wallet, while mentally rehearsing what she'd say to Helen as their cab approached her home.

The cab's on me, providing the liquor and music's on you.

The waiter took the wallet that Ellie had stolen from Helen's handbag. "Sure. If we don't hear from the owner by tomorrow, we'll report it. Can you give me your name?"

"Maggie Evans."

"Okay, Ms. Evans. Thanks for your honesty, and have a nice evening."

Ellie exited the bar.

Helen was standing by a cab and had a glint in her eye. "You like Abba?" Before Ellie could answer, Helen started singing "Dancing Queen" as she opened the door.

Ellie wished that Helen's CIA security ID had been in her handbag. Then again, maybe it was good that it wasn't, because Ellie could give Helen the mother of all hangovers, to the extent that tomorrow she'd think it perfectly plausible that she'd not only left her wallet at the bar, but also her treasured Agency ID. Also, it was probable that Helen would be late for work or call in sick. But that meant that Ellie was going to have to endure Abba, more wine, and inane small talk for several hours until she could steal Helen's ID, leave her home, get changed into a wig and glasses and padding, and briefly pretend to be someone resembling the ID photo of Helen.

Will stood in front of Truro Heights Irving Big Stop, on McClure's Mills Connector Road. It was a 24-7 gas station, but what was important to Will was that it was the largest truck stop in Truro.

The lot was to the left of the station forecourt and shop; despite the driving snow the lights from both gave him glimpses of parked trucks. Will kept away from the lights, moving down one edge of the forecourt and behind the 24-7 until he reached the parking lot. There was a single row of sedans, and two rows of sixteen trucks. Three of them had cab lights on and engines running, the rest were unlit. He imagined that most of the drivers would either be grabbing coffee and provisions while swapping notes with other drivers about destinations and road conditions, or were asleep in their cabs or in a nearby motel. No one from the shop or gas forecourt could see him as he moved in near pitch-darkness from one vehicle to another, checking their registration plates. Fourteen trucks had Canadian plates and were therefore no good to him; two of them had U.S. plates, one from Maine, the other from New Hampshire.

He withdrew the lockpick set he'd retrieved from the Russian cache and started working on the rear door locks of the Maine trailer. Two minutes later, both locks were open. The trailer was full of cardboard boxes with pictures showing their contents were televisions. A full container was no good to him because it meant the American truck was heading farther south into Nova Scotia, rather than returning home after making its delivery. He shut the door, locked it in place, and jogged to the New Hampshire truck.

This one had more basic padlocks and chains, and it took him half as long to open them. He pulled open the trailer door and breathed a sigh of relief. The truck was empty. Unless he was mistaken, this was a truck that had no need to be in Canada anymore, one that had to get home so that its driver could collect a paycheck, grab a day's rest, and get back on the road. Like Will right now, truckers liked to stay on the move.

He entered the cold, long trailer, snapped the padlocks shut when the door was nearly closed, and sealed himself inside the trailer. He was now completely blind. The Canadian border with Maine was approximately 250 miles away. It had seventeen border controls, but the truck driver would be using the International Avenue crossing, since it was the only one that permitted commercial traffic.

He had to assume the cops who'd given him a ride would subsequently establish or be told the real identity of the man they'd picked up outside Truro, and that meant the Canadian border would be reinforced with armed officers. That was bad news for everyone, because if cops stopped the truck and opened the trailer, they'd be confronted by a man at the far end of the container who'd be pointing two pistols at their heads.

Will wondered how long it would take before the driver got it on the move. One hour later, he had an answer. The engine rumbled, causing the trailer to vibrate.

Then the truck started pulling away.

TWENTY-TWO

Though it was four ten A.M. in Washington, D.C., Marsha had no intention of going home to get some rest. Instead, she was working through the night at her desk, making and receiving calls from security service and law enforcement officials who were operating in different time zones.

One of her cell phones rang.

A man spoke to her. "I'm Inspector Campbell, RCMP H Division, Nova Scotia."

"Inspector—what's the latest?"

"Two of my guys picked up a male hitchhiker outside of Truro. His story for being on the road seemed plausible, but we subsequently showed the officers a photo of Cochrane. They think it's a probable match."

Marsha was motionless. "Probable?"

"Yeah. We got a sketch artist to copy the one photo we have of Cochrane, but make his face a bit thinner and add a short beard. My guys are convinced it's him. I've got patrols all over Truro."

Marsha looked at the map above her desk.

"Forget Truro—you won't find him there. He's heading for the border. Get men there ASAP!"

The taxi firm told Ellie Hallowes that a driver would be at the address in thirty minutes. Ellie snapped shut Helen's cell, glanced at the CIA analyst, who was passed out on the sofa, and turned off the alarm clocks that had been programmed into her cell and in the adjacent bedroom's clock. If later challenged by Helen, Ellie would ask her whether she remembered declaring in the early hours that they should carry on drinking until sunrise and to hell with wake-up calls and work.

She opened Helen's closet, selected clothes that were frumpy and similar to those Helen was wearing, unzipped her overnight bag containing the wig and other items, and set to work.

At eight fifty A.M. Ellie Hallowes used Helen Coombs's ID to enter the security gates in the lobby of the CIA headquarters. She felt totally calm and focused, despite the possibility that someone might see through her disguise, grab her, and pin her to the floor. It was the same feeling she always had when going undercover. She likened it to putting on a suit of armor.

Underneath her pleated skirt, jacket, and frilly blouse, she had padding around her hips and stomach. Her wig covered her throat and the sides of her face, to hide the fact that there was nothing she could do to make it puffier. Plus, her thick-rimmed glasses and carefully applied rouge and other makeup had altered her appearance sufficiently, she hoped.

After taking an elevator, she waddled down a corridor in the way that Helen had done when she'd entered the bar yesterday evening. She was fully cognizant of the dangers—Helen could be awake now and on her way to work; she might have realized her CIA ID was missing and alerted Langley's security department; someone could pass Ellie in the corridor and challenge her; hidden cameras in the headquarters could be watching her; and someone at the reception of the place she was headed toward could look at her ID and her face and say, "I know Helen Coombs, and you're not her." But Ellie didn't let any of these possibilities worry her. Worry had no place in her line of work.

Langley was buzzing with people arriving for work, and with others who'd already been here for an hour or so. She stopped by the entrance to the Russian and European Analysis division's archive room. Of all of the archives in Langley, this was without doubt the one that contained the CIA's most sensitive secrets. She was going to try to steal one of them.

She entered the big hall, at the head of which was a wide reception desk with ten computer screens in a row and people behind them, beyond that a room resembling a library that kept all of its books behind combination-locked steel shutters. But in here there were no books; instead there were paper files that recorded all of the developments relating to the Agency's Russian spies as well as ongoing and closed operations against Russia.

The Herald files were in here, containing Ellie's contact reports and intelligence briefings.

She wasn't interested in those files.

She looked at the archive employees. Hundreds of other Agency officers would use this archive, but there was still a real risk that one or more of the people working here knew Helen Coombs.

The place was busy, with officers lining up in front of the reception desk to get access to files they were cleared to read. None of them were allowed beyond the desk, so they had to wait patiently while members of the archive went off to retrieve the files.

Whom to approach? Not the archivists who were approximately Helen's age—they might socialize with the analyst or at least make the effort to engage in small talk with her every time she came in. Or the old guy who looked like he was head of the archive and probably made it his business to get to know the people who came in. That left the bored-looking young man.

She stood in the line, behind another officer who was being served. The officer took a file that was handed to him and moved out of the way. Ellie was in front of the archivist.

She handed Helen's ID over. "I need the Ferryman files."

The receptionist typed the word into his computer, swiped the ID into the system, looked at the photo, and looked at Ellie.

He stared at her for five seconds. "You want both of them?"

"What?"

"Both files."

Ellie smiled. "Yes, please."

"Okay." The archivist handed the ID back to her. "Come with me. System says you can't take them away—got to be read in one of the booths."

Ellie followed him to a series of tiny cubicles, each containing a desk and one chair. "Wait here."

Ellie sat at the desk.

Was the archivist going to return with two burly security guards?

One minute later, he dropped the files on the desk. "They can't leave the booth. You press that button when you're finished and I'll come and get them. Make sure the door's shut."

After he was gone and the closed room secure, Ellie placed her hands on the files and momentarily didn't want to open them. Whatever Ferryman was, the Agency had decided it was important enough to sacrifice Ellie in order to keep Antaeus alive, and to crucify Will Cochrane because he'd broken Ferryman protocols. Inside the files, she'd find whatever secret was more important than her life. She couldn't help but wonder whether learning about Ferryman was pointless, considering Will stood no chance of reaching the States.

But she was a spy, and all spies lust after the truth with the mental and physical yearning of a crack addict searching for another fix.

No matter what the dangers.

She opened the files.

The New Hampshire truck idled in the stationary traffic at the newly built large customs complex on the American side of the International Avenue crossing. The buildings resembled a small airport complex, and to the left of them were six lanes that led to six passport controls, three of which trucks were permitted to use, plus six bays where cargo could be unloaded, examined, and reloaded.

The bays were at capacity and every vehicle going through the complex was being checked.

The driver glanced at his watch, desperate to get moving onto Maine State Route 9 so that he could reach New Hampshire with time to spare for some food and rest before his next pickup.

A tap on the window. A Maine state cop stood there, making no effort to hide the fact that he was holding a pistol in one hand.

Clearly, something really serious was going down.

The driver opened his window.

"You got cargo in the trailer?"

The trucker shook his head. "I dropped off at Truro. Heading back to Concord. What's going on?"

The cop ignored the question and gestured to a bay containing three more police officers, one of them holding a mirror on the end of a pole, all of them carrying pump-action shotguns. "Put her in there, ignition off. We'll need to check inside."

The driver did as he was told. The cop walked alongside the vehicle and once again stood by the window when it was stationary.

The trucker said, "I'll open the trailer for you."

"No you won't. You'll stay here while we get things unlocked. Give me the trailer keys."

The driver handed them to him.

"You pick anyone up en route?"

"No."

"See anything suspicious? Maybe a man on foot in a place where people don't generally take a walk?"

"Nope."

"All right. Don't do it yet, but when I tell you to I want you to immediately turn on the interior trailer lights. *Immediately*, understand?"

"Sure."

The police officer looked at his colleagues. "This one's from Truro. We give it the VIP treatment. All of you, with me."

They moved to the rear of the trailer. Three of them stood back so that they could not be seen by anyone inside. The cop holding the pistol and keys unlocked the container, yanked the doors open, and immediately stepped back while shouting, "Lights on, now! Police. If there's anyone in there, call out your name."

Silence.

The cop holding the mirror on a pole moved it to the entrance and adjusted angles so that he could see everything inside. He shook his head.

His commander held three fingers up, then two, then one. All four men swung their weapons so that they were pointing at the interior of the trailer.

It was brightly illuminated.

And completely empty.

"Okay. Let's check underneath and in the cab."

Forty feet away from the cops, at the front of the trailer, Will released his grip on the undercarriage, dropped to the road, pulled out his handgun, and rolled away from the vehicle until he was on his back. He fired six rounds, all of them aimed with precision so that they struck the truck inches from the police but had no chance of ricocheting and injuring them. The police ducked low, dashed for cover, and started shouting. Will fired two more rounds, jumped to his feet, ran to the head of the truck, and swerved left just before a shotgun boomed and sent pellets into the side of the cab. While changing his magazine clip, he dodged between stationary trucks and other vehicles in the six lanes leading to the passport control booths. Behind him, the police were screaming at passengers to stay in their vehicles and get down.

Will spun around and got to one knee between two trucks, fired at the road to the right of the four encroaching cops, sent three more rounds over their heads, dived under one of the trucks as they returned fire with shotguns and pistols, and leopard-crawled to the other side.

As he emerged, something hit him on the back with tremendous force, causing him to wince in agony. A man was on top of him, wrapping a muscular arm around his throat and squeezing. Will lashed his skull backward into the man's face, making him loosen his grip and allowing Will to twist and smash a hand into his face with sufficient force to crush his nose. The man fell away, writhing on the ground crying. He was a big trucker who'd leapt out of his cabin onto Will the moment Will had crawled from underneath his trailer. Now, he probably wished he'd listened to the cops' orders.

Two police officers peered from behind the

truck and fired their shotguns just as Will rolled away, got to his feet, and jumped onto the roof of an adjacent car. Most of the pellets missed him, but some tore through his jacket and raced alongside the skin of one arm, sending needlelike pain down the limb.

Will ran onto the roof of the next vehicle, leapt forward to another car, jumped down as more shots were fired, and sprinted as fast as he could to the passport booth while wondering if the man in there was armed. He took no chances and fired two warning shots through the glass, close to his head.

"Stop!"

Will dived onto a car as one cop fired again, his body causing the metal beneath him to buckle.

Whoever these cops were, they were tenacious professionals.

Ones that couldn't be deterred by warning shots.

He regretted that as he fired a bullet into the officer's shoulder and watched him twist and drop his shotgun.

He ran alongside the booth, past vehicles containing men, women, and children who were embracing each other and looking at him with mouths open and eyes wide in disbelief and disgust.

They thought he was a criminal.

But not a common one.

Instead, a rabid creature who'd shot a cop and therefore could savage them if they gave him reason to.

The officer in the booth was squatting with his hands on his head while staring at him. He looked middle-aged, overweight, and terrified.

Will shouted, "Stay in there!" as he ran onward. Ahead of him were empty roads and zero cover. But that didn't matter, because he knew he could outpace the three remaining cops and stay beyond the limited range of their shotguns and pistols. All he had to do was keep running.

Two hundred yards later, the roads converged into a two-lane bridge that took drivers into Maine. Will was halfway across the bridge when he heard a police siren and a vehicle approaching fast from behind him. He spun around and saw a cop car with three cops inside, racing toward the bridge.

He stood no chance of reaching the end of the bridge before the cruiser.

Kneeling down, he held his pistol in two hands, and was motionless as he took aim.

The vehicle was one hundred yards away, halfway between him and the border-check booths.

He fired three shots into the car's engine block and two into the front left tire. The vehicle swerved left and shuddered to a halt as Will got to his feet and bolted along the bridge while zigzagging to make himself a difficult target.

Behind him, pistol shots: some rounds raced through the air close to him, others struck the tarmac close to his feet.

But the cops were too far behind him.

He reached the end of the bridge, sprinted off the road, and entered the United States.

Ellie walked at an even pace, away from the archive. What mattered now was getting away from Langley, changing out of the disguise, and praying that Will Cochrane made contact with her.

She entered an elevator that was traveling to the ground floor, and felt her heart miss a beat. Three men were in the elevator.

Jellicoe.

Sheridan.

Parker.

They were talking in hushed tones, but immediately fell silent when she stepped into the elevator.

She turned her back to the men.

"Ma'am, you want the ground floor?" The voice belonged to Parker.

Ellie nodded, and replied with an accent that wasn't hers, "Yes please, sir."

She hoped she was conveying the feeling of unease that many low-ranking officers have when they inadvertently find themselves in the presence of senior management.

"Heading home already?"

God, why did Director Parker have to be so darn sociable? "Yes sir. I was on the night shift."

Parker laughed. "Glad those days are long behind me. But we appreciate your work. What's your name, lady?"

She glanced back, just for a split second and only showing a fraction of her face, knowing the risk in doing so but also knowing that just staring ahead would be odd. "Paula Jones."

"Not seen you around here before."

"It's my first week. I'm in archives."

"Didn't know archives pulled night shifts."

"We're doing a major refiling exercise. It's a round-the-clock job."

"Don't envy you."

"It's a job, sir. I'm grateful." The doors opened at the ground floor. Ellie stepped out and walked toward the security gates in the lobby. At every moment as she crossed the large marble foyer, she expected Parker to shout out something like, "Ellie Hallowes—that's far enough!" But she heard no such thing as she swiped Helen's ID through the turnstile gate's security panel and exited the CIA headquarters.

Outside it was bitterly cold, with bright sunshine causing her to squint and her eyes to hurt. She kept walking toward a lot where her rental was parked, desperate to get as far away from here as possible.

And desperate to tell Will Cochrane that Ferryman was a high-ranking Russian SVR officer named Gregori Shonin who'd been recruited by the CIA in Prague in 2005.

Shonin worked for Antaeus and had direct access to the spymaster's secrets. Antaeus's biggest secret of all was that he was ahead of the West in tracking Cobalt and had ascertained that the terrorist financier was going to be in Afghanistan in two weeks' time. Soon, Ferryman would learn from Antaeus the exact time and location of Cobalt's meeting, at which point he would relay this intel to the CIA so that it could blow Cobalt into pieces.

Ferryman was of incalculable value because of his access to Antaeus.

And Antaeus had to be kept alive because without him the Agency couldn't get to Cobalt.

At face value, there was now no doubt in Ellie's mind that Project Ferryman was infinitely more important than her life, and that Will Cochrane had been wholly wrong to break Ferryman protocols in Norway.

But something wasn't right.

Herald had told her that there was a Russian mole right at the top of the Agency. Even if that mole wasn't privy to the identity of Ferryman, he'd certainly know of Ferryman and that he had a direct line to Antaeus, whose insight was vital to killing Cobalt.

The mole would have told Antaeus that the Agency had access to his secrets.

And somebody as clever and ruthless as Antaeus would have identified Ferryman and killed him by now.

But Ferryman was still alive and working alongside Antaeus.

And that meant one thing: that Antaeus had his own agenda.

The spymaster was a puppeteer with his hand hovering over the Agency, holding strings tied to Langley so strong that he could make it move like a deaf, dumb, and blind doll.

Simply put, he had the United States' national security apparatus by the balls.

PART III

TWENTY-THREE

Retired major Dickie Mountjoy tried not to wince as he got out of his armchair in his small apartment in West Square. Damn limbs were getting old, but that didn't mean he had to gripe about it or show others that he was no longer the army officer who could march for hours in front of Her Majesty and the tourists in Horse Guards Parade. He opened the door and found his neighbors Phoebe and David there. Phoebe was dressed to kill, meaning no doubt she was going out for the evening to watch a middleweight boxing match or attend one of her art gallery's boozy functions. David, on the other hand, was wearing a food-stained T-shirt over his flabby torso, and jeans that had baking flour all over them. For the life of him, Dickie never understood why the mortician spent so much time cooking, considering that he was recently divorced and had no one else in his life.

"What d'ya want?"

Phoebe and David exchanged bemused glances.

"Your notes under our doors. You said you

wanted to see us. This evening." Phoebe wagged a finger. "You're not getting all senile on us, are you, darling?"

"No, and do I look like a *darling* to you?"

Phoebe looked mischievous and replied in a sultry voice, "I think deep down you're an *utter* darling."

Dickie huffed. "That means you know the square root of bugger-all about me. All right, come in."

"Oooh. Nice Christmas tree." Phoebe sat in Dickie's favorite armchair, which annoyed the bejesus out of him, and crossed her legs. "Got any bubbly?"

"Scotch, port, or ale. I've no reason to keep lady drinks in here."

"Oh well. Scotch it is."

Dickie poured three drinks, without bothering to ask David if he wanted one. The retiree thrust the Scotch at the mortician. "Here. Might cut through some of that waistline, and get yer ticker pumping. You think age is on your side, but carry on eating for a regiment and you'll end up on one of your mortuary slabs."

David was unsure what to say, and perched his large frame on the end of the sofa. This also annoyed Dickie because it meant he had to sit next to him, there being no other empty seat.

"You workin' at a brothel tonight? You look and smell like a tart."

Phoebe was unflustered by the comment. "Have you been to many brothels, Dickie?"

"Before I met Mrs. Mountjoy, army took me all

over the world. Ain't much I haven't been to, young lady."

"And after Mrs. Mountjoy . . ." Phoebe cut herself short. Dickie's wife had died two years before. "Sorry, I . . ."

"*Sorry's* for quitters and mess-ups. You don't strike me as either." Dickie took a gulp of his liquor, coughed violently, held a handkerchief to his mouth, examined it, and cleared his throat. "No time to be sorry."

Phoebe frowned. "Is everything okay, Major?"

"Tickadeeboo. But it's not all good for our Will Cochrane, and that's why I wanted to see you both."

"Of course it's not good for Will. The police made that clear when they came here."

Dickie eyed her with a stern expression. "You make a move on that young constable? Go to his station at Southwark and give them some cock and bull about losing your purse just so that constable plod might pop over to your flat and take down details?"

Phoebe rolled her eyes at David. "No."

"That surprises me."

Phoebe asked, "What's bothering you, Dickie?"

The major waved his hand dismissively before allowing it to slowly descend to his knee, where he tapped his fingers. "I've been too hard on Mr. Cochrane in the past."

"You thought he was in life insurance, part of an industry that didn't pay out on your wife's medical bills. You've nothing to feel bad about. Plus, you had no idea he was an MI6 officer."

"It's not MI6 that's changed things." Dickie felt uncharacteristically emotional. "Well, not that much. Just, I misjudged his character."

Phoebe nodded and mimicked Dickie's clipped army officer tone. "He has a *right proper backbone*."

Dickie didn't find that amusing. "Yes, missy."

Phoebe wondered whether David could sense something was wrong with Dickie. "We can't help him now."

"We can."

"The world's hunting him! You're not young enough to do . . ." David tried to think of a military analogy that might resonate with Dickie. ". . . to do a Charge of the Light Brigade or whatever to save him."

Phoebe frowned. "Charge of the Light Brigade? What's that?"

Dickie eyed her with disdain. "What do they teach at schools these days? Crimean War, 1853 to 1856. Great Britain, France, and the Ottoman Empire versus the Russians. Charge of the Light Brigade was the war's biggest suicidal disaster. A fool's errand given to men who deserved better." Dickie pointed at a copy of the Yellow Pages on the side table next to him. "I got an errand that ain't foolish. I was thinking we can help Mr. Cochrane by giving him his home back. Replace the stuff inside that's broke. Trouble is, my eyes aren't so good and I can't find bloody lute sellers and violin makers and upholsterers and the like."

Phoebe leaned forward, all thoughts about her evening ahead now out of her mind. "You want us to buy him stuff? I don't have that kind of money."

"Nor do I." David took a sip of his Scotch, and went bug-eyed as the spirit coursed down his throat.

Dickie smoothed his hand over the phone directory. "Not asking for your money. Just your eyes and"—he nodded toward Phoebe—"legs. I got a guard officer's pension that's sitting in my post office account waiting for me to pop my clogs so that the tax man or some other greedy bastard can get his hands on my cash. Thought I might beat them to it. Spend the money while I still can."

"Are you . . . ill?" Phoebe looked at the little Christmas tree, its lights and handmade parcels with ribbons bound around them, and wondered why Dickie had made the effort to dress the tree.

Dickie shrugged. "Coughing up blood."

David asked, "What has your doctor said?"

"Never been to one before and not going to start now."

"But you have to get an expert opinion!"

"When you get to my age you don't *have* to do anything."

"Oh, Dickie." Phoebe tried not to shed a tear, because she knew Dickie would hate it, but she couldn't help herself. "Dickie . . ."

"It's all right, my love. Just gettin' old and crumbly. Stuff happens."

She smoothed a hand against her face and in doing so rubbed mascara across her cheeks. "Not to you it doesn't." She tried to smile. "Girls love men who've been around the block and who fight to the end. You're a fighter, Dickie, but this time you need help. Medical help."

Dickie leaned forward and took her hand. "Guys like me spend half our lives prancin' around like peacocks and the other half wishing we still had our plumage. But we always know we're going to die. Death nearly happened to me lots of times in the Falklands and Northern Ireland and other places. I was lucky. Some of my pals weren't. We have to get on with death, just like we have to get on with life."

David asked Phoebe, "You okay, Phoebes?"

Phoebe nodded while trying to compose herself. "I'm okay, thanks."

"Phoebes?" Dickie released Phoebe's hand and leaned back. "And I suppose you call him Dave. You two gettin' familiar?"

"No!"

David blushed. "No."

Dickie chuckled, coughed, and turned serious. "No chance of finding exact replicas, but you can both help me source stuff that makes Will want to come home. I don't care if the world's looking for him. Let it find him here, happy."

Phoebe glanced at David. "We'll do it, as long as you let us take you to a doctor."

"No."

"We—"

"The answer's no!"

Phoebe said, "You said you'd been too hard on Will. I've got an idea how you can make amends. You can put your trust in him. When he gets home, let him take you to a doctor."

Dickie was hesitant. "I . . ."

Phoebe held up a finger and adopted an expression of a strict schoolmistress or dominatrix. "The answer's yes."

The retired major was silent for a moment before saying, "You're right that I've been around the block. It's taught me a lot. Man like me doesn't keep all his loot in one place. I've got other savings stashed in places where the sun don't shine and the tax man's too scared to stick his fingers. I'll be all right." He folded his arms and stared at David. "Who you cookin' for tonight?"

"Just me."

Dickie turned his attention on Phoebe. "You havin' much luck finding Mr. Right by going out dressed in not much more than your undies?"

"I . . ." Phoebe didn't know how to answer.

"Bring you happiness?"

Phoebe took a deep breath. "Girl's got to do whatever it takes."

Dickie pointed at David. "Why don't you let him cook for you tonight? Get him to scrub up first so he looks halfway respectable. Might be a better alternative to what you both have planned for this evening."

Phoebe and David exchanged coy glances.

"And if you give it a whirl, then I'll let Mr. Cochrane take me to the doctor."

David half smiled. "You're blackmailing us into a date?"

"No. I'm telling you to see common sense. You two are made for each other. I know it."

David and Phoebe exchanged looks, both feeling

embarrassed, and both thinking that maybe Dickie's idea was a good one. They said, "Okay," in unison.

"Good. That's squared away. Now—after you've done your romance thing, tomorrow I need you to start helping me out with Cochrane's home."

Phoebe felt herself getting teary again. "Dickie—your health, savings . . . Maybe Will won't ever get back here."

Dickie thought for a moment. "When the horse-mounted dragoons, lancers, and hussars of the Light Brigade made ready to charge down the mile-long valley in Balaclava, they must have known that most of them would die. But they went anyway, and were attacked from the sides and far end of the valley by Russian artillery and infantry. A large number of the British cavalry and their horses were slaughtered. It was a suicide run, and the majority of 'em didn't make it home." He took a sip of his whiskey. "But some of them did."

The FBI clerk ran along the labyrinth of corridors in the Bureau's Washington, D.C., headquarters and entered the large ops room. Breathless, he scoured the room. It was bathed in electric blue light from spot lamps in the ceiling that sent laser-like beams to the floor and looked like they could cut a man in half if he walked through them. Two men were sitting at desks in the center of the room, playing chess; a woman was by the wall to their left, working at her station.

She had to be who he was looking for.

The clerk jogged while calling out, "Agent Gage?"

Marsha looked up. "Yeah, that's me."

The clerk walked up to her and thrust a computer memory stick onto her desk. "Maine State Police have just e-mailed our liaison department a CCTV file and told us that they need your opinion ASAP. We copied the file."

Marsha picked up the stick while frowning. "CCTV? Of what?"

"Eight security cameras at the International Avenue border crossing between New Brunswick and Maine. A guy took on four cops and escaped into the U.S. Maine needs to know if he's the man you're looking for."

Though her heart was pounding, Marsha responded to the clerk in a calm and authoritative tone. "Thanks. Leave the room. I'll take it from here."

After he'd left, she slotted the stick into her computer and summoned Alistair and Patrick. When she clicked on the file, her computer showed eight symmetrical squares, within which were black-and-white images of the buildings, roads, and traffic at the International Avenue crossing.

For six seconds, everything seemed like a normal day at the border control.

Then, everything wasn't normal.

Two minutes later, Marsha replayed most of the images before pausing the file. One of the squares showed a close-up image of the gunman who'd engaged with the cops before escaping into the

United States. The man had a short beard; his face was otherwise clearly visible. She turned to Alistair and Patrick.

Both were frowning.

Patrick spoke. "That's him."

Alistair said with resignation, "My boy, Will Cochrane."

Marsha got out of her chair and leaned right up to the screen. "What on earth are you doing, Cochrane?"

Alistair didn't understand Marsha's question. "It's as we suspected—he's coming to the States to get answers."

Marsha turned to face them and leaned against her desk. "Maine police and the Canadian Mounties both told me the same thing: it's easy for a man to cross the border between New Brunswick and Maine without being detected because it's got big spaces of deserted countryside between each security control. All he needs to do is get wet in the St. Croix River. Why take the risk of crossing at International Avenue? Seems a stupid thing to do."

Alistair and Patrick looked at each other. Each knew what the other was thinking, but neither of them voiced their thoughts.

Patrick moved back to his desk while calling out, "Don't feel like doing it, but I gotta notify the Agency that Cochrane's on U.S. soil, and that means calling that ass Sheridan."

Alistair asked Marsha, "What next?"

Marsha sprung to her feet. "I'll alert the media that Cochrane's on U.S. soil. And starting tonight, I need to fill this room with extra Bureau bodies—detectives, analysts, surveillance special-ists." She reached for her phone. "Then we need our best shooters."

The MD 530 Little Bird helicopter banked left and flew fast toward the building on the Quantico Marine Corps base, Virginia. Two operatives sat on foldout external benches on either side of the bird—team leader Pete Duggan and one of his men. The other six members of Duggan's unit were now visible on the ground. All eight specialists were members of the FBI's elite Hostage Rescue Team, America's premier law enforcement special opera-tions unit that was trained to the standard of Spe-cial Forces; indeed, most members of HRT were ex-SF, and Duggan was no exception. He'd spent twelve years in SEAL Team 6 before his wife had successfully convinced him to swap a globetrotting covert life for one that kept him home a bit more.

Like six of his men, he had a .45 pistol and stun grenades strapped to his body and was carrying an MP5/10A3 submachine gun; the seventh man was equipped with a Remington 870 shotgun, and the man speaking on the radio was lying prone four hundred yards from the building while looking through the sight of an M40A1 sniper rifle. All of them were wearing OD green Nomex assault suits, combat boots, gloves, and Kevlar helmets with radio mics hardwired into them.

Inside the building were life-sized wooden cut-outs of men holding guns, some of them static, others on electric-powered pulleys that could make them move. And in one of the rooms, sitting at a desk, was a real person—Jack O'Connor, head of the FBI's Critical Incident Response Group, to whom all members of the HRT reported. It was the fifteenth time this week that the HRT had practiced the assault. Today it was O'Connor's turn to play hostage and hopefully not be killed as the team attempted to rescue him while using live ammunition. Aside from not accidentally shooting his boss, Duggan's objective was to shave ten seconds off previous assault times.

These drills kept him and his men sharp.

And staved off boredom.

But God, Duggan was hoping for some real action soon, because it had been three months since he'd fired a weapon at genuine bad guys.

The Little Bird hovered over the flat roof. It was the signal to assault, and Duggan and his colleague wasted no time, both tossing ropes down so that they were hanging over the building's flat roof.

Five members of the team entered the house at ground level.

Duggan and his number two fast-roped down.

Boots on the roof.

Sectors clear.

Heel through the window skylight.

Flash bang dropped through there.

Abseil gear secure on extractor vents.

Both men flew down the side of the building, rope in one hand, MP5 in the other.

Sound of more flash bangs and machine gun fire inside the building.

Doorframe charges blew open a reinforced fire exit.

Boom.

Enter.

Duggan first. Number two second.

Inside the room.

Two hostiles.

Down. Down.

Move on.

To the corridor.

Target running away.

Short burst in his back; stand over his body; another three rounds in the back of his head.

Second room.

Empty.

Last room on second floor.

Four targets, one live hostage.

Take two on the left.

Fire.

Shit! Weapon malfunction.

Drop to knee, .45 out, fire. Fire.

Wingman takes other two out.

Targets dead.

Hostage alive.

Second floor clear.

Radio mic says first floor also clear.

House is secure.

Jack O'Connor checked his watch. "That's your fastest by seventeen seconds. Excellent work, considering you had a gun malfunction."

Duggan removed his helmet and one glove, smoothed fingers through his matted blond hair, and walked through smoke to examine the targets. All shots had been precise. "Next time I want us to do a fast rope while the Little Bird's still moving. We'll run it again this afternoon."

O'Connor shook his head. "No you won't. While you were in the air, I had a call from HQ. I want you and your team in D.C. in three hours."

"Another training exercise?"

O'Connor smiled. "Not this time."

Antaeus was deep in thought as he walked beside the lake on his large, wooded and heath-covered grounds, fifty miles outside of Moscow. Two things were on the spymaster's mind: Project Ferryman and Will Cochrane. It was imperative that Cochrane didn't learn the truth and destroy Antaeus's strategy to cripple America. Cochrane had to fail and back down, or be killed.

Killing a man was not only distasteful to Antaeus; he also saw it as a sign of weakness, because it usually meant that something had gone wrong. Throughout his career he'd always believed that the most effective weapon in a spy's armory was his mind. Time and time again, he'd proven that his brilliant tactics were infinitely superior to those of his more brutish colleagues. That's why he answered to no one except the premier of Russia. And even the premier rarely dared to challenge or attempt to direct Antaeus. As a result, Antaeus was the real brain and power behind Russia's desire for ascendancy and world dominance. And right now, that brain would not hesitate to issue orders to have Cochrane murdered.

Even though Antaeus highly respected Cochrane and would gain no pleasure from killing him.

He put Cochrane and Ferryman out of his mind and started scrutinizing the land beneath him. After a while he stopped, used the tip of his long walking stick to unearth a barely visible stone, and ignored the pain down one side of his body as he picked it up. After brushing off soil, he smiled. The object was a Stone Age flint axhead, crafted with immaculate precision, and was no doubt the best he'd found during his comprehensive research into the settlement that had existed here twenty-two thousand years ago. Back inside the house, he would mount the tool and draw it so that he could add the illustration to the thesis he was submitting to the Moscow Archaeology Museum. The discovery of the tool would bolster his argument that, contrary to perceived wisdom, Stone Age man was not solely nomadic during the Ice Age in western Russia, but would settle in one place for long periods of time and would rely extensively on the fur, flesh, and bones of mammoths for clothing, food, and the construction of shelters. The tool would have taken days to make and was unlike the crude tools made by people on the move. Its maker was a patient, cunning man who had the wit to let his prey come to him rather than risk death from exposure during a hunt. Despite the severity of his surroundings, he was in control of his environment.

Antaeus's cell phone rang.

A U.S. number.

He listened to the caller for two minutes before saying, "I will alert my team that Cochrane's in the

States. But if the FBI gets to him first, you know what needs to be done."

Charles Sheridan snapped shut his cell phone, poured a large glass of red wine, and slid it across the table just as Senator Jellicoe sat down opposite him in a discrete corner of the D.C. Ritz-Carlton's Westend Bistro. "You're going to need that."

"Bad news?"

"Cochrane's in the U.S."

"What?!" Jellicoe looked around, realizing his raised voice had caught the attention of others in the restaurant. He leaned forward and whispered, "You told me there was no chance he'd head west!"

"I got it wrong."

"But Marsha Gage didn't." Hostility and apprehension were evident on Jellicoe's face. "How did he manage to get this close to us?"

The CIA officer shrugged. "He's resourceful."

"And driven." Jellicoe pointed a finger at Sheridan. "He mustn't disrupt our project. We're this close to Cobalt."

Sheridan thought for a moment. "We could just tell him to give himself up, that no charges will be made against him. Put a statement out to that effect on the networks and print media. Maybe he'd listen."

"Why would he do that?"

"If he knew the true value of Ferryman and its link to getting Cobalt, the professional in him might realize he's not operating in the interest of our national security."

"Perhaps. Or maybe he'll go to the *Washington Post* and tell them that he's been hung out to dry because of something called Ferryman. And once the media's involved, you know where that will lead."

Sheridan smiled. "So that means we stay on track."

"Yep."

"I was hoping you'd say that."

Jellicoe took a sip of his red wine and patted his mouth with a handkerchief. "But, he's too close."

"This could work for us. There was always the risk that if he got caught in Europe, one of the foreign agencies might not have handed him over to us. Here, it's cut and dry."

"But also more exposed."

Sheridan looked around. The Westend Bistro was a favorite among politicians and lobbyists working in Capitol Hill. Some of them were in here right now, and he wondered what they'd think if they knew what he was discussing with Jellicoe. "I got a couple of deniable Agency assets on standby and a place west of here where we can take Cochrane and make his body disappear."

"How deniable and reliable?"

"Grade A to both."

Jellicoe grinned, his flabby face looking reptilian and smug. "Good."

Antaeus's four assassins were sitting in a car on Colorado Avenue, in the Crestwood section of Washington, D.C. The quiet street was lined with family homes that were modern, functional, and medium sized, for those whose paychecks were neither great nor small. All had large front lawns that were immaculately cut and uncluttered. The men were observing one house from a hundred yards away. Two kids were playing while their dad was keeping an eye on them and stamping his feet to stay warm. It was afternoon and the family had returned home ten minutes ago.

One of the two Englishmen asked his compatriot, "How come the boss calls you Scott and me Oates?"

Code name Scott shrugged. "What's wrong with that?"

"Well, for starters it means I'm cursed."

"Why?"

"Captain Oates got out of his tent during the Terra Nova expedition and went walkabout in the Antarctic so that he could die and not be a burden to his mates."

"It was a brave thing to do."

"Whereas Scott got to reach the South Pole. It's not fair."

Scott gestured to their Norwegian colleague. "You're forgetting that I die on the way back, and anyway Amundsen here beat me to the South Pole. Wasted journey."

Amundsen laughed. "I made it to the South *and* North Poles." The Norwegian frowned. "Still, I later die in a rescue mission in the Arctic."

The Irishman ran a hand over his pistol's barrel. "I got no complaints being Shackleton 'cause I got knighted by King Edward VII for getting furthest south before Norwegie Boy later reached the Pole. Plus, I die of natural causes."

"No you don't. The booze gets you in the end. Stops your heart."

"Never proven."

"It's what your doctor said."

"So what? Anyways, what's *unnatural* about booze?"

Oates laughed. "An Irishman to the bitter end."

"Quite right." Shackleton's expression turned serious as he rammed a magazine into his hand-gun, while keeping his gaze on the family. "I give it fifteen minutes maximum before the father tells them to pack it in and get inside 'cause he's freezing his nuts off."

Scott raised a hand. "Showtime."

The four men were motionless as they watched a car pull up into the driveway of the house they were watching.

"Give it five minutes, then we'll put the beacon in the car. And we stay on the target day and night. Got it?"

Scott's colleagues nodded.

"Target leads us to Cochrane. We kill Cochrane." Scott watched the vehicle door open, his expression focused. "And the boss has given us complete authority to clear a path if anyone gets in our way."

Marsha Gage stepped out of the car, greeted her family, and walked with them into their home.

TWENTY-FOUR

Catherine Parker kissed her nine-year-old daughter good night, went downstairs, and was pleasantly surprised to see her husband sitting at the kitchen table. He'd warned her that he might have to work late because the fugitive Will Cochrane was now on U.S. soil. Her surprise turned into concern as she watched him down his Scotch, pour another, and rest his head in his hands while staring at the drink. Outside their Arlington home, it had started to rain hard, and ordinarily that would have been perfect for Ed. After a long day at work, he loved sharing a drink with his wife, and doubly so if he and his family were all toasty while the outside world was chucking everything it could at their sturdy house. But tonight he seemed oblivious to the weather and the presence of Catherine.

"Home early, my dear. Everything okay?"

Ed looked up, tried to smile but failed, and rubbed his hand over his fatigued face. "Just glad to be here."

"Now, now, darling." Catherine grabbed a bottle of Sauvignon Blanc from the refrigerator and poured herself a glass. "You can't fool a spook's wife that easily." She sat opposite him, pulled out the knitting needles that held her long, raggedy gray hair in place when she was gardening and doing other chores, and placed a hand over his. "What's happened?"

Ed took a swig of his whiskey and huffed. "I got overpromoted, that's what happened. Should never have been made director."

Catherine squeezed his hand. "We've spoken about this before."

They had, many times. Though a capable Agency operator, deep down Ed hated the additional responsibilities attached to being in senior management.

Catherine eyed the whiskey, wondering whether she should tell her husband to switch to a softer drink. She decided to let him get his worries out of his system by finishing the Scotch, but after that she'd take the tumbler away from him. "Just a wobbly day?"

Ed sighed while gripping his forehead with the tips of his fingers. "Not just any wobbly day. Things are escalating, and I'm damned if I like the direction they're going in."

"You have a voice and a say. Speak your mind to your peers, if you don't like what they're doing."

"Peers?" Ed looked bitter, swirled his drink, and downed it in one. "Technically, Jellicoe and Sheridan are my peers. But I'm not their equal. At least they don't treat me that way, and they do what they darn well like."

Catherine knew she had to tread carefully on the rare occasions when Ed was like this. Not that he could be a threat to her—on the contrary, he was the gentlest of souls—but he was a sensitive man and always liked to feel that Catherine was his closest ally. Saying the wrong thing could make him doubt that, and therefore give him anguish. Trouble was, sometimes Ed also needed to be told he was wrong. She was sensing that now could be one of those times. "How are things escalating?"

"Marsha Gage is putting together a task force. The Bureau manhunt's about to kick off."

"So?"

"So when she gets Cochrane, we're authorized to take him off her hands. What the Bureau doesn't know is that we're then going to put Cochrane out of his misery and dump his body somewhere it'll never be found."

"You told me days ago this might happen. What's changed things for you?"

"I just . . . just keep thinking that this could be me or one of my officers. Cochrane disobeyed orders in Norway in order to rescue Ellie Hallowes. Sure, he should get a reprimand and be told to keep his mouth shut. But I don't know if I'd have done any different if it was me with a rifle in my hand watching men coming to kill one of our own."

Catherine smiled sympathetically. "I think you're a bit old to be in a situation like that. Plus you were never one for the guns-and-glory stuff."

"Yeah, and look where it's got me: promoted because I spent more time in a suit, mixing with the Capitol Hill folk, than I did out in the field."

Catherine had to snap Ed out of this mood, because he was spiraling. She got an extra glass, filled it with wine, moved the whiskey tumbler out of his reach, and gave him the drink. "Wine always makes you happy."

"Can't promise you that tonight."

Catherine leaned forward and kissed Ed on the cheek. "You trust me, my love?"

"Yeah, always."

"Know that I've got your back?"

Ed smiled, though his eyes were moist. "Sure thing, Mrs. Parker."

"And know that I think Sheridan and Jellicoe aren't even worthy of wiping your ass?"

That comment cheered Ed up. "Now that's an image I don't want stuck in my head. But, yeah, I know what you think of them."

"Then you'll also know that there are times when you should listen to your wife, because she just might get some sense into that head of yours."

"Sense?"

Catherine nodded. "You've always had to make tough decisions, haven't you?"

"Nature of the job."

"It is. And I know for a fact those decisions have to take into account the greater good."

"Doesn't mean the process of getting there's all cherry blossom."

"It doesn't, and I can see you're in that place right now."

Ed was about to speak, but Catherine held up her hand.

"Maybe you've told me more about your work than you should; maybe not. Either way, I do know that if Cochrane does anything to unsettle Ferryman, then it is probable that you'll lose access to Antaeus and in turn will fail to get an exact time and location for Cobalt's meeting in Afghanistan. You may have one window of opportunity to kill Cobalt and save thousands of lives by taking him off planet Earth. Cochrane's in danger of blundering into something he knows nothing about and shutting down that window. I know you don't like it, and I have to say that as your wife I hate the idea of what needs to be done to Cochrane. I *hate* it. And I love you for the fact that you hate it. But I also love you because you're helping people."

"I'm not helping Cochrane, though, am I?"

"Oh, come on, dear." An idea came to Catherine. "You told me Cochrane had saved lives during his career."

"A lot of lives."

"Presumably that means he's the kind of guy who's willing to sacrifice his life for others."

"For sure."

"How many women and children has Cobalt's terrorist funding killed?"

"Can't be exact, but certainly thousands."

"Do you think Will would lay down his life to ensure a similar number or more won't be killed in the future?"

"Without doubt, but . . ."

"Hello, Daddy."

Ed swiveled around and saw his daughter standing at the bottom of the stairs, wearing pink pajamas and clutching her teddy bear while rubbing her sleepy eyes. He beamed. "Hey, sweetie. What are you doing up?"

She came over to him and nuzzled her head against his chest. "I heard you and Mummy talking about things dying. I was worried something bad had happened to Fred and Ginger."

Her pet hamsters.

Ed rubbed her head. "Don't be silly, pumpkin. They're fine." He pretended to look stern. "But they won't be fine if you don't clean out their cage tomorrow." He smiled. "Want me to read you a story?"

Crystal nodded.

"Okay. Deal is, you take yourself back to bed and give me five minutes to finish up down here."

After she'd left, Ed nodded at Catherine. "Thanks. Think I needed that perspective." For the first time today he felt his shoulder muscles start to relax.

TWENTY-FIVE

Sheridan could hear the boars grunting and squealing before he stopped his car at the end of the forest-lined track, in front of the remote farmstead. It was eight P.M., and the CIA officer knew it was the exact time the fifteen swine got their evening feed. He'd witnessed it before, and it was a terrifying and frenzied display of gluttonous savagery. Because their owners had crossbred male boars with domestic pigs, the boars were twice the size of their wild cousins, had large tusks, coarse hair that was painful to touch, and the strength and ferocity to shred a man to pieces in minutes. As Sheridan stepped out of his car into the sodden night air, the animal screams began to sound like hysterical pagans witnessing a sacrifice.

The sounds revolted him.

Not least because the boars' favorite food was flesh.

The officer shivered, turned on his flashlight, and walked on, trying not to get his expensive shoes and suit trousers muddy. The complex was in West

Virginia, approximately one hundred miles west of Langley, in forested, sparsely populated countryside; it had five main buildings and a cluster of outbuildings. As he headed toward the farmhouse, he passed the barn and could smell the boars' stench, a combination of musk, piss, and shit; a brutish odor that oozed from three-hundred-pound beasts whose sole joy was to indulge in an orgy of bacchanalian feasting.

The houses in the town of Springfield, Maine, were all spread far apart from each other; between them, trees ensured that residents had privacy from their neighbors.

Some of the houses had garages where owners' vehicles could be locked away, but others didn't. Will walked from one property to the next, checking the driver's seats of the cars and their distance from the brake and accelerator pedals, and glancing around to ensure none of the houses' lights came on because someone had spotted him.

At the seventh house, he found a vehicle with a driver's seat that looked to be in the position that Will would put it in if he were driving it. He faced the house, could see no signs of an alarm system, so ran around the side of the house and entered the backyard. Placing his head against the back door, he listened for a moment and heard nothing save the rain. He turned the handle— unsurprisingly, it was locked—and withdrew his lockpick set.

One minute later, he was in the kitchen. It was silent. He stayed still for ten seconds, listening for any signs that people were awake and allowing his eyes to adjust to the darkness.

On either side of him were two large rooms. He turned his flashlight on and quickly checked both; they were empty.

At the base of the stairs, he turned off the flashlight and stood still, listening again for any indication that an occupant had heard him and was getting out of bed to grab his shotgun. He slowly moved up the stairs in total darkness while praying the floorboards underneath were not creaky.

On the second floor, there were four rooms that had open doors. He moved to the nearest doorway, crouched down beside it, and glanced inside. It was a study, and no one was in it. He repeated the same drill in the next two rooms. Neither was occupied: one was a cluttered storage room, the other a bathroom. He crouched beside the last door. It had to be the bedroom.

Breathing deeply, he stuck his head into the room.

Inside were a wardrobe, a chest of drawers, and a bed that was empty.

The owner was not at home.

Will opened the wardrobe. Though the position of the car seat suggested its driver was approximately the same height as Will, there was every possibility that its owner was fat or thin. But after checking the length and waist size of a pair of jeans, Will was relieved to see that they were a good fit. Together with the pants, he grabbed a shirt, sweater, and underwear from the drawers.

He'd need a coat as well, and he'd spotted four of them hanging on a rack on the first floor.

He made ready to leave, but paused by the bathroom.

It looked so enticing.

Should he?

He entered the windowless room, shut the door, and stripped out of his clothes.

After filling the sink with hot water, he quickly sponge-washed his body and hair, brushed his teeth with a spare toothbrush, got dressed in his new clothes, grabbed his old ones, went downstairs, and turned the flashlight back on. He chose a winter jacket that looked warm and sturdy but nothing like the kind of thing a man would wear if he'd received specialist military training and was on the run, and moved back into the kitchen. Beside the trash can was a roll of plastic bags. After removing his guns and all other items from his dirty jacket and placing them in his new coat, he chucked all his clothes in the bag. He'd dispose of it somewhere a few miles away. Then he opened the refrigerator and grabbed some food.

He reckoned the clothes he'd stolen and the guilt of eating the man's food called for two hundred dollars' compensation. He withdrew three hundred and left the cash on the table.

As he walked fast away from the house and the town, he felt rejuvenated. Just as important, he looked like an ordinary American civilian and not like the man who'd been seen in Nova Scotia and at the New Brunswick–Maine International Avenue crossing.

He was now confident that he could blend in and get to D.C. within a couple of days by train, bus, or other public transportation.

Trouble was, he was also aware that he could be heading toward his downfall.

Being in the presence of the two men always made Sheridan feel uneasy. Augustus and Elijah were fifty-two-year-old twins and looked nearly identical, with straight shoulder-length black hair, bodies that were diminutive yet very strong, circular spectacles, galoshes, and all-in-one overalls that were covered in pig meal and crap. Though they looked a bit odd, Sheridan supposed they would look harmless enough to anyone else who could see them making mugs of coffee in their kitchen.

But most people didn't know what Sheridan knew—that they were former members of the CIA's Special Activities Division, where they'd specialized in psychological warfare, physical and mental experimentation on foreign prisoners, torture, and execution. They'd honed their skills during every covert and overt war that the States had been involved in during their service. Few people in the Agency had known about their existence, and those who did rarely liked to talk about their role. They were an unpalatable last resort, and were tolerated by CIA senior management in the same way that psychopaths are tolerated in the ranks of an army when every able-bodied man is needed to stave off a country's obliteration. But that had ended nine years before, when the twins went too far on a mission in Afghanistan by reenacting the medieval English punishment of hanging a person to near death before emasculating, disemboweling, beheading, and chopping the person into four pieces. It was done in front of a suspected terrorist who they wanted to confess to a roadside bomb attack against U.S. soldiers. Ordinarily, the hanging, drawing, and quartering might have been hushed up by those members of the Agency who knew about the twins and their work.

But the victim was the eight-year-old son of the alleged terrorist.

They'd gone way too far. Even by the standards of Agency men who had no qualms about sticking their hands in blood and guts to get secrets so that they could protect the American way of life.

Sheridan had stepped in to save their necks, arguing that Agency interests would not be served by making what had happened public, and also suggesting that the twins could still be of use to the CIA, albeit completely off the books. The Agency agreed that the twins could return to the States and live off their pensions. It also said that the twins could not be used again, on or off the books. That hadn't surprised Sheridan, because the Agency says stuff like that a lot, even when it doesn't mean what it says. In situations like that, what the Agency doesn't say is more important, and in this case it didn't say that Sheridan wasn't allowed to meet the twins again. So for nine years Sheridan had been the twins' sole point of contact with the Agency, and he'd drawn upon their skills to do the really nasty stuff that nobody wanted to know about. In particular, anyone on U.S. soil whom the Agency didn't like could be made to vanish when Sheridan involved Augustus and Elijah.

The kitchen looked normal, aside from a work surface that had nineteen large bottles of bleach, an excessive number of meat cleavers hanging from hooks in the ceiling, and clothes racks that were standing next to radiators and had animal skins draped over them.

"What you got for us?" Augustus handed Sheridan a mug of coffee and lit a cigarette that was wrapped in paper as black as his long hair.

Sheridan wondered whether he should drink the coffee, because consuming anything in this place seemed unnatural. "Right now, I haven't got anything for you. Very shortly, though, I may, and I need you to be ready when that happens."

"Man or woman?"

"Man."

Elijah interlocked his fingers, outstretched his sinewy arms, and cracked his knuckles. "Age, nationality, and name?"

Sheridan answered the questions.

"The guy who's been all over the news?"

"Yes. You got a problem with that?"

"Nope. How much does he weigh?"

Sheridan frowned. "What?"

"Simple question."

"I haven't had the opportunity to put him on a scale."

"You know his height and build?"

Sheridan shrugged. "Over six foot. He's big. But athletic. Doubt he's got much fat on him."

Elijah glanced at his brother. "Should we assume two-ten to two-forty pounds?"

Augustus nodded. "I'm thinking so, and that means at least three days in the chest."

"I'd say four and a half to be on the safe side."

Sheridan had no idea what they were talking about. "The chest?"

Augustus inhaled deep on his cigarette. "Chest freezer."

Elijah added four spoons of sugar to his coffee and slowly stirred the drink. "Few months back, me and Augustus conducted a forensic analysis of the site of our last kill. We thought our methods were good enough to cover our tracks, but we were wrong and found traces of the target's DNA. Not much, but enough to get us the needle. So, we've further refined things."

Augustus said, "Day before it happens, we turn up the empty chest freezer to maximum cold."

Elijah added, "When it's at its lowest temperature, we sedate Cochrane."

"And put him in a see-through bag."

"Body length."

"Sealed over the head."

"Then we strangle him."

"No blood."

"Dump him in the freezer."

"For four and a half days."

"Body's going to be rock solid after that."

"Easy to put through the wood chipper."

"Then easy to feed to the boars."

Sheridan smiled. "All trace of Will Cochrane and his DNA disappeared." He stood, checked his watch, and decided he could be back in D.C. in time to get showered and changed before going to the FBI ops room for Marsha Gage's briefing to her newly assembled task force. "What's your price?"

The twins answered in unison. "Fifty thousand."

It was money that would come out of the Agency slush fund under Sheridan's control.

The CIA officer nodded. "You'll get it once your pigs have turned Cochrane into shit."

TWENTY-SIX

Ellie Hallowes got out of her hotel room bed and stared at the cell phone.

Goodness knows how many times per day she'd looked at the cell's screen, desperate to hear it ring or receive an SMS, her mind crying out for Will Cochrane to make contact. But every time she glanced at the blank screen it further reinforced her belief that Will had either decided to turn back and flee, or died in the wilderness somewhere in Europe.

That would mean she'd never see him again. She didn't like that prospect one bit.

And it would mean she would either have to stay quiet about her suspicions that Antaeus knew about Ferryman, or she would have to tell someone else. But who? She recalled what Will had said to her in Norway.

Be very careful. Trust no one.

Maybe she could speak to someone outside the U.S. intelligence community. Perhaps the attorney general or someone like that. She'd seen it happen in the movies, but had never been told how it worked in real life. No instructors on her Agency training course had said to her, "Look, if one of us is a traitor and you can't trust anyone, then this is what you need to do."

And even if she did speak to someone who was wholly independent, she decided that nothing would come of it save her being severely punished for meddling in affairs she wasn't cleared to know about. The president himself had signed some of the documents she'd read in the Ferryman files. So had Senator Jellicoe, Charles Sheridan, and Ed Parker.

Powerful people.

All men.

With huge vested interests in Project Ferryman because it would give them fame and glory when it served up Cobalt's head.

She wondered if Helen Coombs had established that Ellie had deliberately gotten her drunk so she could temporarily steal her identity. If she had, no doubt Helen would report it immediately to the Agency, and Ellie would be grabbed by CIA heavies and locked in a cell. So much depended upon Will getting into the States to meet with Ellie. And it had to happen fast, or everything she'd done and hopefully Will had done would be a waste of time.

She changed out of her nightgown into a bathrobe, started running a shower, and switched on the TV. After flicking through the channels, she settled on a news network's story about a bomb attack in Kabul that had left twenty-two dead and three times that number mutilated. A security

analyst was saying that the bomb used was sophisticated, containing military-grade high explosive.
The type of bomb, Ellie mused, that would be
expensive to buy and would be used by terrorists
with access to a stack of cash—money that in all
probability came from Cobalt.

The anchor cut short the analyst and announced
the show was going live to Washington, D.C.,
where there was breaking news.

Ellie gasped as she saw a grainy black-and-white
close-up shot of a bearded Will Cochrane's face.
At the base of the screen were his name and a text
feed that stated, WANTED FUGITIVE IS IN UNITED
STATES. ARMED AND EXTREMELY DANGEROUS. DO
NOT APPROACH. IF SEEN, CONTACT FBI OR POLICE.

Ellie's heart was pounding, her body tingling
with adrenaline.

The show cut live to a female reporter who
was close to the FBI's headquarters, the J. Edgar
Hoover Building. Standing next to the reporter
was a man Ellie didn't know. He was wearing a
suit, held an umbrella over his head, and looked
pissed to be standing out in the rain and darkness
so early in the morning.

The reporter announced, "I'm with a spokesperson for the FBI. Sir, we understand from Senator
Colby Jellicoe's televised appearance at the Senate
Select Committee on Intelligence that Cochrane
is a member of Great Britain's MI6 intelligence
service."

The man nodded. "That's correct."

"So can you tell us why Cochrane's on the run?"

"Something he did in Norway while operating on a joint CIA-MI6 mission. But I'm not privy to the details."

"You've confirmed Will Cochrane's been sighted at the Canadian border crossing into Maine. Do you have any other confirmed sightings of him?"

The FBI spokesperson shook his head. "We've had one or two possible leads, but nothing substantial. That said, we're fairly sure he's headed to Washington, D.C."

"Why D.C.?"

"I can't answer that, ma'am."

"Is he a danger to members of the public?"

The FBI official looked directly into the camera. "He's a real danger to certain people."

"What advice do you give if he's spotted?"

"Stay well away. Then call us or the cops. We'll send in HRT or SWAT to take him down."

The reporter frowned. "What's HRT?"

The spokesperson replied, "They're the type of men we need to take down Cochrane, and they're embedded in our task force."

"Is that standard procedure?"

"No, but this is a highly unusual case. We need to move very fast and with maximum force if Cochrane's spotted or tracked down."

The reporter asked, "Can you tell us a bit more about Cochrane's capabilities?"

The spokesperson's expression was somber as he answered, "He's a highly trained and effective operator. This is a dangerous manhunt. I can't emphasize that enough. If he's spotted, no members of the public must approach Cochrane. *Nobody*."

• • •

After the hotel room television was turned off, Oates turned to Scott and asked, "What's HRT?"

"Hormone replacement therapy."

The former SAS soldiers laughed.

"Feds are using hormones to capture Cochrane."

"Trying to make him have a sensitive side."

Scott turned serious. "Hostage Rescue Team. Some of my pals in Delta and DEVGRU joined HRT. They're good."

"As good as the Regiment?"

The SAS.

"Don't be a dickhead."

"Thought not," Oates said. "You worried you might have to slot some of those pals of yours?"

Scott shrugged. "Shit happens."

Oates grabbed his knapsack containing food, drink, three cell phones, and two handguns. Scott had already collected his things from his adjacent room. "Where we taking over from Amundsen and Shackleton?"

Scott nodded toward the blank TV screen where moments ago they'd seen the J. Edgar Hoover Building. "Outside the cross-dresser's place."

A reference to the FBI founder's sexual peccadillo.

"Gage already there?"

"Yeah."

"Best we go and keep her company, then."

The long FBI ops room was filled to capacity with Bureau men and women unpacking boxes, arranging their desks, checking phone lines and computer terminals, placing mementos and framed photos of loved ones on their work stations, and catching up with colleagues they hadn't seen for a while. Including Alistair, Patrick, and Sheridan, the room contained fifty-four people, most of whom were wearing suits, with the exception of eight men who were wearing sweaters, jeans, and boots. Unlike all the other agents, Pete Duggan and his seven HRT colleagues had no need to unpack anything. Their two SUVs, both parked in the building's secure basement parking lot, contained everything they needed—Springfield Armory's M1911A1 Professional handguns, Heckler & Koch MP5/10A3 submachine guns with laser aiming devices and SureFire tactical lights, Heckler & Koch HK416 rifles, ammunition, communications and surveillance equipment, stun grenades, plastic cuffs, fire resistant overalls, Kevlar helmets and body armor, and respirators.

The room smelled of coffee, aftershave, perfume, and testosterone, and the combined scent was one that Marsha Gage had been surrounded by on many occasions. As she stood watching her team from one end of the room, she recalled the first time she'd had to give a briefing to a task force. Back then, it had been a daunting prospect, and she remembered the butterflies in her stomach and trying to relax through breathing exercises. But since then, years of detective work, and having kids who didn't give her one second to think about nerves, had made briefings like these a walk in the park.

Still, this was the first time she'd ever been put

on a manhunt to capture a rogue intelligence officer. And though she'd handpicked five agents for the team who were experts in counterintelligence, she knew for a fact that no one on the task force had ever come up against someone like Cochrane. She breathed in deeply. "Okay, everyone. Listen up!"

The room grew silent as all looked at her and ceased their activities. Alistair and Patrick moved to her side, Patrick folding his arms and adopting a look that suggested he was going to kill anyone in the team who asked something dumb, Alistair leaning against a wall with one foot resting over the other and a look of nonchalance.

She pointed at a whiteboard containing two photos of Will Cochrane: one in which he was clean-shaven and wearing a suit and tie, the other the International Avenue border crossing shot. "We're after Will Cochrane. He works—correction, *worked*—for the two gentlemen by my side. Both are spooks, so try to keep hold of your wallets and sanity if you go anywhere near them."

One of the agents called out, "They got names?"

Patrick answered, "We do, but you don't need them. I'm CIA, and"—he gestured toward Alistair—"my friend here's MI6. Cochrane was a joint U.S.-U.K. asset. We're here as advisers to Agent Gage."

Marsha said, "He's been sighted crossing the Canadian border into Maine. It's possible he broke into a house in Springfield, because whoever did stole a set of clothes that matched Cochrane's size, grabbed some food, and left a lot of cash to pay for both. Either way, we believe that Cochrane's heading southwest along the East Coast toward D.C."

One of the team members asked, "Why D.C.?"

Marsha stared at Sheridan, wishing she could hold a gun to his head and make him tell her and everyone else in the room what Ferryman was. "He wants to know details about a CIA mission."

More questions were fired from the team.

"We think he's still armed?"

Marsha nodded. "Yes."

"Any assessment on his mental condition?"

"No doubt he's had better days, but he's trained to operate for long periods in hostile locations."

"Is he wounded?"

"He might have some cuts and bruises, but based on the way he moved during the border crossing, we don't think he's got any serious physical problems."

"How much cash has he got on him?"

"I'm told by my CIA colleagues that he had ten thousand dollars when he was deployed to Norway."

"ID?"

"An alias passport and credit card in the name of Robert Tombs."

"How did he get to Canada from Norway?"

"Most likely he had help from assets we don't know about."

"Has he got assets in the States?"

Marsha glanced at Patrick.

The CIA officer answered, "Before my team was disbanded, two of Cochrane's colleagues were paramilitary Agency."

Roger Koenig and Laith Dia, both of whom had served with Will on three missions.

"They're very loyal to Cochrane, and no doubt would help him if they could. For that reason, I redeployed them overseas as soon as we suspected Cochrane might be heading this way."

Marsha hadn't known that, and wondered if there was anything else the damn spies in her team weren't telling her.

Patrick added, "Cochrane was raised in the States, but his parents are dead and his sister lives in Scotland and doesn't have contact with her brother. As far as we can tell, he's got absolutely no one here who can help him. That's our assumption."

The youngest member of the team—a male who'd been selected by Marsha because of his cyber intercept expertise, but had no idea about old-fashioned detective work—smirked and stated, "We know where he's headed and he's on his own. He's screwed."

Marsha locked her intimidating gaze on the junior. "Millions of people commute along the East Coast every day, and they take thousands of different routes."

The cocky young technician should have kept his mouth shut, but he didn't. "He'll stand out like a sore thumb."

"What, like one of the Boston Marathon bomb suspects did when he went on the run? Boston police traced him to a twenty-block radius and shut down the city. But it still took a day to locate the suspect, and even then he was found by a civilian. Plus, they were hunting an untrained kid."

She walked to a map of the States and pointed at a dot that looked no bigger than a pinhead. "Here's Boston." She swept her arm fully outstretched in a complete circular movement over the map. "And by contrast, this is the area we have to search for Cochrane." She pointed at the technician. "I need you because you're good with algorithms. But beyond that your opinions are useless to me, so keep your head down and your mouth shut unless you've got something important to contribute."

Now he was quiet, with a look on his face that said he'd just been sucker-punched.

Pete Duggan called out from the far end of the room, "Ma'am, would one of your intelligence advisers be able to comment on Cochrane's capabilities?"

Marsha was relieved to be once again fielding questions from seasoned members of the team, and particularly Duggan, whom she deeply admired and had specifically asked to be included. She looked at Patrick, who said nothing. She looked at Alistair.

The MI6 controller pushed himself away from the wall and smiled, his superb intellect encapsulated by the glint in his blue eyes. "Ladies and gentlemen, I'm always reminded on occasions like this to jettison loquaciousness in favor of *dicendi campus*."

Marsha rolled her eyes as she placed a hand on Alistair's forearm. "Speak in words we can all understand."

"That's broadly the English translation of what I just said in Latin." Alistair's eyes changed from charm to steel. "William Cochrane spent five years in French Special Forces."

Duggan asked, "The Legion? GCP?"

"Correct. I didn't care about that when he joined MI6. What mattered to me was that I wanted to put him through a year of hell. I thought it would break him, as it had done to others before him. It didn't." Alistair studied Duggan. "You look like a man who knows a thing or two about hardship."

When Duggan responded, it was in a tone that was neither bragging nor disrespectful, the tone of a professional operator. "I was in SEAL Team 6. Spent most of my career in water. It was a *hardship* and humbling."

"And the longest you'd spent in said water?"

"Thirteen hours and four minutes. Me and another guy, both of us in scuba gear and on the surface of the Indian Ocean with a rope between us while waiting for a mobile U.S. sub's antenna to break through the sea, snag the rope, draw us together as it sailed onward, and put us on its back. Was cold and dark out there."

Alistair nodded. "I'm sure it was. Cochrane's longest time in water during his training program was four days, nine hours, and thirty-two seconds. And it was in the North Atlantic. During November. He had food, and water, and a dry suit and buoyancy aids, but not much else."

One of the agents frowned. "Superspy?"

"No." Alistair wagged his finger. "Human being. Like anyone in their right mind, he doesn't like misery. And that's his strength. His mind can overcome his body's craving for rest and warmth and no further pain. That's why he survived the program I put him through. When he's in the field, he's constantly fighting the very natural desire to give up. He's no *super* anything. He is who he is."

Marsha pointed again at the map of the States. "Non-Bureau law enforcement agencies are taking the lead on trying to capture him while he's still in transit, including being all over public transportation routes. But they've got one heck of a task. We, on the other hand, are going to focus on ground that we can control. The only way he's going to get the answers he wants is to grab someone in the CIA and make that person talk." She looked at Sheridan, imagining Cochrane putting his hand around the officer's throat. "The D.C. area is where we'll get him, and I'll lock down the entire city to do it if necessary." She checked her watch. "Okay. I'm going to task all agents in this room individually. Pete—after that, I want to speak to you and your men so we can run through response and takedown drills."

Pete Duggan nodded. "One thing I'm confused about—how come Cochrane made the International Avenue crossing and showed his face? Strikes me, guy like him would know all about covert infiltration."

Marsha agreed. "It's possible he was desperate or simply made a mistake, though I don't buy that."

"Guess we'll just have to ask him when we got him in a cell."

Alistair was once again leaning against the wall, his eyes closed. "You won't need to. William deliberately chose to use the crossing knowing that it would be reinforced with extra men. He let us see him because he wanted us to know he's in the States."

Marsha turned to the MI6 officer. "What?"

Alistair opened his eyes and looked right at Marsha. "Once he's found out the truth about why he's on the run, he wants you to get very close to him, though I must warn you it will be completely on his terms."

TWENTY-SEVEN

In the rural outskirts of Moscow, Antaeus lit a candle and carried it into his study. He could have availed himself of the room's electric lights or its gas lamps, but sometimes he just liked being in near darkness, with the smell of wick and wax, and light that erratically flickered to produce a partial, indistinct representation of the surroundings.

He sat down at his old wooden desk and lit a cheroot that was a gift from a Dutchman whose tobacco emporium was one of the best in Europe. The shop also happened to have a tunnel to a listening post where the Russians could eavesdrop on the American embassy in The Hague.

The chalkboard was in front of him; names on it appeared and disappeared each time a scant breeze nudged the candle's flame left and right.

Senator Colby Jellicoe.

Charles and Lindsay Sheridan.

Ed Parker.

Gregori Shonin.

Project Ferryman.

Cobalt.

The key players in Antaeus's plan to cause a major catastrophe and derail the United States.

Only Will Cochrane stood in his way of achieving that result.

He looked at Will's name on the other side of the board, drew a circle around it so that the arrow from the code names of his four assassins was touching it, and drew four more arrows pointing at the circle from different angles.

Against the first new arrow, he wrote, STATE & COUNTY POLICE FORCES.

The second arrow, THE MEDIA AND CONCERNED U.S. CITIZENS.

The third, MARSHA GAGE/FBI/HRT.

The fourth, SHERIDAN/CIA/AUGUSTUS & ELIJAH.

Five arrows in total that wanted Will Cochrane incarcerated or dead.

Cochrane stood no chance of getting anywhere near Project Ferryman.

But something was nagging Antaeus.

He held the candle close to the reptile tank containing the chameleon. Its pigmentation had altered to reflect the fact that earlier today Antaeus had cleaned the tank and replenished it with lighter-colored foliage. He was sure the reptile liked to frequently change its appearance. Just like Ellie Hallowes.

Antaeus was sure that Hallowes was the only person who didn't want Cochrane captured or killed. The nature of her deep-cover work made her dislocated from the unconditional loyalty prevalent in mainstream Agency operatives. That meant that even though Cochrane broke rules to protect her, she wouldn't blindly agree with the rules that had put Cochrane on the run.

Instead, she'd help him if she could. And the best way she could do that was to read the Ferry-man files and relay what she had read to Cochrane. Yes, that's what had been troubling him. Hallowes was the threat to his otherwise watertight strategy. But how would she relay what she'd discovered to Cochrane? Not by standard forms of communication, because she'd know that she didn't have the Agency's full trust and it could be monitoring her. That left old-school tradecraft. A dead-letter box. In a location agreed upon by Cochrane and Hallowes. One she could easily access without garnering suspicion from the Agency by being absent for too long. Washington, D.C.

Antaeus smiled and picked up his telephone.

The rolling, frost-covered vista of Middleburg, Virginia, was magnificent and all the better for being seen on horseback. Catherine Parker and Lindsay Sheridan were both proficient riders, and it had been Catherine's idea to get out of D.C. for an afternoon so that the two women could get some bracing air, exercise, and time out from the craziness that came with being married to the Central Intelligence Agency.

Wearing jodhpurs, riding boots, helmets, and warm jackets and gloves, the women rode side by side at a fast trot along a valley that contained pine, ash, and oak trees. The horses were stabled at the

Salamander Resort & Spa, and were their regular mounts when they could get out for a visit. But their last ride together had been over four months ago, so today's venture was long overdue.

They reached a large pond that was glistening under the winter sunshine and looked like a perfect place to let the horses rest and for the women to catch their breath. Catherine called out, "Time for an aperitif?"

Lindsay smiled. "Now you're talking."

They stopped, dismounted, and tethered their horses to trees. Catherine withdrew a hip flask and unscrewed its cap. "I stole some of Ed's best Scotch." She took a swig and handed it to Lindsay. "It can be our little secret."

Lindsay swallowed the fiery liquor and nodded her head in appreciation. "Tastes even better, knowing it's illicit." She removed her helmet and scratched her scalp where the hat had rubbed it. As she looked at the water, she exclaimed, "God, it feels good to get away."

Catherine knew she was referring to her husband, but kept quiet.

"Sometimes it's hard to breathe when I'm around Charles."

"He's not here now."

Lindsay looked at Catherine with a smile that suggested she thought her friend's comment was naive. "Trouble is, I can feel his presence all the time."

So many times, Catherine had wanted to ask Lindsay the question she was contemplating right now, but she'd always feared what reaction she'd get. She hesitated, and asked, "Why don't you just leave him? Start a new life?"

Lindsay bowed her head and said quietly, "Guess you've been waiting to ask me that for a long time."

"I didn't want to meddle, I—"

"It's okay, Cathy." She returned her gaze to the water. "I think about it all the time. Wonder what it would be like to be in a relationship with a nice man. Thing is though—when you're young, it's easy; you just hitch up your skirt, flash a bit of leg, and you've got a crop of men to pick from. Not so easy at our age though, is it?"

Catherine was about to tell her she was wrong, but stopped and placed her hand on Lindsay's back. "Maybe you just have to find out."

Lindsay turned to Catherine, her eyes watering. "I think . . . I think I'm not strong enough to walk out on him. You know, I fantasize that the decision is made for me. It's awful"—tears were now running down her face—"awful, but I keep thinking it would be best if he was dead. Killed. Died. Dead."

"You're not planning anything bad, are you?"

Lindsay shook her head. "No, no. Nothing stupid. Don't worry. This is just us talking and me spouting shit. I can't touch him. I can't do anything bad to him. That's half the problem." She wiped her tears away. "But it doesn't stop me wishing every day that some drunk driver or whoever would wipe him out on his way home. At least then I'd be forced to do something."

• • •

The black London cab stopped in King's Road, in Chelsea. Though it was evening and raining, the popular thoroughfare of designer shops and restaurants was buzzing with well-groomed beautiful people, none of whom looked over the age of forty. As Dickie Mountjoy surveyed his surroundings, the retired major decided that everyone who came here was a scrounger who'd never done a decent day's work and lived off swollen bank balances courtesy of their fathers.

Phoebe paid the cabbie, helped Dickie get out of the vehicle, and exclaimed, "Ooh, I do *love* King's Road."

Dickie huffed. "Thought you might." He steadied himself with his walking stick, swung it under one arm, and followed Phoebe. He was properly dressed for the cold outing—leather gloves, scarf immaculately folded so it looked like a cravat around his throat, and a knee-length blue moleskin coat over his trousers and jacket. Aside from a chic cropped faux-mink-fur jacket, Phoebe, on the other hand, was wearing next to nothing and a pair of platforms. It was a miracle she didn't get hypothermia during her regular evenings out.

She led him to an antique shop that was closed, though its inside lights were still on. She pressed the doorbell. An elderly man unlocked the entrance; he had half-moon spectacles hanging on a chain over his chest, was wearing a red smoking jacket that looked as though it had been made a hundred years ago, and had yellow and silver hair that had been styled to make him look Bohemian and eccentric. An arty type. For the love of Jesus, let's get this over with quickly, thought Dickie.

Phoebe introduced herself as the woman who'd called the shop proprietor earlier in the day and had asked for an after-hours appointment. The man beckoned them in. Dickie was about to follow Phoebe in, but stopped as a newsstand billboard farther up the street caught his eye. He frowned as he tried to decide what it meant, and entered the shop.

On display were antiques that Dickie reckoned were targeted at more-money-than-sense people who wanted to furnish their West London homes with Victorian and Edwardian junk and old stuff from India and China that nobody there wanted anymore. The proprietor led them to a glass counter, on top of which was a musical instrument case. He stood behind the counter and placed his manicured fingers over the case. "I have an interested buyer for this in Vienna."

Major Mountjoy stood ramrod straight, even though it hurt his back and legs to do so. "How much does he want to pay for it?"

"She." The proprietor smiled. "And I rarely discuss money at the outset. In my business, it's a tad gauche to do so."

"In my world, 'gauche' is a word used by poofs, pricks, and the loiterers Phoebe hangs out with in her poncey art gallery."

Phoebe hooked her arm under his, rubbed her

hip against his body, and said in a mock stern tone, "Don't be a naughty Dickie."

The major wished she'd let go. "I'm just sayin' I'm entitled to know how much it costs."

The proprietor smiled with a look of insincerity. "Let me show it to you first." He opened the case; inside was a handcrafted German baroque swan-neck lute. "It's eighteenth century, and I have a certificate of authenticity from the man I purchased it from in Berlin."

Though Dickie knew nothing about music, or art, or indeed anything that seemed to him to be a pointless load of nonsense, he had to admit the instrument looked beautiful. "In good nick?"

The proprietor frowned. "I beg your pardon?"

"Is it in good condition? Does it do what it's supposed to do?"

The shop owner ran his fingers over the strings. "It's perfect."

Phoebe nestled her body closer to Dickie. "I think it's gorgeous. Will would love to play this." She looked sternly at the proprietor, and this time there was nothing false in her expression. "However, I agree with the major that we need to know what we're dealing with. How much?"

The proprietor's smile widened. "It's not easy to put a value on an instrument of such—"

"How much?"

The proprietor pinged one of the strings. "Three thousand pounds."

Phoebe was shocked. "I think you might have mistakenly added an extra naught on the price."

"It has been valued with precision, and my Viennese potential buyer agrees with my valuation." He shut the case. "By all means get an independent assessment of its value. But, I can show you my receipt of purchase, which unequivocally states that I bought it for five hundred pounds less than I'm asking for it. I believe the markup accurately reflects the effort and cost it took for me to source the lute."

Dickie nodded at the case. "We'll take it."

"Dickie?" Phoebe pulled his arm. "You mustn't spend that much money. My—"

"Mind's made up." He withdrew his wallet, containing five thousand pounds that he'd withdrawn from his post office pension fund earlier in the day. "It's worth the price to make Mr. Cochrane happy, and to get out of this faggoty place."

Ten minutes later, Dickie was standing on the sidewalk while Phoebe was holding the encased lute in one hand and hailing a taxi with the other. To Dickie's surprise, she wasn't staying out in the West End to make a night of it, but instead wanted to return to West Square because David was cooking for her. He coughed onto the back of his hand, silently cursed as he saw blood on his glove, and caught the headline on the billboard.

ROGUE MI6 OFFICER SPOTTED IN U.S. NET CLOSING IN.

"Keep going, lad. Don't give up," Dickie muttered to himself.

Traversing New Jersey, the Greyhound bus was 160 miles from Washington, D.C., and was due to arrive in the capital in exactly three hours and ten minutes' time. Outside the bus, nothing was visible in the darkness; inside, every seat was taken and most people were sleeping or talking in the hushed tones that all but the brash and dumb adopt on a bus at night.

Toward the rear of the coach Will Cochrane was in an aisle seat next to a twenty-eight-year-old named Emma, who'd introduced herself to Will when she'd boarded the vehicle in New York City and had told him, somewhat flirtatiously, that she hoped he didn't snore when he slept.

He felt cramped in the seat, and he couldn't get his big frame and head into the right position; every time he tilted his skull back he feared an involuntary snort, and as he drifted into sleep, his head would move forward—slowly at first, but then culminating in a whiplash butt against nothing and an inhalation of air that produced a grunt. He decided it was too embarrassing to continue and stared ahead down the aisle.

"Want a slice of orange?" Emma held up a segment of fruit. "Good for the sinuses."

Will smiled and replied in his Virginian accent, "Sinuses or snoring?"

"Same thing." Emma dropped the orange segment into Will's palm. "Actually, I don't know if orange helps at all. But it sounds about right, doesn't it?"

"Guess so. Thanks. I haven't had fruit for a while." His teeth crushed the segment, sending shots of vitamin C into his mouth.

"You look like you're desperate for sleep."

"That obvious, is it?"

Emma nodded. "Tell you what." She rummaged in her knapsack. "I got a spare travel cushion. They're great for getting comfortable, and"—she grinned—"stopping sinuses getting noisy." She pulled out the pillow and held it out to Will.

"You sure?"

"Totally, because I'd kind of like to get some sleep myself."

Will fixed the cushion around his neck. He knew that he shouldn't sleep, but his whole body and mind were craving a few hours of shutdown. He decided to close his eyes and take a chance.

Ten minutes later, Emma could tell from her fellow passenger's slow, deep breathing that he was asleep. She was relieved that her cushion had done the trick, not just because she wanted some peace and quiet to rest, but also because she'd meant what she'd said to him—the guy really looked dog tired.

He seemed like a nice man, and she was happy to help him.

She looked at him, thinking how odd it was that strangers could sleep next to each other when traveling on public transportation, as if they were sharing a bed. Not that she was complaining; this guy was hot. She decided to go to sleep fantasizing about watching him fall asleep in their bed while caressing his fatigued face.

The image made her feel good.

And made her frown.

Because there was something about his face that was familiar.

Actor? TV personality? Unlikely somebody

from that world would travel on a bus. And the name he'd given her—John Jones—didn't ring any bells. Oh well, in all probability he was a nobody who just happened to have the looks of someone famous.

She closed her eyes, picturing her fantasy, and at the same time wondering, Who are you?

It was nearly 1:00 A.M. when Ed Parker entered the Russian and European Analysis division's archive room at CIA headquarters. He'd considered leaving this inquiry until morning, but couldn't sleep. So he'd gotten out of bed, put on jeans and a sweater, made a call to the head of the archive, and driven over to Langley.

The archivist was already in the room, working on his computer while looking majorly annoyed that he'd been summoned by Ed to work at this ungodly hour. The man—in his early sixties and thin, aside from a belly that came from decades of sitting at a desk and drinking gallons of beer in his off hours—was wearing casual attire and socks that didn't match, and his hair was ruffled. "Director Parker. So pleased to see you."

"No you're not." Parker strode to the archivist's desk. "You got any coffee around here?"

"Nope. But I got a bottle of Jack in my drawer in case of emergencies."

"I have to drive home after this."

"So do I."

"Well, fuck it, then. If we get caught, we can spend a night together in a cell while swapping stories about the good ol' days."

The archivist poured whiskey into mugs, handed one to the director, and returned to his workstation. "What do you want?"

Parker placed a hand on the archivist's computer. "Your password to your database."

The archivist laughed. "Can't give you that."

"Thought you'd say that, which is why I needed you here." He took a sip of the liquor. "The Project Ferryman files: Who last pulled them and when?"

The head of the archive spent a few minutes tapping on his keyboard and glancing at his computer screen before looking at Parker. "Helen Coombs pulled the files three days ago at 0906 hours. As per access protocols for these files, she read them in one of the booths and they were then returned to us at 0957 hours. You know her?"

Parker nodded. "She's cleared to read the files: she's involved in distributing Ferryman intel to our key government contacts. Anyone else read the files in the last few weeks?"

The archivist returned to his screen. "You, Mr. Sheridan, and Senator Jellicoe. No one else."

Parker polished off his drink. "Okay. Send an e-mail to Helen Coombs telling her I want to see her at ten A.M. tomorrow in my office." He checked his watch. "Correction, today. But don't tell her why."

The sight of Washington, D.C., with its neon lights showing glimpses of rain-drenched buildings in the darkness, made Emma feel both euphoric and irritable. The joy was plain and simple, the same elation she always felt when she reached the end of a long journey, and by Christ she'd made this journey enough times to wish away every minute of the time it took. Her irritability came from the fact that she was visiting her parents, meaning she would have to endure her mother's cross-examinations about her love life, dietary intake, fashion sense, and latest hairstyle, as well as her ignorant and snide comments about her vocation. Her father, by contrast, was a head-in-the-sand guy whose prime motivation in life was avoiding confrontation. Trouble was, every time Mom started getting all nosy on her, Dad would tell her she was acting like Perry Mason, and Mom would say she was too young to know who Perry Mason was, and Dad would say she wasn't, and finally Dad would get precisely what he wanted to avoid: confrontation. It happened on every trip she made to see them. And while they were going for each other's throats, she'd sit between them feeling like she was twelve years old.

And the irony was, during her short adulthood she'd experienced far more of the world than her parents. Upon graduating from college, she'd given the finger to their dogmatic belief that a career in law awaited her and instead accepted a position with a charity that specialized in aid to the Third World. She'd chosen the career path because she desired travel, was by nature a person who wanted to make the world a better place, and knew it would shock her mom and dad. Among many things, Emma was a rebel who would frequently eschew sensible paths in favor of impulsive adventure.

She pulled out her cell phone and saw it was nearly 6:00 A.M.

The man by her side was still asleep, or more like unconscious. She'd never seen a guy look this tired, and felt guilty for having to wake him.

But Union Station was minutes away.

She nudged his arm.

Good Lord, it felt like steel.

He remained asleep.

She prodded his thigh.

It was as solid as a mature oak tree.

He was motionless.

What was left? There had to be something he could feel. Not his hands. They looked leathery and immune to pain or any other feeling, since they were covered in scars.

That left the face. Touch him there? Just like she'd fantasized?

She raised a finger and smoothed the back of it against his cheek.

His eyes opened and he exclaimed, "Ulana, too dangerous to make it."

Definitely not the same accent she'd heard before.

British, she decided.

"You okay? We're pulling up to Union Station."

Will collected his thoughts, silently cursing his involuntary outburst.

"You dream in British?"

Will smiled and made no effort to conceal his English accent. "Sometimes, yeah. I often switch between accents without knowing I'm doing it. I'm half and half. Mother was British; father American."

"Was?"

Will nodded. "Was."

The coach pulled into Union Station, and as it did so Emma recalled killing hours in New York City's Penn Station by reading a discarded copy of the *New York Times*. There was something she'd read in the paper that was nagging her, but she'd only been half awake and she was struggling to recall what she'd seen. "Hope you don't mind me asking, but are you on TV? You look familiar."

Will tensed. "I've been asked that before. Guess there must be some actor out there who I resemble."

"Maybe a better way to look at it is that he resembles you." She smiled, and then thought, God, did I just say that?

Will smiled back at her. "Thanks for the pillow. It was a lifesaver, and it really was a very kind gesture." He got to his feet as the coach came to a halt in the station's bus deck and held out his hand. "Nice to meet you, Emma."

Emma shook his hand and kept hold of it as she asked, "You make this trip a lot?"

Will lied. "Too often."

"I hope we bump into each other again."

"Me too. Just make sure you bring your extra travel cushion."

He walked down the aisle, leaving Emma wondering who decided that it was inappropriate for a girl to give a guy her telephone number when he hadn't asked.

She also wondered why her fellow passenger wasn't carrying any luggage.

Strange.

Still, she was envious, because her cruddy backpack felt like it weighed as much as she did; it would be great one day to travel footloose and fancy-free.

She gathered her things and exited the coach into the station's basement bus parking zone. Though it was only recently built, she knew every inch of Union Station's new bus area—it was as big as a cathedral, modern, spacious, and minimalist, had multiple tiers that were accessed by elevators, escalators, and stairwells, and a glass roof over the upper level containing bathrooms and retail outlets. But as she entered the ground floor to head toward the H Street NE pedestrian entrance, she reflected that this was the first time she'd seen cops in the building.

She could see four of them standing in two groups. The nearest pair were approximately fifty yards away and were looking at the faces of the commuters passing them. Farther ahead, two more cops were doing the same.

Ten yards ahead of her, John Jones stopped for a second before continuing on toward the exit and the police who stood in their way.

Why did he stop, she wondered?

She glanced at the cops again; there was no doubt they were looking for someone.

She returned her gaze to the back of John Jones.

He was walking slowly, his hands now in his jacket pockets.

Did cops make him uneasy?

Scare him?

It came crashing home.

The *New York Times* article.

A photo of a handsome man who was described as half English, half American.

An image that matched the face of the guy who'd sat next to her on the bus.

A rogue British intelligence officer.

On the run in the United States.

Her heart beating fast, she tried to decide what to do. Call out to the police, saying an armed fugitive was heading toward them? That was the logical option. Maybe she'd be entitled to some kind of reward for playing a part in the capture of the man named Will Cochrane.

The cops were heavily armed and were wearing body armor. Together, they'd easily overpower him. Plus, he'd looked so tired on the coach that she doubted he had any fight in him.

She was forty yards away from the nearest cops. Though they weren't looking in her direction, they'd easily hear her if she shouted.

The sensible path to take was to do precisely that, and then duck for cover.

Trouble was, the man who'd been so grateful to her for use of her travel pillow never once looked or sounded like he was a threat. He seemed like a good person, someone she'd felt totally comfortable around while she closed her eyes.

To hell with alerting the cops.

She'd never been one to do the sensible thing.

She jogged as fast as her heavy pack would let her until she was side by side with the FBI's Most

Wanted. "Mr. Jones," she said, breathless and smiling, "I've got a favor to ask—you mind carrying my damn bag? It's killing my back."

Will looked at her. His face looked focused and serious. "I'm—"

"Only need you to hold it until we're outside. Maybe payment in kind for the pillow?"

Will hesitated. "Sure." He took the backpack and slung it over one shoulder.

As they walked closer to the first pair of cops, Emma said, "Got another favor to ask: Do you mind holding my hand? Ever since I was a kid and got in a bit of trouble, cops freak me out."

"Your hand?"

Emma grabbed his hand impatiently. "Yes. It would reassure me."

Will was frowning, trying to figure her out.

But she pulled him closer. "I'm just a scared girl, okay?"

As they walked nearer to the cops, looking every bit a couple who were visiting or returning to D.C., Will whispered, "You know who I am."

Emma's heart was now racing, though externally she hoped she looked calm. "Some stuff I read. But I also know you like fruit, dream in another accent, and don't have anyone to look after you anymore. That's more interesting to me."

The first two policemen were now looking at Will. "I can't let you do this. It's too dangerous."

"I don't think you're a danger to me." She pulled him even closer and put on a fake smile. "Just act like you love me."

Urgently, Will replied, "I'm no danger to you, but what could happen next may well be."

Keeping her grin fixed on her face, she muttered, "Use your U.S. accent. Your face looks a bit thinner than in the photo the press is showing, and the clothes help make you look different. We're visiting my folks. You're my new boyfriend and I'm showing you off for the first time. I'm a charity worker, based in NYC. Surname Jones. We met two weeks ago at Huckleberry Bar in Brooklyn. Still getting to know each other. I haven't been to your home yet, because I'm a Bible Belt gal who ain't hopping into bed for any guy until he pops the question. What do you do for a living?"

As they got closer to the police, Will felt respect for Emma's quick thinking, courage, and commitment, but was increasingly worried for her at the same time. "Therapist with my own practice in New York. I counsel trauma victims, particularly war veterans."

"Clever. Cops will like that."

Barely moving his lips, Will responded, "Clever things don't always work out in real life. If anything bad happens, fall to the ground, lie flat with your hands over your head, and after I'm dead tell them that I had a gun pointed at your gut." The police were now staring directly at them. "Why are you doing this?"

Emma squeezed his hand. "Seems to me, someone's got to look after you."

Will used his eye contact in the way he'd been trained to do when operating in hostile environments without wishing to be conspicuous—never keep your head down to avoid looking at anyone, because it looks odd, or fix your gaze on someone, because it may unsettle them and cause a confrontation. Instead, act normal by briefly glancing at people before respectfully looking away. That's what he did with the cops as he and Emma walked past them.

The police, by contrast, made no attempt to hide the fact they were scrutinizing everyone, while their hands rested over their sidearm holsters. They continued staring at the couple as they moved farther along the concourse toward the other two cops who were forty yards ahead.

The first group of police said nothing to Will and Emma, and they were now behind them.

Emma was mightily relieved.

Will wasn't, because he'd known they wouldn't be challenged by the first group of officers; they were the spotters, in place to signal to the second group if they had a possible sighting. And between the two sets of cops was the takedown zone.

Or kill zone.

One of the cops ahead was looking at him; no, looking just slightly to his left, at the officers behind him. Was he receiving a silent signal from one of his colleagues, saying that the man walking between the two sets of cops was Will Cochrane?

He kept walking, and Emma maintained pace and retained her smile.

The two men ahead changed position, not much but enough so that they had good angles of fire should they need them.

Coincidence?

Will breathed in deeply while unslinging the backpack and rubbing his shoulder as if it were aching from the straps. "Emma."

"Yeah."

"You really a Bible Belt girl?"

"Perhaps you'd like to find out."

"Sorry."

"For what?"

"I'm truly sorry that I'll never get the chance to find out, and I'm sorry if I accidentally hurt you."

"Hurt me?"

"Yes."

Will slammed the backpack on the floor so that it acted as a cushion, pushed Emma over it, pulled out his handgun and fired two shots in under one second, saw both cops in front of him drop to the floor as his bullets struck their Kevlar jackets, then spun around and fired again so that the two cops behind him were writhing on the concourse as if they'd been hit in the chest with a sledgehammer. He bolted while men and women around him screamed at the sight of a psychopath who'd gunned down four law enforcement officers with brutal precision and speed.

But Will wasn't a psychopath. He'd aimed at the cops' body armor, knowing his pistol rounds would not reach the officers' bodies, but nevertheless would incapacitate them for a vital few seconds.

Will was almost out of sight as the first cop managed to get to his feet, his face screwed up in agony from the impact to his upper body, which would remain bruised for weeks, his feet unsteady, his mind disoriented but praising the Lord and Kevlar for saving his life. He tried to move, but his legs nearly buckled. One by one, his colleagues got upright, three of them removing their bullet-proof vests and examining the gunshot hole that was dead center in the jacket, the fourth speaking in a near hysterical voice on his radio mic that they needed assistance and mobile patrols to scour Union Station's surroundings.

All around them was chaos, noise, panic, and the acrid smell of discharged rounds.

Emma's ears were in pain from the sound of Will's pistol; she'd never known gunshots were that loud in reality.

But, despite her body shaking from fear and adrenaline and the needlelike pain in her head, she kept her eyes on Will Cochrane until he disappeared from view.

She knew they wouldn't get him.

Not today.

Anyone who could nonlethally immobilize four law enforcement officers in that fraction of time was too good to be caught fleeing this place.

Emma smiled as she imagined her mom inevitably asking her if she had a man in her life. This time she'd be able to respond with words that would finally stop her interference. Something like, "Yeah, lovely guy. I was hoping to introduce him to you, but turned out he was a spy, and we decided to end things after he shot four cops."

Her smile faded when she realized she'd never see Will again.

Just her luck to finally meet a guy who she could sleep next to with a feeling of utter contentment and safety, only for that moment to be snatched away from her.

Still, it gave her some consolation to know that during her visit to her parents he might be nearby this weekend.

In Washington, D.C.

PART IV

TWENTY-EIGHT

Though she loved the city, there were two things that Marsha Gage didn't like about Washington: it had far too many politicians for her liking, and early-morning traffic could be horrendous, particularly when rain was pouring out of the black clouds above the city. Thankfully, her car was tailgating Pete Duggan's SUV as its siren and flashing lights forced a path toward Union Station. Duggan's HRT colleagues weren't in the vehicle because Marsha didn't need them right now; instead she'd told Pete to come with her so that she could draw upon his expertise.

Twenty-three minutes earlier she'd received a call from Commander Bret Oppenheimer of the Metropolitan Police Department of the District of Columbia telling her what had happened at the station, that all police leave had been canceled, that he was increasing the police presence in D.C., and that Will Cochrane had vanished. And while she'd been grabbing her car keys and Pete Duggan, she'd gotten another call from the chief of Washington's

Metro Transit Police Department saying that this morning he'd be unofficially telling every cop who worked for his department that none of them would be reprimanded if they spotted Cochrane at another transportation hub and shot him dead without issuing a warning. The chief had sounded furious, and Marsha didn't blame him because it was his men who'd been shot.

Duggan was driving fast down Massachusetts Avenue, and Marsha kept pace with him as they raced onto the ramp that took them to Union Station's parking zone. Two minutes later they were walking fast across the concourse where the confrontation had taken place. Most of it was cordoned off with police tape; uniformed and plainclothes cops were everywhere, including the four officers who were shot. Though they were merely bruised, the casualties had blankets over their shoulders, were drinking coffee, and were being attended to by paramedics. Beyond the tape, civilians were standing in near silence as they stared at the crime scene.

Marsha and Duggan ducked under the tape, flashed their FBI credentials at two officers who challenged them, and walked to the center of the crime scene. As they did so, Marsha estimated there were approximately fifty police officers on the concourse—a mixture of Transit and Met cops.

"Who's in charge here?" Marsha's voice echoed in the station.

The officers stared at her.

A plainclothes female officer stopped talking to three of her colleagues and called out, "That would be me. Detective Brooks. Met Department."

Marsha and Duggan walked up to her. "We're FBI. My name's Marsha Gage and this is Agent Pete Duggan from HRT. I'm in charge of the Bureau manhunt to catch Will Cochrane." She looked around. "What procedures do you have in place right now?"

Brooks nodded toward the exit. "Detectives and uniform are doing door to door to see if we can pick up Cochrane's trail. We've interviewed a woman who sat next to him on the bus he took from NYC and who was close to him when he opened fire here. She says he was holding a gun on her when they were walking across the concourse. I know she's lying, but I also know she's not an accomplice. At least, nothing more than trying to help a guy who she took a shine to. We know where she lives and who she's visiting, so we let her go with the caveat that we might question her again if we need to."

"You should have asked her about Cochrane's physical and mental state, and anything about where he might be headed."

"I did. He was pleasant, kind, and exhausted when on the coach. She reckoned cops would be able to knock him over with a feather duster, and was very surprised to see how he sprung into action. But he made no mention as to where he was headed. On that point, I know she's telling the truth."

"Have you done anything with the media?"

"No. I was told you were coming here, so knew you'd want to make a decision on how to handle this with the press."

"Forensics?"

Brooks pointed at the men and women who were dressed in all-in-one white overalls and were crouching over a part of the floor that had a small inner cordon and was off limits to everyone else. "That's where he made the shots. Empty cartridges have already been sent off for ballistics analysis. Plus we've taken hair and other samples from a cushion the woman lent him on the coach and from her clothes. It's a formality though—the woman has positively ID'd him as the man she read about in yesterday's *New York Times*. Plus, she said he spoke in a British accent. We're in no doubt he's Will Cochrane."

"Some of my agents are on their way here now to help with picking up his trail. You got a problem with that?"

"No, ma'am. You have jurisdiction. And we need all the help we can get."

Marsha smiled. "Detective Brooks, I can see this crime scene's in capable hands." She pointed at the four officers wearing blankets over their shoulders. "How are they holding up?"

"They're in shock, and they feel like they've been hit by a truck."

"Good."

"Good?"

Marsha nodded. "They'll be at least half as effective as they were before Cochrane opened fire on them." She glanced at Duggan before returning her attention to Brooks. "Can we borrow them for a moment?"

"Sure." Brooks raised a hand and called out,

"Sergeant Kowalski, I need you and your men over here."

The four officers walked over, their faces somber and sheepish.

Marsha said to Kowalski, "I want you all to stand in the exact same positions you were in when Cochrane pulled out his gun. Just before it happened, did you have your hands over your pistols?"

The sergeant nodded. "Our guns were holstered but unstrapped; we were ready to pull them out."

"Okay. Time to stop feeling sorry for yourselves, get rid of the blankets and drinks, and move into position."

The officers moved to the places where Cochrane had knocked them off their feet—two groups of two, spread apart from the area where the forensics team was working.

Marsha said to Duggan, "Stand next to the inner cordon. When I give the command, pull out your handgun and pretend like you're firing on the two cops ahead of you, then the two cops behind. Say 'Bang' for every pretend shot."

The former SEAL Team 6 member turned HRT commander nodded. "Got it."

Marsha raised her voice so that she could be heard by the cops, who were now forty yards apart. "Kowalski—my colleague's going to pretend to be Cochrane and reenact what happened. I want you to do the same, and that means unholstering your weapons if you get a chance."

"We're hardly in the best shape!"

"I know. And that's important to me." She

smiled. "Just make sure your safety catches are on and no one accidentally discharges."

She stared at Duggan, who was standing very close to where Cochrane had opened fire. Within the United States' special operations community, no one was better placed to do this than Duggan. In person, she'd witnessed what he could do with a gun, and on one occasion she'd played hostage in the Quantico antiterrorism training house. It had been a terrifying experience seeing Duggan's explosive precision and speed as he stormed into her room while firing live rounds inches from her face.

Duggan's handgun was concealed under his jacket.

Marsha shouted, "Go!"

The HRT commander dropped low, pulled out his weapon, two "Bangs," spun around, and stopped.

The other two injured cops had their pistols pointing at his chest.

Duggan got upright, put away his weapon, and walked back to Marsha and Brooks. "I'd have been incapacitated or dead before I could fire the third shot."

Marsha nodded. "Killed by men who were half as good as they were earlier this morning."

"Correct."

Marsha's heart beat fast as she looked at Brooks. "If they're not doing so already, make sure every officer on door-to-door detail—detectives included—is wearing body armor." She asked Duggan. "Your assessment?"

The HRT commander looked at the four cops who were now moving back toward their hot drinks, blankets, and colleagues. "Getting up close and personal with Cochrane is a real problem. To be honest, I didn't think I'd get beyond two shots. I'd say we put a net over D.C.—get helos in the air, each carrying one SWAT spotter and one sniper. And get every other sniper-trained SWAT operative on rooftops. The SWAT commander will know where to put them, since this is his turf."

"Can we get extra men from HRT?"

Duggan shook his head. "You were lucky to get eight of us. Half of my colleagues are overseas, protecting U.S. sites from terrorism. The rest need to be on standby for homeland threats."

Marsha silently cursed, wishing she'd been allowed to continue her pursuit of Cobalt so that she could stop his reign of carnage.

"Anyway, I can't afford to put my team on static observation duty. SWAT's perfectly capable for that detail. We need to be ready for a hot takedown once Cochrane's pinned down to one location."

Marsha agreed with Duggan's proposed course of action. She said to Brooks, "Hotels, motels, anywhere that Cochrane can rent a room in D.C.—phone them all, in case he turns up at one of them."

The detective replied, "I've already got officers doing precisely that."

Marsha smiled. "Absolutely no doubt in my mind that you're the right person for this job." Her smile vanished as she looked around the Union

Station concourse. "In a moment, I'm going to tell the media that Cochrane's in D.C., that every transportation hub in the city has been bolstered with extra Transit officers who'll be carrying submachine guns as well as their usual weapons, that the number of Met Department cops on the streets has been increased, that Secret Service is on high alert in case Cochrane's going for high-value targets, that SWAT snipers will be looking over the city from on high, that routes in and out of the city will be heavily monitored, that citizens should go about their normal business but cooperate fully if we give the order for them to stay at home, and that starting right now the city of Washington, D.C., is a police state."

One of the men in the crowd of civilians turned and walked fast away from the Union Station crime scene toward the escalator that would take him to the parking zone. Aside from his good looks and athletic build, he looked like an average guy who had every right to be in the building. His clothes were functional and cheap—jeans, boots, a bomber jacket—and his movement was indicative of someone who'd decided he'd wasted enough time rubbernecking a police incident and needed to get to work. He could have been a construction worker, a courier, or maybe an off-duty cop or security guard.

He wasn't.

As an SAS operative, Oates had hunted down and assassinated terrorists in the backstreets of war-torn Baghdad, been a key participant in the near suicidal yet wholly successful mission to rescue five British army soldiers who'd been held hostage in Sierra Leone, fought toe to toe with tough jihadists in the Tora Bora cave complex, singlehandedly killed twelve rebels in a confrontation on the Pakistani border, and walked into a mosque in Afghanistan and shot its imam in the head for no other reason than that the soldier thought the cleric had been spouting a load of poisonous crap. When unproven suspicion had fallen on him for the murder, he was sacked from the Regiment. At the end of their military careers, Scott, Shackleton, and Amundsen had also stepped into the wrong side of the morally ambiguous gray zone that separated right and wrong in covert combat. Shortly thereafter, all four men became guns for hire. Recognizing their skills and inability to enter the more traditional private-military-contractor career path open to former special operatives, Antaeus had snapped them up and given them additional training in his dark art of espionage.

Oates moved into the vast parking zone and within minutes was sitting next to Scott in their vehicle.

Scott turned on the ignition as he watched Marsha Gage walk quickly to her car. "How did it go?"

Oates pulled out his handgun and fixed it in between his seat and the underside of his thigh. "Lots of cops standing around drinking coffee."

"Doughnuts?"

"Nah."

"What a shame."

"Yeah. Come all this way to America, and you deserve to see cops stuffing doughnuts in their gobs."

"What do you reckon happened in there?"

Oates shrugged. "Gunfight. Cochrane took down four cops."

His fellow former SAS colleague asked, "Killed them?"

Oates shook his head. "Nope. Put them on their asses."

"Shots to vests?"

"Precisely."

"How very generous of him." Scott put the car in gear and slowly moved it out of the lot as Marsha's car began to move. "Could you hear what Gage was saying?"

"No, but I didn't need to. She wanted to examine the scene to find out what Cochrane was capable of. There was a big guy with her. Wasn't wearing uniform, but absolutely no doubt he's Hormone Replacement Therapy."

Scott laughed.

"She used him to see how quick the job could be done."

"Did HRT man pass?"

"Not quite, but he's very fast. We've got to be careful."

"Would you have passed?"

"Of course."

"You saying that just because I'm team leader?"

"Wish you'd fuck off with this *team leader* shit." Oates shook his head. "Next time, I'm going to tell the boss that I should be team leader."

"I'd love to be a fly on the wall when that happens. Antaeus doesn't really get on well with people who try to tell him what to do." Scott drove the car onto Massachusetts Avenue and ensured that three vehicles were between him and Marsha Gage. "What do you reckon Gage is doing now?"

"She had a powwow with the HRT guy and some other cop bird. I think the test scared the shit out of Gage and she's going to escalate matters."

"The media will latch on to what happened at the station."

"Meaning she'll want to speak to them before they speculate."

"Good. When Amundsen and Shackleton take over Gage-stalking duty, let's you and me put our feet up with a nice brew and watch a bit of telly. Sounds like this morning there might be something interesting to watch."

The fact that over six hundred thousand people lived in Washington, and at least three times that many worked here during daytime hours, was little consolation to Will Cochrane as he walked north along Seventh Street NW. He felt totally exposed, as if every passerby were looking at him and he were seconds away from hearing, "Police! Get your hands on your head."

Icy rain was penetrating the gap between his jacket's collar and his back, causing his skin to tingle and rise in goose bumps. His muscles ached from fatigue, his earlier exertions, and stress; his mind was awash with self-doubt and anxiety that Ellie Hallowes wouldn't deliver on her side of the bargain they'd reached in Norway.

Norway.

It seemed that he'd been there in another age.

So much had happened between Scandinavia and here.

And maybe all of it was pointless.

He entered D.C.'s Chinatown as the dark clouds above him clapped and thundered, as if they were summoning sentinels to lash the air beneath them with bolts of electricity.

Will continued walking through a sea of umbrellas held by tourists gawping at the delicious food on display in the restaurant windows. How enticing the rotisserie chickens and other exotic cuisine looked, and he felt engulfed by the urge to step into one of the warm eateries, sit at a table, and order enough food to feed an army. That's where he would be shot, like a mobster taking a reflective and indulgent moment away from death and extortion, eating a meal in the comfort of civilized refinement, unaware that it was his last.

He kept moving, wondering if this place had looked similar when Ellie Hallowes came here.

If she'd come here.

He felt his left eye twitching, an involuntary movement prompted by nerves and tiredness and a body that was crying out for him to finally stop. The feeling made him recall how Chief Inspector Dreyfus's eye would start to twitch as Inspector

Clouseau's unwavering incompetence would escalate in the Pink Panther movies. The image temporarily made him smile, though also made him
question where his mind was.

He tried to settle his thoughts by recalling
memories that meant something to him—whether
they were good or bad.

At home in London, cooking pheasant breasts
and smoked bacon in a dry cider casserole while
listening to Andrés Segovia's classical guitar
recitals; in a scuba suit while drifting peacefully
in the deep, sun-penetrated azure waters of the
Red Sea alongside wrasse, tuna, turtles, and a
British Vanguard–class Trident nuclear sub-
marine; watching an American girl called Kelly
smile and relieve the butterflies in his stomach
when she said yes after he asked her out for a first
date in high school; standing on top of a snow-
covered mountain in the Scottish Highlands and
feeling like he was in heaven, even though he was
barefoot and in red overalls and being pursued by
an MI6 training staff hunter-killer force; being
kicked in the head by high school jocks in his class
who said he was a faggot for playing viola; and
being a sandy-haired and freckled seven-year-old,
sitting on a beach and scraping out whelks from
their shells, and bursting into tears as he saw his
mother cry because she was so sad that two years
earlier Dad had been captured in Iran and was
presumed dead.

These and many other thoughts ran through his
mind as he continued moving through Chinatown.

He broke left into a dark, narrow alleyway full

of trash bins, with fire escapes on the adjacent building walls. He was relieved to see that no one was in here, and moved three-quarters of the way toward the far end. Crouching down, he stared at a part of the wall where a year ago he'd loosened a brick in case of need. He'd done similarly in every city he'd been to in the world. They were his dead-letter boxes, his means to communicate with others like him.

So many times during his odyssey to reach this place he'd mentally pictured this moment. And most times his despairing mind had imagined him pulling out the brick and seeing an empty void.

Part of him didn't want to find out whether his journey and the risks he'd taken had been a complete waste of time, because if there was nothing behind the brick he'd have no choice other than to walk out of the alley and surrender to the nearest cop.

He breathed in, ignoring the rain that was pouring over his body, removed his knife, and eased the loose brick out of its cavity. His hand was shaking as he placed it in the hole.

Something was in there.

Hard.

His fingers gripped it.

A small box.

His heart was pounding, but there was no feeling of elation because he knew that inside could be a note saying, "I'm sorry, Will, but I can't go through with this."

He withdrew the container and held it in the

palm of his hand. It was a cheap black jewelry box with a metal clasp to keep its lid in place. After standing, he looked left and right along the alley in case he was being watched, but saw no one.

Both of his hands were now shaking.

Everything that had happened to him had been about this moment.

He opened the box.

Inside was a small slip of paper.

Keeping his head and upper body over the box so that rain didn't saturate the paper and make illegible the one thing in the world that he wanted right now, he unfolded the paper.

On it was a cell phone number.

One that nobody else had.

Except Ellie Hallowes.

Will snapped the box shut, closed his eyes, and exclaimed, "Thank God!" as he tossed his head back so that rain could wash over his face. "Thank you, God!"

Now he could contact Ellie.

And learn the truth about Ferryman.

Dickie Mountjoy and David sat in a rear room within Phoebe's small art gallery, in London's Pimlico district. Phoebe was with them, strutting back and forth; to Dickie's mind, she was all tits and ass with barely anything to cover them.

The room was head-to-toe white and contained nothing save the chairs they were sitting on, an easel supporting a canvas covered by a white cloth, and a young gay man called Marcel, who was standing next to the painting. Dickie hadn't liked Marcel on sight; thirty seconds after hearing him speak, the retired major wanted to shoot him.

Marcel was wearing Turkish trousers that made him look like he'd had an involuntary bowel movement, sandals without socks, and a collarless purple shirt that was so vivid it made Dickie gag just by looking at the damn thing.

Dickie jabbed his walking stick against the floor. "Stop poncing around and get on with it."

"Dickie!" Phoebe looked sternly at the major. "You can't rush art."

"Yes you bleedin' can. You just work harder, like people do with proper jobs."

Marcel rolled his eyes at Phoebe, and when he spoke it was in the over-the-top tone favored by certain English actors from a bygone era. "Oh, darling. You didn't tell me you'd be bringing Neanderthal Man to our precious gallery."

"Neanderthal Man?!" Dickie pointed his stick at Marcel. "Least I am a man."

"Whatever, Grandpa."

Dickie glanced at David, who was making his rabbit-caught-in-the-headlights expression and looked like he wanted to bolt. "You comfortable with your missus hangin' around with these queer types? They might turn her, you know."

The mortician blurted, "Phoebes isn't my missus . . . not quite yet, anyway."

"Best you stop wasting her time then, Sunny Jim. Phoebe doesn't do subtle. You need to sweep the girl off her feet and get her legs around you *toot sweet.*" Dickie smiled before turning his glare back onto Marcel. "And talking of wasting my time . . ."

Marcel looked at Phoebe. "Kitten, you've no idea how much I've struggled with this. I do abstract paintings, and you know that. This isn't my kind of thing."

Dickie muttered, "You're a walking, talking *abstract.*"

Phoebe ignored the major's comment and said to her artist, "We're not expecting great. Anything's better than what Will's got right now. It's torn to shreds."

Marcel lit a cigarette. That didn't bother Dickie. But when the painter placed the cigarette in a long antique holder, it took all of the major's self-control to stop him from knocking the blasted thing out of Marcel's hand.

Marcel gripped the top of the sheet with two fingers, and hesitated. "If you don't like it, I won't be offended."

Phoebe kissed Marcel on both cheeks . . .

An action that prompted Dickie to nudge David in the ribs and exclaim, "You lettin' her get away with that?"

. . . and she said, "You're such a sweetie, Marcel. If it's awful, we won't hold it against you." She gave Dickie her dominatrix expression. "Will we?"

Dickie huffed.

"Very well then." Marcel sighed and whipped off the cloth.

Underneath was Marcel's oil reproduction of the English artist J. M. W. Turner's classic 1839 painting *The Fighting Temeraire*, depicting the ninety-eight-gun HMS *Temeraire*. The warship had played a distinguished role in the Battle of Trafalgar in 1805, but since then the old warrior had been deemed technologically obsolete. The painting showed a paddle-wheel steam tug towing the ship toward its final berth in London, where it was to be broken up for scrap.

Dickie awkwardly got to his feet, put his reading glasses on, and walked right up to the painting. Nobody in the room spoke as the major bent forward to closely examine the work.

Phoebe and David braced themselves for another of his inappropriate rants.

But Dickie stood upright and tried to stop his eyes from watering as he looked directly at Marcel. "It's . . . it's . . . Mr. Cochrane will be over the moon with this." He glanced at the magnificently vibrant and brushstroke-perfect reproduction before returning his gaze to Marcel. "Well done, sir." He tried to stop the emotion coming out in his voice, but failed. "Well done indeed. You've done us proud."

"You wanted to see me." Helen Coombs stood nervously in the entrance to Director Ed Parker's spacious office in Langley. The CIA analyst wished she'd known she'd be summoned this morning to see the director; she'd have made more of an effort with her clothes and hair. She felt frumpy and fat.

Ed smiled and stood up from behind his desk. "Yes I did, Helen. And don't be concerned—there's nothing to worry about." He gestured to a seat on the opposite side of his desk and sat back down. "By the way, love what you've done with your hair."

She waddled to the chair and sat. "Have I done something wrong?"

Keeping his grin fixed on his face, Ed shook his head. "Ms. Coombs, you're one of my best analysts. Just wish some of your colleagues could learn a thing or two from your work."

The comment reassured Helen, and she felt her body relax, though she knew she had to remain on her guard. Mr. Parker could be all charm, but he was still senior management, and one didn't get to that rank without being canny and fork-tongued.

"Would you like something to drink? Coffee, tea, water?"

"No, I'm fine, sir."

"Okay." Parker interlaced his fingers. "All I have for you is a quick question. First thing in the morning three days ago, you pulled the Ferryman files from archives. You're perfectly entitled to do that, since you have clearance, but I just wanted to check why you did so."

Helen frowned. "Three days ago."

"Just after nine A.M."

Helen tried to get her mind to think clearly, not an easy task when someone as lowly as her was in the presence of such a senior clandestine officer. "I . . ."

"Take your time. Jeez, sometimes I struggle to remember what I've done yesterday."

The frown remained on Helen's face. "No, it's okay. Just . . . just kinda embarrassing."

"Embarrassing?"

"Yeah, I . . ." Helen's palms felt sweaty. "Embarrassing because four nights ago I got drunk."

Parker laughed. "What you get up to in your own time is your business, providing it doesn't become a problem and interfere with your day job."

"That's the embarrassing thing." Helen felt like she wanted to crawl into a hole and disappear. "Having to admit this to management. I got drunk in a bar, lost my Agency security pass, got home, and carried on partying. Truth is, sir, I was too ill to make it in to work the next day. You certain it was three days ago?"

Parker felt his skin crawl and his stomach tighten into knots. "Positive."

"Anyway, I haven't looked at the Ferryman files for at least a couple of weeks. No way did I pull them days ago. Couldn't have. Impossible."

All trace of Parker's geniality had vanished. "When did you report your missing pass to our security department?"

"I . . . I didn't wake up until after lunchtime. I guess it was about midafternoon when I realized the pass was missing. I called the bar I'd been to the night before. They told me someone had found and handed in my wallet. Guess I'd lost it at the same time as I dropped my pass. But unfortunately the pass wasn't found. I made the call to security after that. Told them the loss wasn't suspicious. They said they'd cancel the missing pass and reissue me with a new one."

Parker felt a sharp pain behind his eyes. "Were you accompanied by anyone when you were in the bar and when you went home to continue drinking?"

Helen bowed her head silently, her mind racing.

"Anyone?" The director's tone was stern. "Right now, I don't care if it was a married Agency guy or a Russian spy. But I need a name."

"I'm sorry, I . . ."

"Did you walk home?"

"No, no."

"Drive your own car?"

"No."

"Someone else drive it for you?"

Helen shook her head.

"In that case, you must have taken a cab home. How did you pay for it when you'd lost your wallet? I'm thinking someone else paid. And I need that person's name."

Helen's eyes were watering. "I'm so sorry, Mr. Parker."

"A name!"

She looked up. "Ellie Hallowes."

TWENTY-NINE

As Patrick exited his car on Pennsylvania Avenue and handed the keys to a valet, the sight of the large SWAT truck farther up the road disgorging two snipers and two spotters made the CIA officer feel sick with worry for Will Cochrane. He'd often felt this sensation when Will was deployed on missions, but this was different.

Will wasn't operating for a greater cause, and moreover was almost certainly going to die at the hands of the country he'd protected so many times.

He watched the sniper team disappear from view, wondering where they were going to hide and also wondering how many other snipers remained in the SWAT truck as it pulled away. Above him, he could see three police helicopters, and he knew they contained expert marksmen who could take a man's head off from a distance while moving at speed. In every direction across the city, he could hear emergency vehicles' sirens wailing.

He pulled up the collar of his overcoat to shield

himself from the rain, and walked fast toward the entrance to the Café du Parc. Alistair was drinking a cup of tea within the venue's Le Bar, and he offered no greeting or friendly expression as his colleague removed his coat and slumped into a chair opposite him.

The MI6 controller unnecessarily stirred his tea. "It's a pleasure to be out of Bureau or Agency earshot."

"Damn right it is." Patrick loosened the knot in his tie.

"So, what's happened?"

"I've read an interesting SMS."

"On your telephone?"

"No."

Alistair smiled. "Ah, on Mr. Sheridan's phone."

Patrick nodded.

Ever since the two senior spies had been assigned to Marsha Gage's team and forced to share the Bureau ops room with Sheridan, Alistair and Patrick had challenged each other to see how often they could read Sheridan's messages without getting caught.

"He was in the men's room—just for thirty seconds, but that was long enough for me. Message was from Ed Parker, saying he needs to bring Hallowes into HQ."

Alistair intertwined his fingers. "Ellie Hallowes." He was deep in thought. "She's of no use to anyone in the Agency right now, until she's deployed again overseas. Strange that someone as senior as Parker is bothering someone as senior as Sheridan to waste time tracking down an agent who to all intents and purposes isn't worthy of their time."

"I agree. And that means her importance has just shot through the roof."

"They need her to help them."

"Unlikely."

"So, more likely she's done something that's truly bothered them."

"And they want to put the thumbscrews on her."

Alistair nodded.

Both men had long suspected that Hallowes could be a vital asset to Cochrane, and in particular that she would attempt to access the Ferryman files and relay what she'd read to Cochrane if he made it to the States. One of the first things Patrick had done after the initial meeting with Jellicoe, Sheridan, and Parker—wherein the co-heads were told that their Task Force S was shut down with immediate effect—was to retrieve from the Agency personnel database Hallowes's cell phone number and the name of the D.C. hotel she was staying in. Neither Alistair nor Patrick had contacted her, but they'd kept her details in case of need.

"Matters are drawing to a head."

Patrick agreed. "Rapidly."

"And all you and I can do is gently nudge events."

"But do so in a way that helps our boy."

Their boy, Will Cochrane.

The son of CIA officer James Cochrane, who'd surrendered to revolutionaries in Iran in order to save the lives of Alistair and Patrick; the young boy who'd never known that his widowed mother was secretly given financial support from the two men who would feel lifelong guilt that they were alive and James Cochrane wasn't; the MI6 trainee who would be taken under their wing and subjected to a brutal instruction program that some might think was sadistic, but others in the know would realize was the one thing Cochrane needed at that time to prevent him from losing his soul; the spy who'd stepped up to the plate on their behalf and three times stopped genocide; the man who would forever remind them of their brave former colleague and friend.

At no point were Alistair and Patrick ever going to fully comply with the CIA or Marsha Gage.

It just wasn't in their makeup.

"The SMS to Sheridan?"

Patrick answered, "Deleted by me."

"No more than two hours before Parker sends him another message or tries calling him."

"I'm working on the basis of one hour max."

"And you read Parker's message . . . ?"

Patrick looked at his watch. "Sixteen minutes ago."

"Have you tried calling Hallowes?"

"Yes, from a pay phone. Her cell's switched off."

Alistair stirred his now cold tea and tapped his silver spoon hard on the cup's rim. "That's not good."

Ellie was sitting in her room in the huge Washington Marriott Wardman Park hotel. Ordinarily, she'd love being in a hotel like this—not because it was luxurious, but because it had over a thousand rooms located on ten floors, meaning she could come and go using different entrances and elevators and ultimately could move around the place unnoticed. But now, the vastness of the hotel made her feel that she was an insignificant speck of dust.

She supposed she should show her face in Langley at some point this afternoon. Not that anyone cared whether she checked in to the Agency HQ. Most people in the CIA didn't know her, and the few that did viewed her as a spook without a portfolio who needed to be returned to the shadows because she reminded them that real spying was wholly unreflective of the clean-cut ambience that pervaded Langley.

She switched on her TV and looked for updates about the hunt for Cochrane. She saw live images of D.C.—police helicopters hovering beneath the dark clouds over the city; cop cars racing along the streets; tactical teams carrying assault rifles; and snipers and their spotters on rooftops. The camera switched to an interview with the chief of the Metro Transit Police Department who was standing outside Union Station and saying that he hoped legal charges against Cochrane would lead with his attempted murder of four cops.

Ellie turned off the TV, feeling that all was now hopeless. Even a man like Cochrane wouldn't keep going to get answers within an environment as hostile as this. He'd realize that his only option was to flee. Maybe he'd try to get back to Europe. No, it would be just as bad for him there. Much better would be for him to travel south and covertly cross the border into Mexico. Either way, there was no doubt in Ellie's mind that there was nothing more he could do to get to the bottom of Project Ferryman.

She grabbed her coat and handbag with the intention of heading to Langley, then froze.

A noise was coming from inside her bag.

She knew what it was, but simply couldn't believe she was hearing the sound.

Urgently, she thrust her hand into the bag and withdrew her cell phone.

Not the one the Agency knew about. She had switched that off because nobody called her.

Instead, the one whose number she had secreted in a box in Chinatown.

The screen showed a local landline number.

Someone dialing a wrong number?

She told herself to snap out of it and answer the damn thing.

As Charles Sheridan walked through the entrance to the Wardman Park hotel, his overriding thought was that it was going to be a pleasure putting his hands around the throat of the duplicitous bitch.

Parker had called him twenty minutes earlier, asking why he'd not responded to his SMS. Sheridan hadn't received that message; strange, though he was still struggling to come to grips with this stupid childish cell phone technology. But a good old-fashioned telephone call had cleared things up, and he'd wasted no time in getting over here so that he could haul Ellie Hallowes's ass out of the hotel and take her somewhere quiet for a chat.

• • •

Ellie couldn't believe she was hearing his voice. He sounded tired, and was speaking loudly because there was a lot of background noise. Probably he was calling from a street pay phone somewhere busy. But there was no doubting who he was.

Will Cochrane.

She tried to concentrate as he gave her precise instructions: at three this afternoon she needed to be sitting in Teaism, on Connecticut Avenue at Lafayette Park. Though she wouldn't be able to see him, Will would be watching the café and would approach at a time of his choosing. If he hadn't made the approach by four thirty, it meant he suspected she was under surveillance. If that happened, she needed to leave, and he would call her the same time tomorrow with new instructions.

Will ended the call.

Ellie stared at the phone.

Part of her felt overjoyed.

The rest of her knew Will was insane to remain in D.C.

Sheridan smiled as he rode the elevator to the sixth floor. He and Parker were in no doubt about what had happened a few days ago. Hallowes had deliberately targeted the analyst Helen Coombs because she had clearance to read the Ferryman files. Hallowes had gotten her so drunk that she couldn't make it to work the next morning, had stolen her security pass and used it while Coombs was still sleeping off her hangover, and had pretended to be her so she could read the files.

Sheridan had to admit that Hallowes had displayed incredible bravery by infiltrating one of the Agency's most sensitive archives while in disguise. But that admiration wasn't going to get in the way of what needed to be done to the traitor.

The elevator stopped at the sixth floor. Sheridan exited and walked along the corridor toward Ellie Hallowes's hotel room.

Even though she had two hours to kill before she needed to be in the vicinity of the café, Ellie was desperate to get on the road. But she knew she had to make preparations. She opened her laptop and browsed the Internet. Within seconds, she was staring at a map of the café and its surroundings. Her mind processed street names, points of interest, and routes. It was second nature to her, and within one minute she had a mental picture of the on-foot antisurveillance route she'd be taking to reach the venue. She wholly trusted Cochrane's ability to spot anyone following her, but she also owed it to him not to bring any hostiles close to him.

She deleted her browsing history, exited the Net, snapped shut the laptop, and got ready to leave.

Then she heard the loud ringing of the doorbell to her room.

And someone knocking hard on the door.

Sheridan placed his hand on his gun, deciding that when Hallowes opened the door he'd shove the barrel in her mouth and keep it there when he pushed her onto her back. He imagined the terror in her eyes, her limbs thrashing wildly but to no avail as he pinned her down, and cocking the gun's hammer in order to scare the shit out of her.

Then he'd tell her she had two choices: go calmly with him so that this delicate matter could be dealt with discreetly; or make a fuss, meaning he'd have to keep her in the room until an Agency team could arrive, inject her so that she was unconscious, and remove her body in a bag.

Ellie frowned as she walked toward the door. She had a Do Not Disturb sign hanging outside, and the maids had already cleaned the room while she'd been at breakfast. She hoped it wasn't hotel management stopping by to tell her that her work credit card had been declined again. Damn Agency accounts department had forgotten to top it up with funds a couple of days ago and it had taken her hours of cutting through bureaucratic bullshit to get it sorted out.

She opened the door.

A man stood in front of her and started talking immediately. "Ellie Hallowes. You don't know me but I know you. Name's Patrick. I'm Agency. Cochrane works for me and I'm here to help you 'cause you're in danger."

"What?"

"Immediate danger!" Patrick grabbed her arm, pulled her out of the room, kicked shut the door, and dragged her along the corridor.

"What's going on?!"

"We've got to run! Sheridan's coming for you because you read the Ferryman files." The CIA officer yanked her thin arm. "Trust me! He's on this floor. We gotta get out of here right now!"

Ellie looked over her shoulder, desperately trying to decide what to do. Trust this stranger? Was this a trap? Maybe this guy was working for Sheridan and he was tricking her so that he could lead her right to him.

But his eyes were imploring, his expression urgent.

She had to go on her gut feel.

"Okay. This way." She slung her bag over her shoulder and sprinted alongside the man, who looked like he was in his fifties but seemed to have no problem running at the speed of a man two decades younger. They were moving away from the main lobby elevator that Sheridan would most likely take to her floor and heading toward the fire stairs. As they turned the corner into another corridor, Ellie wondered what they would do if they crashed into Sheridan, but there was no one there aside from maids, who were looking at them with bemused faces. Her breathing was fast and shallow, but adrenaline kept her moving.

Into the stairwell.

Down flights of stairs.

On the third flight down, Ellie tripped and nearly fell headfirst, but Patrick grabbed her and shouted, "Keep moving!"

Thank God she was wearing pants and boots,

because otherwise she'd have snapped her neck by now.

Two more flights, taken at speed, hands grabbing rails, spinning around corners, jumping, and moving legs and feet faster than a line dancer on amphetamines. This was the lobby floor. Was this the best way to get out of the hotel?

Patrick read her thoughts. "Let's get down to basement parking!"

Fifteen seconds later they were running across the garage, this time Patrick leading the way holding his car keys. They got into his sedan and Patrick immediately engaged gears and revved so hard that the car's tires screeched in the vast basement parking lot. He thrust his prepaid parking ticket at the attendant as they reached the exit, and sped onto Connecticut Avenue NW. Glancing in his rearview mirror, he muttered, "Can't see anything unusual. You?"

Ellie fixed her eyes on the side-view mirror. After ten seconds, she said, "Nothing unusual."

Patrick inhaled deeply. "I saw Sheridan arrive almost the same time I did. He was seconds behind me when I knocked on your door."

Ellie nodded. "I'm meeting him at three this afternoon."

"Him?"

"Will Cochrane."

Patrick turned onto Calvert Street NW. "I don't want to know the location of the meeting."

"Understood."

"I'm going to drop you at a metro station. After

that, you're on your own." The CIA officer glanced at Ellie. "I'm sorry, miss, nothing else I can do to help."

"I know. Thank you for this."

"Do me a favor. When you see Cochrane, tell him from me that he's a pain in the fucking ass."

Ellie smiled. "Sure."

"Also, tell him there are people rooting for him. Admittedly, not many, though."

Ellie nodded. "I'm surprised you haven't asked me what I know about Ferryman. I didn't see anyone named Patrick on the file clearance list."

Patrick turned onto Columbia Road NW. "It won't help me to know, because there'd be absolutely nothing I could do with that information. But there is one thing I want to understand: Is Cochrane doing the right thing? For that matter, are *you* doing the right thing?"

"I believe so. I think there's something wrong with Project Ferryman."

"Then that's all I need to know." He stopped the car adjacent to the Columbia Heights metro station, leaned across Ellie, and opened her car. "Time for you to go."

She got out of the vehicle, shut the door, and started walking away.

"Ellie?"

She turned back and saw that Patrick had lowered the passenger window and was leaning toward her.

"Yes?"

"Unless Cochrane can deliver a miracle, you

know your Agency days are over for you now, don't you?"

"I do."

"Got a safe house? Someplace where you can vanish?"

"Of course."

"Then good luck to you, girl." Patrick gunned the car and sped off.

Momentarily, Ellie felt disconcerted. She had many sanctuaries, but all of them were places where she'd need to live alone. So far, she'd managed just fine with her solitary existence, but now was different because she was no longer a CIA operator working for a cause. She had no purpose beyond surviving. No, that wasn't true; not yet, anyway. She still had one true goal: to meet Will Cochrane and tell him what she'd read in the Ferryman files.

THIRTY

"Come on! Come on! Come on!" Marsha Gage was striding down a corridor toward the FBI operations room. "There's got to be a trail."

One of her senior agents was on the end of the line. "So far the trail's gone cold two blocks from Union."

"He can't have just disappeared. Somebody must have seen him escape."

"We've dried up."

"Dried up?!" Marsha made no effort to hide her exasperation. "We don't *dry up*. It's not what we do."

"Yes, Agent Gage."

"Run door-to-door again."

"We were thorough the first time, so—"

"Just do it!"

FBI officers were staring at her with looks of fear and bemusement as she entered the ops room. The place was buzzing, with officers talking fast on phones, hunched over maps of D.C., typing fast on computer keyboards, and jogging back and forth between desks, swapping data with their colleagues. But Alistair, Patrick, and Sheridan were nowhere to be seen.

Marsha placed her hands on her hips, and shouted to everyone, "Where are the spooks?"

One of the agents answered, "Haven't seen them for a couple of hours."

Jesus. She'd spent days cooped up with the three old spies, listening to them bicker like cantankerous retirees in a nursing home, and watching Alistair and Patrick do nothing more productive than flicking screwed-up bits of paper at Sheridan, who in turn would flip them the finger. Now that she actually needed them, they'd disappeared.

She called Alistair, who informed her that he and Patrick were having a lovely cup of tea at a delightful restaurant. She told him that the Bureau had plenty of tea bags, that they were to get their asses back to HQ, and that if they saw Sheridan he was needed as well. She ended the call, thinking that child care was sometimes easier than what she had to put up with here.

As she surveyed the room and all activities within it, she decided that right now she had three options open to her to catch Will Cochrane.

The first was continuing to hit the streets, pursuing every lead, and just hoping they got lucky. Though that remained an essential component of the manhunt, it was partly a reactive role, and if there was one thing Marsha hated about her job it was when it required her to sit on her butt and pray for a lucky result.

To enact the second option, she needed help from the three spies seconded to her team.

But the third option could be green-lighted right now.

"Listen up." She waited for her task force to end phone calls and stop what they were doing. When she had their undivided attention she shouted, "We need all the help we can get, and that includes help from the people of D.C. How are we going to get that?"

One of the younger members of the team put his hand up, as if he were a schoolchild about to answer his teacher's question. "We rely on their law-abiding natures."

"That doesn't mean they'll help."

Pete Duggan called out from the back of the room. "In my experience, fear, and wanting life to get back to normal with no SWAT snipers on rooftops, is usually a big incentive to help cops get fugitives off their streets."

Marsha nodded. "I'm thinking the HRT commander's assessment is a more realistic one." Her gaze darted between each member of her team. "And I'm going to throw in another incentive. It took a bit of browbeating from me to get Director Haupman to agree to this, but I got my way in the end. We're going to put a price on Cochrane's head, and I want you all to spread the word—post it on our Most Wanted list, speak to your contacts in the media, and tell our agents and every other law enforcement team who's on the streets so that they can tell citizens when they're doing door-to-door."

Duggan asked, "The price?"

Marsha smiled. "Two million dollars."

• • •

Ellie Hallowes felt like a fraud as she followed her antisurveillance route to reach the Lafayette Park café. Not that there was anything wrong with her drills. She'd chosen a starting point at the Park Hyatt Washington hotel, approximately one mile northwest of the café; had predetermined five locations along the on-foot route where she could stop without it looking suspicious for her to do so and subtly look for a second or third sighting of someone she'd seen earlier. She ended her walk with absolute certainty that there was no surveillance team on her. As important, had there been a team following her, she would have been able to abort her meeting with Cochrane without the team knowing that she knew they were there.

She'd done similar routes countless times.

But always as a fully paid-up member of the Western intelligence community.

Now, she was an outcast, and that made her feel that she had no right to act like a spy.

She wrapped her arms tightly around her chest, entered the café, and immediately realized why Will had chosen the venue. It was small and quiet, with only two other customers sitting at one of the tables. It would be a devil of a job for surveillance specialists to sit in here without being noticed.

She sat at a table at the far end of the café, her back to the wall so she could see anyone entering or exiting.

She wondered if Will was watching her now.

• • •

Marsha pointed at Alistair and Patrick as they entered the FBI ops room and gestured for them to follow her into the adjacent office. After she shut the door behind them, she asked, "Where have you been?"

Alistair smiled. "I told you on the telephone—partaking of some much-needed refreshments."

"I didn't give you permission to go off site."

"No, you didn't."

Marsha felt exasperated. "If I have to put electronic tags on you and enforce a curfew, then I'll do just that."

Alistair's eyes twinkled. "We'll take them off and break curfew, just to keep you on your toes."

Patrick said, "You know Cochrane's in D.C. and you've got every man, woman, and dog looking for him. You don't need us around right now."

Marsha folded her arms. "Right now, you're wrong. I need to persuade Sheridan to do something he'll plain and simple refuse to do, and you can help me because you know how he thinks."

She told them about the second strategy she wanted to set in place to capture Cochrane.

Alistair and Patrick glanced at each other, both suppressing the desire to smile because what Marsha was suggesting could get Sheridan off Ellie Hallowes's back.

Patrick said, "You got our help. But if I may make a suggestion, let's tweak your idea a bit."

Ellie checked her watch. Four twenty-five P.M.—only five minutes left until she'd have to follow Will's instructions, leave the café, and await a call from him tomorrow. The fact that he hadn't come also meant that there was a strong probability the café was under CIA surveillance and that she'd be grabbed the moment she stepped outside.

If that happened, all would be lost.

She muttered, "Shit," bent down to grab her purse to pay for her tea, sat upright, and let out an involuntary gasp.

Will Cochrane.

Standing right before her.

He was thinner than when she'd last seen him, though he still looked very strong.

"You got here" was all she could blurt, because she was overwhelmed with relief and emotion, but she was also overwhelmed with the knowledge that this was the moment armed men would choose to burst in and gun them down.

"I got here." He sat next to her, his back to the wall, his gaze locked on the entrance. His hand was in his jacket pocket, gripping his pistol.

Ellie too was watching the entrance.

Both operatives were tense.

"You look different. That's a good thing."

"I *feel* different." Will's expression was focused. "Mostly, I feel like shit."

"You and me both."

Will whispered, "Did you access the Ferryman files?"

She hesitated, then responded, "I did."

There was something in Ellie's tone that made Will ask, "At what cost?"

Ellie briefly glanced at him. "Sheridan knows what I did. He's looking for me."

As Charles Sheridan entered Marsha's office next to the ops room, Patrick wanted to stride up to him and punch him in the throat. Despite his age, Patrick knew that he still had the strength and skill to make the devastating blow, and he also knew that a few minutes later Sheridan would stop writhing on the floor and would be dead. Trouble was, Patrick had killed two men in precisely the same way, so none of his peers in the CIA would believe him if he claimed he'd been trying to punch Sheridan in the face but missed.

Sheridan leaned against a wall opposite Patrick, Alistair, and Marsha, who were sitting facing him. "What do you want?"

Marsha made no attempt to hide her anger. "The names of everyone who's Project Ferryman cleared."

"Go fuck yourself."

"Shut up." Marsha's eyes were unblinking and hostile. "The names?"

Sheridan's eyes narrowed. "While you're at it, why don't you ask me who really killed JFK, whether the moon landing was a fraud, the identity of the Zodiac killer, and the location of Jimmy Hoffa's corpse? You're as likely to get answers to those."

Alistair said, "I thought we were on the same side."

"Did you?" Sheridan folded his arms and said

in an over-the-top posh English accent, "Guess all you British *old boys* can't get your head around the fact that the world doesn't revolve around good manners, cups of tea, and fair play."

Alistair's blue eyes were glittering and cold, though he held back a response.

Marsha Gage said, "We need the names of the Ferryman-cleared readership for a reason."

Sheridan looked like he was going to slap her. "And I told you never to use that word again!"

"We don't—"

Sheridan unfolded his arms and took a step closer to her. "You don't know what you're talking about, *policewoman*."

"I'm not a police . . ."

"No, you're not! You didn't have the brains to make it into the Agency, so instead thought you'd play at being a cop."

His last comment genuinely shocked Marsha. She tried to think of a retort, but was lost for words.

Alistair wasn't. "Mrs. Gage has personally removed from American streets three serial killers, fourteen murderers, eight kidnappers, four extortionists, and two foreign spies. You haven't. And during that time, she has also raised two children. Oh, and I nearly forgot: she got the Stanford University School of Law's highest grade point average in twenty-seven years. Had she chosen to apply to the Agency, she would've sailed through its selection and training program."

Marsha glanced at Alistair, wondering how he got that information and why it was that his chivalry constantly caught her by surprise. "Actually, it was twenty-six years."

Alistair placed his fingertips together while keeping his cold gaze fixed on Sheridan. "During which time I know for a fact that Stanford's law exams had become progressively tougher."

Sheridan waved a hand dismissively. "I don't give a shit. She hasn't got what it takes. Too by-the-book. Too much snooping into matters that are way over little missy's head."

Patrick said with deliberation, "Little *missy* has a reason for wanting to know the Ferryman clearance list. Obviously, you know why."

Sheridan was silent.

Alistair smiled. "Please tell me that your superior intellect comprehends the purpose behind Marsha's enquiry."

Sheridan's gaze flickered between the three people in front of him, but his eyes failed to conceal his confusion.

Patrick asked in a voice that mimicked Sheridan's poor attempt at sounding British, "Come on, *old boy*, surely this isn't beyond your capabilities?"

Sheridan now looked like a schoolboy who hadn't done his homework. "I don't answer to you!"

"No, you don't!" This came from Marsha. "But you're a dead man if you don't answer my question."

"Dead?"

Marsha nodded. "Dead."

Alistair closed his eyes while keeping his fingertips pressed together. "Dead, dead, dead." He opened his eyes. "Will Cochrane will tear you and anyone else privy to Ferryman to pieces to get answers. He won't stop. You're dead. So we'd like to put you and everyone else on the Ferryman list under protective custody."

Marsha smiled. "We will put some expert Bureau heavies around you and your pals. Cochrane comes to you for answers. We get the drop on him. Simple."

Sheridan frowned. "You want to lay us out as bait?"

"Yes."

"You're crazy."

"Maybe." Marsha drummed her fingers over her leg. "But I'm told that in days, maybe even hours, you're a dead man walking."

"I can look after myself."

Patrick smiled. "Against Cochrane? Good luck with that. He'll butcher you."

Uncertainty was showing on Sheridan's face. Only one thing was more important to him than Ferryman, and that was his neck. Clearly, the three people in front of him had realized that and had pressed the one button that could make him talk. In any case, he reckoned Patrick would easily be able to access Agency databases to find out who was on the Ferryman clearance list. Sheridan wouldn't be betraying anyone or anything by answering Gage's question. "Senator Colby Jellicoe, me, Ed Parker, an analyst named Helen Coombs, the head of the Agency, the British prime minister, and the American president are cleared to know every detail about Project Ferryman. Others know what it can deliver, but the aforementioned are the only ones who know the key players in the mission."

Marsha nodded. "The premiers are obviously already taken care of, but the rest of you need to be taken out of the equation."

"Equation?"

"Away from danger. Protected."

Alistair pointed a finger at him. "Marsha's original idea was to put Project Ferryman Agency personnel under discreet surveillance. But Patrick and I thought that was far too dangerous, and Mrs. Gage has agreed with us."

However, Marsha didn't know the real reason why Patrick and Alistair had tweaked her idea—that 24-7 protective custody would stop Sheridan from hunting Ellie Hallowes.

Alistair continued. "You can come and go from here as much as you like."

Marsha smiled. "So long as you realize that you'll have armed men around you at all times."

Sheridan nodded. "I'm fine with that."

His observation made Alistair and Patrick frown.

Within the café, Will was motionless and silent as he listened to Ellie recount what she'd read in the Ferryman files.

She told him that a high-ranking Russian SVR officer called Gregori Shonin had been recruited by a CIA officer who was on a posting with his wife in Prague in 2005. Though Shonin was a fabulous asset in his own right, his true value was that he had direct access to his SVR boss, the spymaster Antaeus. Shonin's recruitment had been complex, because he was insistent to his Agency handler that he needed to pretend to Antaeus that he'd recruited an Agency officer and could obtain from that officer American secrets. The CIA officer quite rightly reported these terms to the head of the Agency, who in turn sought clearance from the Senate Select Committee on Intelligence to pass Shonin chicken-feed U.S. secrets that wouldn't damage American interests.

Shonin was given the code name Ferryman.

During the subsequent decade, Ferryman had produced invaluable intelligence, and three people in particular had their careers accelerated on the back of the project. In 2007, Ferryman had supplied the Agency with the name of an American double agent who'd been working for the USSR and subsequently Russia for years. Colby Jellicoe, then a CIA officer, expertly interrogated the traitor, got him to confess, and established every piece of intelligence he'd supplied to the Russians. Jellicoe's career subsequently escalated to director level, and thereafter he became a senator working on the SSCI. In 2009, Russia had discovered that the Americans had built a listening post underneath the political district in central Moscow. Ferryman told the Agency that Russia knew about the post and was likely to find it within forty-eight hours, at which point it would announce the discovery to the world and cause a diplomatic disaster between the two countries. CIA officer Ed Parker was immediately deployed covertly to

Russia and, at great risk, took command of the listening post team, expertly dismantled the post, and covered up all of America's tracks. In 2011, Ferryman had told the CIA that Russia had tasked an assassination squad to hunt down and kill a Russian dissident who intended to go to the press with information that could compromise Russia. The dissident was in hiding in Georgia. CIA officer Charles Sheridan volunteered to rescue him, infiltrated Georgia, located the dissident, and got the man safely out of the country while being pursued by the assassins. During his exfiltration, Sheridan debriefed the dissident and established that the man had a stolen an encrypted computer stick containing data on Russian political intentions toward its neighbors and the West. Once decrypted by the Agency, the data on the stick provided a vital tactical advantage to America on a raft of political negotiations with Russia. For his actions, Sheridan was awarded the Intelligence Star medal.

Three years ago, the CIA had learned that MI6 was planning to assassinate Antaeus. The Agency pretended to assist British Intelligence, whereas in truth it wanted to establish the minutiae of the operation so that it could forewarn Antaeus of the plot via Ferryman. It did precisely that, seconds before Will Cochrane's bomb blew up Antaeus's car. According to Ferryman, Antaeus was disfigured by the blast but survived. His wife and six-year-old daughter did not.

"What?!" Will couldn't believe what he was hearing. "They weren't . . . weren't supposed to be there. Were never there. Never traveled in the same car with him."

Ellie lowered her head. "I know. It said as much in the files. But they were in the car that night and their deaths were hushed up." She stared at him closely. "I'm sorry, Will. There's more."

"I . . ." Will felt sick and incredulous. "Six years old? Dear God. Six years . . ."

"Will."

He felt utterly disgusted with himself and racked with grief. "If I'd known they were there . . ."

"Will! We don't have much time!"

Will tried to compose himself, and nodded.

Ellie continued relaying what she'd read.

Though Ferryman's access to Antaeus's secrets had produced grade-A actionable intelligence, none of it compared to what Ferryman had recently ascertained: Antaeus knew that the terrorism financier Cobalt was holding a secret meeting with the Taliban in Afghanistan. Soon, Antaeus would know the precise date, time, and location of that meeting. This gold data prompted the leaders of Britain and the United States to call off the manhunt for Cobalt, for fear that if they continued they might force Cobalt to abort his Afghanistan meeting. Moreover, without giving details about their source, they persuaded every other Western nation hunting Cobalt to do the same. Ferryman said that Russia didn't have the stomach to attack the Cobalt meeting, given that it would be held underground and would be heavily defended. That didn't matter to America and Britain, because the States would drop a bunker buster on the meeting and kill the world's most wanted terrorist.

Ellie concluded, "Project Ferryman will blow Cobalt into pieces. And that's why you're on the run. By disobeying orders, you could have very nearly jeopardized that outcome."

Will's mind was racing. "But something's wrong with this."

Ellie nodded. "I agree."

"Herald told you about a high-ranking Russian mole . . ."

"In the Agency."

An individual who would surely know that Project Ferryman was key to eliminating Cobalt, and would have relayed that to Antaeus, who in turn would instantly know that someone very close to him was giving the Americans all of Antaeus's secrets.

"What's Antaeus's game?" Will whispered to himself.

"I keep asking myself that. Why hasn't he killed Ferryman? It wouldn't take Antaeus long to establish which member of his SVR team was the traitor working for us."

Will was deep in thought as he asked, "Do you have anything else for me?"

"Before I read the Ferryman files, I found out who's leading the manhunt for you on U.S. soil. Agent Marsha Gage, FBI. She's top of the league, is as honest as they come, and doesn't have any allegiance to the CIA." She held out a slip of paper. "That's her home address."

"Excellent." Will had reasoned that the Bureau could be useful once he'd discovered the truth about Ferryman. But he needed the Bureau to be proactively chasing him on U.S. soil, so that he could learn the identity of the person heading the FBI manhunt and make a decision as to whether that person could be trusted. That was why he'd deliberately shown himself at the Canadian border. Plus he wanted to unsettle the Russian spy in the CIA so that the mole would make a mistake and expose himself. Having Agent Gage's home address was invaluable.

Will knew they'd spent too long in one place and needed to separate. "I presume the CIA officer who was posted with his wife to Prague in 2005 and recruited Ferryman was Charles Sheridan."

Ellie shook her head. "It was Ed Parker."

"Parker?"

"He was there with his wife Catherine. Ed first met Shonin at a U.S. embassy cocktail function."

Will hadn't expected that.

Not at all.

"Did you find out where Ed Parker lives?"

Ellie handed Will a second slip of paper. "As you requested in Norway, I got the addresses of the major Project Ferryman personnel—Parker, Charles Sheridan, and Senator Jellicoe. Also, this is for an apartment I rented for you in D.C." She handed him a key and gave him the address. "I've stored the things you asked for there."

"Excellent. I got a new cell phone." As he gave her the number, Ellie programmed it into the cell phone that only Will knew about. "Call me if you need my help. But I can't promise I'll be able to get to you." He smiled as he nodded toward the exit. "I've got a fair few distractions going on."

Ellie placed the tips of her fingers against his hand. "Why did you disobey orders in Norway?"

Will looked at her fingers. "I felt . . . it was the right thing to do." He pulled out the jewelry box that Ellie had secreted in Chinatown. "Thought you might like this back."

Ellie frowned as she took it from him. She resisted the urge to shed a tear when she saw that inside was a new gold necklace. It was very similar to the one her father had given her and she'd subsequently lost. "Why . . . ?"

"Why not?"

Ellie smiled. "Why not indeed."

He stood. "Are you going to be okay?"

Ellie shrugged. "The Agency trained me too well. If I can get out of D.C., they'll never find me."

From the bottom of his heart, Will said, "I will *never* forget what you've done for me."

Ellie smiled. "Didn't just do it for you. Did it for the good ol' U.S. of A."

Will took her hand and held it. "I hope we meet again."

"You do?"

Will nodded. "I'd like that." He meant every word. Ellie was unlike any woman he'd met before, and he realized now that his feelings for her went way beyond professional admiration.

As she looked at him, Ellie now understood why her cool persona was rattled when she thought about Will. She was attracted to him, plain and simple, and her feelings were intensified by the circumstances and what they were doing. "I'll let you in on a secret: I've always loved sunshine, particularly *Mexican* sunshine."

"Mexico's a big country to find a person who's in hiding."

"Not if the person looking is someone with your skill set." She winked at him.

Just like she'd done in Norway while armed men were waiting to kill her.

"Providing I'm not in jail or dead," Will said, grinning, "consider it a date." He turned to leave, but looked back at her as a thought entered his head. "Was there any description of Gregori Shonin in the Ferryman files?"

Ellie shook her head while placing her hand inside her handbag. "No, but I was a bit of a naughty girl. I stole something I shouldn't have from the archives: Shonin's photo, taken without him knowing, in the early days after his recruitment." She handed the photo to Will.

His heart was pounding as he looked at the image. "I'm the only person in Western intelligence who knows what Antaeus's face looks like," he said. "That's one of the reasons why I was deployed to Moscow to kill him three years ago." He held the photo out to Ellie. "This isn't just a case of not understanding why Antaeus hasn't identified Ferryman and killed him. It's far worse than that. Gregori Shonin doesn't exist. Because the man in this photo is Antaeus."

"Antaeus?!" Ellie's mind was racing. "But surely Ed Parker would have realized that Antaeus and Ferryman were one and the same, when he met Ferryman after your bomb injured Antaeus, and saw that he was disfigured?"

Will agreed, and said, "I think I know what this is all about. In 2005, Parker didn't recruit a man he allegedly believed to be Gregori Shonin. Instead, Antaeus recruited Parker, who knew from the outset who he was dealing with. And that means Herald was right when he told you in Norway that there was a Russian spy at the Agency's top table." He looked away toward the exit while feeling overwhelming anger. "Ed Parker is being run by Antaeus, who's using him to feed us information that will lead to the death of Cobalt. Ed Parker is the mole. And his code name is Ferryman."

"The Russians hate terrorists like Cobalt just as much as we do," Ellie said. "Maybe he's using us because he knows that we're the only ones who can kill Cobalt."

"Maybe." Will was frowning. "But Antaeus wouldn't run an operation this elaborate and dangerous to help America. His career has been built around his primary objective to cripple the States." A thought suddenly entered his head, and his eyes widened.

"Will?"

Will was silent.

"What is it?"

Will shook his head in disbelief as he muttered to himself, "Clever, clever Antaeus."

"I don't understand."

Will looked directly at Ellie. "If I'm right about what's really going on, when the United States of America drops its bomb on Cobalt, what will follow will be nothing short of a disaster."

THIRTY-ONE

The Washington Marriott Wardman Park hotel lobby was buzzing with suited delegates who were attending an advertising conference. Ellie was glad the place was so busy; it meant she could get her things from her room, check out, and leave the place without being noticed.

Then she'd head to Mexico and wait for Will to find her.

She smiled as she walked along the sixth-floor corridor, swiped her key card through her room's lock, and entered the room.

She switched on the light and froze.

A man was sitting in the armchair, staring at her with a smile on his face.

She was about to run, but someone else behind her thrust a thick plastic bag over her head, pulled the bag's drawstrings tight around her throat, and locked her arms in a viselike grip.

She tried to gasp for oxygen inside the airtight bag. She thrashed her legs, but whoever was holding her was too strong and knew exactly what he was doing.

Something else was in the bag.

Cotton wool swabs.

They gave off a toxic odor.

One that made her light-headed.

Of course: a chemical compound that renders humans unconscious when inhaled.

Her legs felt incredibly heavy.

As she lost consciousness, her last thought was that thank goodness she'd met Will when she did.

Augustus looked at Elijah and grinned. "She's out for the count." Like his twin brother, he was wearing a smart suit and had his straight, shoulder-length black hair tied in a ponytail. Anyone looking at them as they'd entered the hotel earlier would no doubt have surmised that they were arty ad exec types.

Elijah got out of the seat and helped Augustus lift Ellie into a straight-backed desk chair and tie her to it with a rope. Then Augustus pulled out a military knife.

At 7:10 P.M., Ed Parker opened his refrigerator door with the intention of pouring himself a large glass of Chablis, but stopped when Catherine came rushing into the room, a look of deep concern on her face.

"Ed, there's four men at the door. They're FBI."

"FBI?" Ed's heart started racing.

"They've asked to speak to you. Said it was serious." She gripped his arm.

Ed's thoughts were in turmoil.

Because when Feds turned up at a spook's home and said they wanted to speak about something serious, it usually had one outcome.

Arrest.

And a life sentence in a maximum-security prison.

"Jesus." Ed's mind was racing.

Catherine frowned. "Have you done something wrong?"

Ed couldn't answer.

"Is this about Project Ferryman?"

Ed rubbed his hand over his face. "I don't know, can't be sure, I . . ."

Catherine gripped him harder. "Ferryman is an Agency matter; the Bureau has no jurisdiction over it, and therefore no jurisdiction over your involvement. You've done nothing wrong and don't need to tell them anything. Hold firm to that fact."

She released her grip.

Ed nodded, inhaling deeply. He wished Catherine was right, but knew that the Bureau could stick its nose wherever it liked if it got the faintest whiff of treachery or corruption or worse. He grabbed a dish towel, used it to mop the sweat off his face, and allowed Catherine to tighten the knot on his tie and use her fingers to straighten his hair. "Where's Crystal?"

"In her room, doing her homework."

"Don't let her come downstairs," he said. He walked to the front door. The four men were all wearing blue FBI Windbreakers and baseball caps.

One of them said, "Mr. Parker?"

Ed nodded, his heart in his throat and his stomach in knots.

"We've been sent to speak to you." He showed

him his ID. "Seems you've been involved in something that's going to get you in trouble."

Ed tried to decide what to say. With no forethought, he blurted, "Trouble is, I don't know what the trouble is."

The agents laughed.

Probably to put him at ease and display the bizarre camaraderie that can sometimes be on show between an arresting officer and the perp he wants to put cuffs on.

"We won't hold that against you." The agent pointed at a black sedan that was parked across the street.

No doubt it was a Bureau car, the one they were going to take him away in.

The FBI officer said, "You're going to see that day and night. Two of us will be in it at all times. We'll work in twelve-hour shifts." The agent smiled. "It's just a precaution, but apparently you and a handful of other Agency folk need to be protected while Will Cochrane's still loose. We'll be following you to and from work, and when you're home we'll be sitting in our car outside, drinking coffee and watching over you. All we ask in return is that you stick to speed limits when driving and call us if you see anything suspicious."

"Suspicious?"

"A man coming to kill you."

Ed didn't know if he felt total relief or abject fear. "Sure, sure. You want me to alert Agency security that you'll be parked outside Langley while I'm at work?"

"That's already taken care of."

Ed glanced back toward his house. "Should we temporarily move someplace else? How serious is this threat?"

The agent patted his jacket. "Mr. Parker, we got enough armaments on us and in our vehicle to take down a gang of professional bank robbers, let alone a single guy. Plus, we got direct lines to D.C. SWAT and their helos. You're going to be fine. Unless you need us, pretend we're not here." He nodded toward the interior of Ed's home. "And please tell Mrs. Parker that we apologize if our presence at your home made her worry."

"Seems to me that we're in good hands." Ed checked his watch. "I got to make some calls, and"—he smiled—"pour myself a large drink."

Lindsay Sheridan poured brandy into two glasses and placed them on a side table between her husband and Senator Jellicoe, in front of the sumptuous living room's roaring fire. "Is there anything else that you need from me, Charles?"

Charles Sheridan glanced at her with an expression of contempt. "No. Just don't disturb us, okay? And if I hear that damn kitchen TV from in here, I'll smash it on the floor."

Lindsay smiled at Jellicoe to hide her embarrassment at Charles's comment and to put the senator at ease. Not that Jellicoe seemed to care one hoot. He seemed as irritated with Lindsay's presence in the room as her husband was.

She said timidly, "I'll stay out of your way," and left the room while wishing she had the courage to lock its door behind her and set fire to the place.

Sheridan swirled his brandy. "My boys have got Hallowes."

Jellicoe smiled. "Good."

"You sure I have your unconditional backing to do this?"

Jellicoe placed a chubby finger into his liquor and sucked on it like a child with a Popsicle. He glanced toward the window. Outside were two vehicles containing their newly acquired FBI protection detail. "So long as you keep matters discreet, I don't care what you have to do to her to make her talk."

Antaeus was sitting in his study making the final amendments to his thesis on Stone Age settlements in western Russia. He was extremely pleased with the way he'd pulled his research together to form a document that would poleax Russian archaeological societies' received wisdom that people back then were solely nomadic. But he had two other reasons for feeling happy.

Parker had just told him that Sheridan's men had captured Hallowes and would use her to flush out Cochrane.

In return, Antaeus had told Parker that he'd just learned that Cobalt would be attending the meeting with the Taliban at noon the day after tomorrow. He'd given the CIA agent the precise location in Afghanistan, and Parker had told him America would now spring into action and ensure that everyone at the meeting was killed.

He couldn't predict whether total war and

genocide would follow the air strike. But he did know one thing for certain.

The United States of America would have its head separated from its body.

The two men were sitting in front of Ellie with grins on their faces. After she fully regained consciousness, she wanted to tell them that if they wanted to kill her they should get it over with. But she couldn't speak, because a leather strap was tightly wrapped around her mouth and her head, in place to secure the sock that was screwed into a ball inside her mouth in order to prevent anyone standing outside her hotel room from hearing her screams.

Though her heart was pounding, Ellie refused to let fear take hold.

The men were obviously twins, and she estimated they were in their fifties. They were quite small, and if she'd seen them anywhere else but here and under different circumstances she would have assessed that they looked a bit unconventional, but otherwise perfectly harmless.

With two exceptions.

Their eyes were glistening, agitated, and excited.

And their smiles were just plain wrong.

They were the smiles you see on sadists, rapists, and mad-dog killers.

Both of them were holding big military knives that looked razor sharp; their jet-black hair was now out of ponytails and hung straight down to their shoulders.

"My name's Augustus." The twin nodded toward his brother. "And this is Elijah. We'd tell you not to be scared, but that would be a dumb thing to say given your predicament." He laughed, then his expression changed. "We take the sock out when we need you to speak. We put it back in when we want a bit of peace and quiet. You get that?"

Ellie nodded.

"At any point, if you call for help or make any kind of noise to attract anyone, punishment will be instant and severe. You get that as well?"

Ellie tried to speak, but all she could emit was a barely audible muffled sound.

"Get it?"

Ellie nodded quickly.

"That's my pretty little gal."

Elijah moved to her side; his smell reminded her of a dirty zoo.

Augustus tapped the tip of his knife over Ellie's two cell phones, which were lying on the bed by his side. "We think you've got a way to get in touch with Cochrane, and that way is inside one of these two phones." He nodded at Elijah, who undid the strap and pulled out the sock. "Which phone is it?"

When she spoke, drool ran down her chin. "Don't know what you're talking about."

Augustus smiled and said, while tapping his blade over each phone in quick succession, "Eeny, meeny, miny, moe." He stared at Ellie.

She said nothing.

Elijah shoved the sock ball back into Ellie's

mouth as Augustus chanted, "Catch a tiger by the toe."

Elijah whipped Ellie's right shoe off her foot and used his knife to slice off her big toe.

Ellie's back arched as agony seared from her foot to her central nervous system. The ropes kept her fixed to the chair, which Elijah was now gripping with tensile steel strength. Her head was shaking wildly as unbelievable pain made her retch.

As the pain receded to a fearsome but barely tolerable ache, the sock was removed from her mouth.

Augustus grinned. "Catch a tiger by the toe. If he hollers, let him go. Unless we wish him to suffer so." His eyes intensified. "This phone has only got one number programmed into it. I'm thinking that makes it a special phone. Am I right?"

Ellie spat, "Screw you!"

Elijah shoved the sock back into her mouth.

Ellie braced herself.

Elijah placed his knife by her injured foot and touched her four remaining toes while saying, "This little piggy went to market, this little piggy stayed home, this little piggy had roast beef, this little piggy had *none*." He sliced her little toe off and held it in front of her face so that blood dripped from it onto her lap.

Elijah stepped away and pulled out the sock.

Ellie said between gritted teeth, "You're wasting your time."

This made the twins laugh hysterically.

"So, let's try again." Augustus tapped one of her cells. "Is this the number Cochrane's got?"

Ellie tried to decide what to do. She was certain she could withstand a lot more torture without breaking. She was also sure the men wouldn't leave the room until they'd gotten the answers they sought. They'd keep torturing her until she was dead. Her best option was to maintain the upper hand by manipulating them into believing that she couldn't take anymore, and giving them half truths and half lies that would help her and Cochrane.

Though she felt nothing but focus and anger, she had to act like she was scared.

It could well be her last curtain call.

She lowered her head to look resigned, and whispered, "Yes. It's the number Cochrane has."

Augustus clapped. "That's my girl!" He tossed the phone to Elijah, while keeping his eyes on Ellie. "You're going to call him and say you want to meet with him tomorrow—ten fifteen A.M. outside the Friendship Heights metro on Wisconsin Avenue. Don't use any odd words, make yourself sound weird, tell him what's really happening, or hang up midsentence. By all means sound scared, to make him concerned, but if you say or do anything to make him think you're not making the call on your own, then today won't be your best."

Elijah placed the tip of his knife a millimeter away from Ellie's eyeball, and held the palm of his other hand inches away from the blade's hilt, ready to thrust it deep into her socket.

She rang Will's number.

It went straight to voice mail, which didn't

surprise her because Will would be preserving his cell's battery life for as long as possible, and no doubt would be turning it on later to check for messages.

She spoke for twenty-three seconds while Elijah craned his neck next to her so that he could hear if anything was being spoken back on the other end of the line.

Elijah stuck his thumb up. "All good. We're done."

Augustus stood. "We are, indeed."

Ellie closed her eyes after she saw Augustus moving across the room toward her, because his visage was the last thing she wanted to see right now. She knew what was coming.

She wasn't scared, because she'd lived her whole adult life expecting a moment like this.

But she did regret that she'd never have the chance to sit in a Mexican beach bar, watch the warm sea ebb and flow while she drank a bottle of beer, feel a man's hand on hers, maybe Will Cochrane's.

That would have been nice.

When Augustus's knife entered Ellie's stomach, of course she felt absolute pain.

But as the blade sliced upward, she kept her eyes shut and held on to the image.

She imagined holding Will's hand as they walked from the bar, along a white sandy beach, as if she were already in heaven.

It was her picture.

No one could take it away from her.

Certainly not the repulsive scum who were with her now.

And as the visceral savagery took her life away, she felt relief that the twins hadn't noticed that her message to Will contained two words that would hopefully warn him off.

THIRTY-TWO

It was the last two words in Ellie's voice message that made Will's stomach knot and his mind swirl.

Good-bye, William.

She'd never called him William, meaning she'd given him a signal to let him know all was not well. And the tone of her voice was not one that was simply signing off a call. Instead, she sounded like she was saying her final farewell to him. He was in no doubt that her request to meet at the Friendship Heights metro in the morning was one that was made under extreme duress, meaning Sheridan or men working for him had caught her. But that wasn't why Will felt so much despair. It was the fact that she'd said good-bye that made him fear the worst about her safety and future.

He turned off his cell, feeling ashamed of himself for involving Ellie in his quest for the truth.

No—*shame* wasn't the right word for how he felt about himself.

Revulsion and *abject guilt* were better words.

If it turned out that anything had happened to Ellie, he knew how he'd react.

Utter sorrow and self-loathing would be inevitable.

So too would be the death his hands would deliver to anyone involved in hurting Ellie.

He sucked in oxygen to focus his thoughts and stared at Marsha Gage's house on Colorado Avenue. It was nearly nine P.M., and yet it didn't surprise him that her car wasn't parked outside her house. She was leading the FBI's most significant manhunt in decades and would be working as close to 24-7 as possible. But he hoped that she'd be home at some point soon, if nothing else than to grab a quick shower and a change of clothes. That's when he'd speak to her. Face-to-face. A gun pointed at her skull if the situation warranted.

When Ed Parker finished the call with Charles Sheridan, he shook his head and began sobbing.

Catherine entered the living room, frowned as she looked at her husband, switched off the TV, and placed a hand over his forearm. "What's happened?"

Ed looked at her, his face flushed red, eyes wet and streaming, bottom lip quivering. "We've gone . . . gone . . . gone too far. Much too far."

Catherine tried not to cry because her husband was so emotional, but she felt her eyes welling up. "Too far?"

Ed nodded. "Ellie Hallowes. Sheridan's men got to her. But . . . but . . ."

"But?"

Ed blurted, "They were only supposed to get her to flush out Cochrane. End there. Not do anything else, apart from keeping her quiet until after

Cochrane was caught. But Augustus and Elijah couldn't stop. Wouldn't."

Catherine felt disbelief. "They killed her?"

Ed rubbed his moist eyes. "Slaughtered."

"What . . . Jesus . . . what does Sheridan think of that?"

"He doesn't care. It's what he wanted."

"Dear God!"

"Sheridan doesn't care about God." Ed placed his head in his hands. "But he acts like him. At least, acts like His disciple. Jellicoe's the one who pulls all the strings. Jeez, what have we done?"

Catherine placed her arm around her husband. She loved him and hated seeing him like this. She'd always loved Ed, even though a decade before she'd been unfaithful to him while they were in Prague—not just once, but twice. Things had been bad between them at that time. But since then she'd gotten her thinking straight and had cherished what Ed had given her. Poor Lindsay Sheridan had also snuck into another guy's bed at around the same time, but her reasons for doing so were wholly different, and Lindsay never suspected that Catherine had been less the perfect wife and more like her than she knew. "As far as I can work out, what you've done has been for your country and your family."

Ed pulled out his cell phone while muttering, "I wish I could turn back the clock."

Catherine pulled his head against her chest. "You want me to leave you alone?"

Ed held onto his wife, still crying. "Just need to make a call. After that, stay with me. Please."

• • •

Antaeus gently lifted the chameleon out of the tank. Parker's call had offended his sensibilities and dignity.

Ellie Hallowes was dead.

Killed by Charles Sheridan's goons.

That was unacceptable.

Wrong.

After this was over, he hoped Sheridan and Jellicoe would be forced to face up to their maker. They didn't work for Antaeus, knew nothing about the truth behind Project Ferryman, were mere callous and ignorant foot soldiers in Antaeus's grand scheme, and were self-serving swine who relished inflicting misery on others.

He kissed the reptile on its back. To him, the chameleon had come to represent Ellie. He stared through his study's window at the starlit night sky. "My daughter's name was Anna. She'd be nine by now if she hadn't been killed by the man who saved you in Norway." A tear ran down the disfigured side of his face as he said, "Retribution is an intractable merry-go-round of inevitable pain." He returned his attention to the chameleon while feeling deeply sad. "Tomorrow, my beauty, I promise you I'll get you a much bigger tank, one that will give you lots of room to explore. It'll make you feel free."

Will walked across the street toward Marsha Gage's house, with the intention of secreting himself in a place where he could get to her quickly once she pulled up in her car and got out. He was midway across the street when he heard a vehicle driving at speed toward him.

Marsha Gage?

Other law enforcement officers who wanted to apprehend him?

Shots were fired from the vehicle.

No, these were people who wanted him dead.

He dived to the ground, rolled, and pulled out his handgun. The car was eighty yards away, its headlights off despite the road being in near darkness. But the streetlamps gave him just enough light to see that there were two men in the car: one driving, one shooting.

Shackleton and Amundsen.

Two exceptional assassins.

Not that Will knew who they were.

Or what they were capable of.

He fired at the windshield, but the car swerved and his bullets went wide of their mark. Whoever was driving was clearly an expert. He maintained traction and increased speed as he got the car back into position so that it was hurtling toward Will.

Will was about to fire again, but the headlights were now turned on, blinding him. The vehicle screeched to a halt as Will sprinted left to get behind the cover of a stationary car. Around him he heard dogs barking and doors opening and slamming shut as people came out to see what was causing the noise before fleeing back into their homes as they realized the commotion was a head-to-head gun battle. He pointed his pistol at the car, trying to adjust his vision so that he could catch any signs of movement. Nothing. He fired a couple of warning shots, with no idea if they'd hit the assailants, and broke cover, his only chance being to flank the car and get away from its dazzling headlights.

Running over a front lawn in near darkness with his eyesight still temporarily diminished, he crashed into someone large. Both men fell away from each other but quickly got to their feet. The man opposite Will had a handgun and was raising it to shoot Will in the head. He was one of the assailants. Will was a fraction of a second quicker, shot him in the leg, dashed forward, grabbed him, spun him around, kicked the man's gun away after he dropped it, and placed the muzzle of his pistol under the man's chin.

He could have just as easily killed him, but needed him alive to act as a human shield against the second assailant, who was now walking fast toward him with his handgun held in both hands at eye level.

Will backed away, gripping his captive with all his strength, dragging him because the injured hostile's leg was completely useless, ignoring his moans of pain as he kept his eyes fixed on the encroaching killer. "I'll shoot him again if you come any closer!"

"Will you now?" The man was under a lamppost, his face fully visible. "That would be a shame."

Irish accent.

Who the hell were these guys?

Will moved faster. "Back off!"

"We've not come all this way to back off from anything."

The moment the Irishman had said the words,

Will knew in an instant what the assailant was going to do. He released his grip on his captive and dived right just as three rounds sliced through the captive's chest and exited his back. Had he remained standing behind him, Will would now be dead.

He was dealing with men who'd shoot through each other to kill him.

Jumping to his feet, he sprinted away, zigzagging as rounds raced through the air, narrowly missing him. Once on the other side of the road, he threw himself behind a low wall and trained his weapon back across the street to where he'd last seen his pursuer.

His eyes were back to normal; he could see everything.

Police sirens were loud at one end of the street. Will frantically glanced in that direction and saw three cop cars, then four. He glanced back and saw the Irishman drag his dead colleague into his car, get into the driver's seat, and accelerate away.

The act was incredibly brave, because it wasted valuable seconds of his getaway. It was also the professional thing to do—remove as much compromising material as possible from the scene of a fight, including dead colleagues.

But the cop cars now stood a very good chance of catching up with the Irishman.

Will couldn't let that happen.

He strode out into the middle of the street and barked, "Get back inside!" as Marsha Gage's husband opened his front door.

Will stood stock-still as he fired controlled shots at the cop cars.

Some of his rounds hit tires; others engine blocks. All of the vehicles swerved out of control, hitting white picket fences and each other before shuddering to a halt. The cops got out of their damaged cars, but they were too far away to pose a threat to Will.

He turned and ran from them.

The Irishman's car was now out of sight.

As Will escaped into the night, he knew there'd be at least another two men in the team he'd confronted tonight. They were watching Gage with the hope that her efforts would lead them to Will. Two on surveillance; two off. That's how it worked. And that meant there were three killers still out there who were not only highly trained, but also utterly ruthless. Will doubted he'd be able to take on all three of them. Together, they'd be too good. He stood no chance of speaking to Marsha Gage while they were watching her; the odds of him confronting Ed Parker were now ridiculous; and the probability that he would survive the next day was near zero.

Probably the men who'd attacked him tonight belonged to Antaeus and were his insurance that Will was killed even if the FBI failed to get him.

Either way, there was no doubt in Will's mind that they were hired assassins.

Antaeus and Ferryman had won.

Will had lost.

Unless he could pull off what he was planning.

A piece of utter madness.

Colorado Avenue was in chaos as Marsha drove home. Cop cars were everywhere, their lights flashing; police officers were on foot, moving back and forth between the numerous residents who were standing outside their homes wearing coats, blankets, or nightgowns.

An officer banged his flashlight on the bonnet of her car and shouted, "Ma'am—stop!"

She did what he told her to do and lowered her window. "What's happened?"

"You can't drive along here." The officer looked young, and the tone of his voice was both aggressive and nervous. "There's been an incident."

"Incident?" Marsha looked toward her home, feeling panic. "Is anyone hurt?"

"That's none of your concern."

Marsha turned off her engine and got out of her car. The officer shouted, "Ma'am, get back in your vehicle!"

Marsha looked up and down the road.

"Ma'am!" The officer had his hand on his holster and looked completely unsure what to do.

She saw her husband emerge from their home, and called out to him, "Paul! The kids?"

Paul held a hand over his eyes and squinted in her direction. "Marsha. Thank God! They're fine. No one's hurt."

The cop repeated, "Ma'am. Get back in your vehicle."

Marsha spun to face him and pulled out her ID. "My name's Agent Marsha Gage, Federal Bureau of Investigation. I live on this street and have more right to be here tonight than anyone in uniform."

The cop looked terrified.

By contrast, Marsha was furious. "Whoever's

the highest-ranking officer here had better tell me what the fuck's happened outside *my* home!"

Will entered the tiny apartment in the outskirts of D.C., smelled must as he turned on the light, and felt sorrow that the person who'd been here before him was Ellie Hallowes. A tear ran down his face as he saw that she'd made up the single bed and had placed some granola energy bars and a can of Coca-Cola on its sheets.

He moved to the sole window in the place and heard police sirens and helicopters all around the city. They wanted him. Needed his head.

On the center of the bed was a plastic bag. He tore it open and emptied the contents onto the floor. Some of the items that Ellie had procured during the last three weeks of her being in D.C. were not needed. Others were most certainly what he required for tomorrow.

Goodness knows how Ellie had gotten them.

He looked at the bed and wondered if Ellie had lain in it.

He lay down on top of the sheets and held the can of cola over his chest as he closed his eyes and thought about drifting through the sky above Norway's northern archipelago.

The image faded and was replaced by a long and bustling shopping thoroughfare.

Wisconsin Avenue.

Would Ellie be there at ten fifteen tomorrow morning?

He'd be crazy to find out.

THIRTY-THREE

The following morning, Major Dickie Mountjoy placed his handcrafted replica of the *Cutty Sark* on Kensington Palace's Round Pond and smiled as he watched a cold breeze catch its sails and glide it across the water. It had taken him nearly a year to construct the hull, cut and stitch the sails, and create figurines that represented the real sailors who'd manned the tea clipper as it took provisions to the colonies in record-breaking times, before the advent of the Suez Canal made routes shorter and the invention of steamships made the likes of the *Sark* obsolete.

His smile faded as he saw it moving gracefully across the pond.

He'd first sailed this ship in the 1960s and had continued to do so every year thereafter, even when Mrs. Mountjoy was alive and felt he was living in the past.

But this time was different. He couldn't help thinking that Cochrane was captaining his own *Cutty Sark*. One last voyage across oceans. A desperate swan song.

He sat on a park bench next to Phoebe and David. They were holding hands, and that was a good thing as far as Dickie was concerned. Phoebe needed David to bring her down from the exuberant excesses of London life. Plus, he embalmed bodies for a living, which meant he knew too well where excess could lead. By contrast, David needed Phoebe's irreverence, heart, and warm thighs to make him understand that death was the end of matters rather than the beginning.

Dickie thought about his own inevitable death and wished he could perpetuate his soldierly bravado to convince himself that it didn't matter.

Cling onto a moment that stuck two fingers up to death and captured all that was final about life.

He imagined how that might look.

Him wearing an immaculate British army officer's uniform.

A cigarette in his mouth.

Inhaled deeply and with panache and machismo.

A wink at his terrified young soldiers who were about to follow him over the top at Passchendaele or the Somme, charge behind him through the woods at the Bulge, follow him into battle against incensed Mau Mau warriors in the jungles of Kenya, or watch him with disbelief as he singlehandedly destroyed an Argentine machine gun nest at Goose Green during the Falklands War before he was put on his ass by two nine-millimeter rounds.

The last action was a real personal memory; the ones before it belonged to other men he didn't know.

But they all shared the same human spirit.

Now he was an old man, no longer invincible; not the chap who had endless spunk and charm and strength.

He looked at Phoebe and smiled.

She was a good girl. Admittedly, she needed to stop wearing skimpy outfits all the time. But that was just a woman thing that had no depth beyond showing that she had the interests of mankind at heart. He started coughing uncontrollably. Blood sprayed over his chin.

"Dickie!" Phoebe placed her hand around the major's head while dabbing his face with her favorite chiffon scarf.

Dickie held a hand up while trying to control his cough and stop more flecks of blood from coming out of his mouth. "It's okay. Okay."

David looked shocked. "It's not okay!"

Dickie wagged a finger, suppressing the urge to cough again, and smiled. "Rule of thumb—two pints 'o the red stuff minimum before a soldier starts feeling light-headed and needs a transfusion. Anything less is codswallop." He gently stroked Phoebe's face while maintaining his smile. "Girls do it every month and don't bleat like cowardly Argies who've been caught out by Guardsmen on Mount Tumbledown."

David now looked horrified. "You can't talk about women like . . ."

"It's a fact of life for them and it's a fact of life for me!" Dickie watched his *Cutty Sark* hit the pond's perimeter and stay there as if it had been roped to a wharf. "No one cares when you bleed. It's what happens after that can sometimes make others get all sensitive and scared, and . . ."

"We care." Phoebe squeezed Dickie's hand while looking at him with eyes that the major reckoned were better than the Koh-i-Noor diamond he'd seen while recuperating from war by helping to guard the crown jewels in the Tower of London. "Very much."

"I'm not letting you take me to a doctor. Cochrane will do that when he gets back. He understands death, and I need a man like that by my side if a quack tells me I'm on the way out."

David slapped his legs with frustration. "You're a bloody fool. Haven't you seen the news? Pigs will learn to fly before Will escapes Washington, D.C., alive."

Dickie stood awkwardly while grimacing, composed himself, and marched as best he could alongside the pond. His back ached as he bent down to collect his boat, though he kept his expression stoic and dignified. Upon his return, he held the *Sark* in two hands diagonally across his chest, like a rifle belonging to a soldier on guard duty, and said to David, "He'll come back."

At 6:20 A.M., Marsha entered the FBI ops room. The place was at full capacity. It didn't surprise her that Pete Duggan, his HRT colleagues, and all Marsha's analysts were here, but she was shocked to see that every agent who was supposed to be hitting the streets was also in the room. Most of them were huddled over maps of D.C. "What's going on?"

One of the analysts pointed at Charles Sheridan. "You better ask him."

Marsha made no effort to hide the hostility on her face. "Charles?"

Sheridan grinned as he looked up from a map. "Hey, Marsha Gage has decided to join the party."

She repeated, "What's going on?"

Sheridan's grin widened. "I decided to demote myself while you were away, and take over your job. And you know what, turns out your job's a walk in the park. I've achieved more in the last few hours than you've done in weeks."

No way was Marsha going to let him speak to her like that in front of her team. "You pick up your prescription pills yet?"

"What?"

"The Bureau health center keeps calling me to remind you."

"My prescription?"

"Your Viagra pills. Come on, Charles, you mustn't forget to start taking them, because I know your wife's desperate for something to finally start moving down there." She nodded toward his crotch.

Sheridan looked furious as he walked fast toward her.

So furious that Marsha placed a hand on her sidearm.

But Pete Duggan stepped into Sheridan's path. "You take one more step toward Agent Gage, and you'll have other reasons for needing to visit the health center."

Marsha came to his side. "It's all right, Pete. I

can handle this." Everyone in the room was looking at her, and you could hear a pin drop. She raised her voice as she stared at the task force. "If anyone in this room *ever* takes orders from a CIA officer again, you'll not only be off my team; I'll make sure you spend the rest of your careers working as a night-duty security guard, patrolling the outside of the J. Edgar building. Now, back to work!" Her eyes locked on Sheridan. "Precisely what have you achieved in my absence?"

Sheridan composed himself. "I got me a source, and that source has told me that Cochrane's going to be outside the Friendship Heights metro on Wisconsin Avenue at ten fifteen this morning."

"A source?" She frowned. "How would a source be able to predict Cochrane's exact location?"

"That's none of your darn business."

Marsha's eyes narrowed. "Maybe that source is an intelligence operative. A friend of Cochrane's. Someone who's met him and given him important information. An individual who you've suspected and have put the thumbscrews on to flush him out."

Sheridan smiled, though said nothing.

Patrick and Alistair moved to Marsha's side, having overheard the conversation.

Patrick said between gritted teeth, "And maybe that person is a she."

Sheridan's eyes twinkled.

Alistair asked, "What have you done to her?"

Sheridan folded his arms. "The traitor's been taken care of. That's all that matters."

Marsha darted a look at Alistair and Patrick. "You know who she is?"

They answered in unison, "Yes."

"American citizen?"

They nodded.

Marsha pointed at Sheridan. "The CIA has no authority to act on U.S. soil. If I find out you've broken the law, it'll be my pleasure to personally put cuffs on you."

"You're out of your depth, girlie." Sheridan was grinning again. "Your laws don't apply to me. Never have and never will. Anyway, my actions have been fully supported by Senator Jellicoe."

Alistair took a step closer to Sheridan and said, "Her name's Ellie Hallowes. What have you done to her?"

Sheridan laughed. "You think I'm going to answer that question truthfully while standing in the headquarters of the FBI?"

Marsha looked at Alistair and Patrick. "You know where Hallowes lives?"

Patrick answered, "She's staying at the Washington Marriott Wardman Park hotel. I'll get hotel security on the line." He moved to his desk, browsed the Internet to get the hotel switchboard, and made the call. Everyone else in the ops room was silent. Six minutes later, he replaced the handset, walked fast across the room, and grabbed Sheridan by the throat. "You bastard!"

Marsha frowned. "What's happened?"

Sheridan tried to break Patrick's hold.

But Patrick held firm. "Hotel's checked her room. Found her dead body in there. Of the four hotel staff who entered the room while I stayed on the line, two of them fainted when they saw what had been done to her." He tightened his grip on Sheridan.

Marsha placed a hand over Patrick's arm. "Let me take over from here. Please."

Patrick was motionless for ten seconds, then released his grip and stepped away while keeping his venomous gaze on Sheridan. "I'll make you pay for this, Sheridan!"

Sheridan rubbed his throat, composed himself, and smiled. "For what? I've done nothing wrong."

"Liar!"

Marsha said, "We'll do a forensic analysis of her hotel room. Your DNA . . ."

"My DNA ain't anywhere near that room, so go ahead and do what you have to." Sheridan took a step closer to Marsha. "Do what you want."

Marsha was in no doubt that Sheridan had covered his back by getting someone else to kill Ellie. She recalled Alistair once advising her that she should keep her powder dry for a time when it could best be used against the CIA officer. Now was that time. She smiled. "Great work, Charles. Thanks to you, sounds like we're going to have this manhunt wrapped up this morning. Of course, we'll need all the manpower we can get." She pulled out her cell phone. "Manpower that includes the agents I put on your protection detail. You don't need them anymore because in a few hours Cochrane's going to be behind bars or dead." She pretended to look quizzical. "Thing is though—Cochrane paid my home a visit last night. My husband positively identified him. I wonder how he got the location of my house."

She shrugged. "Guess it must have come from the source you tortured. I suppose Hallowes also gave Cochrane your address and the addresses of anyone else involved in the mysterious Project Ferryman. And since she took such risks to help Cochrane, I'm betting he's seriously loyal to her and would be severely pissed with anyone who's hurt her."

As she rang Sheridan's Bureau protectors, her smile broadened. "There's a lot riding on this morning. But if it doesn't come off, best you put a gun to your head before Cochrane gets to you."

Sheridan's face paled.

THIRTY-FOUR

Most of the spaces in the parking lot at 1403 Wisconsin Avenue NW were taken, but only one of them contained a nondescript sedan occupied by assassins.

Oates and Shackleton were munching on sandwiches, killing time.

Speaking with his mouth full, Oates said, "I think you should be the one to dig Amundsen's grave."

"It's quicker if we all do it."

The Londoner said, "Yeah, but you shot him. Me and Scott reckon you might be in danger of getting post-traumatic stress disorder or something, that giving Norwegie a decent burial might help stop the trauma. And no one wants an Irishman with trauma; you have enough crazy shit going on in your brains already."

"I don't have PTSD!"

"That's the trouble with trauma. Doesn't always show itself for a while. Festers inside you like a parasite feeding off your organs. You only know it's there when it grows bigger."

Shackleton was annoyed. "After this morning, we drive to a forest, remove Amundsen from the trunk, and dig a hole for him together."

Oates took another bite of his food. "You thought about words?"

"Words?"

"Got to pay your respects at the graveside. Say something nice about him. Maybe throw in a tiny bit of humor, or an anecdote, just to make him sound human and put a brief smile on the mourners' faces."

"There's only going to be three of us there, and we're hardly mourners."

"Maybe you should sing a hymn."

"Now you're really starting to fuck me off!"

Oates laughed to himself as Scott opened the rear door and got into the backseat.

Scott leaned forward. "You save me any of the sarnies?"

Oates replied, "Sorry. Shackleton ate them all. He needs a lot of comfort food 'cause he's feeling a bit down."

"No I'm cocking not."

Scott slumped back into the seat. "Well, you're both a bunch of cunts." He beamed and held out a BLT baguette. "I spotted a nice little deli up the road. Just as well I didn't get you greedy bastards anything while I was there."

Oates asked, "Anything else you spot of interest?"

Scott ripped a chunk of the baguette off with his teeth. "They got uniform foot patrols on the ground, but nothing out of the ordinary that'll spook Cochrane. Plus, there's a shitload of interceptor squad cars and uniform cops hidden up in four of the parking lots at the bottom of Wisconsin. But they're backup. The juicy stuff's already in situ. Three SWAT sniper units on rooftops overlooking the avenue, eight guys milling around the metro—plainclothes, and I reckon they're HRT."

"Means they probably got body armor under their jackets."

"That's what I'm thinking. All of them are carrying small packsacks."

"Submachine guns inside."

"Yeah, also plastic cuffs, and maybe some flash bangs." Scott examined his baguette and frowned. "Why do Americans put mayonnaise in everything? Statistically, there must be some of them who don't like this cum shit."

The comment made Shackleton's good humor return. "Me and Oates won't tell a soul that you're putting it down your throat." He turned serious. "Gage? Bureau agents?"

Scott answered, "She's in a van, parked up on the avenue about one hundred yards south of the metro. Three other agents are with her—two males, one female. But she ain't of interest to me, because we don't need her anymore."

Parker had told Antaeus that Cochrane would be at the Friendly Heights metro this morning, so there was no need for Scott's team to continue following Gage.

"Other agents are stretched out along the entire route, in cars and on foot. They're kitted out like proper civvies—no black suits and Ray-Bans and all that crap. I counted twenty-three of them, but reckon there's a lot more." He finished his baguette and rubbed his hands. "Either of you two need to study the map or data again?"

"Nah."

"Nope."

All three assassins had memorized everything they needed to know. Wisconsin Avenue traveled directly north from Georgetown and the Potomac River, and was one of the main shopping streets in D.C. It was several miles long, in the heart of the city, typically had slow-moving traffic due to having only two travel lanes, was usually busy with shoppers and commuters during daylight hours, and had enough entrances and exits to make a tart blush. Ordinarily, it was a nightmare environment for a surveillance team or assassination squad to operate. But that didn't matter today, because there was a ring of steel around the place, within which Scott's unit would be prowling with lethal intent.

Scott looked at his watch. "One hour until showtime. Best we get on foot and in our positions."

Shackleton asked, "If cops or agents get in our way?"

Scott smiled as he checked the workings of his sound-suppressed handgun. "Slot 'em. All that matters is that we kill Will Cochrane."

The Metropolitan Police Department beat cop was relieved that the rain had stopped pouring over Wisconsin Avenue.

He'd spent three hours patrolling the avenue, being a friend rather than an enemy to citizens around him, wanting to help the good people he served. He was like many other beat cops, men and women who'd joined the police because they wanted to make people safe, not because they were closet bullies who hid behind their uniforms and badges so that they could bang heads together.

He wondered if some of the numerous cops and plainclothes agents who'd been drafted into the area this morning were thugs. Sure, they were here to catch the British Intelligence officer, but all beat cops feel resentful when other law enforcement officers are drafted at short notice to serve on their patch. They simply didn't understand the nuances of the neighborhood or know its people, and were driven by the desire to arrest or shoot anyone they thought was a criminal.

Then there were the SWAT sniper teams that were on his rooftops, and the plainclothes HRT men who were strategically and discretely mingling within shoppers and commuters near the metro. They'd be very tough men—people who should have stayed in the army, rather than briefly putting on a cop uniform for police training before taking it off after graduation and replacing it with Kevlar. They weren't cops; they were shooters who had no understanding of community policing.

And finally there were the FBI agents who were running the show: college-educated know-it-alls who conducted law enforcement as if it was a white-collar corporate business. They didn't know what it was really like on the streets and rarely got their hands dirty. Still, the local police had been told there'd be plenty of Bureau agents on Wisconsin

Avenue today, so maybe the FBI would experience what real cop work was like.

The officer sighed as he continued his leisurely patrol. The sun started to break through clouds, and he tilted his cap to shield his eyes. The weather was turning for the better, but that was no compensation for the probability that this morning his patch was going to turn to shit.

Pete Duggan was tense and alert as he exited the Friendship Heights metro to take up position farther up the avenue. Every five minutes, he and his seven HRT colleagues rotated locations to avoid arousing suspicion, not that they stood out—the metro and the street were bustling with civilians, many of whom were dressed like them and were carrying bags. Above him, out of sight on the roof top of the Microsoft Corporation building, was a SWAT sniper and spotter who had a clear sightline to the Metro entrance. Two other sniper teams were farther north and south on the avenue. He could hear them communicating with each other in his earpiece—brief, calm updates about the movement of vehicles and people in the vicinity.

Helos with additional SWAT snipers were hovering low over the city, but not too close to the avenue. They couldn't be visible or audible to Cochrane when he came here, but they could reach Wisconsin in one minute if needed.

Traffic was crawling along the route, and that was a good and bad thing: good that Cochrane couldn't attempt to do a speedy drive-by of the metro to see if Hallowes was standing outside; bad that all mobile law enforcement units would be severely hindered by the traffic.

The fact that there were hundreds of plain-clothes and uniformed officers in the vicinity gave Duggan little comfort, because he kept hold of the thought that he was hunting a man who could expertly take down four fit and alert cops, whereas he'd only managed to train his gun on two of the injured officers before the remaining two had gotten the drop on him. During his time in SEAL Team 6, he'd been graded as an outstanding operator, and within HRT he was considered the agent who was the best with a pistol and submachine gun. And he was up against someone who was better than him.

Of course, Cochrane stood no chance of survival this morning. But collateral damage worried Duggan. There were so many civilians in and around the avenue; so many opportunities for them to get caught in crossfire.

He checked his watch.

Five minutes past ten.

Marsha Gage was in a van with three of her agents. Like them, she was wearing jeans, a bulletproof vest underneath her Windbreaker jacket, and tactical boots. She said to her colleagues, "Time for you to get on foot. Keep your distance from the metro, and don't stand in one place for too long." After they'd left, Marsha returned her gaze to the Friendship Heights metro. She was south of the station, and in between were hundreds of people; a few of them were her colleagues, most were not.

How much easier her task would've been had she been able to evacuate the avenue of all but personnel carrying guns. But if she'd done that, Cochrane wouldn't have come near the place. She had to make him feel at ease, keep things normal, make him think that he was an anonymous pinhead in a sea of dots.

It seemed like she'd been tracking him forever, and she couldn't help but feel deep professional admiration that he'd evaded capture—and not by fleeing, but by coming toward her. Part of her felt it was unfair that she was now using a sledgehammer approach to finally bring him to justice. Still, she had a job to do, and the bottom line was that Cochrane needed to be taken off the streets.

She spoke into her throat mic. "Five minutes until zero hour. Everyone stand by."

Scott, Oates, and Shackleton looked every bit like politicians stepping out of their offices to grab some breakfast or coffee—dark woolen overcoats, sharp suits, white shirts, silk ties, brogues, and hair that was just the right length to make female voters respect their professional appearance but also make them a bit wobbly at the knees. Not that any self-respecting woman would vote for men like this if she knew how they really spoke and thought when not pretending to be wealthy businessmen or politicos.

As they walked along Wisconsin Avenue, their smiles showed off their immaculate white teeth, and they were talking in American accents they'd borrowed from the multitude of Hollywood movies they'd watched while waiting for the right time to kill people.

They felt exhilarated. None of them had any fear, despite being fully cognizant of the dangers around them. In part, this was because their entire adult lives had been suffused with the threat of death; after a while, worrying about it got boring. But more important, they were fatalists who knew they'd die by the bullet; it would happen today, tomorrow, or some other time, but it would happen. It was a liberating feeling because it gave them certainty. That was crucial, because men like this needed to be in control at all times.

They were two hundred yards from the metro and knew full well that they were walking toward eight undercover HRT operatives, Marsha Gage's vehicle, other FBI agents, and a SWAT sniper post.

None of them cared.

What mattered to them was that Will Cochrane was due here in less than two minutes.

The D.C. beat cop walked from north to south down the avenue while wondering if he should join in if there was any action to be had. Nobody had told him one way or the other what to do, and he was sure that other cops like him were in the same ignorant position.

Treated like mushrooms.

Constantly in the dark and fed shit.

As he drew nearer to the Friendship Heights metro station, he tried to spot undercover law enforcement agents lurking near the two lanes of nose-to-tail traffic that was now barely moving, or on the crowded sidewalks. But a cop like him didn't have the skills or experience to clock such agents.

Even though he was wearing shades to protect his eyes from the glaring sunlight, he had to squint as he glanced at the rooftops. He couldn't see a police sniper anywhere, but guessed the whole point was that they weren't to be spotted.

Police sniper.

It was a sad reflection of the times that it could be considered policing to shoot a man in the head from five hundred yards away, rather than walking up to him and talking him out of doing something bad.

He supposed his style of policing was on the wane. Soon all cops would be kitted out like Judge Dredd; enacting justice with the dispassionate and unwavering logic of a robot.

He nodded and smiled at passersby, walked past the metro and parked vehicles—empty sedans and a van with a woman behind the wheel—and continued walking through the crowd toward three men who looked like young politicians or investment bankers.

It surprised him that he felt unwanted and invisible, on a patch that belonged to him.

That was a sad thought.

He checked his watch.

Ten fifteen A.M.

The men who looked like politicians passed him and kept walking toward the station.

He sighed again, because it was time to go off duty and leave this beat to visiting tourists, Republicans and Democrats who were out grabbing a cappuccino, and cops who didn't know these streets.

They were the thoughts of an honest beat cop who'd devoted his life to ensuring that a square mile of land was kept safe.

Not that Will Cochrane would truly know how that felt.

He was just playing the part.

Will spun around, pulled out his sidearm, shot the Irish assassin in the leg, turned back, and ran south while shouting, "Three armed men! Get to cover! Run!"

Chaos erupted.

"Shot fired! Shot fired!" Duggan dropped to a crouch, ripped open the Velcro cover on his pack-sack, and withdrew his Heckler & Koch MP5 submachine gun. He shouted into his throat mic, "All units. Metro station. Go! Go!"

Every cop, Bureau agent, SWAT operative, and HRT agent had been given the green light to race to the place where gunfire had sounded.

"Get down! Down!" Duggan was dodging screaming pedestrians as he sprinted while holding his gun at eye level. His HRT colleagues were close by, moving in exactly the same way. "Bravo One. What do you see?"

Bravo One. The SWAT sniper.

Bravo One responded. "One man down. Civilian clothes. Pistol in his hand. Two guys with him, also armed."

"Are they FBI?"

"How the hell would I know?"

• • •

Marsha dashed out of her vehicle, her handgun drawn. She looked up the street. Thirty yards away, with their backs to her, were the three men the SWAT sniper had referenced. One was lying injured, the other two were by his side with weapons drawn.

Her heart pumped rapidly and she said into her mic, "I can't see their faces! If anyone's hearing this and is injured, for God's sake say so now because otherwise you're likely to have your head taken off by Bravo One!"

What had just happened? She looked in the other direction. Uniformed cops were now on the avenue, rushing toward civilians to get them to cover, barking orders; everywhere was movement, noise; people were abandoning their cars and running; police sirens were sounding from every direction.

One of the uniform cops was running away from the scene, shouting at people to get to cover, his priority to get people to safety, knowing that the area around the metro was a kill zone.

Maybe he was the beat cop who'd passed her transit vehicle moments ago.

A man who was now running.

Away from the scene.

Shit!

"Bravo One. Uniform cop! Running south. I think that's Cochrane!"

She sprinted after him.

"This is Bravo One. Which cop? Every cop I can see is running in different directions."

Marsha cursed. The cop was at least two hundred yards away, appearing and disappearing in the writhing mass of hysterical bodies that were between him and her. She ran faster, desperate not to lose sight of him.

Scott was calm as he placed a hand on Shackleton's shoulder and said, "Head shots to all the fuckers."

"Damn right." Lying on his uninjured leg, Shackleton pointed his handgun at the approaching HRT operatives while ignoring the screaming civilians all around the trio of assassins.

Scott winked at Oates. "Time to go loud. Be a good chap and take out the sniper for me."

Both secreted their handguns and pulled out from under their overcoats SCAR-H 7.62 mm battle rifles. Not only could the devastatingly powerful weapons be fired on automatic, just one round could penetrate body armor and kill a man.

Scott stepped forward, his gun held high, and squeezed the trigger. The sustained volley tore through four HRT operatives, three FBI agents, and six civilians.

Oates got to his knee, took aim, and sent shorter, controlled bursts at the sniper nest on top of the Microsoft building. He smiled because the sniper and spotter were now dead. He stood up and opened fire at everything in front of him.

Marsha was near breathless as she shouted, "SWAT helos: I need you over Wisconsin now! In pursuit of a cop. Possible target. He's heading south, two hundred yards ahead of me. Now, now, now!"

She crashed into a civilian, fell, rolled, got to her feet, and continued running. "Bravo One. Update!"

Silence in her earpiece.

"Update!"

It was Duggan who answered. "Bravo One's down! We're in a firefight with three unknown hostiles!"

Duggan dived behind a car as more bullets came his way and punched through the vehicle and the wall behind him. He knew the gunfire sound—SCAR weapons, upgraded to larger rounds; ones that don't injure a soldier and require two of his mates to carry him off, meaning three combatants have been taken out of the battlefield equation. The bullets were killers, the same ones used by the British SAS. Lessons learned from fighting fanatics in Afghanistan who don't give a shit about casualty evacuations of their injured comrades.

He grimaced as shards of metal raced close to his face, crouched, and spun out of cover.

A handgun bullet walloped him in the chest with the impact of a sledgehammer being swung full strength.

But the bullet was no match for the Kevlar under his jacket.

Duggan held firmly in position as he aimed his gun and sent two bursts of bullets into Shackleton's head.

He moved his gun's sight toward the remaining two assassins, but they were largely obscured by men, women, and kids running around like headless chickens, or crouching or standing like statues, or draped over stationary cars while waiting to die. An FBI agent and uniform cop ran from his right flank toward the gunmen. The cop flipped backward as bullets smashed into his throat and face; the agent yelped and hit the ground dead as SCAR rounds turned his internal organs into mush.

It was no good. Duggan decided he had to get much closer to the assassins.

The noise around Marsha was deafening as she ran, holding her gun while shouting, "FBI! FBI!" in case any of the numerous cops or hundreds of civilians thought she was one of the hostiles. She could still see the policeman she was pursuing as she dodged through the crowd, flapping one arm to tell people to get down. But he was faster than her, and she was losing ground. "The policeman who's running away from me! Stop him!" No one heard her. No one cared, because all that mattered to them was that farther up the street it sounded like a regiment of Russian airborne troops was advancing on Capitol Hill.

Somewhere behind her she heard a helo.

"Delta Two. We got visual on you, Agent Gage." This came from the SWAT sniper in the helicopter.

Thank God! "The uniform cop. About two fifty yards ahead of me heading south. Take him down!" Marsha tried to run faster, but her legs felt as if they might buckle from her exertions. "Take him down!"

"One hundred percent confirmation cop is Cochrane?"

"Negative."

"Then I've no clearance to proceed."

"Wound him then!"

"Negative."

"What?!"

"Bullet in the leg can still kill. Man might be a legitimate cop."

Jesus! The SWAT sniper was right, but she was now losing all hope. "Okay. Take out the gunmen in the north."

"Roger that." The helo turned away.

Marsha leapt on top of a stationary car and began running along the row of vehicles that had been abandoned by terrified drivers and passengers. The extra height gave her better visibility and the ability to move without constantly bumping into people. Either side of the vehicles was still chaos, with people racing into shops, falling over each other, wailing; and the drone of police sirens was all pervasive.

She jumped to another car and saw the cop dash off of Wisconsin Avenue into a side alley.

Scott and Oates were expertly holding their ground, covering angles, one of them opening fire while the other changed magazines, crouching while shooting, moving, sending short and long bursts of death at anything that might be a threat to them.

The former SAS operatives knew there was no way out of this.

It was their last stand.

Their day of the bullet.

And they were making it a memorable one for every person here.

Duggan sprinted into open ground, shouting, "Out of the way!" at civilians he had to swerve around to get closer to the gunmen. Some of them did as he commanded, others dropped to the tarmac because assassins' bullets had just entered their brains.

"Delta Two. I got one of them in my sights."

Duggan yelled into his throat mic. "Do it! Now!"

As the sniper's high-velocity round bored a hole through Oates's head, Duggan ran faster than he'd ever done in his life, and hurled himself through air to grab Scott.

But the assassin sidestepped.

Duggan crashed to the sidewalk and rolled onto his back.

Scott was standing over him, his SCAR pointing at Duggan. "Got to be quicker than that, sunshine." He smiled. "But I guess that was the point."

It was the point. Duggan's clever strategy had laid Scott momentarily open to anyone and everyone. Even if it meant he was putting his life at the feet of a highly trained killer.

But Scott knew he'd been outwitted.

He took his eyes off Duggan and looked toward the sky.

Allowing Duggan time to lift his submachine gun.

Scott closed his eyes.

Duggan's rounds hit Scott's chest at exactly the same time as Delta Two's sniper bullet entered the assassin's head.

• • •

Marsha had to slow down as she reached the entrance to the alley; her breathing was too fast, her legs felt like lead, but more than anything she felt abject fear as she held her gun in two hands and entered the dark and narrow passageway. She moved cautiously down the alley. Trash containers were sporadically positioned on both sides; fire escape ladders hung down the tall walls above them; water poured from roof gutters that were overflowing from the day's earlier heavy rainfall. No one was visible in the alley, but there were plenty of places for a man to hide while he changed his appearance from that of a cop to an ordinary citizen.

In her earpiece she heard Duggan saying that the three gunmen were dead, that all law enforcement officers needed to scour the area in case there were more of them, and that every paramedic in D.C. was needed on Wisconsin Avenue.

She could still hear the sirens and the commotion on the avenue, but the noises grew quieter with every step she took. And despite the fact that thirty yards behind her was the start of what was temporarily the most heavily policed zone in the U.S., right now she felt completely alone.

She wondered if she should call for backup; even just one or two cops would make a difference.

But every able-bodied man and woman was needed on the avenue.

People were injured.

Dying.

Dead.

And there was the possibility that there were more gunmen loose.

But they weren't the only reasons she didn't call for assistance.

If Cochrane was in the alley, she couldn't signify her presence here to him by allowing him to hear her voice.

She kept walking, estimating that she had another twenty yards to go before she reached the ten-foot-high wall that blocked the end of the alley—a wall that Cochrane would easily be able to scale in order to disappear into the hectic throngs of the city.

Part of her now hoped that was what had happened, because the prospect of confronting a cornered Will Cochrane terrified her.

But she was in no way going to back down from her duty.

After another forty yards, she stopped and listened but heard nothing. And she had a clear view of the remainder of the alley and could see nothing out of the ordinary.

He wasn't here.

She was sure.

She breathed in deeply; her heartbeat began to slow; her muscles started to relax.

Then she tensed again as she heard a clanging noise behind her, and spun with her gun ready to fire.

But it was merely a pigeon that had landed on one of the rusty fire escapes.

She silently cursed, turned to complete her search of the alley, and involuntarily gasped in shock.

Will Cochrane was standing right in front of her.

His gun's muzzle inches from her forehead.

A nondescript brown jacket covered his police tunic, the cap was gone, and sunglasses were clipped to his collar; he no longer looked anything like a cop. In a flash, he ripped the gun out of her hand, pulled out the radio set that was clipped to her waist, and smashed it against the wall. "Any secondary weapons on you?"

She shook her head.

"Prove it."

"You . . . you want me to strip?"

"Not in this weather. You'd catch your death from cold. Frisk yourself—firmly."

Marsha ran her hands tightly around her arms, legs, and the rest of her body.

As she did so, Will threw her handgun as far as he could down the alley behind her. He nodded toward the weapon as it rolled to a halt. "You can pick that up after I'm gone. I know you cops give each other a lot of grief if someone disarms you."

"Thank . . ." God, was she really about to thank him? "I'm not a cop."

"FBI?"

Marsha nodded.

"You work for Marsha Gage?"

Should she lie? Would he put a bullet in her brain if she answered honestly? She recalled what Alistair had said to her.

Once he's found out the truth about why he's on the run, he wants you to get very close to him, though I must warn you it will be completely on his terms.

It made sense. He'd tried to come to her home last night but was confronted by men with guns—probably the same men who'd been killed today. And he had no gripe with Marsha, because he'd know that she and the rest of the FBI were as much in the dark about Project Ferryman as he was.

She made a decision.

Not an easy one, but she just made it.

"I'm Marsha Gage. I was warned you might come for me once you had answers."

Will smiled, though his expression remained menacing. "Between Norway and here, time and time again you considerably inconvenienced me."

"The feeling's mutual."

"I'm sure it is." He was motionless, his gun still pointing directly at her head. "What have you done with Ellie Hallowes?"

Marsha's eyes widened, but she stayed silent.

"What have you done to her?!"

Marsha shook her head, fear coursing through her body. "Until this morning, I'd never heard of Hallowes."

"And yet you wouldn't be here unless you or someone like you made Ellie set this up!"

The fury on Will's face was easily recognizable, but as she stared at him she also saw absolute concern in his eyes. She'd been right about him. He was extremely loyal to Hallowes. What was the right thing to say and do? She settled on what her heart was telling her: truth and justice. "I had nothing to do with this. If you ever meet them again, Patrick and Alistair will attest to that because they've been assigned to my team for the duration of our manhunt. The men responsible for capturing Hallowes are Charles Sheridan and Colby Jellicoe."

"That doesn't surprise me." Will's eyes narrowed as he cocked his gun's hammer. "But I need to know that Ellie's okay."

Marsha lowered her head.

"Head up!"

She lifted her gaze, and her voice trembled as she said, "We can't prove it, but we know for sure that Sheridan had her killed. She was murdered in her hotel room. We've taken possession of her body."

Will's eyes were unblinking. His lack of movement and silence were more terrifying than if he'd done or said something.

In a split second, Marsha could be dead.

Murdered, for being vaguely associated with Hallowes's killers.

But Will asked, "You still believe in the reasons you joined the FBI? Fidelity, Bravery, Integrity?"

The Bureau motto.

Marsha nodded.

"I want to hear your answer on your lips!"

"Yes, yes."

"Good." Will's greenish blue eyes looked intense. "When you get home today, you'll find a package in your mailbox. It's from me, but don't be alarmed—there's nothing dangerous inside. Just make sure it's used no later tonight than the time I've written on the box. And when you do, ensure that the attorney general and the directors of the FBI and CIA are standing next to you." He took a step back. "I'm going to deliver you the most dangerous double agent who's ever operated in the States. He's a high-ranking CIA officer, working for the Russians. But in order for him not to be warned off, I need you to do something." He explained his thinking. "Can you do that for me?"

Marsha's head was spinning. Here she was, face-to-face with Public Enemy Number One, and he was asking for her help, and she was seriously considering giving it to him.

"When it's done, you can arrest the double agent. It will be *your* success, *your* glory, and *your* career that goes sky high as a result."

"I don't care about any of those things."

Will smiled, and this time the menace seemed diminished. "In which case, I judged you correctly." His smile vanished. "Will you do what I ask?"

"No!"

Will was exasperated when he said, "All I need is a window of a few hours. After that you can do what you want, maybe say that you were mistaken."

"The answer's still no!"

Frustration coursed through him. There was only one option left to him. He told her about the link between Antaeus, Ferryman, the proposed American assassination of Cobalt, and what he suspected could happen after the bomb detonated in Afghanistan.

But he omitted telling her that Ferryman was Ed Parker.

Marsha was shocked. She knew that her career

could be ruined if she agreed to do what he was asking. But sometimes you just have to go with your gut. And right now, her gut was telling her that if she didn't do what Will wanted, U.S. national security and dominance in the world were screwed. "I'll do it."

"Good."

"But I'll need to get approval from the Bureau director. I can't make this call on my own. It's too big."

"Fine, but do it fast and make sure no one else knows—in particular anyone in or associated with the CIA."

"Okay. But I ain't going to promise that I'll back off from hunting you after you're done."

"I wouldn't expect you to."

Marsha frowned. "I think you knew Hallowes wasn't going to be here today."

Will said nothing.

"And yet, you came here anyway and shot one of the men who were after you, so you could have his team taken out by my colleagues."

Marsha was right. Will had deliberately kept alive the Irish assassin he'd confronted the night before and had fended off the cops who showed up on the street where Marsha lived so that the assassin could escape, because he wanted to identify him today and establish who was with him.

It took a few seconds for Marsha to work this all out, then she said, "Smart."

"Or, just plain stupid." Anguish was on Will's face. "I heard SCAR automatic gunfire when I was running down the avenue. To my knowledge, they're not weapons used by the FBI or SWAT. I'm hoping you're not going to tell me that civilians got caught in the crossfire."

The last update she had from Duggan was that the civilian body count was twenty-two and rising. Should she tell him? Cochrane looked like he was in so much pain. "Some of my men were shot. But we're still trying to establish whether there were any fatalities."

Will knew she was lying. He'd thought that the assassins would only be armed with handguns and would easily have been taken down by HRT. No way would he have triggered an assault on them in a crowded place if he'd known they were packing battle weapons. "Turn around."

She did so, wondering if his words had been a trick and if he was now going to execute her by putting a bullet in the back of her head.

In the distance she could see a tiny glimpse of the terror and panic that was still prevalent on Wisconsin Avenue.

Was this going to be the last thing she ever saw?

Death and carnage.

Twenty seconds passed.

Nothing happened to her.

She turned back.

Will Cochrane was gone.

THIRTY-FIVE

By noon the next day, Parker, code name Ferryman, would be of no further use to Antaeus. Until that time, he needed Parker's treachery to remain undiscovered and for the information Antaeus had relayed to his asset to continue to be taken as the truth. The Americans had to believe that bombing Cobalt's meeting in Afghanistan tomorrow was the right thing to do.

Whereas in reality it would make America's entry into the Vietnam War look like a brilliant yet brief skirmish.

Afghanistan was nine and a half hours ahead of Washington time. Noon tomorrow in Afghanistan was two thirty A.M. in the U.S. capital. And given that it was currently eleven A.M. in D.C., that meant he only needed Ferryman to remain intact for the next fifteen and a half hours.

Only Will Cochrane could ruin everything.

But by now, he should be dead.

If he wasn't, Antaeus would have no choice other than to tell Parker to go into hiding. It wasn't an ideal option, because Cochrane could take his suspicions to someone else, a powerful and law-abiding official, who'd then see red flags if the asset whom Will was accusing of treachery had run away.

He entered his living room and turned on a television that had been state of the art in the 1980s but now looked like a decrepit box of junk. Still, it got the news and history channels—as well as the one that showed his favorite repeats of *Only Fools and Horses* and *Monty Python's Flying Circus*—and that was all he needed.

RT news network, one of the largest in Russia, was showing scenes that were akin to a war zone in Washington, D.C. American civilians were being interviewed while shaking with tears and pointing back to a barricaded street.

He didn't care about that.

The camera cut to a police officer saying that three men had been killed in a gun battle outside the Friendship Heights metro station, and that a fourth, believed to be their colleague, had been found dead in the trunk of a car in a parking lot close by.

That would be Antaeus's assassins. The spymaster turned the volume up.

The camera cut to a woman with matted hair and wide eyes. The banner beneath her read in Cyrillic, AGENT MARSHA GAGE: HEAD OF THE FBI MANHUNT FOR WILL COCHRANE.

The interviewer asked, "Agent Gage. What happened here today?"

Gage looked straight at the camera. The expression on her exhausted face suggested she didn't care she looked a mess while appearing on global TV. "What happened is we killed Will Cochrane. We got him. It's over."

Antaeus tried to smile as he turned off the TV, but something felt wrong. For three years he'd wanted to avenge the death of his wife and daughter by killing Will Cochrane. He'd dreamt about it, visualized it, and planned it; but now that Cochrane was dead, he felt no satisfaction. Instead, he felt like a brute.

He forced his mind to snap out of these ruminations, lit a cheroot, and inhaled deeply on the aromatic tobacco. No need to get Parker to go into hiding now that Cochrane's dead, he thought. And yes, Agent Gage; it's over. But at noon tomorrow there'll be a new beginning. You won't like it, though.

In the United States Air Force's Shindand base in Afghanistan, a USAF ground crew was making final checks of the large predator drone. A CIA officer was standing nearby, drinking beer from a bottle as he looked at the five-hundred-pound bunker-destroying bomb on the drone's undercarriage. He had no role or expertise in preparing the lethal craft, but he did need to be here to make sure the drone was fully functional and ready for takeoff at exactly the right time tomorrow. And though he wasn't like the new breed of Agency officers, who thought that spying was all about neutralizing enemies rather than obtaining secrets from them, he had to admit that the sight of the bomb made him feel good. It would kill Cobalt. A man whose secrets were no doubt hugely valuable. But more important than that, a man whose death was priceless.

He sipped his beer.

Noon tomorrow, the drone would be high above the target.

Its bomb hurtling downward.

Catherine Parker saw the last bit of the sun disappear over the horizon and beamed. "It's official. Cocktail hour!"

Ed tossed his newspaper onto the kitchen table, having been unable to read anything in it because his mind was so distracted. "Not for me, thanks. Got to stay sharp tonight. I've got a very important day tomorrow."

Catherine rubbed her husband's knotted shoulders. "Maybe we should have an early night." She nibbled his earlobe. "Or does the Agency operate the same rules as football teams—no sex before a big match?"

"To be honest, babes, I'm not sure I'd be much use to you there, either." He tried to smile. "Anyway, I've still got to fix that darn bed frame. Can't have Crystal hearing all that squeaking."

Catherine poured herself a glass of wine. "Crystal's on a sleepover at her friend Cherry's house tonight, so we can squeak as much as we like." She smiled, and said with sympathy, "It's okay, my dear. I know you've got a lot on your plate. Just trying to lighten the mood."

Ed rubbed his temples. "My brain feels like it's going to explode."

Catherine smoothed a hand against his cheek. "Try to relax. After tomorrow, you're going to be man of the moment. Man of a very *long* and exciting moment."

"I'm just a cog in the machine. Bigger men than me will get the real glory."

"You're not . . ." Catherine felt anger as she tapped her hand on his shoulder. "You're not insignificant. I love you. We love you. Tomorrow the Agency will love you."

Ed looked embittered. "You have no idea what you're talking about."

Will stood in total darkness at the end of the driveway, watching the house and in particular the illuminated room containing the two men. He hadn't anticipated they'd both be here, but it made no difference. He had a job to do, and there was no chance he could come back later. He felt calm, and that was normal for him. Anger would come; right now was not a time for blind, unproductive fury.

He walked to the large home's front door and tried the handle. Locked. He put on his most charming smile and rang the bell.

A woman opened the door.

Will's smiled broadened. "Good evening."

He pushed past her, walked along the corridor, and entered the living room.

Colby Jellicoe and Charles Sheridan were seated in leather armchairs next to a roaring fire. Jellicoe stood quickly, horror on his flabby face as he exclaimed, "You're supposed to be dead!"

"I got better." Will punched him with sufficient

force to render him unconscious, then grabbed Sheridan by the jaw and hurled him full force across the room.

The CIA officer smacked against a wall and slumped down onto his ass. He looked terrified.

Will crouched nonchalantly and placed the muzzle of his handgun against Sheridan's belly. "Who killed her?"

Sheridan's face was screwed up; his whole body was in agony. "Fuck you!"

Will repeated the question. "Ellie Hallowes. I know you ordered her death. Got people to torture her to set up today's meeting. Thing is, though, she was a very brave and clever woman. She let me know she was calling me under duress."

Will prodded his gun into Sheridan's gut. "Try to imagine that kind of bravery. Who killed her?"

Sheridan gritted his teeth and looked venomous. "I don't know what you're talking about."

With deliberation, Will said, "You. Don't. Know."

Sheridan nodded, his eyes wide, sweat pouring down his face.

"That means you're of no use to me." Will stood and pointed his gun at Sheridan's head. "Best we get this over with."

"Stop! Stop!" Sheridan was shaking his head wildly. "You won't kill me if I tell you?"

Will answered, "All I care about is knowing the identity and location of her murderer."

Sheridan lowered his head and whimpered, "The twins did it. They weren't supposed to kill her."

"Where are they?"

Sheridan told him.

"Look at me."

Sheridan glanced up, his eyes now pleading and expectant. "That's all you wanted?"

"Yes. Thing is, though, I don't believe you."

"The farm! Approximately one hundred miles west of Langley. They're in the forest. It's the truth!"

Will nodded. "I don't doubt that. You're lying about not wanting her dead."

"Jellicoe made me do it!"

"That means you're both in the shit."

"Please. I was following orders."

"I've heard that before from other psychopaths."

"I'm begging you."

Will smiled, though his eyes remained cold. "Please don't beg. It's very undignified and shows weakness of character."

Sheridan's expression became defiant. "You're not going to kill me." His voice grew louder as he said, "I'm a senior CIA officer. You wouldn't dare hurt me on U.S. soil."

"You're not a senior CIA officer."

"I am!"

"No you're not. At least, not anymore." Will pulled the trigger, saw bits of Sheridan's brain splatter into the fire, then walked over to Jellicoe's prone body and shot him twice in the head.

He turned to leave but froze as he saw the woman who'd answered the door, standing in the entrance. Her eyes showed fear and uncertainty.

"I'm not going to hurt you. I came for these men, and now I want to leave. You're safe."

Tears were streaming down Lindsay Sheridan's face as she asked, "Safe?"

Will nodded. "Safe."

"Safe . . . safe . . ."

Will watched the woman.

Her voice strengthened. "You're the man on the news. I thought they killed you today."

"Not yet." He sighed. "I'm sorry I took your husband away. He killed a woman I cared about."

Lindsay moved into the room, picked up her husband's brandy glass, sipped from it, and spat the liquor into the fire. The flames roared up from the fuel as she said, "He killed me a long time ago." She moved back toward the door. "I saw an intruder enter my home this evening. He wasn't Caucasian, over six foot, or English. And I'll stick to that version until my dying day."

"Why?"

Lindsay shrugged. "Because you've done what I didn't have the courage to do. I'm going out now—late-night shopping—and I won't be back for a few hours. That's when I'll discover that my husband and Jellicoe were murdered by a burglar who was still ransacking the place and fled when he saw me. In the meantime, I suggest you make a mess of my house and steal something." She nodded toward a side table containing the dead men's car keys. "Maybe something you can use."

Lindsay Sheridan left the room, feeling that finally someone had made the decision for her.

No more bastard husband.

And a future that was hers.

• • •

Two hours later, Will drove Sheridan's car very slowly along a farm track, headlights off, before bringing the vehicle to a halt and getting out. Most of the remote farmstead's buildings were in darkness, though lights were on in the barn and the main house. The barn had a large annex alongside it, and Will could hear snorting and grunting coming from inside. The noises had to be from the huge boars Sheridan had told him about; their sulfurous stench poisoned the forest's air. As Will walked silently past the annex, the boars sounded agitated and anxious.

It was, after all, nearly eight P.M., meaning they were desperate to be released into their feeding pit where the twins would drop their delicious mix of scraps, blood, and flesh.

He drew nearer to the farmhouse and could see the twins in the kitchen, standing at either end of a large table, chopping vegetables into chunks with meat cleavers before tossing the food into a barrel of blood. The twins' long black hair thrashed in time with each downward stroke of the blades.

He knew it was impossible for them to see him or anything else outside the brightly illuminated room, but nevertheless he moved cautiously in case an external security light came on, or he accidentally made a noise that would alert them.

Everyone Will had killed during his career had been given a quick death, because he took zero pleasure from that side of his job. On the contrary, it gave him great sadness and guilt, which is why he let the souls of his victims waft around him, sometimes to torment him, other times to forgive him. But he never forgot that they were there.

Yet these mad men in the kitchen had no souls.

They were rabid beasts.

Murderers who relished their job.

Foul demons who were willing to desecrate something pure and lovely.

Right now, Will was about to cross the line that divided right and wrong.

And he didn't care.

Couldn't care.

Avenging Ellie Hallowes was all that mattered to him right now.

He had to make the twins' evil savagery pay in a way that was fitting.

He pulled out his handgun, walked to the kitchen door, opened it, and held his weapon at eye level. He stood stock-still as Augustus and Elijah ran toward him, shrieking some kind of war cry, their eyes wild and crazy, their meat cleavers held high. His first shot struck Augustus in the arm, causing him to drop his weapon and scream. His second shot did the same to Elijah. Both stopped dead in their tracks, their good arms clutching their burning injuries. But Will knew they were still dangerous, and so shot their good arms as well.

As he drew nearer to them, they spat, uttered obscenities, and tried to kick him before realizing the sudden movements were causing them agony.

Will pocketed his weapon and withdrew from

his jacket two lengths of rope, at the end of which were choker nooses. He placed the loops over the twins' heads and said, "Let's go."

As he dragged them out of the kitchen and headed toward the barn, their legs moved fast to avoid strangulation and their arms were limp and useless by their sides. Will pulled them into the barn and opened an inner door that led to a pit surrounded by an eight-foot concrete wall. In the center of the pit was the steel stake that the twins used to tether live animals. Will lashed the ropes around the stake, so that the twins couldn't escape.

He looked down at them.

Their eyes were still wide with astonishment.

And now they had grins on their faces, continuing to spit and curse.

Will ignored them as he ripped off their upper garments, exposing their blood-covered torsos. "You're monsters."

Augustus laughed.

Elijah's expression was intense as he said, "And right now, what are you?"

"I don't know." Will walked to the door leading to the pigpen, slid back bolts, pulled the door open, and sprinted to the pit's exit as he heard the boars charge in, their grunts replaced by shrieks of ecstasy.

When Will reached his car, he heard another sound rising over the noise of the boars.

Two men screaming.

Will drove off the road, ten miles away from Arlington, and gripped the steering wheel tight.

The vehicle shuddered while it moved over rough land and into a wooded area of deserted country-side. When he was satisfied he was far enough in, he stopped the car in a clearing. From the trunk, he removed two jerricans of spare fuel he'd stolen from Sheridan's garage, doused the gasoline over the inside and outside of the vehicle, removed the car's gas cap so its fuel tank was exposed, and tossed an ignited Zippo lighter onto the passenger seat.

He ran fast.

In part to get away from the burning vehicle in case it exploded.

But far more important, he needed to cover ten miles on foot to finish a journey that had started in Norway.

THIRTY-SIX

Although it was five minutes after midnight, Ed Parker had no thoughts of going upstairs to join his wife in bed. In less than two and a half hours, it would be noon in Afghanistan.

The time when Cobalt would be blown to pieces.

A defining moment in history.

The CIA director turned the TV off and rubbed his clammy face, feeling restless and impatient, willing time to move more quickly. A glass of milk, he decided, might calm him down. He went into the kitchen opened the large refrigerator door, withdrew a milk carton, shut the door, and dropped the carton.

Will Cochrane was standing before him.

His pistol held in two hands and pointing at Ed's face.

Ed showed fear but also resignation. "Looks like you struck a deal with Marsha Gage. And in order for you to get her to agree to that, you must have told her the truth."

Will nodded. "Sit at the table and put your hands flat over it."

Ed did as he was told. "My wife's asleep upstairs. Please don't let her see anything . . . bad."

"I won't kill you unless I have to." Will stood on the opposite side of the table, keeping his gun trained on Ed. "You're Ferryman. Antaeus's spy. And your treachery is about to trigger something that will devastate the United States."

"I'm not . . . not Ferryman. Gregori Shonin is that man."

"He doesn't exist, and you know that! As far as the Agency was concerned, Ferryman was the link to Antaeus. What it didn't know was that in truth, you were that link."

All trace of resignation was gone from Ed's expression and was replaced by what looked to be genuine confusion. "No, no. This can't be right. I thought you'd come here because you'd discovered that—"

"Enough, Ed!" Catherine was standing in the entrance, pointing a handgun at Will. "Keep your mouth shut!"

But Ed spun around to face her. "What is he talking about? Shonin doesn't exist?"

The questions made Will's mind race. As he kept his eyes on Catherine and his gun trained on Ed, he stated, "Catherine Parker is Ferryman."

Catherine laughed. "I don't have to say anything. Looks to me like we've caught ourselves America's Most Wanted."

Ed stood and looked imploringly at her. "What's going on?"

Catherine's expression was venomous, but she stayed silent.

Things were starting to make sense to Will. "It appears, Mr. Parker, that you didn't recruit Shonin. Your wife did, while you were both posted to Prague in 2005. I'm guessing she told you back then that Shonin would only work for her, but that didn't matter because you could pretend to the Agency that it was you who were running Shonin."

Ed took a step closer to Catherine, and Will let him do so. "We knew the Agency would never let Catherine run someone so important, since she's not a trained case officer. But we also knew the wonders it would do to my career if there was some way we could keep Shonin on board. I thought you'd discovered this and that's why you came for me tonight. Catherine, what does he mean when he says Shonin doesn't exist?"

She remained quiet, a hostile look on her face.

So Will answered for her. "Antaeus was pretending to be Shonin. Catherine knew that from the outset, or he told her sometime thereafter when he had his hooks into her. Either way, he recruited her rather than the other way around. Your wife's been working for Antaeus all along. She's a Russian spy."

Catherine placed her finger on the trigger to shoot Will, but as she did so Ed rushed at her, screaming, "Spy?"

There was no doubt it was an accident.

She didn't mean for it to happen.

As she pulled the trigger, Ed moved in front of her, staring into her eyes with an expression of shock on his face.

Too late, she realized he was in her line of fire.

And too late, Ed lowered his gaze and saw what was happening.

Urgently, she released her finger, but the trigger was by now too far back.

Her gun fired.

She screamed and dropped her gun as Ed fell to the floor.

Tears poured out of her as she cradled her husband. "What have I done?" She looked up and didn't care that Will had his gun on her. "Oh. Dear God, no! What have I done?" Catherine rocked back and forth while holding her dead husband.

Will rushed forward and grabbed her gun. "There's no time for this!"

Catherine looked at her husband with tear-filled, bloodshot eyes.

"In two hours, Cobalt's not going to be at the Afghanistan meeting. Someone else is. Who?"

Catherine looked around, desperation and misery written across her face.

"It's all over for you now. Time's running out!"

Catherine used the back of her sleeve to rub tears away. "The Russian deputy prime minister and the head of the United Nations. It's a top-secret meeting. They're trying to negotiate with the Taliban to ensure free movement of international aid into Afghanistan."

Will nodded. "Antaeus knew about this meeting and told you to tell the Agency that Cobalt was the person going there. But Antaeus only recently found out the exact day, time, and location of the meeting."

"Two days ago."

"How could you do this?"

Catherine started slapping her forehead, her face screwed up. "In 2005, Antaeus discovered that I'd been unfaithful to Ed. He used that against me, seduced me. We had a brief affair."

"And after that ended, he told you who he was and you went along with that because it gave the Parkers a chance to make it big time in the Agency."

"That was the main reason. I told Antaeus that I wanted to get my marriage back on track, and he told me that was a good thing but we'd need all the help we could get." She lifted her head. "Another reason was that Antaeus gave me something that Ed couldn't."

"A child."

"Crystal."

"Did Ed know?"

"He didn't know, and Antaeus didn't know. As far as Ed was concerned, Crystal was his. Anyway, a few months later Antaeus got married and had a child of his own. It wouldn't have served anyone's interests for me to share the truth. To this day, Antaeus doesn't know he's Crystal's father."

Will placed his finger over the trigger. "When the bomb drops, big time in the Agency comes to an end. You must have known that, so why agree to pass on false intelligence about Cobalt's presence in Afghanistan?"

Catherine held her husband's hand while smoothing her thumb over his skin and staring at him with glazed eyes. When she spoke, her voice sounded distant. "Antaeus's strategy about reputation building. He had to make Project Ferryman an irresistible and fundamental truth to the CIA so that when Ferryman said Cobalt was in Afghanistan, the United States wouldn't hesitate to act."

"Colby Jellicoe, Charles Sheridan, and your husband all had their careers accelerated on intelligence fed to you by Antaeus. *Good* intelligence."

Catherine's voice was dead, her tears still streaming. "It *was* good intelligence—genuine Russian operations that Antaeus was willing to sell out to make Project Ferryman the Agency's most credible and vital mission."

Will opened his jacket and turned the radio set that was attached to his belt off Transmit and onto Transmit and Receive. Loudly, he asked, "You getting all of this?"

Out of the speaker, Marsha's voice responded. "All of it. And the attorney general and heads of the Agency and Bureau did too. They're witnesses, and we've recorded everything that's been said. We're calling off the drone strike right now."

Will felt total relief. "I'll keep Mrs. Parker here. Come and get her." He switched the radio back onto transmit.

Catherine looked perturbed. "Prison, not death? Right now, I'd prefer the latter."

"Not tonight. One thing that's always interested me about Cobalt is that a lot of the intelligence pertaining to him has been Russian information that we've intercepted or learned about from Russian sources. I've got a hunch you might know something about this."

Catherine was silent.

"Speak!"

Catherine looked at him, no terror in her eyes, instead a look that suggested her mind was disassociated from her body. "Antaeus used me to feed intelligence about Cobalt into the CIA. I'm not stupid; I thought something was odd about it all. One day I confronted him about it, told him I thought he had big lies up his sleeve. He didn't grace me with an answer."

"Of course not."

"So, when he instructed me to pass on the intel about Cobalt's location in Afghanistan, I told him no."

"Because you suspected something was wrong with that intelligence."

"It sounded to me like a setup. I quickly decided that Ferryman had always been about this. I've always worked for Antaeus because of what it could give my family. But I've never hated my country. On the contrary."

Will lowered his gun because Catherine was no longer a threat. "You knew that if America dropped its bomb, the backlash from the international community would be severe. At best, America would be kicked out of the UN Security Council, made to abandon every overseas U.S. military base, and have its balls cut off to the extent that its days of being a superpower were forever dead. At worst, Russia, its allies, and countries that were previously not its allies, would go to war with the States."

Catherine bowed her head. "It was Antaeus's master plan. Cripple America."

"A country you love. I'll ask you one last time: How could you do this?"

Catherine kissed Ed's forehead and began rocking back and forth. "When I told Antaeus about my suspicions that something was wrong with Cobalt and that I wouldn't tell the CIA that Cobalt was going to be in Afghanistan, Antaeus looked genuinely flummoxed. But he's clever, very clever. He asked me how my husband was faring in the spotlight of Ferryman glory. I told him the truth." She held her husband close. "That Ed hated being overpromoted and this exposed; that he was a good man." She started crying uncontrollably.

"If I were Antaeus, I'd have seen that as an opportunity to tell you the truth and give you and Ed a way out."

"Seems you and Antaeus are the same man." Catherine was shaking. "He did tell me the truth. Said he'd manipulated me to feed crap about Cobalt, but had also used other means to build Cobalt's profile. He called them his 'dominos': snippets of intelligence, conversations that he knew could be eavesdropped, information placed in certain places that could be picked up by others. All of it was crafted by him. He could stand his dominos up facing the West, and with no effort he could make them topple over toward you. You see, he'd spent years planning this. Of course, it was only recently that he learned about the joint Russian-UN trip to Afghanistan. But he'd always believed an opportunity like that would one day come along. When it did, he had to have Cobalt right where he wanted him."

Will nodded, because this was the final missing piece of the jigsaw.

One that had been crafted by a brilliant Russian spymaster.

"Your sole motivation to work for Antaeus was to better your family. But over time you realized the one thing you hoped for your husband was the one thing that he hated. Promotion. So, Antaeus told you the truth to change your mind about not relaying the intel about Cobalt's Afghan meeting. And the hook was that the fallout after the bomb was dropped would destroy Ed's career, and give you your husband back. I suppose there was an SVR retirement fund in place too."

"Ten million dollars."

"Where do you think Cobalt is right now?"

Catherine placed her cheek against Ed's. "I've no idea. Laying low I guess."

Will shook his head. "Wrong guess."

Catherine frowned.

Will crouched before her and placed his hand over hers and Ed's. He didn't know why, because Catherine had very nearly caused untold pain. Perhaps it was because he felt sorry for all pawns manipulated by the minds of the greatest intelligence officers.

"I'm so sorry, Mr. Cochrane." Catherine's regret was tangible.

"So am I. You knew Gregori Shonin was a myth. Thing is though, he wasn't the only one, and you've been completely played for a fool. Terrorist activities that had been attributed to Cobalt were in truth atrocities that had been conducted by thousands of other terrorists. There wasn't one man who was financing the majority of them."

Catherine stared at him, openmouthed, shock written across her face.

Will ran a finger against her tears, stood, and threw his handgun across the room. He'd learned the truth and felt nothing but disgust that the world of espionage reduced people to winners and losers and the dead. "Cobalt doesn't exist."

THIRTY-SEVEN

One week later, Will was wearing an orange jumpsuit, had shackles on his ankles and wrists, and was shuffling along a brightly illuminated corridor inside ADX Florence—a Federal Bureau of Prisons supermax penitentiary in Colorado. Four burly armed guards surrounded him as they led him through the part of the facility where he'd been kept for seven days in solitary confinement.

They forced him into a room that was bare of anything save a metal table and four chairs, all of which were molded to the floor to prevent them from being used as impromptu weapons. He was pushed down into one of the chairs so that he was facing the seats on the opposite side of the table. The guards took up positions in each corner of the room.

He waited for approximately twenty minutes, no one speaking, no explanation given as to why he'd been dragged out of his cell and brought here. He supposed it could be another meeting with the prison governor, who'd already told him that sometime soon he'd be moved to another high-security prison so that he didn't have time to plan his escape, and that he'd keep being moved until a decision was made about his fate. Or it could be another tedious interview with a Bureau agent or CIA officer, wherein they'd barrage him with questions about what had happened during the last few weeks before walking out of the room and threatening to throw away the key to his cell because all he'd given them were lies, manipulation, and crap.

So he was surprised when the door opened and Marsha, Alistair, and Patrick walked in and sat opposite him.

Marsha was clutching a white envelope, and she looked considerably different than when he'd last seen her in the alley off Wisconsin Avenue. Her hair was immaculate, and she was wearing an elegant suit. It didn't surprise him that Alistair was also nicely dressed. The MI6 controller rarely liked to be seen in public in anything less formal than a three-piece suit, topped off with a Royal Navy tie and hair that was always cut at the two-hundred-year-old Truefitt & Hill barbershop in London's St. James's Street. But the fact that Patrick was also wearing a suit worried Will, because the CIA officer was normally a roll-your-sleeves-up guy. He never dressed up unless something bad was about to happen and he needed to look the part.

Marsha said, "I know my colleagues have asked you the same questions countless times during the last few days, but now that I'm here in person, I'm going to ask the same things. How did you get to Canada?"

"I flew first class with British Airways." Will smiled. "It was a lovely flight. Very peaceful."

"You know anything about a Norwegian trawler vessel berthing and being boarded by Danish police in Denmark?"

"Why would I? Sea travel makes me queasy."

"A downed aircraft off the coast of Nova Scotia containing a dead Russian female intelligence operative?"

Will remembered Ulana telling him that all paperwork had been approved for her to adopt a baby boy. "No."

"If circumstances had been different, would you have killed any of the police officers you encountered in Nova Scotia, at the Canadian border crossing, or in Union Station?"

"I'm not a cop killer."

"You shot one of them in the shoulder."

"He was trying to stop me entering your beautiful country. I was rather displeased with that. I presume he's recovered?"

"He'll live." Marsha tapped the envelope on the table. "Final question: You know anything about the deaths of Sheridan, Jellicoe, or twins called Augustus and Elijah?"

Will glanced at Alistair and Patrick before returning his gaze to Marsha. "Their deaths are a terrible tragedy."

Alistair laughed.

Marsha did not. "All four were"—she frowned

while trying to think of the right word—"*executed* in the space of a few hours, the same evening you later confronted Ed and Catherine Parker. Was that your Night of the Long Knives?"

A reference to when Nazis killed many of their German political opponents in a purge in 1934.

Will moved his hands onto the metal table, causing the chain between them to rattle against the surface and the guards to take a step toward him.

But Will held the palms of his hands up and smiled. "Now, Agent Gage: I can forgive you for accusing a gentleman like me of murder. However, tut tut: Comparing me to a Nazi? My grandfather and his brothers killed Nazis for a living."

"I'm drawing a comparison to the event, not the personalities involved. Did you kill Sheridan, Jellicoe, and the twins?"

Will kept her gaze, his eyes unblinking. "Has Ellie Hallowes been laid to rest?"

Marsha nodded. "In a grave next to her parents. The Director of the CIA personally placed the Distinguished Intelligence Cross in Ellie's hands before the casket was sealed."

The Distinguished Intelligence Cross was the Agency's highest decoration, awarded for extraordinary heroism. Only a handful of officers had received the medal since the creation of the Agency in 1947.

The act touched Will deeply, though he wondered if Ellie cared about medals. He thought about the jewelry box he'd returned to her, wishing he'd been able to place it in her hands. "You went out of your way to help me."

"Not help you, but help get to the truth behind Ferryman."

"Fair enough, but nevertheless it was help that you didn't need to give and could have prompted severe repercussions against you if it hadn't paid off. So, I'm going to give you something in return. If you choose to ask your question about the deaths of Jellicoe, Sheridan, and the twins one more time . . ."

The guards placed their hands on the butts of their pistols.

". . . I promise you that I will answer your question truthfully."

Patrick and Alistair frowned.

Marsha stared back at Will, oblivious to everyone else in the room. "The truth?"

"The truth."

The room was silent. Everyone was motionless.

It seemed like minutes later that Marsha broke her gaze on Will and put her finger on the white envelope. "In here is a joint letter from the president of the United States of America and the prime minister of Canada. They've signed it, and it's stamped with the seals of their offices. The letter has been witnessed and countersigned by the U.S. attorney general and the chief justice of Canada. It says that, due to your outstanding devotion to Western national security, you are pardoned of all crimes known to be committed by you in their countries. But there's a catch. Both premiers have told me not to give the letter to you if there are other crimes you've committed that they don't know about and that would need to be investigated, particularly if those crimes involve murder."

Will nodded slowly. "I respect their position, and I respect your authority. I'm prepared to give you the truth, no matter what the consequences."

"Why?"

Will sighed. "Because I of all people know that the truth matters. I've spent the last two weeks thinking about nothing else."

All eyes were on Marsha.

Nobody spoke.

Finally, she said, "There's only one witness to one of the incidents, and her description of the man who broke into her home doesn't match yours." Marsha's eyes flickered.

Will knew Marsha didn't believe Lindsay Sheridan's version of events.

But she thrust the envelope across the table. "So that's case closed as far as you're concerned." She looked at the guards. "Get him out of these darn shackles. This man's saved the States from a shit storm and deserves to be treated better than this." The guards tried to object, but Marsha barked, "Do it, or you're messing with an executive order from the president."

After he was liberated from his cuffs, Marsha stood and held out her hand.

Will got to his feet and placed his scarred hand in hers.

She shook his hand firmly, turned, and walked out of the room while calling out, "If you come to my jurisdiction again and cause trouble, I'll be the first one to put you back in here."

Will smiled.

"Sit down, Will." Alistair intertwined his fingers and looked at the guards. "Leave us." When the guards were gone, Alistair said, "Task Force S has been shut down. There's no future for you in MI6 or the CIA."

Will shrugged. "Up to a moment ago, I thought I was facing life imprisonment or the needle. Thoughts about my future career were the least of my worries."

Alistair studied him. "Patrick and I still carry a lot of power in our agencies. Plus, no one can touch the rather healthy slush fund that we've tucked away for a rainy day." He smiled at the inadvertent poetry. "You're unemployable in the normal world, and the secret world can't afford to lose someone of your capabilities. So here's what we're thinking: you become self-employed but we're your only clients. When we want a deniable job done, we pay you one-third up front, the balance on results. But we won't want to know how you get those results."

"And you'll stand in a court of law and deny any association with me if things go wrong?"

"Correct."

Will looked around the room. "Rather strange place to be conducting a job interview."

Alistair had a genteel smile on his face. "Will, I think this is probably the least strange thing that has happened to you."

Will thought Alistair had a point. "Have you established how Catherine Parker communicated with Antaeus?"

Patrick answered, "We have. Cell phone calls

to set up meetings. And encrypted bursts between two covert comms transmitters, for use when they couldn't meet but intelligence needed to be relayed."

"You got Parker's transmitter and her key code to operate the system?"

"Yep. Doesn't help us, though."

"What's going to happen to Parker?"

"Life imprisonment. No chance of parole." Patrick sighed. "Her daughter's been put into temporary foster care. Reckon she'll be moved from family to family, rather than staying put somewhere permanent, 'cause not many parents want to adopt the child of a traitor." His expression steeled. "After what he nearly pulled off, I just wish we'd got Antaeus. Maybe that'll be the first job we give you: get the bastard."

Will shook his head. "He was merely doing his job. In any case, last time I tried to kill him, I lost, Antaeus lost, and his family lost. Do you have a pen and paper?"

Alistair withdrew his fountain pen and a notepad. "What are you thinking?"

Will wrote carefully on a sheet of paper and put the note in front of the men. "This."

Alistair read the note before handing the paper to Patrick, who frowned.

Will asked, "Do you think you can pull this off?"

Patrick laughed. "I'll move heaven and earth to get this done. Will, this is brilliant."

"I don't care about brilliance." Will looked at Alistair. He'd been through so much with this man, who meant more to him than just being a high-ranking colleague. Sometimes Alistair was a pain in the ass, other times a pompous mandarin whose superb intellect could think in Latin, French, Arabic, and a host of other languages; and then there were his eccentricities, including his love of falconry during his retreats to his Scottish mansion, where he fed his beloved kestrels with dead baby chicks that he, and any other foolish guest who stupidly dared to come and stay for the weekend, had to spend evenings peeling the skin off before feeding them to the birds of prey. God had broken the mold after creating Alistair.

But he was so much more than what you saw on the surface.

To Will, he was a surrogate father.

And Patrick was Will's surrogate uncle.

Both men had served alongside his real father and were there at the end.

They'd subsequently supported his family, without Will or his sister knowing.

They were complex, tough, yet ultimately magnificent men.

Will looked at them both and felt like their child.

A kid who was all bravado and uncaring of scratches and bruises caused during his imagination-driven adventures in the forests surrounding his home. And yet one who also needed love and security.

Now that security was being taken away from him.

By men who were acting like a mother who knew the time was right to cut her apron strings.

He had to trust their judgment.

THIRTY-EIGHT

Dickie Mountjoy grumbled under his breath as his front doorbell rang. No doubt it was the postman again, who'd come with some soddin' special delivery or whatever else it was these days that was no better than a good old stamp with the queen's image on it, stuck like it should be on a bit of paper and shoved through a red pillar box. Military men, he'd long ago decided, understand change just fine: new weapons, tactics, wars, blundering politicians telling them what to do and them doing it anyway because soldiers know duty even when it means supporting a blithering stack of spineless ignorance. But civvies like change because it keeps their boring lives on their toes. New this, new that; special or recorded deliveries; change for the ruddy sake of change.

As he reached for the door, he decided he was going to tell the postman that, no, he wasn't going to put his signature on some cruddy electronic screen just so that he could be given a package that belonged to him, because the screen didn't work and nobody seemed to care that his signature never came out looking like it was supposed to.

He pulled open the door, ready to give the post-man a dressing down as if he were a young Guards-man who had a hair out of place while standing to attention in Wellington Barracks.

But the man before him wasn't the postman.

It was Will Cochrane.

Wearing a suit and overcoat.

No hair out of place.

He was smiling. Looked thinner than when Dickie had last seen him.

Dickie's bottom lip trembled as he stood ram-rod straight, his hands clasped behind his back, his immaculate civilian clothes pressed to the standards of an off-duty major partaking of a glass of port in the officers' mess. "You . . . you got here then."

"It took me a while."

"And I suppose you're here to flog me some of your dodgy life insurance?"

Will's smile broadened. "Something like that."

"Except, everyone knows your cover as a sales-man was all a big fib." Dickie pointed at the ceiling. "Been to your home?"

"I have."

"Like what you see?"

"I called Phoebe on my way over here. She told me my place had been trashed. You didn't need to . . ."

"Do you like what you see, or not?"

Will was overwhelmed with gratitude. "I like what I see."

Dickie held out his hand, keeping his expression gruff to suppress the true emotions that were searing within him. "Good to have you back, soldier."

Will shook his hand.

No embraces for Englishmen like these.

Just a brief eye contact to recognize that both men knew exactly what the other was thinking and feeling, and that no fuss needed to be made of those sensations.

Will said, "Phoebe also told me that you'd only let me take you to a doctor. I've pulled some strings and fast-tracked an appointment."

"When do we go?"

"Grab your coat. You're on parade in ten minutes."

They left the apartment block, neither man speaking, their breath steaming in the cold London air, walking side by side over snow-covered ground, passing trees that had Christmas lights draped over them. Minutes later they entered the Princess Street healthcare clinic.

They were inside for an hour. Sitting in the waiting room while ignoring each other and reading back issues of *National Geographic* magazine; sitting in a doctor's consulting room while tests were made on Dickie; back in the waiting room to read about volcano eruptions and indigenous tribes in Botswana; and back in the consulting room.

That's when Dickie was given the news.

They left in silence.

Despite his arthritis, Dickie marched alongside Will with the vigor and precision of a commanding officer who was determined that his last-ever inspection of his troops should be one of his best.

As they entered West Square and headed toward their apartment house, music was playing from one of the nearby houses.

Dean Martin's "Let it Snow."

The song that had played in a loop in Will's head as he'd staggered through treacherous weather in Greenland, thinking that soon he would be dead.

The communal front door to the apartment house opened. Phoebe and David were there, Phoebe wearing clothes that wouldn't have looked out of place at a strip club, David wearing a food-stained apron over jeans and a sweater that had a reindeer stitched on it. They were holding each other, looks of concern on their faces.

Dickie placed a hand on Will's arm and stopped. Will stayed with him.

They were surrounded by the gorgeous Edwardian square.

Ten yards away from Phoebe and David.

Dickie looked at Will. "You gonna tell 'em, or should I?"

Will placed his hand on top of Dickie's hand. "Major Mountjoy, you're the highest-ranking officer here."

Dickie nodded, took a step forward, stood to attention, and smiled. "False alarm. Just a poncey bronchial infection. Antibiotics will sort it. This old boy ain't heading for the heavens just yet."

Phoebe had tears of joy running down her face as she ran as fast as her heels would let her and gave the major a hug.

Dickie looked flummoxed, then smiled with genuine warmth as he tenderly put his arms around her and patted her back. "There, there, my dear. Everything's going to be okay."

She rushed to Will, leapt into his arms, wrapped her legs around him, and exclaimed, "Will, Will!"

Will laughed as he lowered her to the ground. "And it's good to see you too, Phoebe." He kissed her on the cheek.

"None of that nonsense!" Phoebe seized the back of Will's head and planted a big kiss on his lips. She grabbed his hand and Dickie's. "Come on, you two: David's cooked some mince pies and we've got some mulled wine on the go." She walked with them toward David, who was now her bona fide boyfriend and had a huge smile on his face.

It was a smile matched by those on Will's and Dickie's faces.

They were all together.

Home.

And this was just what Will wanted more than anything else in the world.

THIRTY-NINE

The Russian man stood outside the FBI head-quarters in Washington, D.C.

He knew that if he entered the J. Edgar Hoover Building there'd be no turning back. He would be a traitor to the motherland, give America an enormous tactical advantage on all matters of West versus East espionage, and would change the rest of his life forever because he would live it in the States.

A new identity.

An American salary that would be given to him in return for every Russian secret he knew. Protection if it was needed. A nice house, hopefully one that was in the countryside and overlooking water. A place where he could live peacefully while doing his studies and writing.

None of those things meant his life in America would be better. But there was something else here that would make a world of difference to him.

The thing that Will Cochrane's message had told him he could have if he came to the States.

At face value, the message was proof that

Cochrane had not only beaten him, but also had the guile to deliver something very special to the West. But the Russian knew that wasn't the real reason why Cochrane had crafted the secret communication. Once, the MI6 officer had inadvertently taken something utterly dear away from the Russian. Now he was making amends.

He entered the building, approached the security desk, and spoke to one of the Bureau guards. "Agent Marsha Gage should be expecting me. I'm here to betray my country and collect my daughter."

The guard frowned. "Name?"

"My real name's of no use to anyone." He smiled. "Tell Agent Gage that there's a Russian intelligence officer in the FBI lobby, and he calls himself Antaeus."

GLOSSARY

11e Brigade Parachutiste—An airborne unit containing most of the parachute units in the French army. The brigade numbers around 8,500 personnel and includes eight regiments. It is under command of a *général de brigade* (brigadier general). French paratroopers wear a red beret, except for the 2e Régiment Étranger de Parachutistes, which wears the French Foreign Legion beret (light green).

Agency—An abbreviation that refers to the Central Intelligence Agency (CIA).

Agenzia Informazioni e Sicurezza Interna—Italy's domestic intelligence agency.

AK-47—A selective-fire, gas-operated 7.62×39 mm assault rifle, first developed in the Soviet Union by Mikhail Kalashnikov.

Army Ranger Wing—The Special Forces unit of the Irish Defense Forces. It is Ireland's premier hostage rescue unit.

Attorney General (U.S.)—As head of the Department of Justice, the attorney general is the top law enforcement officer and lawyer for the federal government of the United States.

Bureau—An abbreviation that refers to the Federal Bureau of Investigation (FBI).

Centro Nacional de Inteligencia—The intelligence agency of Spain.

CIA—The United States' Central Intelligence Agency. One of only a handful of agencies worldwide that have global reach and presence, the CIA primarily obtains secret intelligence by recruiting and running foreign spies, though it is also active in a range of other espionage activities including covert paramilitary direct actions.

Coldstream Guards—The oldest regiment in the British army.

Critical Incident Response Group (CIRG)—A division of the Criminal, Cyber, Response, and Services Branch of the FBI.

Delta Force—Alongside DEVGRU (SEAL Team 6), the United States' premier tier-1 special operations unit. Correctly termed 1st Special Forces Operational Detachment-Delta (1st SFOD-D), the organization is usually referred to by its members as "The Unit" or "Delta." It is modeled on Great Britain's SAS.

DGSE—Direction Générale de la Sécurité Extérieure. France's premier overseas intelligence agency, comparable to the CIA and MI6.

Directorate of Intelligence (CIA)—The division within the Agency that has responsibility for the recruitment and running of foreign spies with a view to obtaining intelligence from them.

DLB—Dead-letter box. A covert means of communication whereby two persons can pass information or items to each other without having to meet.

DO—Duty Officer. Typically a high-ranking intelligence officer who is required to man the headquarters of an intelligence agency at night or during holiday periods, in case urgent matters are communicated to the agency during those periods by one of its overseas stations.

Dragoons—The light cavalry units contained within most European armies.

FBI—Federal Bureau of Investigation. The United States' domestic criminal investigation and counterintelligence agency.

French Foreign Legion—The part of the French army that comprises foreign volunteers who are commanded by French officers. Established in 1831, the Legion is renowned for its harsh training, deployment to some of the harshest and most dangerous parts of the world, and successful combat history.

French Foreign Legion 2e Régiment Étranger de Parachutistes—The elite airborne regiment within the Legion. All members of the regiment are parachute qualified.

FSB—Federal Security Service of the Russian Federation. Broadly equivalent to the U.S. FBI.

G7—A group consisting of the finance ministers of seven developed nations: the U.S., Japan, France, Germany, Italy, the U.K., and Canada (the seven wealthiest developed nations on earth by national net wealth).

GCHQ—The Government Communications Headquarters is the British intelligence agency responsible for providing signals intelligence to the British government and army. It is directly comparable to the United States' National Security Agency (NSA).

Groupement des Commandos Parachutistes (GCP)—An elite pathfinder commando parachute unit in the 11e Brigade Parachutiste of the French army.

GRU—Glavnoye Razvedyvatel'noye Upravleniye, or Main Intelligence Directorate. The primary military foreign intelligence service of the Russian Federation.

Heckler & Koch HK416 rifle—An assault rifle designed and manufactured by Heckler & Koch.

Heckler & Koch MP5/10A3 submachine gun—A selective-fire submachine gun manufactured by Heckler & Koch.

Horse Guards Parade—A large parade ground in Whitehall, central London. It is the site of the annual ceremony of Trooping the Color, which commemorates the British monarch's official birthday.

HRT—Hostage Rescue Team. The counterterrorism and hostage rescue unit of the Federal Bureau of Investigation. HRT is trained to rescue American citizens and allies who are held by hostile forces, usually terrorist and/or criminal.

Hussars—The light cavalry unit that originated in Hungary during the fifteenth century. The title and distinctive dress of these horsemen was subsequently widely adopted by light cavalry regiments in European and other armies. A number of armored or ceremonial mounted units in modern armies retain the designation of hussars.

Intelligence Star—The award given by the Central Intelligence Agency for a "voluntary act or acts of courage performed under hazardous conditions or for outstanding achievements or services rendered with distinction under conditions of grave risk." The citation is the second-highest award for valor in the Central Intelligence Agency, after the Distinguished Intelligence Cross.

IO—Intelligence Officer.

ISI—The Directorate for Inter-Services Intelligence (more commonly known as Inter-Services Intelligence or simply by its initials ISI), is the premier intelligence agency of Pakistan, operationally responsible for providing critical national security and intelligence assessment to the government of Pakistan.

Kevlar—The registered trademark for a para-aramid synthetic fiber. Developed at DuPont in 1965, this high-strength material was first commercially used in the early 1970s as a replacement for steel in racing tires. Kevlar has many applications, ranging from bicycle tires and racing sails to body armor, because of its high tensile strength-to-weight ratio; by this measure it is five times stronger than steel on an equal weight basis.

Lancers—A type of cavalryman who fought with

a lance. The weapon was widely used in Asia and Europe during the Middle Ages and the Renaissance by armored cavalry, before being adopted by light cavalry, particularly in eastern Europe. In a modern context, a lancer regiment usually denotes an armored regiment.

Langley—Located in Virginia, it is a suburb of Washington, D.C. Because the headquarters of the CIA is located here, "Langley" is also a shorthand reference to the Agency.

Light Brigade—The nineteenth British light cavalry force. It mounted light, fast horses that were unarmored and equipped with lances and sabers. Optimized for maximum mobility and speed, they were intended for reconnaissance and skirmishing. They were also ideal for cutting down retreating infantry and artillery units.

M40A1 sniper rifle—A 7.62-caliber rifle, favored by the United States Marine Corps due to its high accuracy up to a range of one thousand yards.

Marinejegerkommandoen (MJK)—The Norwegian maritime special operations force. MJK is employed in many kinds of operations, such as unconventional warfare, guerrilla warfare, special reconnaissance, recovery or protection of ships and oil installations, various counterterrorism missions, hostage rescue, and direct action.

MD 530 Little Bird helicopter—A light helicopter used for special operations by the United States army and elite law enforcement units.

Metropolitan Police Department of the District of Columbia (MPD)—Commonly referred to as the D.C. Police or Metropolitan Police, MPD is the municipal police force of Washington, D.C. Formed in 1861, it is one of the ten largest police forces in the United States.

Metro Transit Police Department—The policing agency of the Washington Metropolitan Area Transit Authority (WMATA). Created in 1976, the Metro Transit Police Department is unique in American law enforcement, as it is the only U.S. police agency that has full local police authority in three different jurisdictions (Maryland, Virginia, and Washington, D.C.)

MI6—Great Britain's overseas intelligence agency. Correctly titled the Secret Intelligence Service, MI6 is the oldest and arguably most experienced intelligence service with a global reach and presence. Its tasking and tactics are comparable to the CIA's.

MI6 Controller—A high-ranking MI6 officer with responsibility for running a strategic clandestine division within MI6.

National Clandestine Service—The CIA directorate for clandestine activities, including the recruitment and running of foreign spies.

NSA—National Security Agency. The United States' intelligence agency with responsibility for collecting signals intelligence.

NYC—New York City.

NYPD—New York Police Department.

Overseas Station—An intelligence agency's unit within a foreign country. An overseas agency can employ from one to upward of twenty intelligence officers. Stations can be either "declared" to their host countries or "undeclared," depending on the station's activities.

Politiets Sikkerhetstjeneste—The Norwegian Police Security Service.

Quantico—A town in Prince William County, Virginia, Quantico is the site of one of the largest U.S. Marine Corps bases in the world: MCB Quantico. The base is the site of the Marine Corps Combat Development Command and HMX-1 (the presidential helicopter squadron). The United States Drug Enforcement Administration's training academy, the FBI Academy, the FBI Laboratory, and the Naval Criminal Investigative Service headquarters are on the base.

Remington 870 shotgun—A pump-action shotgun manufactured by Remington Arms Company, LLC. It is commonly used by law enforcement and military organizations worldwide.

Rigspolitiet—The state national police force of Denmark, with responsibility for policing all regions governed by Denmark, including the Faroe Islands and Greenland.

Royal Canadian Mounted Police (RCMP)—The national police force of Canada.

Säkerhetspolisen—The security service of Sweden.

SCAR H 7.62 mm battle rifle—A modular rifle made by FN Herstal (FNH) for the United States Special Operations Command (SOCOM).

Scotland Yard—The headquarters for Great Britain's Metropolitan Police Service.

SEALs—The United States Navy's Sea, Air, Land teams, commonly known as the Navy SEALs, are the U.S. Navy's principal special operations force and a part of the Naval Special Warfare Command and United States Special Operations Command.

SEAL Team 6—The United States Naval Special Warfare Development Group (NSWDG), or DEVGRU, is a U.S. Navy component of Joint Special Operations Command. It is often referred to as SEAL Team Six, the name of its predecessor organization, which was officially disbanded in 1987. DEVGRU is administratively supported by Naval Special Warfare Command and operationally commanded by the Joint Special Operations Command.

Secret Intelligence Service (SIS)—Commonly referred to as MI6 (see "MI6" on page 447).

SF—Special Forces. In the United States, the term "Special Forces" is specific to a special operations organization within the U.S. Army that carries that name and is colloquially known as the Green Berets. Elsewhere in the world, the term is more generally used to describe elite military commando units.

Special Activities Division—A division of the CIA's National Clandestine Service responsible for covert operations, such as tactical paramilitary operations and covert political action.

Special Air Service (SAS)—The inspiration for all special operations military units around the world, Great Britain's SAS is the most experienced and arguably—alongside its maritime sister, the Special Boat Service—the best Special Forces unit in the world.

Special Branch—The term used to identify units responsible for matters of national security in British and Commonwealth police forces. A Special Branch unit acquires and develops intelligence, usually of a political nature, and conducts investigations to protect the state from perceived threats of terrorism and other extremist activity.

Special Operations Group (SOG)—The department within the CIA's Special Activities Division responsible for operations that include the collection of intelligence in hostile countries, and high-threat military or intelligence operations with which the U.S. government does not wish to be overtly associated.

Springfield Armory's M1911A1 Professional handgun—A reliable, high-quality pistol used by the FBI Hostage Rescue Team, regional SWAT teams, and many other federal and local special operations units.

SSCI—Senate Select Committee on Intelligence. An organization created in 1976 after Congress had investigated CIA operations on U.S. soil and established that some had been illegal. The SSCI comprises fifteen senators who are drawn from both major political parties and whose remit includes oversight of U.S. intelligence activities and ensuring transparency between the intelligence community and Congress.

SureFire tactical light—Portable lights favored by law enforcement and military units, manufactured by American company SureFire LLC.

SWAT—"Special Weapons and Tactics" is a commonly used proper name for U.S. law enforcement units that use military-style light weapons and specialized tactics in high-risk operations that fall outside of the capabilities of regular, uniformed police.

United Nations Security Council (UNSC)—One of the six principal organs of the United Nations, the UNSC is charged with the maintenance of international peace and security. The permanent members of the UNSC are the United States, United Kingdom, France, Russia, and China.

Wellington Barracks—These barracks are located close to Buckingham Palace so the Foot Guards they house can reach the palace quickly if necessary.

ACKNOWLEDGMENTS

With thanks to my wife for being such an enthusiastic proofreader of my book; and my two brilliant mentors, David Highfill and Luigi Bonomi, and their second-to-none teams at William Morrow/ HarperCollins Publishers and LBA Literary Agency, respectively.